THE WORLD'S

A JOURNAL OF THE PLAGUE YEAR

DANIEL DEFOE was born in London in 1660, the son of a tallow-chandler. He was educated for the Presbyterian ministry at Newington Dissenting Academy, but quickly abandoned this intention. Thereafter he embarked on a life of several careers and great complexity. He was captured by Algerian pirates and took part in Monmouth's Rebellion; his early engagement in commerce ended in bankruptcy but he later dealt in ship-insurance, wool, oysters and linen; he became a secret agent, a political pamphleteer and was several times arrested. He died 'of a lethargy' in 1731.

Defoe was the author of some 500 works, ranging over politics, economics, history, biography, and crime. Among his best-known novels are *Robinson Crusoe* (1719), *Moll Flanders* (1722), and *Roxana* (1724).

The late LOUIS LANDA, Professor of English Emeritus at Princeton University, was the author of *Swift and the Church of Ireland* (Clarendon Press) and numerous other studies of eighteenth-century literature.

DAVID ROBERTS has taught at the universities of Bristol, Oxford, and Kyoto, and is now Visiting Lecturer at Osaka University, Japan. His publications include *The Ladies: Female Patronage of Restoration Drama* (OUP, 1989) and the introduction to Defoe's *Colonel Jack* for the World's Classics series (1989).

DANIEL DEFOE

A JOURNAL OF
THE PLAGUE YEAR

being Observations or Memorials
of the most Remarkable Occurrences,
as well Publick as Private,
which happened in London
during the last Great Visitation
in 1665.
Written by a Citizen who continued
all the while in London.

Edited by
LOUIS LANDA

With a new Introduction by
DAVID ROBERTS

Oxford New York
OXFORD UNIVERSITY PRESS
1990

Oxford University Press, Walton Street, Oxford OX2 6DP

Oxford New York Toronto
Delhi Bombay Calcutta Madras Karachi
Petaling Jaya Singapore Hong Kong Tokyo
Nairobi Dar es Salaam Cape Town
Melbourne Auckland
and associated companies in
Berlin Ibadan

Oxford is a trade mark of Oxford University Press

British Library Cataloguing in Publication Data
Defoe, Daniel 1660 or 1–1731
A journal of the plague year: being observations or
memorials of the most remarkable occurrences as well
publick as private, which happened in London during the
last great visitation in 1665. – (The world's classics) –
(Oxford paperbacks).
I. Title II. Landa, Louis A., 1901–89
823'.5
ISBN 0–19–282682–4

Library of Congress Cataloging-in-Publication Data
Defoe, Daniel 1661?–1731.
p.   cm. — (The world's classics)
Includes bibliographical references.
1. Plague—England—London—Fiction. 2. London (England)—
History—17th century—Fiction. I. Landa, Louis A., 1901–89.
II. Title. III. Series.
PR3404.J6 1990   823'.5—dc20   90–30244
ISBN 0–19–282682–4

Printed in Great Britain by
BPCC Hazell Books
Aylesbury, Bucks

CONTENTS

ACKNOWLEDGEMENTS

I am grateful to Dr Peter Davidson, Dr Stephanie Blackden, Professor Yutaka Senba, and Professor Toshiharu Yamamoto for helping me to find medical and other books; to Dr Richard Luckett for information about Pepys and Paul Lorrain; and to Dr Peter Robinson for his comments on the first draft of my introduction.

D. R.

INTRODUCTION

A Journal of the Plague Year has endured a long crisis of classification. Like many readers since, Sir Walter Scott recognized its power and its oddity; he thought it Defoe's finest work after *Robinson Crusoe* and described it as 'one of those peculiar character of compositions which hover between romance and history'. Until recently it seemed that oddity had triumphed over power: poised between fact and fiction, the *Journal* was thought less influential than *Moll Flanders* and *Roxana* in the rise of the novel. Now, many critics have dispensed with the problem by relaxing their generic terms, so that the book is often treated as simply another 'narrative'. This compensates too far; we need a sense of its oddity as well.

The best way of answering that need is to call the *Journal* what it most obviously is: a classic of plague literature, worthy of comparison with Thucydides and Boccaccio. As such, it prompts critical questions more urgent than those attendant on its not being a novel. One historian of the Black Death of 1348–9 comments on his mass of evidence, 'The same phrases are used to describe the appearance of the disease, the same exaggerated estimates of mortality appear, the same passions are aroused, the same economic and social consequences ensue.'[1] Plague literature, in other words, exhibits striking rhetorical consistency in describing strikingly consistent events. Modern literary theory has emphasized the gap between words and the things they indicate. Some of Defoe's words are the accretion of other people's on the same subject, but the subject's own repetitive nature is medically verifiable. If

---

[1] Philip Ziegler, *The Black Death* (Penguin, 1988), p. 112.

the oddity of the *Journal* manifests itself today as a test of theoretical criticism, it may be at last that in its oddity will be found the key to its power; for Defoe's conviction that the suffering of plague victims could be recorded is constantly threatened by the inadequacy of words to the task. This threat sets the *Journal* apart from much of Defoe's fiction, for where his novels often allow somewhat facile access to human experience, *A Journal of the Plague Year* approaches it with critical reticence.

Defoe had been writing about plague for over ten years before the publication of the *Journal* in March 1722. He began by dealing not with the London epidemic of 1665, but with the danger of plague from the Continent. In six numbers of his *Review* between 22 October and 6 December 1709, he warned of the risk of infection if British troops went to assist Sweden in the wars against the Second Coalition, while in August 1712, in the same paper, he showed how many European countries had suffered outbreaks of plague over the previous eight years. In the next issue, of 26 August, he gave a thunderous reminder of the disaster that had once befallen London: there appeared a copy of the Mortality Bill for the week beginning 12 September 1665, the worst of the whole epidemic, when over seven thousand people are recorded as having died of plague. His warnings of the spread of plague in Europe eleven days later were his last words on the subject until the disease broke out in Marseilles in July 1720.

A Journal of the Plague Year was topical in many ways, but especially in its response to the Marseilles plague. Defoe had been concerned before about the threat of plague (others had as well), but then the threat had not been so great. An epidemic in a major trading port was a serious matter, and Walpole's government had to defy commercial interests by introducing an Act of Quarantine which would keep out vessels suspected of carrying the disease. In a series of ten articles for *The Daily Post*, *Mist's Journal*, and *Applebee's Journal*, Defoe argued in favour of the Act, which received the royal assent on 12 February 1722, four days after the publication of Defoe's first major work on the plague, *Due Preparations for the Plague, as well for Soul as Body*, and less than two months before *A Journal of the Plague Year*. Defoe was concerned about the risk of plague and wanted to alert people to it, as well as to support the Government; but this prolific professional author must also have wanted to write something of commercial value. Accordingly, the *Journal* dramatizes its divided loyalties, admitting to and trying to check its prurience. The narrator's curiosity often takes him to places where, to use his own pun, he has no business, and he makes a point of concealing names so that surviving members of families whose stories he tells will not be embarrassed.

Topical the subject certainly was. The Marseilles plague not only vindicated Defoe's previous warnings, but provided him with a wealth of published medical opinion, some of it reprinted from the aftermath of the Great Plague itself. The *Journal* quotes and takes issue with some of these works directly. The theories it advances about the origin and nature of the plague are drawn chiefly from two medical tracts, Richard Mead's *A Short Discourse Concerning Pestilential Contagion* (1720), and *Loimologia*, translated in 1720 from the Latin of Nathaniel Hodges by John Quincy. Defoe had already made use of the weekly Bills of Mortality for his *Review* article of 26 August 1712; a collection of Bills for 1665 had been published in that year as *London's Dreadful Visitation*. His new plague book was a polemic, a powerful response to a topical issue, and much of its power lay in its being a hoax. Defoe's name did not appear on the title-page of the first edition; he seems to have hoped that his audience would believe that the *Journal* was indeed written 'by a Citizen who continued all the while in London'. The most vivid warning of the terrors of plague was also the most marketable; in that sense Defoe's moral and commercial ambitions were one.

The idea that Defoe obtained inside information from someone who had remained in London is attractive and long-standing. We know from the last page of the *Journal* that its narrator's initials are H. F., and from other sources that

Defoe had an uncle called Henry Foe who in 1665 was, like H. F., a Whitechapel saddler in the middle years of life. We also know that Henry Foe died when his nephew was 14, so it is possible that Defoe had the benefit of personal reminiscences from his uncle, although there is no proof that Foe stayed in London during the plague (Defoe, then a child of 5, was evacuated) and none that he kept a journal.

A better-documented source of information connects Defoe with the author of the other famous journal of the plague year, Samuel Pepys. The responses to plague of the self-effacing H. F. and the festive, increasingly libidinous Pepys have little in common. Their journals, however, share a number of details which are not in any of Defoe's recognized sources. Given that Pepys's diary was not deciphered until more than a century after the *Journal* appeared, the obvious explanation for this is that Defoe got his information first-hand from survivors of the epidemic who happened to have visited the same parts of London as Pepys; yet there appears to be a more intriguing solution which is also more likely. In 1703 Defoe was interned in Newgate prison for writing *The Shortest Way with the Dissenters*; at that time the Ordinary was Paul Lorrain, who achieved fame by writing up and selling the dying speeches of condemned criminals. Use is made of these pieces in a volume of 1724, *A General History of the Pirates*, apparently by 'Captain Charles Johnson', although many take the true author to be Defoe. Lorrain's stance as a commentator differs sharply from Defoe's, and there is evidence of personal hostility between the two men. None of this would matter as far as the *Journal* is concerned were it not for one of the most remarkable records of employment in literary history: when Lorrain became Ordinary of Newgate in 1698 he had for the previous twenty years been an amanuensis and library clerk in the service of Samuel Pepys, a position he retained with his Newgate job until Pepys's death in 1703.[2] From at least as early as 1683, Pepys's

---

[2] For information concerning Lorrain's employment by Pepys, I am indebted to Dr Richard Luckett, Fellow and Pepys Librarian of Magdalene College, Cambridge. For documentation, see Select Bibliography.

diary was on the shelves of his library in York Buildings, off the Strand; it was catalogued, and Lorrain was partly responsible for the reorganizations of the library which took place between 1678 and Pepys's death. There are indications that he was able to read Pepys's far from difficult shorthand code. Even if Lorrain and Defoe were not always the best of friends, the author of *A Journal of the Plague Year* spent six months in close proximity to a man who might easily have read Pepys's diary.

If Defoe was helped by the records of one eminent citizen who did continue all the while in London, he was not concerned simply to create an authentic period atmosphere. In harking back to a time when Londoners were resourceful, tolerant, and charitable in a time of dire stress, Defoe was lending support to the plea made by George I at the state opening of Parliament in October 1721 for a renewed sense of industry and public welfare among merchants; the *Journal* makes its own plea for improved relations between London and the rest of the country, and dwells upon the political threat of the London mob. It is infused with the rhetoric of the other big news story of the early 1720s, the collapse of the South Sea Company, and certain passages vindicate the initiative of the Government in April 1721 to locate 'scandalous clubs and societies of young persons' who blasphemed drunkenly day and night.[3] Defoe's novels often allude to the contemporary world rather freely, but the *Journal*'s focus on London in 1665 is accompanied by an unusually precise sense of the capital in 1722. This does not mean that Defoe treated the past as if it were the present. He took care to reconstruct London as it existed before the Great Fire of 1666, so that anachronisms should not cast doubt on the authenticity of the account; explicit contrasts between the layout of London past and present are frequently made. He seems to have realized, too, that the *Journal* would be more disturbing if he often drew his reader's attention to the things that were still there in 1722: the

---

[3] See the articles by Schonhorn, Novak, and Rogers listed in Select Bibliography; also M. Dorothy George, *London Life in the Eighteenth Century* (Penguin, 1987), pp. 44–8.

churches where people of different denominations had once prayed together, and the plague-pits which had since been built upon. Defoe's investigations were not free from error; but, whatever the risks of assigning the book to a genre, it is plain that he approached the problems of the historical novel with tact and ingenuity.

The writing of history is not only an ambition of the *Journal*, but also one of its themes. All of Defoe's best-known novels are introduced by a fictitious editor, who claims to have printed the manuscript autobiography of the protagonist. In the *Journal*, the editor *is* the protagonist. He marshals his evidence from the Mortality Bills, Lord Mayor's Orders, and medical tracts. He has anecdotes to hand, waiting their turn to be recounted. The editor of the novels always claims that the text speaks for itself, but the many texts which confront the editor of the *Journal* require constant interpretation. The figures on the Mortality Bills, baldly horrifying, can be shown to be false; oral history is inspected for its bias or conventionality. We share the perspective not of the castaway, kept woman, or pickpocket, but of the historian dispelling myths and rumours with the retrospective immediacy which characterizes Defoe's novels. He is, however, an historian who believes that history is what happens beyond the four walls of his own home. Like Crusoe, Moll, Roxana, and Jack, H. F. has a personal memoir, but we are told that he has derived the book from it instead of simply transcribing it. Some of it is said not to be suitable for public consumption: the private 'meditations' which occupy the days of his confinement at home are edited out, as if there were something indecent, given the subject of the book, about the solipsistic form of Defoe's other narratives. It has been said that Defoe does not make much of the device of the narrator's diary, as he does in *Robinson Crusoe*. Better to say that the diary, like all the other documents available, cannot be reproduced without comment; it, too, must be carefully explained and its contribution to written history assessed. H. F.'s individuality, which he tries to suppress, is in precisely this sceptical approach to evidence and to his own worth. Defoe adapts the resources of his novels and in doing so appears conscious of their narrow scope.

H. F.'s low profile is meant to serve history, but the history of this subject is dominated, for each of its participants, by a single question: how can *I* survive? The *Journal* opens, strikingly for a work by Defoe, not with a summary of the narrator's family background, but with public facts which submerge him into his community: for the first six pages we have more 'everybody' and 'we' than 'I', and it is not until page 7 that we are told who the narrator is (he is, moreover, the only one of Defoe's narrators whose death is recorded—buried, as it were, in his own story). The book ends, however, on a more starkly personal note than any other by Defoe: *'yet I alive!'* Throughout the book, people abandon their public offices to save themselves; H. F. does so too. The *Journal* itself charts the same course, suppressing the assertive 'I' of Defoe's other works only to assert it yet more intensely. It is not only the public responsibilities of the narrative which reduce the role of the private man and make H. F. a less vivid presence than Defoe's other narrators. The subject of plague collapses everything to a question of survival, so that where Defoe's other narrators distinguish themselves for their recklessness or ingenuity, part of H. F.'s distinction is that he simply remains alive.

The instinct to remain separate and alive pervades the book's collective narrative as well. In a startling biblical reference, H. F. says of the survivors of plague that they were like 'the Children of Israel, after their being delivered from the Host of *Pharoah*, when they passed the *Red-Sea*, and look'd back, and saw the *Egyptians* overwhelmed in the Water' (p. 248); fellow sufferers have become conquered enemies. For the first six pages of the *Journal*, we have the fears not of all Londoners about the onset of plague, but of the inhabitants of the Eastern part of the city. It may be ethically as well as geographically simplistic to talk, as many have done, of the *Journal* as a tragedy of London, so precarious is its sense of community. Since the beginning of the seventeenth century,

Londoners had spoken of their city as if it were two places, East and West. As if to reconcile them, the capital's double nature is here seen as providential as well as factional, since West can recover while East suffers, and vice versa. A plethora of doubles appears in Defoe's final novel of 1722, *Colonel Jack*. They replicate the hero's experiences and distance him from suspicion or implication, reminding him of the favours providence has bestowed on him. It was a fatal presumption, 'Turkish pre-destinarianism', for individuals to count on such favours in 1665; in this work of public responsibilities the providential double is the city itself.

This does not mean that London is celebrated as merely an infinite resource of human population, unconquerable for its sheer size. After the plague has finally abated, 'wonderful it was to see how populous the City was again all on a sudden; so that a Stranger could not miss the Numbers that were lost . . .' (p. 229). This courts the suggestion that the plague made no difference, but dismisses it: 'Stranger' reminds us of the actual and remembered loss of lives. Yet simply remembering the dead may in the *Journal* demand the impossible. H. F. attempts to list those who died while performing their duties, only to abandon it for want of evidence (p. 237). Sometimes lives just vanished: 'some whole Families were so entirely swept away, that there was no Remembrance of them left' (p. 230). Such vanishings at times of calamity mark the boundaries of our sympathy; we need the representative unknown soldier to understand. H. F. tracks down individual suffering behind the statistics of the Mortality Bills, and he also tries to extend his and our compassion to those who had not even that memorial. In that sense the *Journal* educates us in the meaning of its limits as history. Kenneth Clark once observed, 'We are used to catastrophes; we see them every day on television.' The *Journal* retains its power to alert us to what is narrow and habituated in our response to human suffering.

The search for individual loss emphasizes the diversity of human behaviour. H. F.'s favoured descriptive formula is 'some . . . some . . . others'. He balances his knowledge of individual cases against common generalizations; he shows how people experienced the disease differently. He states that he will not vouch for particulars, but still prefers to track them down where possible. His preference may lead him to admit to the almost impossible magnitude of his task: the standard of 'true in the general' is invoked where particulars are lacking. The magnitude of the task is that of London itself with its half million inhabitants. Defoe's book is particular in its view of human behaviour where Albert Camus's *La Peste* is mythical, and where the *Journal* sprawls in pursuit of its participants all over Essex, *La Peste* is confined to an insignificant walled town; Camus's containment of moral particulars had first to be a question of geography. Spurning myths, H. F. may still be overwhelmed by them. He may lose sight of individual suffering in the oblivion not of familial extinction, but of common rumour, death's second self in the *Journal*: 'nor is it easy to give any Story of this, or that Family, which there was not divers parallel Stories to [be] met with of the same Kind' (p. 120). As the plague increases and communication lessens, even these stories are harder to come by; all that can be trusted is the first-hand observation of the narrator, roaming the streets which others fear. The commerce of the *Journal* with the problems of writing history makes instant commercial sense; it is self-advertising, a rich metaphor for what Defoe himself was so involved with—the birth of the newspaper. In H. F. we have an acute prototype of the heroic reporter, risking all for truth in the drive to satisfy his own guilty curiosity.

The diversity of the subject required a diversity of technical means. Defoe's handling of fictional time is always problematic; he needed strict limitations of time and space to achieve his best. In the *Journal* he had them as nowhere else, yet this appears the most randomly organized of all his major works. There is little respect for chronological sequence; Defoe takes his reader back to the beginning of the story and to his favourite themes throughout the narrative. This is partly offset by the vividly realized fear of an indifferent audience and of the insufficiency of words. Such fear makes a virtue of repetition:

'it is impossible to say any Thing that is able to give a true Idea of it to those who did not see it, other than this; that it was indeed *very*, *very*, *very* dreadful, and such as no Tongue can express' (p. 60). Here, Defoe's endeavour is a tribute to what modern historians of plague prefer not to consider: its *failure* to make a lasting impact on people's minds. The *Journal* also discloses the interrelatedness of its evidence. H. F. the historian is reluctant to close off the repercussions of any given event; paragraphs often begin with 'This puts me in mind of', or 'Here I must observe', and he returns to matters already dealt with so that they can be seen in a fresh light.

This is not to suggest that the *Journal* simply ignores the reader's demand for some sense of chronology; far from it. It would have been hard to write about the plague year without indicating some overall narrative clock. In the *Journal*, calendar time is often what is indicated by the Mortality Bills, the 'tale', as Peter Conrad has observed, corresponding to the 'tally' of the dead. But this means that calendar time is also local time, so often do the Bills show losses in particular parishes. The Eastern perspective lends the book its most embracing narrative clock: H. F. often divides the year into 'the first Part of the time', which is 'till the Beginning of August', and the second part, which is when the plague reached the Eastern parishes with most virulence. If time in the *Journal* is topographical, topography is the chart of the epidemic's progress, and there Defoe's attention is drawn to the horror of individual cases. The book abounds with episodes of individuals evading the watchmen, bringing death to their own families, or roaming the streets with marks of the plague upon them. This episodic tendency, a weakness in Defoe's other works where it can prevent him from seeing the overall scope of the narrative, is in the *Journal* an asset. Each story has its own rhythm and time-span, alerting us to the passage of time in a variety of circumstances. In that sense the proliferation of local and individual narrative clocks reflects H. F.'s compassionate intentions, submerging calendar time beneath that of his individual subjects.

However, just as plague reduces human concerns to the question of survival, it focuses our consciousness of time upon the shockingly few days which victims have left. In this there is little variety, yet here Defoe's hauntingly deliberate sense of time is most resonant. A family living near H. F.'s house in Aldgate 'were all seemingly well on the Monday, being Ten in Family', but 'by Saturday at Noon, the Master, Mistress, four Children and four Servants were all gone, and the House left entirely empty' (pp. 173–4). If the *Journal* is most disturbing when its narrator can no longer account for individual loss, there are few more disturbing moments in it than when the most precise narrative time engulfs a mass of individual cases: 'this was the time when it was reported, that above 3000 People died in one Night; and they that wou'd have us believe they more critically observ'd it, pretend to say, that they all died within the space of two Hours, (*viz*) Between the Hours of One and three in the Morning (p. 173). Compassionate attention to the individual subject is overwhelmed by the 'tally' which is narrative time; yet from H. F.'s sceptical report it is impossible to know what the tally is. Plague shapes narrative time to its own form: relentless, diffuse, and beyond reckoning. As before, the *Journal* combines the allure of journalism with the conscience of scrupulous history, all along declaring its provisional nature.

Defoe's attention to particulars leads to an uneasy relationship with the rich symbolic potential of the subject. Hasty comparisons between the *Journal* and the desolate New York of Edward Hopper or the iconography of the Last Judgment diminish its variety and complexity. Defoe certainly shows unnerving skill in rendering the outward signs of desolation in the once-busy city—the doors which there was no one to shut and the windows left 'shattering with the Wind' (p. 171)—but the streets of the *Journal* are not always deserted; its sense of locality sees to that. When H. F. goes to visit the 'terrible Pit' at Aldgate, the apocalyptic sight is conditional (like Defoe's providential view of plague) upon worldly causes, 'for Coffins were not to be had' (pp. 62–3). When the abusive men in the Pye Tavern catch the disease they are 'every one of them carried into the great Pit, which I have mentioned above, before it was quite fill'd up' (pp. 66–7). The unobtrusive subordinate clause cautions us not to think too readily of hell, but the allusion in the final clause to the ultimate sealing of its gates reassures us that we may. Two pages on, H. F. prays to God to pardon the men. To see the Aldgate pit as the inferno would be to usurp God's judgment and to consign everyone, good and bad, to the same fate (the old difficulty of the view which called plague an instrument of divine anger against the sinful), but Defoe's style exhibits his debt to such a view. His doctrinal position is insufficiently clear to support consistently a non-symbolic version of events.

The same uneasy relationship with symbolism has different implications elsewhere. H. F.'s favourite subject, the shutting-up of houses, makes the Englishman's home not his castle but a lethal prison; the Dutch merchants ape the indigenous tradition by actually fortifying their homes against all intruders. Many readers have noticed that the *Journal* is full of grim puns. These threaten to make the symptoms and consequences of plague a metaphor, and sometimes an explanation, for other things: on page 6 we are told that the numbers of people suffering from 'Feaver, Spotted-Feaver, and Teeth, began to swell'. Rumour imitates the plague; people try to conceal it, but as word is passed from one person to the next, everyone knows. Anything that is circulated is deadly; in *Robinson Crusoe*, the hero reflects on the pointlessness of his store of coins, and in *Colonel Jack* on its encumbrance. In the *Journal*, money is an infection to be sterilized before use. Communication is a deadly disease, and people walk down the middle of the street and shun passers-by to avoid it. Made representative of all human behaviour, Defoe's account of the plague year would be a grisly satire. Swift drew on the success of *Robinson Crusoe* in writing his satiric masterpiece of travel literature, and in the repatriated Gulliver, unable to bear the stench of humanity, we are reminded of Defoe's Londoners of 1665, at large in the streets only if they can carry scent to protect their nostrils. The mythical potential of the *Journal* is often satirical, so the compassionate narrator must do his best to suppress it.

His problem is partly that plague attacks not only the constitution but the conscience; it brings the worst out of many people. H. F. himself bribes someone to take over his dangerous but responsible job as parish examiner; others become violent in order to survive. The narrator's attitude is forgiving in the extreme. He tries to separate plague behaviour from his general sense of human nature; so much so that his reasoning may appear confused, as if pressurized by the magnitude of the event. Appeals to God's greater mercy offer no relief, for H. F. must sort out his own judgments before making any such appeal; the inner life of the *Journal* is often in the effort to record the ramifications of other people's actions. There are, however, some incidents which exceed even this narrator's powers of forgiveness—ones which suggest, for all H. F.'s optimism, a depravity in human nature itself. The houses of the dead are looted; workers at the burial ground strip linen from corpses; nurses smother their patients to lessen the risk of infection to themselves, and make off with their goods; it is even suggested, in unobtrusive parenthesis (H. F.'s grammar subordinates what he would prefer not to admit to), that some people were shut up in their houses 'maliciously': a litany of chaos to satisfy Shakespeare's Timon. Some of these incidents may be explained as mere rumour. H. F. notes that murderous nurses always seem to operate on the other side of town, wherever one lives, and he seeks to contain the horror of the episodes within statistical probability: 'I must say I believe nothing of its being so common a Crime, as some have since been pleas'd to say' (p. 83). The worst of these tales of depravity are those which suggest that the infected tried deliberately to pass the disease on to the healthy. H. F. returns to the question almost as obsessively as he does to the shutting-up of houses. It is a matter of public debate: some think it is in the nature of the disease, some in the nature of humanity, 'which cannot bear to see itself more miserable than others of its own Species' (p. 154). H. F.'s solution is to dispose of the question by attacking the evidence for it: it is, he says, a fiction born from the fears of country people of being infected by those fleeing from the city, and from popular ignorance of the fact that one could have the disease without knowing it. But here the narrator stands convicted by his own frequent admission that it was impossible to 'come at all the particulars' of any story. The scandal remains through want of evidence. When he seeks to reverse another myth of the plague year, that bodies remained unburied in the open streets, he defends the local magistrates against the scandalous imputation that they failed to fulfil their duties (p. 181). By proposing that deliberate infection was a product of rumour, he defends human nature itself.

   A Journal of the Plague Year was responsive to its time in a number of obvious ways, but it also has a deeper sense of the currents of the age which better represents its distinction and recommends it more forcibly to readers today. Defoe is often portrayed as a writer of practical concerns, incapable of engaging with ideas. In his defence of human nature, however, he probes the central philosophical issues of the early eighteenth century in England, indeed of the Enlightenment itself. The decade preceding Defoe's *Journal* had seen the publication of two enormously influential works, Shaftesbury's *Characteristics* (revised in 1714), and Mandeville's *Fable of the Bees* (also 1714, and reissued in 1723). Defoe owes more to Shaftesbury's optimism than to Mandeville's cynical vision of public good supported by private vice, but his debt is troubled: placed in the extreme conditions of a plague-ridden city, the dicta of natural philosophy seem shallow and complacent. Shaftesbury argues that man is inherently sociable and that public good means private good, but in the world of the *Journal* the equation is suicidal; he writes of the pleasure of affections such as 'pity, succour, or whatever else is of a social or friendly sort', where in 1665 these affections could be mere luxuries. He holds that what we call 'evil' or 'unnatural' reflects deficiencies in our thinking, that we should always be able to explain the reasons why crimes are committed in terms of natural (and therefore good) feelings. Defoe is more sceptical.

His concern with a wholly independent evil is evident in the exchanges between Crusoe and Man Friday and in the contrast between the three boy-thieves in *Colonel Jack*; in the *Journal* he admits that some actions cannot be explained by natural philosophy: 'What natural Reason could be given, for so wicked a Thing, at a Time, when they might conclude themselves just going to appear at the Barr of Divine Justice, I know not: I am very well satsify'd, that it cannot be reconcil'd to Religion and Principle, any more than it can be to Generosity and Humanity' (p. 54). H. F. stands by what Shaftesbury had rejected: a religion based on rewards and punishments.

Keeping Shaftesbury at arm's length also meant doubting the political efficacy of his ideas. Recent commentaries have stressed the role of 'sentimentalism', inspired by Shaftesbury's work, in shaping eighteenth-century notions of human society.[4] The *Journal* gives scope to feelings of compassion, forgiveness, and tolerance (unlike the more admonitory *Due Preparations for the Plague*) but it does not suppose that everyone will share them; conciliation of rival religious interests it considers almost impossible. It hopes that its terrors will make the stoutest heart bleed, and emphasizes the natural bonds of sympathy between people; yet it often contrasts the behaviour of the compassionate with that of the 'hardened', who are as incapable of pity as they are of seeing the danger of the disease to themselves. One of H. F.'s most important qualifications as a narrator is that he remains 'surprized', 'curious' and 'tender' for all his exposure to scenes of horror. The episode in the *Journal* that best exhibits its sentimental inheritance is H. F.'s meeting with the impoverished but virtuous waterman. Resolving to find out about people who have fled to ships moored on the Thames, he encounters a boatman who supports his plague-ridden family by rowing provisions across the river. Accused of abandoning his wife and children, the boatman casts his eyes up to heaven in thanks for having been preserved

---

[4] See John Mullan, *Sentiment and Sociability* (1988); for Shaftesbury, his *Characteristics of Men, Manners, Opinions and Times* edited by J. M. Robertson, 2 vols. (repr. 1964), vol. i, pp. 263–336.

in order to support them. H. F. is provoked not only to tears but to dig into his pocket—the two actions are inseparable: 'As I could not refrain contributing Tears to this Man's Story, so neither could I refrain my Charity for his assistance' (p. 109). The boatman responds with his own tears and repeated thanks to God. H. F. reminds his audience that 'the Cries of the poor were most lamentable to hear' (p. 95); he also praises, perhaps in ignorance of history, the charity of affluent people in supporting them. But the *Journal* also asserts everywhere what the scene of the boatman implies: that the poor must work hard and depend on faith through reason to deserve either tears or charity. Sentimentalism was later to develop strong democratic tendencies, but there is little sign of them here.

Yet the *Journal* not only challenges the sentimental ethos but also strengthens it. Sentimental literature usually rewards the penitent and attempts mawkishly to realize tragic experience in ordinary lives. Where Moll Flanders and Colonel Jack repent of their crimes in the balm of prosperity, the penitents of the *Journal* are denied all material help: 'none durst stop ... administer Comfort to the poor Creatures' (p. 34); and in this book, where mothers pass infected milk to their babies, and fathers spread plague through their families by seeking to protect them, almost anyone is liable to incur the appalling, ironic fate of the protagonists of ancient drama. Defoe stresses the bonds of sympathetic and familial attachment between people, but he also exposes us to the horrors of their rupture. Even in its medical uncertainties, its search for explanations of the mysterious affliction, the *Journal* suggests the atmosphere of tragedy. Defoe's *Tour through the Whole Island of Great Britain* is often referred to as the true epic of eighteenth-century English literature. The oddity of *A Journal of the Plague Year* may make it hard to classify, but its power is that of tragedy, such as we find nowhere else in the literature of its time.

D. R.

NOTE ON THE TEXT

A Journal of the Plague Year was first published in 1722, the only edition to appear during Defoe's life. A second edition appeared in 1755. The present text is that of 1722, printed from a xerox reproduction of the Huntington Library copy, through the kindness of Mr. James Thorpe, Director of the Huntington Library. The long 's' of the first edition has been eliminated, and I have silently corrected obvious errors of the press. In a very few instances where the text of the first edition is unintelligble, the result of an omitted word, I have supplied an obvious reading in square brackets. I have occasionally reduced the excessive punctuation of the original to avoid confusion. Aldgate, or Algate, the parish inhabited by Defoe and by the narrator of the *Journal*, I have printed consistently as *Aldgate*.

L. L.

SELECT BIBLIOGRAPHY

JOHN ROBERT MOORE's *Checklist of the Writings of Daniel Defoe* (2nd edn., 1971) includes more than five hundred titles, most of which are available from University Microfilms Ltd. His bibliographical methods are challenged by P. N. Furbank and W. R. Owens in *The Canonisation of Daniel Defoe* (1988). Defoe's major works (including the *Journal* and *Due Preparations for the Plague*) are collected in *Romances and Narratives of Daniel Defoe*, ed. G. S. Aitken, 16 vols. (1895, repr. 1974). Other useful collections are *Works*, ed. G. H. Maynadier, 16 vols. (1903–4); and *Novels and Selected Writings*, 14 vols. (Shakespeare Head, 1927–8). Defoe's *Review* is available in the facsimile edition of A. W. Secord, 22 vols. (1938).

The first edition of *A Journal of the Plague Year* appeared in 1722; the second in 1755. E. W. Brayley's edition of 1835 was based on the first and makes no corrections; it was reprinted many times in the nineteenth century. The Everyman edition, first published in 1908, uses Aitken's text. Anthony Burgess and Christopher Bristow prepared a modernized text for Penguin in 1966 which has been reprinted many times since. Louis Landa's Oxford English Novels edition was published in 1969.

Defoe's other writings on plague may be found in his *Review* of 1709, nos. 86 (22 Oct.), 87 (25 Oct.), 88 (27 Oct.), 89 (29 Oct.), 91 (3 Nov.), 105 (6 Dec.); of 1712, nos. 7 (23 Aug.), 8 (26 Aug.), and 11 (6 Sept.); items from *Applebee's Journal*, *Mist's Journal*, and *The Daily Post* are reprinted in William Lee, *Daniel Defoe: His Life and Recently Discovered Writings* (1869), vol. ii, pp. 265, 277, 281, 284, 291, 294, 296, 378, 399, and 407. Those from *Applebee's Journal* also appear in Michael F.

Shugrue (ed.), *Selected Poetry and Prose of Daniel Defoe* (1968), pp. 204–14. The Quarantine Act is discussed by A. J. Henderson, *London and the National Government* (1945).

We await a major modern biography of Defoe. The most useful is still James Sutherland's *Defoe* (2nd edn., 1950). John Robert Moore's *Daniel Defoe: Citizen of the Modern World* (1958) is factually rich but unpredictable in judgement, the reverse of Paul Dottin's *Daniel Defoe et ses romans* (1924). Defoe's whereabouts during the plague year are discussed in F. Bastian, *Defoe's Early Life* (1981), pp. 18–31, and 'James Foe, Merchant, Father of Daniel Defoe', *Notes and Queries*, ccix (1964), 83.

The *Journal*'s changing reputation may be traced in *Defoe: The Critical Heritage*, ed. Pat Rogers (1972). For recent discussion, see the following general studies: Maximilian E. Novak, *Realism, Myth and History in Defoe's Fiction* (1983), *Economics and the Fiction of Daniel Defoe* (1962), and *Defoe and the Nature of Man* (1963); J. Paul Hunter, *The Reluctant Pilgrim* (1966); Michael M. Boardman, *Defoe and the Uses of Narrative* (1983); Ian A. Bell, *Defoe's Fiction* (1985); Paula R. Backscheider, *Daniel Defoe. Ambition and Innovation* (1986); John J. Richetti, *Defoe's Narratives* (1975) and *Daniel Defoe* (1988); G. A. Starr, *Defoe and Spiritual Autobiography* (1965) and *Defoe and Casuistry* (1971); James Sutherland, *Daniel Defoe: A Critical Study* (1971); Arthur W. Secord, *Studies in the Narrative Method of Defoe* (1924); Michael Shinagel, *Defoe and Middle Class Gentility* (1968); E. Anthony James, *Daniel Defoe's Many Voices* (1972); Paul K. Alkon, *Defoe and Fictional Time* (1979); Barbara Foley, *Telling the Truth* (1986), discusses the *Journal* in terms of the theory and practice of 'documentary fiction'.

Studies devoted to the *Journal* include Maximilian E. Novak, 'Defoe and the Disordered City', *Publications of the Modern Language Association of America*, vol. 92 (1977), 241–52, which pre-empts Pat Rogers's '"This Calamitous Year"' in his *Eighteenth Century Encounters* (1985), 151–66. Everett Zimmerman's 'H. F.'s Meditations: *A Journal of the Plague Year*', *Publications of the Modern Language Association of America*, vol. 87 (1972), 417–23, reappears in his full-length study, *Defoe and the Novel* (1975). W. Austin Flanders, 'Defoe's *Journal of the Plague Year* and the modern urban experience', *Centennial Review*, xvi (1972), 328–48, is reprinted in Max Byrd (ed.), *Daniel Defoe: A Collection of Critical Essays* (1976), 150–69. F. Bastian, 'Defoe's *Journal of the Plague Year* Reconsidered', *Review of English Studies*, NS, xvi (1965), 151–73, considers the historical veracity of the *Journal*; Watson Nicholson, *The Historical Sources of Defoe's Journal of the Plague Year* (1919, reissued in 1966), reprints a selection of Defoe's source material. Manuel Schonhorn, 'Defoe's *Journal of the Plague Year*: Topography and Intention', *Review of English Studies*, NS, xix (1968), 387–402, shows how Defoe reconstructed the London of 1665. Some of the liveliest Defoe criticism ever written may be found in ch. 20 of Peter Conrad, *The Everyman History of English Literature* (1985); pp. 338–41 deal with *A Journal of the Plague Year*.

Pepys's employment of Paul Lorrain is recorded in *Letters and the Second Diary of Samuel Pepys*, ed. R. G. Howarth (1932), pp. 109, 246, 314–15; and in *Private Correspondence and Miscellaneous Papers of Samuel Pepys*, ed. J. R. Tanner, 2 vols. (1926). For Defoe and Lorrain, see Robert R. Singleton, 'Defoe, Moll Flanders, and the Ordinary of Newgate', *Harvard Library Bulletin*, xxiv (1976), no. 4, pp. 407–13; and Lincoln B. Faller, 'In Contrast to Defoe: The Rev. Paul Lorrain, Historian of Crime', *Huntington Library Quarterly*, 60 (1976), 59–78.

Defoe's medical sources are listed in the Explanatory Notes. For the Great Plague as others saw it, the following are historically interesting but medically dubious: Charles Creighton, *A History of Epidemics in Britain* (1891, repr. 1965); Walter George Bell, *The Great Plague in London in 1665* (1924, rev. 1951); Charles F. Mullett, *The Bubonic Plague in England* (1956); J. F. D. Shrewsbury, *A History of Bubonic Plague in the British Isles* (1970). More accurate are L. Fabian Hirst, *The Conquest of Plague* (1953); Charles-Edward Amory Winslow, *The Conquest of Epidemic Disease* (1943), which devotes a chapter to one of Defoe's chief sources, Richard Mead; Christopher Morris, 'The Plague in Britain', *Historical Journal*, xiv (1971), 205–15, and 'The Plague', *The Diary of Samuel Pepys*, ed. Robert Latham and William Matthews, 11 vols. (1970) x, 328–37; *The Plague Reconsidered*, Local Population Studies Supplement (1977); P. Slack, 'The Disappearance of Plague: An Alternative View', *Economic History Review*, 2nd ser., 34 (1981), 469–76 and *The Impact of Plague in Tudor and Stuart England* (1985); and Ronald Hutton, *The Restoration* (1985), 225–30.

For those interested in modern epidemiology in general, the following works are both readable and reliable: Sir Macfarlane Burnet and David O. White, *Natural History of Infectious Disease* (1972); J.–N. Biraben, *Les Hommes et la Peste*, 2 vols. (1975); William H. McNeill, *Plagues and Peoples* (1976); G. Melvyn Howe, *Man, Environment and Disease in Britain* (1976); Philip Ziegler, *The Black Death* (1969); Robert S. Gottfried, *The Black Death* (1984). Elias Canetti, *Crowds and Power* (1973), 317–24, dramatizes the psychological and social effects of epidemic disease.

D. R.

A CHRONOLOGY OF
DANIEL DEFOE

THIS is based mainly upon the detailed 'Chronological Outline' in John Robert Moore's *Daniel Defoe: Citizen of the Modern World* (1958), a work indispensable to all students of Defoe.

<table>
<tr><td></td><td></td><td>Age</td></tr>
<tr><td>1660</td><td>Born, London, son of James Foe, a tallow chandler, later a member of the Butchers' Company</td><td></td></tr>
<tr><td>1662</td><td>Act of Uniformity. The Foe family left the Church of England and became Presbyterians</td><td>2</td></tr>
<tr><td>1665</td><td>The Great Plague of London</td><td>5</td></tr>
<tr><td>1666</td><td>The Great Fire of London</td><td>6</td></tr>
<tr><td>c. 1671</td><td>Attended a school in Dorking, Surrey, run by the Reverend James Fisher</td><td>11</td></tr>
<tr><td>1674(?)–79(?)</td><td>Attended the Dissenting Academy run by the Reverend Charles Morton at Newington Green. Planned to prepare for the ministry, but rejected the plan in 1681</td><td>14–19</td></tr>
<tr><td>c. 1683</td><td>Established as a merchant near the Royal Exchange in London, probably in the hosiery trade. About this time he was captured by Algerian pirates but was soon released</td><td>23</td></tr>
<tr><td>1684</td><td>Married Mary Tuffley</td><td>24</td></tr>
<tr><td>1685</td><td>Took part briefly in Monmouth's Rebellion</td><td>25</td></tr>
<tr><td>1685–92</td><td>A merchant, dealing in hosiery, an importer of wine and tobacco, part-owner of ships. He travelled for business purposes in England and on the Continent</td><td>25–32</td></tr>
<tr><td>1688</td><td>Admitted to the Butchers' Company by virtue of his father's membership. Supported the Revolution of 1688 by publishing a pamphlet and joining the forces of William of Orange, then advancing on London</td><td>28</td></tr>
<tr><td>1690–1</td><td>Contributed to John Dunton's Athenian Mercury</td><td>30–1</td></tr>
<tr><td>1692</td><td>First bankruptcy</td><td>32</td></tr>
<tr><td>1697</td><td>Published An Essay upon Projects</td><td>37</td></tr>
<tr><td>1697–1701</td><td>An agent for William III in England and Scotland. Owned brick and pantile works near Tilbury in Essex. This failed in 1703</td><td>37–41</td></tr>
</table>

A

JOURNAL

OF THE

Plague Year:

BEING

Observations or Memorials,

Of the most Remarkable

OCCURRENCES,

As well

PUBLICK *as* PRIVATE,

Which happened in

LONDON

During the last

GREAT VISITATION
In 1665.

Written by a CITIZEN who continued all the
while in *London*. Never made publick before

LONDON:
Printed for E. *Nutt* at the *Royal-Exchange*; *J. Roberts*
in *Warwick-Lane*; A. *Dodd* without *Temple-Bar*;
and *J. Graves* in St. *James's-street*. 1722.

Title-page of the first edition, 1722

A JOURNAL OF
THE PLAGUE YEAR

IT was about the Beginning of *September* 1664, that I, among the Rest of my Neighbours, heard in ordinary Discourse, that the Plague was return'd again in *Holland*;[1] for it had been very violent there, and particularly at *Amsterdam* and *Roterdam*, in the Year 1663, whither *they say*, it was brought, some said from *Italy*, others from the *Levant* among some Goods, which were brought home by their Turkey Fleet; others said it was brought from *Candia*;[2] others from *Cyprus*. It matter'd not, from whence it come;[3] but all agreed, it was come into *Holland* again.

We had no such thing as printed News Papers[4] in those Days, to spread Rumours and Reports of Things; and to improve them by the Invention of Men, as I have liv'd to see practis'd since. But such things as these were gather'd from the Letters of Merchants, and others, who corresponded abroad, and from them was handed about by Word of Mouth only; so that things did not spread instantly over the whole Nation, as they do now. But it seems that the Government had a true Account of it, and several Counsels were held about Ways to prevent its coming over; but all was kept very private. Hence it was, that this Rumour died off again, and People began to forget it, as a thing we were very little concern'd in, and that we hoped was not true; till the latter End of *November*, or the Beginning of *December* 1664, when two Men, said to be

French-men, died of the Plague in *Long Acre*, or rather at the upper End of *Drury-Lane*. The Family they were in, endeavour'd to conceal it as much as possible; but as it had gotten some Vent in the Discourse of the Neighbourhood, the Secretaries of State got Knowledge of it. And concerning themselves to inquire about it, in order to be certain of the Truth, two Physicians and a Surgeon were order'd to go to the House, and make Inspection. This they did; and finding evident Tokens[1] of the Sickness upon both the Bodies that were dead, they gave their Opinions publickly, that they died of the Plague: Whereupon it was given in to the Parish Clerk, and he also return'd them to the Hall;[2] and it was printed in the weekly Bill of Mortality[3] in the usual manner, thus,

Plague 2. Parishes infected 1

The People shew'd a great Concern at this, and began to be allarm'd all over the Town, and the more, because in the last Week in *December* 1664, another Man died in the same House, and of the same Distemper: And then we were easy again for about six Weeks, when none having died with any Marks of Infection, it was said, the Distemper was gone; but after that, I think it was about the 12th of *February*, another died in another House, but in the same Parish, and in the same manner.

This turn'd the Peoples Eyes pretty much towards that End of the Town; and the weekly Bills shewing an Encrease of Burials in St. *Giles*'s Parish more than usual, it began to be suspected, that the Plague was among the People at that End of the Town; and that many had died of it, tho' they had taken Care to keep it as much from the Knowledge of the Publick, as possible: This possess'd the Heads of the People very much, and few car'd to go thro' *Drury-Lane*, or the other Streets suspected, unless they had extraordinary Business, that obliged them to it.

This Encrease of the Bills stood thus; the usual Number of Burials in a Week, in the Parishes of St. *Giles*'s in the Fields,

and St. *Andrew*'s Holborn were from 12 to 17 or 19 each few
more or less; but from the Time that the Plague first began
in St. *Giles*'s Parish, it was observ'd, that the ordinary Burials
encreased in Number considerably. *For Example,*

From *Dec.* 27th to *Jan.* 3.	St. *Giles*'s - - - - - - 16
	St. *Andrew*'s - - - - 17
Jan. 3. to — 10.	St. *Giles*'s - - - - - - 12
	St. *Andrew*'s - - - - 25
Jan. 10. to — 17.	St. *Giles*'s - - - - - - 18
	St. *Andrew*'s - - - - 18
Jan. 17. to — 24.	St. *Giles*'s - - - - - - 23
	St. *Andrew*'s - - - - 16
Jan. 24. to — 31.	St. *Giles*'s - - - - - - 24
	St. *Andrew*'s - - - - 15
Jan. 30. to *Feb.* 7.	St. *Giles*'s - - - - - - 21
	St. *Andrew*'s - - - - 23
Feb. 7. to — 14.	St. *Giles*'s - - - - - - 24

whereof one of the Plague.

The like Encrease of the Bills was observ'd in the Parishes
of St. *Brides*, adjoining on one Side of *Holborn* Parish, and in
the Parish of St. *James Clarkenwell*, adjoining on the other Side
of *Holborn*; in both which Parishes the usual Numbers that
died weekly, were from 4 to 6 or 8, whereas at that time they
were increas'd, as follows.

From *Dec.* 20. to *Dec.* 27.	St. *Brides* - - - - - - 0
	St. *James* - - - - - - 8
Dec. 27. to *Jan.* 3.	St. *Brides* - - - - - - 6
	St. *James* - - - - - - 9
Jan. 3. to — 10.	St. *Brides* - - - - - - 11
	St. *James* - - - - - - 7
Jan. 10. to — 17.	St. *Brides* - - - - - - 12
	St. *James* - - - - - - 9
Jan. 17. to — 24.	St. *Brides* - - - - - - 9
	St. *James* - - - - - - 15
Jan. 24. to — 31.	St. *Brides* - - - - - - 8
	St. *James* - - - - - - 12

From *Jan.* 31.	to *Feb.* 7.	St. *Brides* ------ 13
		St. *James* ------ 5
Feb. 7.	to — 14.	St. *Brides* ------ 12
		St. *James* ------ 6

Besides this, it was observ'd with great Uneasiness by the People, that the weekly Bills in general encreas'd very much during these Weeks, altho' it was at a Time of the Year, when usually the Bills are very moderate.

The usual Number of Burials within the Bills of Mortality for a Week, was from about 240 or thereabouts, to 300. The last was esteem'd a pretty high Bill; but after this we found the Bills successively encreasing, as follows.

		Increased
Dec. the 20. to the 27th,	Buried 291. —	
27. to the 3 *Jan.*	—— 349.	— 58
January 3. to the 10.	—— 394.	— 45
10. to the 17.	—— 415.	— 21
17. to the 24.	—— 474.	— 59

This last Bill was really frightful, being a higher Number than had been known to have been buried in one Week, since the preceeding Visitation of 1656.

However, all this went off again, and the Weather proving cold, and the Frost which began in *December*, still continuing very severe, even till near the End of *February*, attended with sharp tho' moderate Winds, the Bills decreas'd again, and the City grew healthy, and every body began to look upon the Danger as good as over; only that still the Burials in St. *Giles*'s continu'd high: From the Beginning of *April* especially they stood at 25 each Week, till the Week from the 18th to the 25th, when there was buried in St. *Giles*'s Parish 30, whereof two of the Plague, and 8 of the Spotted-Feaver,[1] which was look'd upon as the same thing; likewise the Number that died of the Spotted-Feaver in the whole increased, being 8 the Week before, and 12 the Week above-named.

This alarm'd us all again, and terrible Apprehensions were among the People, especially the Weather being now chang'd and growing warm, and the Summer being at Hand:[1] However, the next Week there seem'd to be some Hopes again, the Bills were low, the Number of the Dead in all was but 388, there was none of the Plague, and but four of the Spotted-Feaver.

But the following Week it return'd again, and the Distemper was spread into two or three other Parishes (*viz.*) St. *Andrew*'s-*Holborn*, St. *Clement*'s-*Danes*, and to the great Affliction of the City, one died within the Walls, in the Parish of St. *Mary-Wool-Church*, that is to say, in *Bearbinder-lane* near the *Stocks market*; in all there was nine of the Plague, and six of the Spotted-Feaver. It was however upon Inquiry found, that this *French-man* who died in *Bearbinder-lane*, was one who having liv'd in *Long-Acre*, near the infected Houses, had removed for fear of the Distemper, not knowing that he was already infected.

This was the beginning of *May*, yet the Weather was temperate, variable and cool enough—and People had still some Hopes: That which encourag'd them was, that the City was healthy, the whole 97 Parishes buried but 54, and we began to hope, that as it was chiefly among the People at that End of the Town, it might go no farther; and the rather, because the next Week which was from the 9th of *May* to the 16th there died but three, of which not one within the whole City or Liberties,[2] and St. *Andrew*'s buried but 15, which was very low: 'Tis true, St. *Giles*'s buried two and thirty, but still as there was but one of the Plague, People began to be easy, the whole Bill also was very low, for the Week before, the Bill was but 347, and the Week above-mentioned but 343: We continued in these Hopes for a few Days, But it was but for a few; for the People were no more to be deceived thus; they searcht the Houses, and found that the Plague was really spread every way, and that many died of it every Day: So that now all our Extenuations abated, and it was no more to be concealed, nay it quickly appeared that the Infection had spread it self beyond all Hopes of Abatement; that in the Parish of St. *Giles*'s, it was gotten into several Streets, and several Families lay all sick together; And accordingly in the Weekly Bill for the next Week, the thing began to shew it self; there was indeed but 14 set down of the Plague, but this was all Knavery and Collusion, for in St. *Giles*'s Parish they buried 40 in all, whereof it was certain most of them died of the Plague, though they were set down of other Distempers; and though the Number of all the Burials were not increased above 32, and the whole Bill being but 385, yet there was 14 of the Spotted-Feaver, as well as 14 of the Plague; and we took it for granted upon the whole, that there was 50 died that Week of the Plague.

The next Bill was from the 23d of *May* to the 30th, when the Number of the Plague was 17: But the Burials in St. *Giles*'s were 53, a frightful Number! of whom they set down but 9 of the Plague: But on an Examination more strictly by the Justices of the Peace, and at the Lord Mayor's Request, it was found there were 20 more, who were really dead of the Plague in that Parish, but had been set down of the Spotted-Feaver or other Distempers, besides others concealed.

But those were trifling Things to what followed immediately after; for now the Weather set in hot,[1] and from the first Week in *June*, the Infection spread in a dreadful Manner, and the Bills rose high, the Articles of the Feaver, Spotted-Feaver, and Teeth,[2] began to swell: For all that could conceal their Distempers, did it to prevent their Neighbours shunning and refusing to converse with them; and also to prevent Authority shutting up their Houses, which though it was not yet practised, yet was threatned, and People were extremely terrify'd at the Thoughts of it.

The Second Week in *June*, the Parish of St. *Giles*'s, where still the Weight of the Infection lay, buried 120, whereof though the Bills said but 68 of the Plague; every Body said there had been 100 at least, calculating it from the usual Number of Funerals in that Parish as above.

Till this Week the City continued free, there having never any died except that one *Frenchman*, who I mention'd before, within the whole 97 Parishes. Now there died four within the City, one in *Wood street*, one in *Fenchurch street*, and two in

Crooked-lane: *Southwark* was entirely free, having not one yet died on that Side of the Water.

I liv'd without *Aldgate*[1] about mid-way between *Aldgate Church* and *White-Chappel-Bars*, on the left Hand or North-side of the Street; and as the Distemper had not reach'd to that Side of the City, our Neighbourhood continued very easy: But at the other End of the Town, their Consternation was very great; and the richer sort of People, especially the Nobility and Gentry, from the West part of the City throng'd out of Town,[2] with their Families and Servants in an unusual Manner; and this was more particularly seen in *White-Chapel*; that is to say, the Broad-street where I liv'd: Indeed nothing was to be seen but Waggons and Carts, with Goods, Women, Servants, Children, &c. Coaches fill'd with People of the better Sort, and Horsemen attending them, and all hurrying away; then empty Waggons, and Carts appear'd and Spare-horses with Servants, who it was apparent were returning or sent from the Country to fetch more People: Besides innumerable Numbers of Men on Horseback, some alone, others with Servants, and generally speaking, all loaded with Baggage and fitted out for travelling, as any one might perceive by their Appearance.

This was a very terrible and melancholy Thing to see, and as it was a Sight which I cou'd not but look on from Morning to Night; for indeed there was nothing else of Moment to be seen, it filled me with very serious Thoughts of the Misery that was coming upon the City, and the unhappy Condition of those that would be left in it.

This Hurry of the People was such for some Weeks, that there was no getting at the Lord-Mayor's Door without exceeding Difficulty; there was such pressing and crouding there to get passes and Certificates of Health,[3] for such as travelled abroad; for without these, there was no being admitted to pass thro' the Towns upon the Road, or to lodge in any Inn: Now as there had none died in the City for all this time, My Lord Mayor gave Certificates of Health without any Difficulty to all those who liv'd in the 97 Parishes, and to those within the Liberties too for a while.

This Hurry, I say, continued some Weeks, that is to say, all the Month of *May* and *June*, and the more because it was rumour'd that an order of the Government was to be issued out, to place Turn-pikes[1] and Barriers on the Road, to prevent Peoples travelling; and that the Towns on the Road, would not suffer People from *London* to pass, for fear of bringing the Infection along with them, though neither of these Rumours had any Foundation, but in the Imagination; especially at first.

I now began to consider seriously with my Self, concerning my own Case, and how I should dispose of my self; that is to say, whether I should resolve to stay in *London*, or shut up my House and flee, as many of my Neighbours did. I have set this particular down so fully, because I know not but it may be of Moment to those who come after me, if they come to be brought to the same Distress, and to the same Manner of making their Choice and therefore I desire this Account may pass with them, rather for a Direction to themselves to act by, than a History of my actings, seeing it may not be of one Farthing value to them to note what became of me.

I had two important things before me; the one was the carrying on my Business and Shop; which was considerable, and in which was embark'd all my Effects in the World; and the other was the Preservation of my Life in so dismal a Calamity, as I saw apparently was coming upon the whole City; and which however great it was, my Fears perhaps as well as other Peoples, represented to be much greater than it could be.

The first Consideration was of great Moment to me; my Trade was *a Saddler*,[2] and as my Dealings were chiefly not by a Shop or Chance Trade, but among the Merchants, trading to the *English* Colonies in *America*, so my Effects lay very much in the hands of such. I was a single Man 'tis true, but I had a Family of Servants, who I kept at my Business, had a House, Shop, and Ware-houses fill'd with Goods; and in short, to leave them all as things in such a Case must be left, that is to say, without any Overseer or Person fit to be trusted with them, had been to hazard the Loss not only of my Trade, but of my Goods, and indeed of all I had in the World.

I had an Elder Brother at the same Time in *London*, and not many Years before come over from *Portugal*; and advising with him, his Answer was in three Words the same that was given in another Case quite different, (*viz.*) *Master save thy self.*[1] In a Word, he was for my retiring into the Country, as he resolv'd to do himself with his Family; telling me, what he had it seems, heard abroad, that the best Preparation for the Plague was to run away from it. As to my Argument of losing my Trade, my Goods, or Debts, he quite confuted me: He told me the same thing, which I argued for my staying, (*viz.*) *That I would trust God with my Safety and Health*, was the strongest Repulse to my Pretentions of losing my Trade and my Goods; for, says he, is it not as reasonable that you should trust God with the Chance or Risque of losing your Trade, as that you should stay in so imminent a Point of Danger, and trust him with your Life?

I could not argue that I was in any Strait, as to a Place where to go, having several Friends and Relations in *Northampton-shire*,[2] whence our Family first came from; and particularly, I had an only Sister in *Lincolnshire*, very willing to receive and entertain me.

My Brother, who had already sent his Wife and two Children into *Bedfordshire*, and resolv'd to follow them, press'd my going very earnestly; and I had once resolv'd to comply with his Desires, but at that time could get no Horse: For tho' it is true, all the People did not go out of the City of *London*; yet I may venture to say, that in a manner all the Horses did; for there was hardly a Horse to be bought or hired in the whole City for some Weeks. Once I resolv'd to travel on Foot with one Servant; and as many did, lie at no Inn, but carry a Soldiers Tent with us, and so lie in the Fields, the Weather being very warm, and no Danger from taking cold: I say, as many did, because several did so at last, especially those who had been in the Armies in the War which had not been many Years past; and I must needs say, that speaking of second Causes, had most of the People that travelled, done so, the Plague had not been carried into so many Country-Towns and Houses, as it was, to the great Damage, and indeed to the Ruin of abundance of People.

But then my Servant who I had intended to take down with me, deceiv'd me; and being frighted at the Encrease of the Distemper, and not knowing when I should go, he took other Measures, and left me, so I was put off for that Time; and one way or other, I always found that to appoint to go away was always cross'd by some Accident or other, so as to disappoint and put it off again; and this brings in a Story which otherwise might be thought a needless Digression, (viz.) about these Disappointments being from Heaven.

I mention this Story also as the best Method I can advise any Person to take in such a Case, especially, if he be one that makes Conscience of his Duty, and would be directed what to do in it, namely, that he should keep his Eye upon the particular Providences which occur at that Time, and look upon them complexly, as they regard one another, and as altogether regard the Question before him, and then I think, he may safely take them for Intimations from Heaven of what is his unquestion'd Duty to do in such a Case; I mean as to going away from, or staying in the Place where we dwell, when visited with an infectious Distemper.

It came very warmly into my Mind, one Morning, as I was musing on this particular thing, that as nothing attended us without the Direction or Permission of Divine Power, so these Disappointments must have something in them extraordinary; and I ought to consider whether it did not evidently point out, or intimate to me, that it was the Will of Heaven I should not go. It immediately follow'd in my Thoughts, that if it really was from God, that I should stay, he was able effectually to preserve me in the midst of all the Death and Danger that would surround me; and that if I attempted to secure my self by fleeing from my Habitation, and acted contrary to these Intimations, which I believed to be Divine, it was a kind of flying from God, and that he could cause his Justice to overtake me when and where he thought fit.

These thoughts quite turn'd my Resolutions again, and when I came to discourse with my Brother again I told him, that I enclin'd to stay and take my Lot in that Station in which God had plac'd me; and that it seem'd to be made more especially my Duty, on the Account of what I have said.

My Brother, tho' a very Religious Man himself, laught at all I had suggested about its being an Intimation from Heaven, and told me several Stories of such fool-hardy People, *as he call'd them*, as I was; that I ought indeed to submit to it as a Work of Heaven, if I had been any way disabled by Distempers or Diseases, and that then not being able to go, I ought to acquiesce in the Direction of him, who having been my Maker, had an undisputed Right of Soveraignity in disposing of me; and that then there had been no Difficulty to determine which was the Call of his Providence, and which was not: But that I should take it as an Intimation from Heaven, that I should not go out of Town, only because I could not hire a Horse to go, or my Fellow was run away that was to attend me, was ridiculous, since at the same Time I had my Health and Limbs, and other Servants, and might, with Ease, travel a Day or two on foot, and having a good Certificate of being in perfect Health, might either hire a Horse, or take Post on the Road, as I thought fit.

Then he proceeded to tell me of the mischievous Consequences which attended the Presumption of the *Turks* and *Mahometans* in *Asia* and in other Places, where he had been (for my Brother being a Merchant, was a few Years before, as I have already observ'd, returned from abroad, coming last from *Lisbon*) and how presuming upon their profess'd predestinating Notions,[1] and of every Man's End being predetermin'd and unalterably before-hand decreed, they would go unconcern'd into infected Places, and converse with infected Persons, by which Means they died at the Rate of Ten or Fifteen Thousand a Week, whereas the *Europeans*, or Christian Merchants, who kept themselves retired and reserv'd, generally escap'd the Contagion.

Upon these Arguments my Brother chang'd my Resolutions again, and I began to resolve to go, and accordingly made all things ready; for in short, the Infection increased round me, and the Bills were risen to almost 700 a-Week, and my Brother told me, he would venture to stay no longer. I desir'd him to let me consider of it but till the next Day, and I would resolve; and as I had already prepar'd every thing as well as I could, as to my Business, and who to entrust my Affairs with, I had little to do but to resolve.

I went Home that Evening greatly oppress'd in my Mind, irresolute, and not knowing what to do; I had set the Evening wholly apart to consider seriously about it, and was all alone; for already People had, as it were by a general Consent, taken up the Custom of not going out of Doors after Sun-set, the Reasons I shall have Occasion to say more of by-and-by.

In the Retirement of this Evening I endeavoured to resolve first, what was my Duty to do, and I stated the Arguments with which my Brother had press'd me to go into the Country, and I set against them the strong Impressions which I had on my Mind for staying; the visible Call I seem'd to have from the particular Circumstance of my Calling, and the Care due from me for the Preservation of my Effects, which were, as I might say, my Estate; also the Intimations which I thought I had from Heaven, that to me signify'd a kind of Direction to venture, and it occurr'd to me, that if I had what I might call a Direction to stay, I ought to suppose it contain'd a Promise of being preserved, if I obey'd.

This lay close to me, and my Mind seemed more and more encouraged to stay than ever, and supported with a secret Satisfaction, that I should be kept: Add to this that turning over the Bible, which lay before me, and while my Thoughts were more than ordinarily serious upon the Question, I cry'd out, WELL, *I know not what to do, Lord direct me!* and the like; and [at] that Juncture I happen'd to stop turning over the Book at the 91*st Psalm*,[1] and casting my Eye on the second

Verse, I read on to the 7th Verse exclusive; and after that, included the 10th, as follows. *I will say of the Lord, He is my refuge, and my fortress, my God, in him will I trust. Surely he shall deliver thee from the snare of the fowler, and from the noisom pestilence. He shall cover thee with his feathers, and under his wings shalt thou trust: his truth shall be thy shield and buckler. Thou shalt not be afraid for the terror by night, nor for the arrow that flieth by day: Nor for the pestilence that walketh in darkness: nor for the destruction that wasteth at noon-day. A thousand shall fall at thy side, and ten thousand at thy right hand: but it shall not come nigh thee. Only with thine Eyes shalt thou behold and see the reward of the wicked. Because thou hast made the Lord which is my refuge, even the most High, thy habitation: There shall no evil befal thee, neither shall any plague come nigh thy dwelling,* &c.

I scarce need tell the Reader, that from that Moment I resolv'd that I would stay in the Town, and casting my self entirely upon the Goodness and Protection of the Almighty, would not seek any other Shelter whatever; and that as my Times were in his Hands, he was as able to keep me in a Time of the Infection as in a Time of Health; and if he did not think fit to deliver me, still I was in his Hands, and it was meet he should do with me as should seem good to him.

With this Resolution I went to Bed; and I was farther confirm'd in it the next Day, by the Woman being taken ill with whom I had intended to entrust my House and all my Affairs: But I had a farther Obligation laid on me on the same Side; for the next Day I found my self very much out of Order also; so that if I would have gone away, I could not, and I continued ill three or four Days, and this intirely determin'd my Stay; so I took my leave of my Brother, who went away to *Dorking* in *Surry*, and afterwards fetch'd a Round farther into *Buckinghamshire*, or *Bedfordshire*, to a Retreat he had found out there for his Family.

It was a very ill Time to be sick in, for if any one complain'd, it was immediately said he had the Plague; and tho' I had indeed no Symptoms of that Distemper, yet being very

ill, both in my Head and in my Stomach, I was not without
Apprehension, that I really was infected; but in about three
Days I grew better, the third Night I rested well, sweated a
little, and was much refresh'd; the Apprehensions of its
being the Infection went also quite away with my Illness, and
I went about my Business as usual.

These Things however put off all my Thoughts of going
into the Country; and my Brother also being gone, I had
no more Debate either with him, or with my self, on that
Subject.

It was now mid-*July*, and the Plague which had chiefly
rag'd at the other End of the Town, and as I said before, in
the Parishes of St. *Giles*'s, St. *Andrews Holbourn*, and towards
Westminster, began now to come *Eastward* towards the Part
where I liv'd. It was to be observ'd indeed, that it did not come
strait on towards us; for the City, that is to say within the
Walls, was indifferent healthy still; nor was it got then very
much over the Water into *Southwark*; for tho' there died that
Week 1268 of all Distempers, whereof it might be suppos'd
above 900 died of the Plague; yet there was but 28 in the whole
City, within the Walls; and but 19 in *Southwark*, *Lambeth*
Parish included; whereas in the Parishes of St. *Giles*, and St.
Martins in the Fields alone, there died 421.

But we perceiv'd the Infection kept chiefly in the out-
Parishes, which being very populous, and fuller also of Poor,
the Distemper found more to prey upon than in the City, as
I shall observe afterward; we perceiv'd I say, the Distemper
to draw our Way; (*viz.*) by the Parishes of *Clerken-Well*,
Cripplegate, *Shoreditch*, and *Bishopsgate*; which last two
Parishes joining to *Aldgate*, *White-Chapel*, and *Stepney*, the
Infection came at length to spread its utmost Rage and vio-
lence in those Parts, even when it abated, at the *Western*
Parishes where it began.

It was very strange to observe, that in this particular Week,
from the 4th to the 11th of *July*, when, as I have observ'd, there
died near 400 of the Plague in the two Parishes of St. *Martin's*,
and St. *Giles in the Fields* only, there died in the Parish of

Aldgate but four, in the Parish of *White-Chapel* three, in the Parish of *Stepney* but one.

Likewise in the next Week, from the 11th of *July* to the 18th, when the Week's Bill was 1761, yet there died no more of the Plague, on the whole *Southwark* Side of the Water than sixteen.

But this Face of things soon changed, and it began to thicken in *Cripplegate* Parish especially, and in *Clerken-Well*; so, that by the second Week in *August*, *Cripplegate* Parish alone, buried eight hundred eighty six, and *Clerken-Well* 155; of the first eight hundred and fifty, might well be reckoned to die of the Plague; and of the last, the Bill it self said, 145 were of the Plague.

During the Month of *July*, and while, as I have observ'd, our Part of the Town seem'd to be spar'd, in Comparison of the *West* part, I went ordinarily about the Streets, as my Business requir'd, and particularly went generally, once in a Day, or in two Days, into the City, to my Brother's House, which he had given me charge of, and to see if it was safe: And having the Key in my Pocket, I used to go into the House, and over most of the Rooms, to see that all was well; for tho' it be something wonderful to tell, that any should have Hearts so hardned, in the midst of such a Calamity, as to rob and steal; yet certain it is, that all Sorts of Villanies, and even Levities and Debaucheries were then practis'd in the Town, as openly as ever, I will not say quite as frequently, because the Numbers of People were many ways lessen'd.

But the City it self began now to be visited too, I mean within the Walls; but the Number of People there were indeed extreamly lessen'd by so great a Multitude having been gone into the Country; and even all this Month of *July* they continu'd to flee, tho' not in such Multitudes as formerly. In *August* indeed, they fled in such a manner, that I began to think, there would be really none but Magistrates and Servants[1] left in the City.

As they fled now out of the City, so I should observe, that the Court removed early, (*viz.*) in the Month of *June*,[2] and

went to *Oxford*, where it pleas'd God to preserve them; and
the Distemper did not, *as I heard of*, so much as touch them;
for which I cannot say, that I ever saw they shew'd any great
Token of Thankfulness, and hardly any thing of Reformation,[1]
tho' they did not want being told that their crying Vices might,
without Breach of Charity, be said to have gone far, in bringing that terrible Judgment[2] upon the whole Nation.

The Face of *London* was now indeed strangely alter'd, I
mean the whole Mass[3] of Buildings, City, Liberties, Suburbs,
Westminster, *Southwark* and altogether; for as to the particular
Part called the City, or within the Walls, that was not yet
much infected;[4] but in the whole, the Face of Things, I say,
was much alter'd; Sorrow and Sadness sat upon every Face;
and tho' some Part were not yet overwhelm'd, yet all look'd
deeply concern'd; and as we saw it apparently coming on, so
every one look'd on himself, and his Family, as in the utmost
Danger: were it possible to represent those Times exactly to
those that did not see them, and give the Reader due Ideas of
the Horror that every where presented it self, it must make
just Impressions upon their Minds, and fill them with Surprize. *London* might well be said to be all in Tears; the
Mourners did not go about the Streets indeed, for no Body
put on black, or made a formal Dress of Mourning for their
nearest Friends; but the Voice of Mourning was truly heard
in the Streets; the shriecks of Women and Children at the
Windows, and Doors of their Houses, where their dearest
Relations were, perhaps dying, or just dead, were so frequent
to be heard, as we passed the Streets, that it was enough to
pierce the stoutest Heart in the World, to hear them. Tears
and Lamentations were seen almost in every House, especially
in the first Part of the Visitation; for towards the latter End,
Mens Hearts were hardned, and Death was so always before
their Eyes, that they did not so much concern themselves for
Loss of their Friends, expecting, that themselves should be
summoned the next Hour.

Business led me out sometimes to the other End of the
Town, even when the Sickness was chiefly there; and as the

thing was new to me, as well as to every Body else, it was a most surprising thing, to see those Streets, which were usually so thronged, now grown desolate, and so few People to be seen in them, that if I had been a Stranger, and at a Loss for my Way, I might sometimes have gone the Length of a whole Street, I mean of the by-Streets, and see no Body to direct me, except Watchmen, set at the Doors of such Houses as were shut up; of which I shall speak presently.

One Day, being at that Part of the Town, on some special Business, Curiosity led me to observe things more than usually; and indeed I walk'd a great Way where I had no Business; I went up *Holbourn*, and there the Street was full of People; but they walk'd in the middle of the great Street, neither on one Side or other, because, as I suppose, they would not mingle with any Body that came out of Houses, or meet with Smells and Scents from Houses that might be infected.

The Inns-of-Court were all shut up;[1] nor were very many of the Lawyers in the Temple, or *Lincolns-Inn*, or *Greyes-Inn*, to be seen there. Every Body was at peace, there was no Occasion for Lawyers; besides, it being in the Time of the Vacation too, they were generally gone into the Country. Whole Rows of Houses in some Places, were shut close up; the Inhabitants all fled, and only a Watchman or two left.

When I speak of Rows of Houses being shut up, I do not mean shut up by the Magistrates; but that great Numbers of Persons followed the Court, by the Necessity of their Employments, and other Dependencies: and as others retir'd, really frighted with the Distemper, it was a mere desolating of some of the Streets: But the Fright was not yet near so great in the City, abstractly so called; and particularly because, tho' they were at first in a most inexpressible Consternation, yet as I have observ'd, that the Distemper intermitted often at first; so they were as it were, allarm'd, and unallarm'd again, and this several times, till it began to be familiar to them; and that even, when it appear'd violent, yet seeing it did not presently spread into the City, or the *East* and *South* Parts, the People

began to take Courage, and to be, as I may say, a little hardned:
It is true, a vast many People fled, as I have observ'd, yet they
were chiefly from the *West* End of the Town; and from that
we call the Heart of the City, that is to say, among the wealth-
iest of the People; and such People as were unincumbered with
Trades and Business: But of the rest, the Generality stay'd,
and seem'd to abide the worst: So that in the Place we call the
Liberties, and in the Suburbs, in *Southwark*, and in the *East*
Part, such as *Wapping*, *Ratclif*, *Stepney*, *Rotherhith*, and the
like, the People generally stay'd, except here and there a few
wealthy Families, who, as above, did not depend upon their
Business.

It must not be forgot here, that the City and Suburbs were
prodigiously full of People,[1] at the time of this Visitation, I
mean, at the time that it began; for tho' I have liv'd to see a
farther Encrease, and mighty Throngs of People settling in
London,[2] more than ever, yet we had always a Notion, that
the Numbers of People, which the Wars being over, the
Armies disbanded, and the Royal Family and the Monarchy
being restor'd, had flock'd to *London*, to settle into Business;
or to depend upon, and attend the Court for Rewards of
Services, Preferments, *and the like*, was such, that the Town
was computed to have in it above a hundred thousand people
more than ever it held before; nay, some took upon them to
say, it had twice as many, because all the ruin'd Families of
the royal Party, flock'd hither: All the old Soldiers set up
Trades here, and abundance of Families settled here; again,
the Court brought with them a great Flux of Pride, and new
Fashions; All People were grown gay and luxurious; and the
Joy of the Restoration had brought a vast many Families to
London.

I often thought, that as *Jerusalem* was besieg'd[3] by the
Romans, when the *Jews* were assembled together, to celebrate
the Passover, by which means, an incredible Number of
People were surpriz'd there, who would otherwise have been
in other Countries: So the Plague entred *London*, when an
incredible Increase of People had happened occasionally, by

the particular Circumstances above-nam'd: As this Conflux of the People, to a youthful and gay Court, made a great Trade in the City, especially in every thing that belong'd to Fashion and Finery; So it drew by Consequence, a great Number of Work-men, Manufacturers, and the like, being mostly poor People, who depended upon their Labour, And I remember in particular, that in a Representation to my Lord Mayor, of the Condition of the Poor, it was estimated, that, there were no less than an Hundred Thousand Ribband Weavers[1] in and about the City; the chiefest Number of whom, lived then in the Parishes of *Shoreditch*, *Stepney*, *White-chapel*, and *Bishopsgate*; that namely, about *Spittle-fields*;[2] that is to say, as *Spittle-fields* was then; for it was not so large as now, by one fifth Part.

By this however, the Number of People in the whole may be judg'd of; and indeed, I often wondred, that after the prodigious Numbers of People that went away at first, there was yet so great a Multitude left, as it appear'd there was.

But I must go back again to the Beginning of this Surprizing Time, while the Fears of the People were young, they were encreas'd strangely by several odd Accidents, which put altogether, it was really a wonder the whole Body of the People did not rise as one Man, and abandon their Dwellings, leaving the Place as a Space of Ground designed by Heaven for an Akeldama,[3] doom'd to be destroy'd from the Face of the Earth; and that all that would be found in it, would perish with it. I shall Name but a few of these Things; but sure they were so many, and so many Wizards and cunning People propagating them, that I have often wonder'd there was any, (Women especially) left behind.

In the first Place, a blazing Star or Comet[4] appear'd for several Months before the Plague, as there did the Year after another, a little before the Fire; the old Women, and the Phlegmatic Hypocondriac Part of the other Sex, who I could almost call *old Women* too, remark'd (especially afterward tho' not till both those Judgments were over) that those two Comets pass'd directly over the City, and that so very near the Houses, that it was plain, they imported something peculiar to the City alone; that the Comet before the Pestilence, was of a faint, dull, languid Colour,[1] and its Motion very heavy, solemn and slow: But that the Comet before the Fire, was bright and sparkling, or as others said, flaming, and its Motion swift and furious; and that accordingly, One foretold a heavy Judgment, slow but severe, terrible and frightful, as was the Plague;[2] But the other foretold a Stroak, sudden, swift, and fiery as the Conflagration; nay, so particular some People were, that as they look'd upon that Comet preceding the Fire, they fancied that they not only saw it pass swiftly and fiercely, and cou'd perceive the Motion with their Eye, but even they heard it; that it made a rushing mighty Noise, fierce and terrible, tho' at a distance, and but just perceivable.

I saw both these Stars; and I must confess, had so much of the common Notion of such Things in my Head, that I was apt to look upon them, as the Forerunners and Warnings of Gods Judgments;[3] and especially when after the Plague had followed the first, I yet saw another of the like kind; I could not but say, God had not yet sufficiently scourg'd the City.

But I cou'd not at the same Time carry these Things to the heighth that others did, knowing too, that natural Causes are assign'd by the Astronomers for such Things; and that their Motions, and even their Revolutions are calculated, or pretended to be calculated; so that they cannot be so perfectly call'd the Fore-runners, or Fore-tellers, much less the procurers of such Events, as Pestilence, War, Fire,[4] and the like.

But let my Thoughts, and the Thoughts of the Philosophers be, or have been what they will, these Things had a more than ordinary Influence upon the Minds of the common People, and they had almost universal melancholly Apprehensions of some dreadful Calamity and Judgment coming upon the City; and this principally from the Sight of this Comet, and the little Allarm that was given in *December*, by two People dying at St. *Giles*'s, as above.

The Apprehensions of the People, were likewise strangely encreas'd by the Error of the Times; in which, I think, the

People, from what Principle I cannot imagine, were more addicted to Prophesies, and Astrological Conjurations, Dreams, and old Wives Tales, than ever they were before or since: Whether this unhappy Temper was originally raised by the Follies of some People who got Money by it; that is to say, by printing Predictions, and Prognostications I know not; but certain it is, Books frighted them terribly; such as *Lilly*'s Almanack, *Gadbury*'s Astrological Predictions; Poor *Robin*'s Almanack[1] and the like; also several pretended religious Books;[2] one entituled, *Come out of her my People, lest you be partaker of her Plagues*; another call'd, Fair Warning; another, *Britains* Remembrancer, and many such; all, or most Part of which, foretold directly or covertly the Ruin of the City: Nay, some were so Enthusiastically bold, as to run about the Streets, with their Oral Predictions, pretending they were sent to preach to the City; and One in particular, who, like *Jonah* to *Ninevah*,[3] cry'd in the Streets, *yet forty Days, and LONDON shall be destroy'd*. I will not be positive, whether he said yet forty Days, or yet a few Days. Another run about Naked,[4] except a pair of Drawers about his Waste, crying Day and Night; like a Man that *Josephus* mentions,[5] who cry'd, woe to *Jerusalem!* a little before the Destruction of that City: So this poor naked Creature cry'd, *O! the Great, and the Dreadful God!* and said no more, but repeated those Words continually, with a Voice and Countenance full of horror, a swift Pace, and no Body cou'd ever find him to stop, or rest, or take any Sustenance, at least, that ever I cou'd hear of. I met this poor Creature several Times in the Streets, and would have spoke to him, but he would not enter into Speech with me, or any one else; but held on his dismal Cries continually.

These Things terrified the People to the last Degree; and especially when two or three Times, as I have mentioned already, they found one or two in the Bills, dead of the Plague at St. *Giles*.

Next to these publick Things, were the Dreams of old Women: Or, I should say, the Interpretation of old Women upon other Peoples Dreams; and these put abundance of People even out of their Wits: Some heard Voices warning them to be gone, for that there would be such a Plague in *London*, so that the Living would not be able to bury the Dead: Others saw Apparitions in the Air;[1] and I must be allow'd to say of both, I hope without breach of Charity, that they heard Voices that never spake, and saw Sights that never appear'd; but the Imagination of the People was really turn'd wayward and possess'd: And no Wonder, if they, who were poreing continually at the Clouds, saw Shapes and Figures, Representations and Appearances, which had nothing in them, but Air and Vapour. Here they told us, they saw a Flaming-Sword held in a Hand, coming out of a Cloud, with a Point hanging directly over the City. There they saw Herses, and Coffins in the Air, carrying to be buried. And there again, Heaps of dead Bodies lying unburied, and the like; just as the Imagination of the poor terrify'd People furnish'd them with Matter to work upon.

> So Hypocondriac Fancy's represent
> Ships, Armies, Battles, in the Firmament;
> Till steady Eyes, the Exhalations solve,
> And all to its first Matter, Cloud, resolve.[2]

I could fill this Account with the strange Relations, such People gave every Day, of what they had seen; and every one was so positive of their having seen, what they pretended to see, that there was no contradicting them, without Breach of Friendship, or being accounted rude and unmannerly on the one Hand, and prophane and impenetrable on the other. One time before the Plague was begun, (otherwise than as I have said in St. *Giles*'s,) I think it was in *March*, seeing a Crowd of People in the Street, I join'd with them to satisfy my Curiosity, and found them all staring up into the Air, to see what a Woman told them appeared plain to her, which was an Angel cloth'd in white, with a fiery Sword in his Hand, waving it, or brandishing it over his Head. She described every Part of the Figure to the Life; shew'd them the Motion, and the Form;

and the poor People came into it so eagerly, and with so much Readiness; YES, *I see it all plainly*, says one. *There's the Sword as plain as can be*. Another saw the Angel. One saw his very Face, and cry'd out, What a glorious Creature he was! One saw one thing, and one another. I look'd as earnestly as the rest, but, perhaps, not with so much Willingness to be impos'd upon; and I said indeed, that *I could see nothing*, but a white Cloud, bright on one Side, by the shining of the Sun upon the other Part. The Woman endeavour'd to shew it me, but could not make me confess, that I saw it, which, indeed, if I had, I must have lied: But the Woman turning upon me, look'd in my Face, and fancied I laugh'd; in which her Imagination deceiv'd her too; for I really did not laugh, but was very seriously reflecting how the poor People were terrify'd, by the Force of their own Imagination. However, she turned from me, call'd me prophane Fellow, and a Scoffer; told me, that it was a time of God's Anger, and dreadful Judgments were approaching; and that Despisers, such as I, should *wander and perish*.[1]

The People about her seem'd disgusted as well as she; and I found there was no perswading them, that I did not laugh at them; and that I should be rather mobb'd by them, than be able to undeceive them. So I left them; and this Appearance pass'd for as real, as the Blazing Star it self.

Another Encounter I had in the open Day also: And this was in going thro' a narrow Passage from *Petty-France* into *Bishopsgate* Church Yard, by a Row of Alms-Houses; there are two Church Yards to *Bishopsgate* Church, or Parish; one we go over to pass from the Place call'd *Petty-France* into *Bishopsgate* Street, coming out just by the Church Door, the other is on the side of the narrow Passage, where the Alms-Houses are on the left; and a Dwarf-wall with a Palisadoe on it, on the right Hand; and the City Wall on the other Side, more to the right.

In this narrow Passage stands a Man looking thro' between the Palisadoe's into the Burying Place; and as many People as the Narrowness of the Passage would admit to stop, without hindring the Passage of others; and he was talking mighty eagerly to them, and pointing now to one Place, then to another, and affirming, that he saw a Ghost walking upon such a Grave Stone there; he describ'd the Shape, the Posture, and the Movement of it so exactly, that it was the greatest Matter of Amazement to him in the World, that every Body did not see it as well as he. On a sudden he would cry, *There it is: Now it comes this Way:* Then, *'Tis turn'd back*; till at length he persuaded the People into so firm a Belief of it, that one fancied he saw it, and another fancied he saw it; and thus he came every Day making a strange Hubbub, considering it was in so narrow a Passage, till *Bishopsgate* Clock struck eleven; and then the Ghost would seem to start; and as if he were call'd away, disappear'd on a sudden.

I look'd earnestly every way, and at the very Moment, that this Man directed, but could not see the least Appearance of any thing; but so positive was this poor man, that he gave the People the Vapours in abundance, and sent them away trembling, and frighted; till at length, few People, that knew of it, car'd to go thro' that Passage; and hardly any Body by Night, on any Account whatever.

This Ghost, as the poor Man affirm'd, made Signs to the Houses, and to the Ground, and to the People, plainly intimating, or else they so understanding it, that Abundance of the People, should come to be buried in that Church-Yard; as indeed happen'd: But that he saw such Aspects, I must acknowledg, I never believ'd; nor could I see any thing of it my self, tho' I look'd most earnestly to see it, if possible.

These things serve to shew, how far the People were really overcome with Delusions; and as they had a Notion of the Approach of a Visitation, all their Predictions run upon a most dreadful Plague, which should lay the whole City, and even the Kingdom waste; and should destroy almost all the Nation, both Man and Beast.

To this, as I said before, the Astrologers added Stories of the Conjunctions of Planets in a malignant Manner,[1] and with a mischievous Influence; one of which Conjunctions was to happen, and did happen, in *October*; and the other in *November*; and they filled the Peoples Heads with Predictions on these Signs of the Heavens, intimating, that those Conjunctions foretold Drought, Famine, and Pestilence;[1] in the two first of them however, they were entirely mistaken, For we had no droughty Season, but in the beginning of the Year, a hard Frost, which lasted from *December* almost to *March*; and after that moderate Weather, rather warm than hot, with refreshing Winds, and in short, very seasonable Weather; and also several very great Rains.

Some Endeavors were used to suppress the Printing of such Books as terrify'd the People, and to frighten the dispersers of them, some of whom were taken up, but nothing was done in it, as I am inform'd; The Government being unwilling to exasperate the People, who were, *as I may say*, all out of their Wits already.

Neither can I acquit those Ministers, that in their Sermons, rather sunk, than lifted up the Hearts of their Hearers;[2] many of them no doubt did it for the strengthning the Resolution of the People; and especially for quickning them to Repentance; but it certainly answer'd not their End, at least not in Proportion to the injury it did another Way; and indeed, as God himself thro' the whole Scriptures, rather draws to him by Invitations, and calls to turn to him and live, than drives us by Terror and Amazement; So I must confess, I thought the Ministers should have done also, imitating our blessed Lord and Master in this, that his whole Gospel, is full of Declarations from Heaven of Gods Mercy, and his readiness to receive Penitents, and forgive them; complaining, *ye will not come unto me, that ye may have Life*;[3] and that therefore, his Gospel is called the Gospel of Peace, and the Gospel of Grace.

But we had some good Men, and that of all Persuasions and Opinions, whose Discourses were full of Terror; who spoke nothing but dismal Things;[4] and as they brought the People together with a kind of Horror, sent them away in Tears, prophesying nothing but evil Tidings; terrifying the

People[1] with the Apprehensions of being utterly destroy'd, not guiding them, at least not enough, to Cry to Heaven for Mercy.

It was indeed, a Time of very unhappy Breaches[2] among us in matters of Religion: Innumerable Sects, and Divisions, and separate Opinions prevail'd among the People; the Church of *England* was restor'd indeed with the Restoration of the Monarchy, about four Years before; but the Ministers and Preachers of the Presbyterians, and Independants, and of all the other Sorts of Professions, had begun to gather separate Societies, and erect Altar against Altar, and all those had their Meetings for Worship apart, as they have [now] but not so many then, the Dissenters being not thorowly form'd into a Body as they are since, and those Congregations which were thus gather'd together, were yet but few; and even those that were, the Government did not allow, but endeavour'd to suppress them, and shut up their Meetings.

But the Visitation reconcil'd them again, at least for a Time, and many of the best and most valuable Ministers and Preachers of the Dissenters, were suffer'd to go into the Churches,[3] where the Incumbents were fled away, as many were, not being able to stand it; and the People flockt without Distinction to hear them preach, not much inquiring who or what Opinion they were of: But after the Sickness was over, that Spirit of Charity abated, and every Church being again supply'd with their own Ministers, or others presented, where the Minister was dead, Things return'd to their old Channel again.

One Mischief always introduces another: These Terrors and Apprehensions of the People, led them into a Thousand weak, foolish, and wicked Things, which, they wanted not a Sort of People really wicked, to encourage them to; and this was running about to Fortune-tellers, Cunning-men, and Astrologers,[4] to know their Fortune, or, as 'tis vulgarly express'd, to have their Fortunes told them, their Nativities calculated, and the like; and this Folly, presently made the Town swarm with a wicked Generation of Pretenders to

Magick, to the *Black Art*, *as they call'd it*, and I know not what; Nay, to a Thousand worse Dealings with the Devil, than they were really guilty of; and this Trade grew so open, and so generally practised, that it became common to have Signs and Inscriptions set up at Doors; here lives a Fortune-teller; here lives an Astrologer; here you may have your Nativity calculated, and the like; and Fryar *Bacons*'s Brazen-Head,[1] which was the usual Sign of these Peoples Dwellings, was to be seen almost in every Street, or else the Sign of Mother *Shipton*,[2] or of *Merlin*'s Head,[3] and the like.

With what blind, absurd, and ridiculous Stuff, these Oracles of the Devil pleas'd and satisfy'd the People, I really know not; but certain it is, that innumerable Attendants crouded about their Doors every Day; and if but a grave Fellow in a Velvet Jacket, a Band,[4] and a black Cloak, which was the Habit those Quack Conjurers generally went in, was but seen in the Streets, the People would follow them, in Crowds and ask them Questions, as they went along.

I need not mention, what a horrid Delusion this was, or what it tended to; but there was no Remedy for it, till the Plague it self put an End to it all; and I suppose, clear'd the Town of most of those Calculators themselves. One Mischief was, that if the poor People ask'd these mock Astrologers, whether there would be a Plague, or no? they all agreed in the general to answer, *Yes*, for that kept up their Trade; and had the People not been kept in a Fright about that, the Wizards would presently have been rendred useless, and their Craft had been at an end: But they always talked to them of such and such Influences of the Stars, of the Conjunctions of such and such Planets, which must necessarily bring Sickness and Distempers, and consequently the Plague: And some had the Assurance to tell them, the Plague was begun already, which was too true, tho' they that said so, knew nothing of the Matter.

The Ministers, to do them Justice, and Preachers of most Sorts, that were serious and understanding Persons, thundred against these, and other wicked Practises, and exposed the Folly as well as the Wickedness of them together; And the most sober and judicious People despis'd and abhor'd them: But it was impossible to make any Impression upon the midling People, and the working labouring Poor; their Fears were predominant over all their Passions; and they threw away their Money in a most distracted Manner upon those Whymsies. Maid-Servants especially and Men-Servants, were the chief of their Customers; and their Question generally was, after the first demand of, *Will there be a Plague?* I say, the next Question was, *Oh, Sir! For the Lord's Sake, what will become of me? Will my Mistress keep me, or will she turn me off? Will she stay here, or will she go into the Country? And if she goes into the Country, will she take me with her, or leave me here to be starv'd and undone.* And the like of Men-Servants.

The Truth is, the Case of poor Servants was very dismal, as I shall have occasion to mention again by and by; for it was apparent, a prodigious Number of them would be turn'd away, and it was so; and of them abundance perished; and particularly of those that these false Prophets had flattered with Hopes, that they should be continued in their Services, and carried with their Masters and Mistresses into the Country; and had not publick Charity provided for these poor Creatures, whose Number was exceeding great, and in all Cases of this Nature must be so, they would have been in the worst Condition of any People in the City.

These Things agitated the minds of the common People for many Months, while the first Apprehensions, were upon them; and while the Plague, was not, as I may say, yet broken out: But I must also not forget, that the more serious Part of the Inhabitants behav'd after another Manner: The Government encouraged their Devotion, and appointed publick Prayers, and Days of fasting and Humiliation,[1] to make publick Confession of Sin, and implore the Mercy of God, to avert the dreadful Judgment, which hung over their Heads; and it is not to be express'd with what Alacrity the People of all persuasions embraced the Occasion; how they flock'd to

the Churches and Meetings, and they were all so throng'd,
that there was often no coming near, no, not to the very Doors
of the largest Churches; Also there were daily Prayers
appointed Morning and Evening at several Churches, and
Days of private praying at other Places; at all which the
People attended, I say, with an uncommon Devotion: Several
private Families also, as well of one Opinion as of another,
kept Family Fasts, to which they admitted their near Relations only: So that in a Word, those People, who were really
serious and religious, apply'd themselves in a truly Christian
Manner, to the proper Work of Repentance and Humiliation,
as a Christian People ought to do.

Again the publick shew'd, that they would bear their Share
in these Things; the very Court, which was then Gay and
Luxurious, put on a Face of just Concern, for the publick
Danger: All the Plays and Interludes, which after the Manner
of the *French* Court, had been set up, and began to encrease
among us, were forbid to Act; the gaming Tables, publick
dancing Rooms, and Music Houses which multiply'd, and
began to debauch the Manners of the People, were shut up
and suppress'd; and the Jack-puddings, Merry-andrews,
Puppet-shows, Rope-dancers,[1] and such like doings, which
had bewitch'd the poor common People, shut up their Shops,
finding indeed no Trade; for the Minds of the People, were
agitated with other Things; and a kind of Sadness and Horror
at these Things, sat upon the Countenances, even of the common People; Death was before their Eyes, and every Body
began to think of their Graves, not of Mirth and Diversions.

But even those wholesome Reflections, which rightly
manag'd, would have most happily led the People to fall upon
their Knees, make Confession of their Sins, and look up to
their merciful Saviour for Pardon, imploreing his Compassion
on them, in such a Time of their Distress; by which, we
might have been as a second *Nineveh*,[2] had a quite contrary
Extreme in the common People; who ignorant and stupid in
their Reflections, as they were brutishly wicked and thoughtless before, were now led by their Fright to extremes of Folly;

and as I have said before, that they ran to Conjurers and Witches, and all Sorts of Deceivers, to know what should become of them; who fed their Fears, and kept them always alarm'd, and awake, on purpose to delude them, and pick their Pockets: So, they were as mad, upon their running after Quacks, and Mountebanks, and every practising old Woman, for Medicines and Remedies; storeing themselves with such Multitudes of Pills, Potions, and Preservatives, as they were call'd; that they not only spent their Money, but even poison'd themselves before-hand, for fear of the Poison of the Infection, and prepar'd their Bodies for the Plague, instead of preserving them against it. On the other Hand, it is incredible, and scarce to be imagin'd, how the Posts of Houses, and Corners of Streets were plaster'd over with Doctors Bills, and Papers of ignorant Fellows; quacking and tampering in Physick, and inviting the People to come to them for Remedies; which was generally set off, with such flourishes as these, (*viz.*) IN-FALLIBLE preventive Pills against the Plague. NEVER FAILING Preservatives against the Infection. SOVERAIGN Cordials against the Corruption of the Air. EXACT Regulations for the Conduct of the Body, in Case of an Infection: Antipestilential Pills. INCOMPARABLE Drink against the Plague, never found out before. An UNIVERSAL Remedy for the Plague. The ONLY-TRUE Plague-Water.[1] The ROYAL-ANTIDOTE against all Kinds of Infection; and such a Number more that I cannot reckon up; and if I could, would fill a Book of themselves to set them down.

Others set up Bills, to summons People to their Lodgings for Directions and Advice in the Case of Infection: These had spacious Titles also, such as these.

An eminent High-Dutch *Physician, newly come over from* Holland, *where he resided during all the Time of the great Plague, last year, in* Amsterdam; *and cured multitudes of People, that actually had the Plague upon them.*

An Italian *Gentlewoman just arrived from* Naples, *having a choice Secret to prevent Infection, which she found out by her great Experience, and did wonderful Cures with it in the late Plague there; wherein there died 20000 in one Day.*

An antient Gentlewoman having practised, with great Success, in the late Plague in this City, Anno 1636, gives her advice only to the Female Sex. To be spoke with, &c.

An experienc'd Physician, who has long studied the Doctrine of Antidotes against all Sorts of Poison and Infection, has after 40 Years Practise, arrived to such Skill, as may, with God's Blessing, direct Persons how to prevent their being touch'd by any Contagious Distemper whatsoever. He directs the Poor gratis.

I take notice of these by way of Specimen: I could give you two or three Dozen of the like, and yet have abundance left behind. 'Tis sufficient from these to apprise any one, of the Humour of those Times; and how a Set of Thieves and Pickpockets, not only robb'd and cheated the poor People of their Money, but poisoned their Bodies with odious and fatal preparations; some with Mercury,[1] and some with other things as bad, perfectly remote from the Thing pretended to; and rather hurtful than servicable to the Body in case an Infection followed.

I cannot omit a Subtilty of one of those Quack-operators, with which he gull'd the poor People to croud about him, but did nothing for them without Money. He had it seems, added to his Bills, which he gave about the Streets, this Advertisement in Capital Letters, (*viz.*) *He gives Advice to the Poor for nothing*.

Abundance of poor People came to him accordingly, to whom he made a great many fine Speeches; examin'd them of the State of their Health, and of the Constitution of their Bodies, and told them many good things for them to do, which were of no great Moment: But the Issue and Conclusion of all was, that he had a preparation, which if they took such a Quantity of, every Morning, he would pawn his Life, they should never have the Plague, no, tho' they lived in the House with People that were infected: This made the People all resolve to have it; But then the Price of that was *so much*, I think 'twas half a Crown: But, Sir, says one poor Woman, I am a poor Alms-Woman, and am kept by the Parish, and your Bills say, you give the Poor your help for nothing. Ay, good Woman, says the Docter, so I do, as I publish'd there. I give my Advice to the Poor for nothing; but not my Physick. Alas, Sir! says she, that is a Snare laid for the Poor then; for you give them your Advice for nothing, that is to say, you advise them gratis, to buy your Physick for their Money; so does every Shop-keeper with his Wares. Here the Woman began to give him ill Words, and stood at his Door all that Day, telling her Tale to all the People that came, till the Doctor finding she turn'd away his Customers, was oblig'd to call her up Stairs again, and give her his Box of Physick for nothing, which, perhaps too was *good for nothing when she had it*.

But to return to the people, whose Confusions fitted them to be impos'd upon by all Sorts of Pretenders, and by every Mountebank. There is no doubt, but these quacking Sort of Fellows rais'd great gains out of the miserable People; for we daily found, the Crouds that ran after them were infinitely greater, and their Doors were more thronged than those of Dr. *Brooks*, Dr. *Upton*, Dr. *Hodges*, Dr. *Berwick*,[1] or any, tho' the most famous Men of the Time: And I was told, that some of them got five Pound a Day by their Physick.

But there was still another Madness beyond all this, which may serve to give an Idea of the distracted humour of the poor People at that Time; and this was their following a worse Sort of Deceivers than any of these; for these petty Thieves only deluded them to pick their Pockets, and get their Money; in which their Wickedness, *whatever it was*, lay chiefly on the Side of the Deceiver's deceiving, not upon the Deceived: But in this Part I am going to mention, it lay chiefly in the People deceiv'd, or equally in both; and this was in wearing Charms, Philters, Exorcisms, Amulets,[2] and I know not what Preparations, to fortify the Body with them against the Plague; as if the Plague was not the Hand of God, but a kind of a Possession of an evil Spirit; and that it was to be

kept off with Crossings, Signs of the Zodiac, Papers tied up
with so many Knots; and certain Words, or Figures written
on them, as particularly the Word *Abracadabra*,[1] form'd in
Triangle, or Pyramid, thus.

ABRACADABRA	
ABRACADABR	Others had the Jesuits
ABRACADAB	Mark in a Cross.
ABRACADA	
ABRACAD	I H
ABRACA	S[2]
ABRAC	
ABRA	Others nothing but this
ABR	Mark thus.[3]
AB	
A	

I might spend a great deal of Time in my Exclamations
against the Follies, and indeed Wickedness of those things,
in a Time of such Danger, in a matter of such Consequences
as this, of a National Infection, But my Memorandums of
these things relate rather to take notice only of the Fact, and
mention that it was so: How the poor People found the
Insufficiency of those things, and how many of them were
afterwards carried away in the Dead-Carts,[4] and thrown into
the common Graves of every Parish, with these hellish Charms
and Trumpery hanging about their Necks, remains to be
spoken of as we go along.

All this was the Effect of the Hurry the People were in,
after the first Notion of the Plague being at hand was among
them: And which may be said to be from about *Michaelmas*
1664, but more particularly after the two Men died in St.
Giles's, in the Beginning of *December*. And again, after another
Alarm in *February*; for when the Plague evidently spread it
self, they soon began to see the Folly of trusting to those
unperforming Creatures, who had Gull'd them of their
Money, and then their Fears work'd another way, namely, to
Amazement and Stupidity, not knowing what Course to take,

or what to do, either to help or relieve themselves; but they ran about from one Neighbours House to another; and even in the Streets, from one Door to another with repeated Cries, of, *Lord have Mercy upon us, what shall we do?*

Indeed, the poor People were to be pity'd in one particular Thing, in which they had little or no Relief, and which I Desire to mention with a serious Awe and Reflection; which perhaps, every one that reads this, may not relish: Namely, that whereas Death now began not, *as we may say*, to hover over every ones Head only, but to look into their Houses, and Chambers, and stare in their Faces: Tho' there might be some stupidity, and dullness of the Mind, and there was so, a great deal; yet, there was a great deal of just Alarm, sounded into the very inmost Soul, *if I may so say* of others: Many Consciences were awakened; many hard Hearts melted into Tears; many a penitent Confession was made of Crimes long concealed: [it] would wound the Souls of any Christian, to have heard the dying Groans of many a despairing Creature, and none durst come near to comfort them: Many a Robbery, many a Murder, was then confest aloud, and no Body surviving to Record the Accounts of it. People might be heard even into the Streets as we pass'd along, calling upon God for Mercy, thro' Jesus Christ, *and saying*, I have been a Thief, I have been an Adulterer, I have been a Murderer, and the like; and none durst stop to make the least Inquiry into such Things, or to administer Comfort to the poor Creatures, that in the Anguish both of Soul and Body thus cry'd out. Some of the Ministers did Visit the Sick at first, and for a little while, but it was not to be done; it would have been present Death, to have gone into some Houses: The very buryers of the Dead, who were the hardnedest Creatures in Town, were sometimes beaten back, and so terrify'd, that they durst not go into Houses, where the whole Families were swept away together, and where the Circumstances were more particularly horrible as some were; but this was indeed, at the first Heat of the Distemper.

Time enur'd them to it all; and they ventured every where

afterwards, without Hesitation, as I Occasion to mention at large hereafter.

I am supposing now, the Plague to be begun, as I have said, and that the Magistrates began to take the Condition of the People, into their serious Consideration; what they did as to the Regulation of the Inhabitants, and of infected Families, I shall speak to by it self; but as to the Affair of Health, it is proper to mention it here, that having seen the foolish Humour of the People, in running after Quacks, and Mountebanks, Wizards, and Fortune-tellers, which they did as above, even to Madness. The Lord Mayor, a very sober and religious Gentleman appointed Physicians and Surgeons for Relief of the poor;[1] I mean, the diseased poor; and in particular, order'd the College of Physicians to publish Directions for cheap Remedies,[2] for the Poor, in all the Cirumstances of the Distemper. This indeed was one of the most charitable and judicious Things that could be done at that Time; for this drove the People from haunting the Doors of every Disperser of Bills; and from taking down blindly, and without Consideration, Poison for Physick, and Death instead of Life.

This Direction of the Physicians was done by a Consultation of the whole College, and as it was particularly calculated for the use of the Poor; and for cheap Medicines it was made publick, so that every Body might see it; and Copies were given *gratis* to all that desired it: But as it is publick, and to be seen on all Occasions, I need not give the Reader of this, the Trouble of it.

I shall not be supposed to lessen the Authority or Capacity of the Physicians, when, I say, that the Violence of the Distemper, when it came to its Extremity, was like the Fire the next Year; The Fire which consumed what the Plague could not touch, defy'd all the Application of Remedies; the Fire Engines were broken, the Buckets thrown away; and the Power of Man was baffled, and brought to an End; so the Plague defied all Medicine; the very Physicians were seized with it, with their Preservatives in their Mouths; and Men went about prescribing to others and telling them what to do, till the Tokens were upon them, and they dropt down dead, destroyed by that very Enemy, they directed others to oppose. This was the Case of several Physicians, even some of them the most eminent; and of several of the most skilful Surgeons;[1] Abundance of Quacks too died, who had the Folly to trust to their own Medicines, which they must needs be conscious to themselves, were good for nothing; and who rather ought, like other Sorts of Thieves, to have run away, sensible of their Guilt, from the Justice that they could not but expect should punish them, as they knew they had deserved.

Not that it is any Derogation from the Labour, or Application of the Physicians, to say, they fell in the common Calamity; nor is it so intended by me; it rather is to their Praise, that they ventured their Lives so far as even to lose them in the Service of Mankind; They endeavoured to do good, and to save the Lives of others; But we were not to expect, that the Physicians could stop God's Judgments, or prevent a Distemper eminently armed from Heaven, from executing the Errand it was sent about.

Doubtless, the Physicians assisted many by their Skill, and by their Prudence and Applications, to the saving of their Lives, and restoring their Health: But it is no lessening their Character, or their Skill, to say, they could not cure those that had the Tokens upon them, or those who were mortally infected before the Physicians were sent for, as was frequently the Case.

It remains to mention now what publick Measures were taken by the Magistrates for the general Safety, and to prevent the spreading of the Distemper, when it first broke out: I shall have frequent Occasion to speak of the Prudence of the Magistrates, their Charity, their Vigilance for the Poor, and for preserving good Order; furnishing Provisions, and the like, when the Plague was encreased, as it afterwards was. But I am now upon the Order and Regulations they published for the Government of infected Families.

I mention'd above shutting of Houses up; and it is needful to say something particularly to that; for this Part of the History of the Plague is very melancholy; *but the most grievous Story must be told.*

About *June* the Lord Mayor of *London*, and the Court of Aldermen, as I have said, began more particularly to concern themselves for the Regulation of the City.

The Justices of Peace for *Middlesex*, by Direction of the Secretary of State, had begun to shut up Houses in the Parishes of St. *Giles's in the Fields*, St. *Martins*, St. *Clement Danes*, &c. and it was with good Success; for in several Streets, where the Plague broke out, upon strict guarding the Houses that were infected, and taking Care to bury those that died, immediatly after they were known to be dead, the Plague ceased in those Streets. It was also observ'd, that the Plague decreas'd sooner in those Parishes, after they had been visited to the full, than it did in the Parishes of *Bishopsgate*, *Shoreditch*, *Aldgate*, *White-Chappel*, *Stepney*, and others, the early Care taken in that Manner, being a great means to the putting a Cheque to it.

This shutting up of Houses was a method first taken, as I understand, in the Plague, which happened in 1603, at the Coming of King *James* the First to the Crown, and the Power of shutting People up in their own Houses, was granted by Act of Parliament, entitled, *An Act for the charitable Relief and Ordering of Persons infected with the Plague*.[1] On which Act of Parliament, the Lord Mayor and Aldermen of the City of *London*, founded the Order they made at this Time, and which took Place the 1st of *July* 1665, when the Numbers infected within the City, were but few, the last Bill for the 97 Parishes being but four; and some Houses having been shut up in the City, and some sick People being removed to the Pest-House beyond *Bunhill-Fields*,[2] in the Way to *Islington*; I say, by these Means, when there died near one thousand a Week in the Whole, the Number in the City was but 28, and the City was preserv'd more healthy in Proportion, than any other Places all the Time of the Infection.

These Orders of my Lord Mayor's were publish'd, as I have said, the latter End of *June*, and took Place from the first of *July*, and were as follows, (*viz.*)

ORDERS *Conceived and Published by the* Lord MAYOR
and Aldermen *of the City of* London, *concerning the Infection
of the* Plague. 1665[1]

'WHEREAS in the Reign of our late Sovereign King *James*, of
happy Memory, an Act was made for the charitable Relief
and ordering of Persons infected with the Plague; whereby
Authority was given to Justices of the Peace, Mayors, Bayliffs
and other head Officers, to appoint within their several Limits,
Examiners, Searchers, Watchmen, Keepers, and Buriers for
the Persons and Places infected, and to minister unto them
Oaths for the Performance of their Offices. And the same
Statute did also authorize the giving of other Directions, as
unto them for the present Necessity should seem good in their
Discretions. It is now upon special Consideration, thought
very expedient for preventing and avoiding of Infection of
Sickness (if it shall so please Almighty God) that these
Officers following be appointed, and these Orders hereafter
duly observed.

Examiners to be appointed in every Parish[2]

'FIRST, It is thought requisite, and so ordered, that in
every Parish there be one, two, or more Persons of good
Sort and Credit, chosen and appointed by the Alderman,
his Deputy, and common-Council of every Ward, by the
Name of Examiners, to continue in that Office the Space of
two Months at least: And if any fit Person so appointed, shall
refuse to undertake the same, the said parties so refusing, to
be committed to Prison until they shall conform themselves
accordingly.

The Examiners Office[3]

'THAT these Examiners be sworn by the Aldermen, to
enquire and learn from time to time what Houses in every
Parish be Visited, and what Persons be Sick, and of what
Diseases, as near as they can inform themselves; and upon

doubt in that Case, to command Restraint of Access, until it
appear what the Disease shall prove: And if they find any
Person sick of the Infection, to give order to the Constable
that the House be shut up; and if the Constable shall be found
Remiss or Negligent, to give present Notice thereof to the
Alderman of the Ward.

Watchmen

'THAT to every infected House there be appointed two
Watchmen, one for every Day, and the other for the Night:
And that these Watchmen have a special care that no Person
go in or out of such infected Houses, whereof they have the
Charge, upon pain of severe Punishment. And the said Watch-
man to do such further Offices as the sick House shall need
and require: and if the Watchmen be sent upon any Business,
to lock up the House, and take the Key with him: And the
Watchman by Day to attend until ten of the Clock at Night:
And the Watchman by Night untill six in the Morning.

Searchers[1]

'THAT there be a special care to appoint Women-Searchers in
every Parish, such as are of honest Reputation, and of the best
Sort as can be got in this kind: And these to be sworn to make
due Search, and true Report to the utmost of their Knowledge,
whether the Persons whose Bodies they are appointed to
Search, do die of the Infection, or of what other Diseases, as
near as they can. And that the Physicians who shall be
appointed for Cure and Prevention of the Infection, do call
before them the said Searchers, who are, or shall be appointed
for the several Parishes under their respective Cares; to the
end they may consider, whether they are fitly qualified for that
Employment; and charge them from time to time as they shall
see Cause, if they appear defective in their Duties.

'That no Searcher during this time of Visitation, be permitted to use any publick Work or Employment, or keep any
Shop or Stall, or be employed as a Laundress, or in any other
common Employment whatsoever.

Chirurgeons

'FOR better assistance of the Searchers, for as much as there hath been heretofore great abuse in misreporting the Disease, to the further spreading of the Infection: It is therefore ordered, that there be chosen and appointed able and discreet Chirurgeons, besides those that do already belong to the *Pest-House*: Amongst whom the City and Liberties to be quartered as the places lie most apt and convenient; and every of these to have one Quarter for his Limit: and the said Chirurgeons in every of their Limits to join with the Searchers for the View of the Body, to the end there may be a true Report made of the Disease.

'And further, that the said Chirurgeons shall visit and search such like Persons as shall either send for them, or be named and directed unto them, by the Examiners of every Parish, and inform themselves of the Disease of the said Parties.

'And forasmuch as the said Chirurgeons are to be sequestred from all other Cures, and kept only to this Disease of the Infection; It is order'd, That every of the said Chirurgeons shall have Twelvepence a Body searched by them, to be paid out of the Goods of the Party searched, if he be able, or otherwise by the Parish.

Nurse-keepers

'IF any Nurse-keeper shall remove her self out of any infected House before twenty eight Days after the Decease of any Person dying of the Infection, the House to which the said Nurse-keeper doth so remove her self, shall be shut up until the said twenty eight Days be expired.

ORDERS concerning infected Houses, and Persons sick of the Plague

Notice to be given of the Sickness

'THE Master of every House, as soon as any one in his House complaineth, either of Botch, or Purple,[1] or Swelling in any part of his Body, or falleth otherwise dangerously Sick, without apparent Cause of some other Disease, shall give knowledge thereof to the Examiner of Health, within two Hours after the said Sign shall appear.

Sequestration of the Sick

'As soon as any Man shall be found by this Examiner, Chirurgeon or Searcher to be sick of the Plague, he shall the same Night be sequestred in the same House, and in case he be so sequestred, then, though he afterwards die not, the House wherein he sickned, should be shut up for a Month, after the use of the due Preservatives taken by the rest.

Airing the Stuff

'For Sequestration of the Goods and Stuff of the Infection, their Bedding, and Apparel, and Hangings of Chambers, must be well aired with Fire, and such Perfumes[1] as are requisite within the infected House, before they be taken again to use: This to be done by the Appointment of the Examiner.

Shutting up of the House[2]

'If any Person shall have visited any Man, known to be infected of the Plague, or entred willingly into any known infected House, being not allowed: The House wherein he inhabiteth, shall be shut up for certain Days by the Examiners Direction.

None to be removed out of infected Houses, but, &c.

'Item, That none be remov'd out of the House where he falleth sick of the Infection, into any other House in the City, (except it be to the *Pest-House* or a Tent, or unto some such House, which the Owner of the said visited House holdeth in his own Hands, and occupieth by his own Servants) and so as Security be given to the Parish, whither such Remove is made; that the Attendance and Charge about the said visited Persons shall be observed and charged in all the Particularities before expressed, without any Cost of that Parish, to which any such

Remove shall happen to be made, and this Remove to be done by Night: And it shall be lawful to any Person that hath two Houses, to remove either his sound or his infected People to his spare House at his choice, so as if he send away first his Sound, he not after send thither the Sick, nor again unto the Sick the Sound. And that the same which he sendeth, be for one Week at the least shut up, and secluded from Company, for fear of some infection, at the first not appearing.

Burial of the Dead

'THAT the Burial of the Dead by this Visitation, be at most convenient Hours, always either before Sun-rising, or after Sun-setting,[1] with the Privity of the Church-wardens or Constable, and not otherwise; and that no Neighbours nor Friends be suffered to accompany the Corps[2] to Church, or to enter the House visited, upon pain of having his House shut up, or be imprisoned.

'And that no Corps dying of Infection shall be buried, or remain in any Church in time of Common-Prayer, Sermon, or Lecture. And that no Children be suffered at time of burial of any Corps in any Church, Church-yard, or Burying-place to come near the Corps, Coffin, or Grave. And that all the Graves shall be at least six Foot deep.[3]

'And further, all publick Assemblies at other Burials are to be forborn during the Continuance of this Visitation.

No infected Stuff to be uttered

'THAT no Clothes, Stuff, Bedding or Garments be suffered to be carried or conveyed out of any infected Houses, and that the Criers and Carriers abroad of Bedding or old Apparel to be sold or pawned, be utterly prohibited and restrained, and no Brokers of Bedding or old Apparel be permitted to make any outward Shew, or hang forth on their Stalls, Shopboards or Windows towards any Street, Lane, Common-way or Passage, any old Bedding or Apparel to be sold, upon pain of Imprisonment. And if any Broker or other Person shall buy any Bedding, Apparel, or other Stuff out of any infected

House, within two Months after the Infection hath been there, his House shall be shut up as Infected, and so shall continue shut up twenty Days at the least.

No Person to be conveyed out of any infected House

'IF any Person visited do fortune by negligent looking unto, or by any other Means, to come, or be conveyed from a Place infected, to any other Place, the Parish from whence such Party hath come or been conveyed, upon notice thereof given, shall at their Charge cause the said Party so visited and escaped, to be carried and brought back again by Night, and the Parties in this case offending, to be punished at the Direction of the Alderman of the Ward; and the House of the Receiver of such visited Person, to be shut up for twenty Days.

Every visited House to be marked

'THAT every House visited, be marked with a red Cross[1] of a Foot long, in the middle of the Door, evident to be seen, and with these usual printed Words, that is to say, *Lord have Mercy upon us*, to be set close over the same Cross, there to continue until lawful opening of the same House.

Every visited House to be watched

'THAT the Constables see every House shut up, and to be attended with Watchmen, which may keep them in, and minister Necessaries unto them at their own Charges (if they be able,) or at the common Charge, if they be unable: The shutting up to be for the space of four Weeks after all be whole.

'That precise Order be taken that the Searchers, Chirurgeons, Keepers and Buriers are not to pass the Streets without holding a red Rod or Wand[2] of three Foot in Length in their Hands, open and evident to be seen, and are not to go into any other House than into their own, or into that whereunto they are directed or sent for; but to forbear and abstain from Company, especially when they have been lately used in any such Business or Attendance.

Inmates

'THAT where several Inmates are in one and the same House, and any Person in that House happens to be Infected; no other Person of Family of such House shall be suffered to remove him or themselves without a Certificate from the Examiners of Health of that Parish; or in default thereof, the House whither he or they so remove, shall be shut up as in case of Visitation.

Hackney-Coaches

'THAT care be taken of Hackney-Coach-men, that they may not (as some of them have been observed to do) after carrying of infected Persons to the *Pest-House*, and other Places, be admitted to common use, till their Coaches be well aired, and have stood unemploy'd by the Space of five or six Days after such Service.

ORDERS for cleansing and keeping of the Streets Sweet

The Streets to be kept clean

'FIRST, it is thought necessary, and so ordered, that every Housholder do cause the Street to be daily prepared before his Door, and so to keep it clean swept all the Week long.

That Rakers take it from out the Houses

'THAT the Sweeping and Filth of Houses be daily carry'd away by the Rakers, and that the Raker shall give notice of his coming, by the blowing of a Horn, as hitherto hath been done.

Laystalls to be made far off from the City

'THAT the Laystalls be removed as far as may be out of the City, and common Passages, and that no Nightman or other be suffered to empty a Vault into any Garden near about the City.

Care to be had of unwholsome Fish or Flesh, and of musty Corn

'THAT special care be taken, that no stinking Fish, or un-wholesome Flesh, or musty Corn, or other corrupt Fruits, of what Sort soever be suffered to be sold about the City, or any part of the same.

'That the Brewers and Tippling-houses be looked unto, for musty and unwholsome Casks.

'That no Hogs, Dogs, or Cats, or tame Pigeons, or Conies, be suffered to be kept within any part of the City, or any Swine to be, or stray in the Streets or Lanes, but that such Swine be impounded by the Beadle or any other Officer, and the Owner punished according to Act of Common-Council, and that the Dogs be killed by the Dog-killers appointed for that purpose.

ORDERS concerning loose Persons and idle Assemblies

Beggers

'FORASMUCH as nothing is more complained of, than the Multitude of Rogues and wandring Beggars, that swarm in every place about the City, being a great cause of the spreading of the Infection, and will not be avoided, not-withstanding any Order that have been given to the con-trary: It is therefore now ordered, that such Constables, and others, whom this Matter may any way concern, take special care that no wandring Begger be suffered in the Streets of this City, in any fashion or manner, whatsoever, upon the Penalty provided by the Law to be duely and severely executed upon them.

Plays

'THAT all Plays, Bear-Baitings, Games, singing of Ballads, Buckler-play, or such like Causes of Assemblies of People, be utterly prohibited, and the Parties offending severely punished by every Alderman in his Ward.

Feasting Prohibited

'THAT all publick Feasting, and particularly by the Companies of this City, and Dinners at Taverns, Alehouses, and other Places of common Entertainment be forborn till further Order and Allowance; and that the Money thereby spared, be preserved and employed for the Benefit and Relief of the Poor visited with the Infection.

Tipling-Houses

'THAT disorderly Tipling in Taverns,[1] Ale-houses, Coffehouses, and Cellars be severely looked unto, as the common Sin of this Time, and greatest occasion of dispersing the Plague. And that no Company or Person be suffered to remain or come into any Tavern, Ale-house, or Coffe-house to drink after nine of the Clock in the Evening, according to the antient Law and Custom of this City, upon the Penalties ordained in that Behalf.

'And for the better execution of these Orders, and such other Rules and Directions as upon further consideration shall be found needful; It is ordered and enjoined that the Aldermen, Deputies, and Common-Council-men shall meet together weekly, once, twice, thrice, or oftner, (as cause shall require) at some one general Place accustomed in their respective Wards (being clear from Infection of the Plague) to consult how the said Orders may be duly put in Execution; not intending that any, dwelling in or near Places infected, shall come to the said Meeting whiles their coming may be doubtful. And the said Aldermen, and Deputies, and Common-Councilmen in their several Wards may put in Execution any other good Orders that by them at their said Meetings shall be conceived and devised, for Preservation of His Majesty's Subjects from the Infection.'

Sir *John Lawrence* Lord Mayor. } Sir *George Waterman* Sir *Charles Doe*. } Sheriffs.

I need not say, that these Orders extended only to such Places as were within the Lord Mayor's Jurisdiction; so it is requisite to observe, that the Justices of Peace, within those Parishes, and Places as were called the *Hamlets*, and Out-parts, took the same Method: As I remember, the Orders for shutting up of Houses, did not take Place so soon on our Side, because, as I said before, the Plague did not reach to these Eastern Parts of the Town, at least, nor begin to be very violent, till the beginning of *August*. For Example, the whole Bill, from the 11th to the 18th of *July*, was 1761, yet there dy'd but 71 of the Plague, in all those Parishes we call the *Tower-Hamlets*; and they were as follows.

Aldgate	14		34		65
Stepney	33	the next	58	and to the	76
White Chappel	21	Week was	48	1st of *Aug.*	79
St. *Kath. Tower*	2	thus.	4	thus.	4
Trin. Minories	1		1		4
	71		145		228

It was indeed, coming on a main; for the Burials that same Week, were in the next adjoining Parishes, thus,

St. *Len. Shorditch*	64	the next Week	84	to the 1*st*.	110
St. *But. Bishopsg.*	65	prodigiously	105	of *Aug.*	116
St. *Giles Crippl.*	213	encreased, as	421	thus.	554
	342		610		780

This shutting up of houses was at first counted a very cruel and Unchristian Method, and the poor People so confin'd made bitter Lamentations: Complaints of the Severity of it, were also daily brought to my Lord Mayor, of Houses cause-lessly, (and some maliciously) shut up: I cannot say, but upon Enquiry, many that complained so loudly, were found in a Condition to be continued, and others again Inspection being made upon the sick Person, and the Sickness not appearing infectious, or if uncertain, yet, on his being content to be carried to the Pest-House, were released.

It is true, that the locking up the Doors of Peoples Houses, and setting a Watchman there Night and Day, to prevent their stirring out, or any coming to them; when, perhaps, the sound People, in the Family, might have escaped, if they had been remov'd from the Sick, looked very hard and cruel; and many People perished in these miserable Confinements, which 'tis reasonable to believe, would not have been distemper'd if they had had Liberty, tho' the Plague was in the House; at which the People were very clamorous and uneasie at first, and several Violences were committed, and Injuries offered to the Men, who were set to watch the Houses so shut up; also several People broke out by Force, in many Places, as I shall observe by and by: But it was a publick Good that justified the private Mischief; and there was no obtaining the least Mitigation, by any Application to Magistrates, or Government, at that Time, at least, not that I heard of. This put the People upon all Manner of Stratagem, in order, if possible, to get out, and it would fill a little Volume, to set down the Arts us'd by the People of such Houses, to shut the Eyes of the Watchmen, who were employ'd, to deceive them, and to escape, or break out from them; in which frequent Scuffles, and some Mischief happened; of which by it self.

As I went along *Houndsditch* one Morning, about eight a-Clock, there was a great Noise; it is true indeed, there was not much Croud, because People were not very free to gather together, or to stay long together, when they were there, nor did I stay long there: But the Outcry was loud enough to prompt my Curiosity, and I call'd to one that look'd out of a Window, and ask'd what was the Matter.

A Watchman, it seems, had been employed to keep his Post at the Door of a House, which was infected, or said to be infected, and was shut up; he had been there all Night for two Nights together, as he told his Story, and the Day Watchman had been there one Day. and was now come to relieve him: All this while no Noise had been heard in the House, no Light had been seen; they call'd for nothing, sent him of no Errands, which us'd to be the chief Business of the Watchman; neither had they given him any Disturbance, as he said, from the *Monday* afternoon, when he heard great crying and screaming in the House, which, as he supposed, was occasioned by some of the Family dying just at that Time: it seems the Night before, the Dead-Cart, as it was called, had been stopt there, and a Servant-Maid had been brought down to the Door dead, and the Buriers or Bearers, as they were call'd, put her into the Cart, wrapt only in a green Rug, and carried her away.

The Watchman had knock'd at the Door, it seems, when he heard that Noise and Crying, as above, and no Body answered, a great while; but at last one look'd out and said with an angry quick Tone, and yet a Kind of crying Voice, or a Voice of one that was crying, *What d'ye want, that ye make such a knocking?* He answer'd, *I am the Watchman! how do you do? What is the Matter?* The Person answered, *What is that to you? Stop the Dead-Cart.* This it seems, was about one a-Clock; soon after, *as the Fellow said*, he stopped the Dead-Cart, and then knock'd again, but no Body answer'd: He continued knocking, and the Bellman call'd out several Times, *Bring out your Dead*; but no Body answered, till the Man that drove the Cart being call'd to other Houses, would stay no longer, and drove away.

The Watchman knew not what to make of all this, so he let them alone, till the Morning-Man, or Day Watchman, as they call'd him, came to relieve him, giving him an Account of the Particulars, they knock'd at the Door a great while, but no body answered; and they observ'd, that the Window, or Casement, at which the Person had look'd out, who had answer'd before, continued open, being up two Pair of Stairs.

Upon this, the two Men to satisfy their Curiosity, got a long Ladder, and one of them went up to the Window, and look'd into the Room, where he saw a Woman lying dead upon the Floor, in a dismal Manner, having no Cloaths on her but her Shift: But tho' he call'd aloud, and putting in his long Staff, knock'd hard on the Floor, yet no Body stirr'd or answered; neither could he hear any Noise in the House.

He came down again, upon this, and acquainted his Fellow, who went up also, and finding it just so, they resolv'd to acquaint either the Lord Mayor, or some other Magistrate of it, but did not offer to go in at the Window: The Magistrate it seems, upon the Information of the two Men, ordered the House to be broken open, a Constable, and other Persons being appointed to be present, that nothing might be plundred; and accordingly it was so done, when no Body was found in the House, but that young Woman, who having been infected, and past Recovery, the rest had left her to die by her self, and were every one gone, having found some Way to delude the Watchman, and get open the Door, or get out at some Back Door, or over the Tops of the Houses, so that he knew nothing of it; and as to those Crys and Shrieks, which he heard, it was suppos'd, they were the passionate Cries of the Family, at the bitter parting, which, to be sure, it was to them all; this being the Sister to the Mistress of the Family. The Man of the House, his Wife, several Children, and Servants, being all gone and fled, whether sick or sound, that I could never learn; nor, indeed, did I make much Enquiry after it.

Many such escapes were made, out of infected Houses, as particularly, when the Watchman was sent of some Errand; for it was his Business to go of any Errand, that the Family sent him of, that is to say, for Necessaries, such as Food and Physick; to fetch Physicians, if they would come, or Surgeons, or Nurses, or to order the Dead-Cart, and the like; But with this Condition too, that when he went, he was to lock up the Outer-Door of the House, and take the Key away with him; to evade this, and cheat the Watchmen, People got two or three Keys made to their Locks; or they found Ways to unscrew the Locks, such as were screw'd on, and so take off the Lock, being in the Inside of the House, and while they sent away the Watchman to the Market, to the Bakehouse, or for one Trifle or another, open the Door, and go out as often as they pleas'd: But this being found out, the Officers afterwards had Orders to Padlock up the Doors on the Outside, and place Bolts on them as they thought fit.

At another House, as I was inform'd, in the Street next

within *Aldgate*, a whole Family was shut up and lock'd in, because the Maid-Servant was taken sick; the Master of the House had complain'd by his Friends to the next Alderman, and to the Lord Mayor, and had consented to have the Maid carried to the Pest-House, but was refused, so the Door was marked with a red Cross, a Padlock on the Outside, as above, and a Watchman set to keep the Door according to publick Order.

After the Master of the House found there was no Remedy, but that he, his Wife and his Children were to be lockt up with this poor distempered Servant; he call'd to the Watchman, and told him, he must go then and fetch a Nurse for them, to attend this poor Girl, for that it would be certain Death to them all to oblige them to nurse her, and told him plainly, that if he would not do this, the Maid must perish either of the Distemper, or be starv'd for want of Food; for he was resolv'd none of his Family, should go near her; and she lay in the Garret four Story high, where she could not Cry out, or call to any Body for Help.

The Watchman consented to that, and went and fetch'd a Nurse as he was appointed, and brought her to them the same Evening; during this interval, the Master of the House took his Opportunity to break a large Hole thro' his Shop into a Bulk or Stall, where formerly a Cobler had sat, before or under his Shop-window; but the Tenant as may be supposed, at such a dismal Time as that, was dead or remov'd, and so he had the Key in his own keeping; having made his Way into this Stall, which he cou'd not have done, if the Man had been at the Door, the Noise he was obliged to make, being such as would have alarm'd the Watchman; I say, having made his Way into this Stall, he sat still till the Watchman return'd with the Nurse, and all the next Day also; but the Night following, having contriv'd to send the Watchman of another trifling Errand, which as I take it, was to an Apothecary's for a Plaster for the Maid, which he was to stay for the making up, or some other such Errand that might secure his staying some Time; in that Time he conveyed himself, and all his

Family out of the House, and left the Nurse and the Watchman to bury the poor Wench; that is, throw her into the Cart, and take care of the House.

I cou'd give a great many such Stories as these, diverting enough, which in the long Course of that dismal Year, I met with, *that is* heard of, and which are very certain to be true, or very near the Truth; that is to say, true in the General, for no Man could at such a Time, learn all the Particulars: There was likewise Violence used with the Watchmen, *as was reported* in abundance of Places; and I believe, that from the Beginning of the Visitation to the End, there was not less than eighteen or twenty of them kill'd, or so wounded as to be taken up for Dead, which was suppos'd to be done by the People in the infected Houses which were shut up, and where they attempted to come out, and were oppos'd.

Nor indeed cou'd less be expected, for here were just so many Prisons in the Town, as there were Houses shut up; and as the People shut up or imprison'd so, were guilty of no Crime, only shut up because miserable, it was really the more intollerable to them.

It had also this Difference; that every Prison, as we may call it, had but one Jaylor; and as he had the whole House to Guard, and that many Houses were so situated, as that they had several Ways out, some more, some less, and some into several Streets; it was impossible for one Man so to Guard all the Passages, as to prevent the escape of People, made desperate by the fright of their Circumstances, by the Resentment of their usage, or by the raging of the Distemper it self; so that they would talk to the Watchman on one Side of the House, while the Family made their escape at another.

For example, in *Coleman-street*, there are abundance of Alleys, as appears still; a House was shut up in that they call *Whites*-Alley, and this House had a back Window, not a Door into a Court, which had a Passage into Bell-Alley; a Watchman was set by the Constable, at the Door of this House, and there he stood, or his Comrade Night and Day, while the Family went all away in the Evening, out at that Window into the Court, and left the poor Fellows warding, and watching, for near a Fortnight.

Not far from the same Place, they blow'd up a Watchman with Gun-powder, and burnt the poor Fellow dreadfully, and while he made hideous Crys, and no Body would venture to come near to help him; the whole Family that were able to stir, got out at the Windows one Story high; two that were left Sick, calling out for Help; Care was taken to give them Nurses to look after them, but the Persons fled were never found, till after the Plague was abated they return'd, but as nothing cou'd be prov'd, so nothing could be done to them.

It is to be consider'd too, that as these were Prisons without Barrs and Bolts, which our common Prisons are furnish'd with, so the People let themselves down out of their Windows, even in the Face of the Watchman, bringing Swords or Pistols in their Hands, and threatening the poor Wretch to shoot him, if he stir'd, or call'd for Help.

In other Cases, some had Gardens, and Walls, or Pales between them and their Neighbours; or Yards, and back-Houses; and these by Friendship and Entreaties, would get leave to get over those Walls, or Pales, and so go out at their Neighbour's Doors; or by giving Money to their Servants, get them, to let them thro' in the Night; so that in short, the shutting up of Houses, was in no wise to be depended upon; neither did it answer the End at all; serving more to make the People desperate, and drive them to such Extremities as that they would break out at all Adventures.

And that which was still worse, those that did thus break out, spread the Infection farther by their wandring about with the Distemper upon them, in their desperate Circumstances, than they would otherwise have done; for whoever considers all the Particulars in such Cases must acknowledge; and we cannot doubt but the severity of those Confinements, made many People desperate; and made them run out of their Houses at all Hazards, and with the Plague visibly upon them, not knowing either whither to go, or what to do, or indeed, what they did; and many that did so, were driven to dreadful

Exigences and Extremities, and Perish'd in the Streets or Fields for meer Want, or drop'd down, by the raging violence of the Fever upon them: Others wandred into the Country, and went forward any Way, as their Desperation guided them, not knowing whither they went or would go, till faint and tir'd, and not getting any Relief; the Houses and Villages on the Road, refusing to admit them to lodge, whether infected or no; they have perish'd by the Road Side, or gotten into Barns and dy'd there, none daring to come to them, or relieve them, tho' perhaps not infected, for no Body would believe them.

On the other Hand, when the Plague at first seiz'd a Family, that is to say, when any one Body of the Family, had gone out, and unwarily or otherwise catch'd the Distemper and brought it Home, it was certainly known by the Family, before it was known to the Officers, who, as you will see by the Order, were appointed to examine into the Circumstances of all sick Persons, when they heard of their being sick.

In this Interval, between their being taken Sick, and the Examiners coming, the Master of the House had Leisure and Liberty to remove himself, or all his Family, if he knew whither to go, and many did so: But the great disaster was, that many did thus, after they were really infected themselves, and so carry'd the Disease into the Houses of those who were so Hospitable as to receive them, which it must be confess'd was very cruel and ungrateful.

And this was in Part, the Reason of the general Notion, or scandal rather, which went about of the Temper of People infected; Namely, that they did not take the least care, or make any Scruple of infecting others; tho' I cannot say, but there might be some Truth in it too, but not so general as was reported. What natural Reason could be given, for so wicked a Thing, at a Time, when they might conclude themselves just going to appear at the Barr of Divine Justice, I know not: I am very well satisfy'd, that it cannot be reconcil'd to Religion and Principle, any more than it can be to Generosity and Humanity; but I may speak of that again.

I am speaking now of People made desperate, by the Apprehensions of their being shut up, and their breaking out by Stratagem or Force, either before or after they were shut up, whose Misery was not lessen'd, when they were out, but sadly encreased: On the other Hand, many that thus got away, had Retreats to go to, and other Houses, where they lock'd themselves up, and kept hid till the Plague was over; and many Families foreseeing the Approach of the Distemper, laid up Stores of Provisions, sufficient for their whole Families, and shut themselves up, and that so entirely, that they were neither seen or heard of, till the Infection was quite ceased, and then came abroad Sound and Well: I might recollect several such as these, and give you the Particular of their Management; for doubtless, it was the most effectual secure Step that cou'd be taken for such, whose Circumstance would not admit them to remove, or who had not Retreats abroad proper for the Case; for in being thus shut up, they were as if they had been a hundred Miles off: Nor do I remember, that any one of those Families miscary'd; among these, several *Dutch* Merchants were particularly remarkable, who kept their Houses like little Garrisons besieged, suffering none to go in or out, or come near them; particularly one in a Court in *Throckmorton* Street, whose House looked into *Drapers Garden*.

But I come back to the Case of Families infected, and shut up by the Magistrates; the Misery of those Families is not to be express'd, and it was generally in such Houses that we heard the most dismal Shrieks and Out-cries of the poor People terrified, and even frighted to Death, by the Sight of the Condition of their dearest Relations, and by the Terror of being imprisoned as they were.

I remember, and while I am writing this Story, I think I hear the very Sound of it, a certain Lady had an only Daughter, a young Maiden about 19 Years old, and who was possessed of a very Considerable Fortune; they were only Lodgers in the House where they were: The young Woman, her Mother, and the Maid, had been abroad on some Occasion, I do not remember what, for the House was not shut up; but about two Hours after they came home, the young Lady complain'd she was not well; in a quarter of an Hour more, she vomited, and had a violent Pain in her Head. Pray God, says her Mother in a terrible Fright, my Child has not the Distemper! The Pain in her Head increasing, her Mother ordered the Bed to be warm'd, and resolved to put her to Bed; and prepared to give her things to sweat, which was the ordinary Remedy[1] to be taken, when the first Apprehensions of the Distemper began.

While the Bed was airing, the Mother undressed the young Woman, and just as she was laid down in the Bed, she looking upon her Body with a Candle, immediately discovered the fatal Tokens on the Inside of her Thighs. Her Mother not being able to contain herself, threw down her Candle, and shriekt out in such a frightful Manner, that it was enough to place Horror upon the stoutest Heart in the World; nor was it one Skream, or one Cry, but the Fright having seiz'd her Spirits, she fainted first, then recovered, then ran all over the House, up the Stairs and down the Stairs, like one distracted, and indeed really was distracted, and continued screeching and crying out for several Hours, void of all Sense, or at least, Government of her Senses, and as I was told, never came thoroughly to herself again: As to the young Maiden, she was a dead Corpse from that Moment; for the Gangren which occasions the Spots had spread [over] her whole Body, and she died in less than two Hours: But still the Mother continued crying out, not knowing any Thing more of her Child, several Hours after she was dead. It is so long ago, that I am not certain, but I think the Mother never recover'd, but died in two or three Weeks after.

This was an extraordinary Case, and I am therefore the more particular in it, because I came so much to the Knowledge of it; but there were innumerable such like Cases; and it was seldom, that the Weekly Bill came in, but there were two or three put in *frighted*,[2] that is, *that may well be call'd*, frighted to Death: But besides those, who were so frighted to die upon the Spot there were great Numbers frighted to other

Extreams, some frighted out of their Senses, some out of their Memory and some out of their Understanding: But I return to the shutting up of Houses.

As several People, *I say*, got out of their Houses by Stratagem, after they were shut up, so others got out by bribing the Watchmen, and giving them Money to let them go privately out in the Night. I must confess, I thought it at that time, the most innocent Corruption, or Bribery, that any Man could be guilty of; and therefore could not but pity the poor Men, and think it was hard when three of those Watchmen, were publickly whipt thro' the Streets, for suffering People to go out of Houses shut up.

But notwithstanding that Severity, Money prevail'd with the poor Men, and many Families found Means to make Salleys out, and escape that way after they had been shut up; but these were generally such as had some Places to retreat to; and tho' there was no easie passing the Roads any whither, after the first of *August*, yet there were many Ways of retreat, and particularly, as I hinted, some got Tents and set them up in the Fields, carrying Beds, or Straw to lie on, and Provisions to eat, and so liv'd in them as Hermits in a Cell; for no Body would venture to come near them; and several Stories were told of such; some comical, some tragical, some who liv'd like wandring Pilgrims in the Desarts, and escaped by making themselves Exiles in such a Manner as is scarce to be credited, and who yet enjoyed more Liberty than was to be expected in such Cases.

I have by me a Story of two Brothers and their Kinsman, who being single Men, but that had stay'd in the City too long to get away, and indeed, not knowing where to go to have any Retreat, nor having wherewith to travel far, took a Course for their own Preservation, which, tho' in it self at first, desperate, yet was so natural, that it may be wondred, that no more did so at that Time. They were but of mean Condition, and yet not so very poor, as that they could not furnish themselves with some little Conveniencies, such as might serve to keep Life and Soul together; and finding the Distemper increasing in a terrible Manner, they resolved to shift, as well as they could, and to be gone.

One of them had been a Soldier in the late Wars,[1] and before that in the *Low Countries*, and having been bred to no particular Employment but his Arms; and besides being wounded, and not able to work very hard, had for some Time been employ'd at a Bakers of Sea Bisket in *Wapping*.

The Brother of this Man was a Seaman too, but some how or other, had been hurt of one Leg, that he could not go to Sea, but had work'd for his Living at a Sail Makers in *Wapping*, or there abouts; and being a good Husband, had laid up some Money, and was the richest of the Three.

The third Man was a Joiner or Carpenter by Trade, a handy Fellow; and he had no Wealth, but his Box, or Basket of Tools, with the Help of which he could at any Time get his Living, such a Time as this excepted, wherever he went, and he liv'd near *Shadwel*.

They all liv'd in *Stepney* Parish, which, as I have said, being the last that was infected, or at least violently, they stay'd there till they evidently saw the Plague was abating at the West Part of the Town, and coming towards the East where they liv'd.

The Story of those three Men, if the Reader will be content to have me give it in their own Persons, without taking upon me to either vouch the Particulars, or answer for any Mistakes, I shall give as distinctly as I can, believing the History will be a very good Pattern for any poor Man to follow, in case the like Publick Desolation should happen here; and if there may be no such Occasion, which God of his infinite Mercy grant us, still the Story may have its Uses so many Ways as that it will, I hope, never be said, that the relating has been unprofitable.

I say all this previous to the History, having yet, for the present, much more to say before I quit my own Part.

I went all the first Part of the Time freely about the Streets, tho' not so freely as to run my self into apparent Danger, except when they dug the great Pit in the Church-Yard of our

Parish of *Aldgate*; a terrible Pit it was, and I could not resist my Curiosity to go and see it; as near as I may judge, it was about 40 Foot in Length, and about 15 or 16 Foot broad; and at the Time I first looked at it, about nine Foot deep; but it was said, they dug it near 20 Foot deep afterwards, in one Part of it, till they could go no deeper for the Water: for they had it seems, dug several large Pits before this, for tho' the Plague was long a-coming to our Parish,[1] yet when it did come, there was no Parish in or about *London*, where it raged with such Violence as in the two Parishes of *Aldgate* and *White Chapel*.[2]

I say they had dug several Pits in another Ground, when the Distemper began to spread in our Parish, and especially when the Dead-Carts began to go about, which was not in our Parish till the beginning of *August*. Into these Pits they had put perhaps 50 or 60 Bodies each, then they made larger Holes, wherein they buried all that the Cart brought in a Week, which by the middle, to the End of *August*, came to, from 200 to 400 a Week; and they could not well dig them larger, because of the Order of the Magistrates, confining them to leave no Bodies within six Foot of the Surface; and the Water coming on, at about 17 or 18 Foot, they could not well, I say, put more in one Pit; but now at the Beginning of *September*, the Plague raging in a dreadful Manner, and the Number of Burials in our Parish increasing to more than was ever buried in any Parish about *London*, of no larger Extent, they ordered this dreadful Gulph to be dug; for such it was rather than a Pit.

They had supposed this Pit would have supply'd them for a Month or more, when they dug it, and some blam'd the Church-Wardens for suffering such a frightful Thing, telling them they were making Preparations to bury the whole Parish, and the like; but Time made it appear, the Church-Wardens knew the Condition of the Parish better than they did; for the Pit being finished the 4th of *September*, I think, they began to bury in it the 6th, and by the 20, which was just two Weeks they had thrown into it 1114 Bodies,[3] when they were obliged to fill it up, the Bodies being then come to lie within six Foot of the Surface: I doubt not but there may be some antient Persons alive in the Parish, who can justify the Fact of this, and are able to shew even in what Part of the Church-Yard, the Pit lay, better than I can; the Mark of it also was many Years to be seen in the Church-Yard on the Surface lying in Length, Parallel with the Passage which goes by the West Wall of the Church-Yard, out of *Houndsditch*, and turns East again into *White-Chappel*, coming out near the three Nuns Inn.[1]

It was about the 10th of *September*, that my Curiosity led, or rather drove me to go and see this Pit again, when there had been near 400 People buried in it; and I was not content to see it in the Day-time, as I had done before; for then there would have been nothing to have been seen but the loose Earth; for all the Bodies that were thrown in, were immediately covered with Earth, by those they call'd the Buryers, which at other Times were call'd Bearers; but I resolv'd to go in the Night and see some of them thrown in.

There was a strict Order to prevent People coming to those Pits, and that was only to prevent Infection: But after some Time, that Order was more necessary, for People that were Infected, and near their End, and delirious also, would run to those Pits wrapt in Blankets, or Rugs, and throw themselves in, and as they said, bury themselves: I cannot say, that the Officers suffered any willingly to lie there; but I have heard, that in a great Pit in *Finsbury*,[2] in the Parish of *Cripplegate*, it lying open then to the Fields; for it was not then wall'd about, came and threw themselves in, and expired there, before they threw any Earth upon them; and that when they came to bury others, and found them there, they were quite dead, tho' not cold.

This may serve a little to describe the dreadful Condition of that Day, tho' it is impossible to say any Thing that is able to give a true Idea of it to those who did not see it, other than this; that it was indeed *very*, *very*, *very* dreadful, and such as no Tongue can express.

I got Admittance into the Church-Yard by being acquainted with the Sexton, who attended, who tho' he did not refuse me at all, yet earnestly perswaded me not to go; telling me very seriously, for he was a good religious and sensible Man, that it was indeed, their Business and Duty to venture, and to run all Hazards; and that in it they might hope to be preserv'd; but that I had no apparent Call to it, but my own Curiosity, which he said, he believ'd I would not pretend, was sufficient to justify my running that Hazard. I told him I had been press'd in my Mind to go, and that perhaps it might be an Instructing Sight, that might not be without its Uses. Nay, says the good Man, if you will venture upon that Score, *'Name of God go in*; for depend upon it, 'twill be a Sermon to you, it may be, the best that ever you heard in your Life. 'Tis a speaking Sight, says he, and has a Voice with it, and a loud one, to call us all to Repentance; and with that he opened the Door and said, Go, if you will.

His Discourse had shock'd my Resolution a little, and I stood wavering for a good while; but just at that Interval I saw two Links come over from the End of the *Minories*, and heard the Bell-man,[1] and then appear'd a Dead-Cart, *as they call'd it*, coming over the Streets so I could no longer resist my Desire of seeing it, and went in: There was no Body, as I could perceive at first, in the Church-Yard, or going into it, but the Buryers, and the Fellow that drove the Cart, or rather led the Horse and Cart, but when they came up, to the Pit, they saw a Man go to and again, mufled up in a brown Cloak, and making Motions with his Hands, under his Cloak, as if he was in a great Agony; and the Buriers immediately gathered about him, supposing he was one of those poor delirious, or desperate Creatures, that used to pretend, as I have said, to bury themselves; he said nothing as he walk'd about, but two or three times groaned very deeply, and loud, and sighed as he would break his Heart.

When the Buryers came up to him they soon found he was neither a Person infected and desperate, as I have observed above, or a Person distempered in Mind, but one oppress'd with a dreadful Weight of Grief indeed, having his Wife and several of his Children, all in the Cart, that was just come in with him, and he followed in an Agony and excess of Sorrow. He mourned heartily, as it was easy to see, but with a kind of Masculine Grief, that could not give it self Vent by Tears, and calmly desiring the Buriers to let him alone, said he would only see the Bodies thrown in, and go away, so they left importuning him; but no sooner was the Cart turned round, and the Bodies shot into the Pit promiscuously, which was a Surprize to him, for he at least expected they would have been decently laid in, tho' indeed he was afterwards convinced that was impractible; I say, no sooner did he see the Sight, but he cry'd out aloud unable to contain himself; I could not hear what he said, but he went backward two or three Steps, and fell down in a Swoon: the Buryers ran to him and took him up, and in a little While he came to himself, and they led him away to the *Pye-Tavern* over-against the End of *Houndsditch*, where, it seems, the Man was known, and where they took care of him. He look'd into the Pit again, as he went away, but the Buriers had covered the Bodies so immediately with throwing in Earth, that tho' there was Light enough, for there were Lantherns and Candles in them, plac'd all Night round the Sides of the Pit, upon the Heaps of Earth, seven or eight, or perhaps more, yet nothing could be seen.

This was a mournful Scene indeed, and affected me almost as much as the rest; but the other was awful, and full of Terror, the Cart had in it sixteen or seventeen Bodies, some were wrapt up in Linen Sheets, some in Rugs, some little other than naked, or so loose, that what Covering they had, fell from them, in the shooting out of the Cart, and they fell quite naked among the rest; but the Matter was not much to them, or the Indecency much to any one else, seeing they were all dead, and were to be huddled together into the common Grave of Mankind, as we may call it, for here was no Difference made, but Poor and Rich went together; there was no other way of Burials, neither was it possible there should, for

Coffins were not to be had[1] for the prodigious Numbers that fell in such a Calamity as this.

It was reported by way of Scandal upon the Buriers, that if any Corpse was delivered to them, decently wound up as we call'd it then, in a Winding Sheet Ty'd over the Head and Feet, which some did, and which was generally of good Linen; I say, it was reported, that the Buriers were so wicked as to strip them in the Cart, and carry them quite naked to the Ground: But as I can not easily credit any thing so vile among Christians, and at a Time so fill'd with Terrors, as that was, I can only relate it and leave it undetermined.

Innumerable Stories also went about of the cruel Behaviours and Practises of Nurses, who tended the Sick, and of their hastening on the Fate of those they tended in their Sickness: But I shall say more of this in its Place.

I was indeed shock'd with this Sight, it almost overwhelm'd me, and I went away with my Heart most afflicted and full of the afflicting Thoughts, such as I cannot describe; just at my going out of the Church, and turning up the Street towards my own House, I saw another Cart with Links, and a Bellman going before, coming out of *Harrow-Alley*, in the *Butcher-Row*, on the other Side of the Way, and being, as I perceived, very full of dead Bodies, it went directly over the Street also toward the Church: I stood a while, but I had no Stomach to go back again to see the same dismal Scene over again, so I went directly Home, where I could not but consider with Thankfulness, the Risque I had run, believing I had gotten no Injury; as indeed I had not.

Here the poor unhappy Gentleman's Grief came into my head again, and indeed I could not but shed Tears in the Reflection upon it, perhaps more than he did himself; but his Case lay so heavy upon my Mind, that I could not prevail with my self, but that I must go out again into the Street, and go to the *Pye-Tavern*, resolving to enquire what became of him.

It was by this Time one a-Clock in the Morning, and yet the poor Gentleman was there; the Truth was, the People of the House knowing him, had entertain'd him, and kept him there all the Night, notwithstanding the Danger of being infected, by him, tho' it appear'd the Man was perfectly sound himself.

It is with Regret, that I take Notice of this Tavern; the People were civil, mannerly, and an obliging Sort of Folks enough, and had till this Time kept their House open, and their Trade going on, tho' not so very publickly as formerly; but there was a dreadful Set of Fellows that used their House, and who in the middle of all this Horror met there every Night, behaved with all the Revelling and roaring extravagances, as is usual for such People to do at other Times, and indeed to such an offensive Degree, that the very Master and Mistress of the House grew first asham'd and then terrify'd at them.

They sat generally in a Room next the Street, and as they always kept late Hours, so when the Dead-Cart came cross the Street End to go into *Hounds-ditch*, which was in View of the Tavern Windows; they would frequently open the Windows as soon as they heard the Bell, and look out at them; and as they might often hear sad Lamentations of People in the Streets, or at their Windows, as the Carts went along, they would make their impudent Mocks and Jeers at them, especially if they heard the poor People call upon God to have Mercy upon them, as many would do at those Times in their ordinary passing along the Streets.

These Gentlemen being something disturb'd with the Clutter of bringing the poor Gentleman into the House, as above, were first angry, and very high with the Master of the House, for suffering such a Fellow, as they call'd him, to be brought out of the Grave into their House; but being answered, that the Man was a Neighbour, and that he was sound, but overwhelmed with the Calamity of his Family, and the like, they turned their Anger into ridiculing the Man, and his Sorrow for his Wife and Children; taunted him with want of Courage to leap into the great Pit, and go to Heaven, as they jeeringly express'd it, along with them, adding some very profane, and even blasphemous Expressions.

They were at this vile Work when I came back to the House,

and as far as I could see, tho' the Man sat still, mute and dis-consolate, and their Affronts could not divert his Sorrow, yet he was both griev'd and offended at their Discourse: Upon this, I gently reprov'd them, being well enough acquainted with their Characters, and not unknown in Person to two of them.

They immediately fell upon me with ill Language and Oaths; ask'd me what I did out of my Grave, at such a Time when so many *honester Men* were carried into the Church-Yard? and why I was not at Home saying my Prayers, against the Dead-Cart came for me? and the like.

I was indeed astonished at the Impudence of the Men, tho' not at all discomposed at their Treatment of me; however I kept my Temper; I told them, that tho' I defy'd them, or any Man in the World to tax me with any *Dishonesty*, yet I acknow-ledg'd, that in this terrible Judgment of God, many better than I was swept away, and carried to their Grave: But to answer their Question directly, the Case was, that I was mercifully preserved by that great God, whose Name they had Blasphemed and taken in vain, by cursing and swearing in a dreadful Manner; and that I believed I was preserv'd in particular, among other Ends, of his Goodness, that I might reprove them for their audacious Boldness, in behaving in such a Manner, and in such an awful Time as this was, especially, for their Jeering and Mocking, at an honest Gentle-man, and a Neighbour, for some of them knew him, who they saw was overwhelm'd with Sorrow, for the Breaches which it had pleas'd God to make upon his Family.

I cannot call exactly to Mind the hellish abominable Raillery, which was the Return they made to that Talk of mine, being provoked, it seems, that I was not at all afraid to be free with them; nor if I could remember, would I fill my Account with any of the Words, the horrid Oaths, Curses, and vile Expressions, such, as at that time of the Day, even the worst and ordinariest People in the Street would not use; (for except such hardened Creatures as these, the most wicked wretches that could be found, had at that Time some

Terror upon their Minds of the Hand of that Power which could thus, in a Moment destroy them.)

But that which was the worst in all their devilish Language was, that they were not afraid to blaspheme God, and talk Atheistically; making a Jest at my calling the Plague the Hand of God, mocking, and even laughing at the Word Judgment, as if the Providence of God had no Concern in the inflicting such a desolating Stroke; and that the People calling upon God, as they saw the Carts carrying away the dead Bodies was all enthusiastick,[1] absurd, and impertinent.

I made them some Reply, such as I thought proper, but which I found was so far from putting a Checque to their horrid Way of speaking, that it made them rail the more, so that I confess it fill'd me with Horror, and a kind of Rage, and I came away, as I told them, lest the Hand of that Judgment which had visited the whole City should glorify his Vengeance upon them, and all that were near them.

They received all Reproof with the utmost Contempt, and made the greatest Mockery that was possible for them to do at me, giving me all the opprobrious insolent Scoffs that they could think of for preaching to them, *as they call'd it*, which indeed, grieved me, rather than angred me; and I went away blessing God, however, in my Mind, that I had not spar'd them, tho' they had insulted me so much.

They continued this wretched Course, three or four Days after this, continually mocking and jeering at all that shew'd themselves religious, or serious, or that were any way touch'd with the Sence of the terrible Judgment of God upon us, and I was inform'd they flouted in the same Manner, at the good People, who, notwithstanding the Contagion, met at the Church, fasted, and prayed to God to remove his Hand from them.

I say, they continued this dreadful Course three or four Days, *I think it was no more*, when one of them, particularly he who ask'd the poor Gentleman *what he did out of his Grave?* was struck from Heaven with the Plague, and died in a most deplorable Manner; and in a Word they were every one of them carried into the great Pit, which I have mentioned above, before it was quite fill'd up, which was not above a Fortnight or thereabout.

These Men were guilty of many extravagances, such as one would think, Human Nature should have trembled at the Thoughts of, at such a Time of general Terror, as was then upon us; and particularly scoffing and mocking at every thing which they happened to see, that was religious among the People, especially at their thronging zealously to the Place of publick Worship, to implore Mercy from Heaven in such a Time of Distress; and this Tavern, where they held their Club, being within View of the Church Door, they had the more particular Occasion for their Atheistical profane Mirth.

But this began to abate a little with them before the Accident, which I have related, happened; for the Infection increased so violently, at this Part of the Town now, that People began to be afraid to come to the Church, at least such Numbers did not resort thither as was usual; many of the Clergymen likewise were Dead, and others gone into the Country; for it really required a steady Courage, and a strong Faith, for a Man not only to venture being in Town at such a Time as this, but likewise to venture to come to Church and perform the Office of a Minister to a Congregation, of whom he had reason to believe many of them, were actually infected with the Plague, and to do this every Day, or twice a Day, as in some Places was done.

It is true, the People shew'd an extraordinary Zeal in these religious Exercises, and as the Church Doors were always open, People would go in single at all Times, whether the Minister was officiating or no, and locking themselves into separate Pews, would be praying to God with great Fervency and Devotion.

Others assembled at Meeting-Houses, every one as their different Opinions in such Things guided, but all were promiscuously the Subject of these Mens Drollery, especially at the Beginning of the Visitation.

It seems they had been check'd for their open insulting

Religion in this Manner, by several good People of every perswasion, and that, and the violent raging of the Infection, I suppose, was the Occasion that they had abated much of their Rudeness, for some time before, and were only rous'd by the Spirit of Ribaldry, and Atheism, at the Clamour which was made, when the Gentleman was first brought in there, and perhaps, were agitated by the same Devil, when I took upon me to reprove them; tho' I did it at first with all the Calmness, Temper, and Good-Manners that I could, which, for a while, they insulted me the more for, thinking it had been in fear of their Resentment, tho' afterwards they found the contrary.

I went Home indeed, griev'd and afflicted in my Mind, at the Abominable Wickedness of those Men not doubting, however, that they would be made dreadful Examples of God's Justice; for I look'd upon this dismal Time to be a particular Season of Divine Vengeance, and that God would, on this Occasion, single out the proper Objects, of his Displeasure, in a more especial and remarkable Manner, than at another Time; and that, tho' I did believe that many good People would, and did, fall in the common Calamity, and that it was no certain Rule to judge of the eternal State of any one, by their being distinguish'd in such a Time of general Destruction, neither one Way or other; yet I say, it could not but seem reasonable to believe, that God would not think fit to spare by his Mercy such open declared Enemies, that should insult his Name and Being, defy his Vengeance, and mock at his Worship and Worshipers, at such a Time, no not tho' his Mercy had thought fit to bear with, and spare them at other Times: That this was a Day of Visitation; a Day of God's Anger; and those Words came into my Thought. *Jer.* v. 9. *Shall I not visit for these things, saith the Lord, and shall not my Soul be avenged of such a Nation as this?*

These Things, I say, lay upon my Mind; and I went home very much griev'd and oppress'd with the Horror of these Mens Wickedness, and to think that any thing could be so vile, so hardened, and so notoriously wicked, as to insult God and his Servants, and his Worship, in such a Manner, and at such a Time as this was; when he had, as it were, his Sword drawn in his Hand, on purpose to take Vengeance, not on them only, but on the whole Nation.

I had indeed, been in some Passion, at first, with them, tho' it was really raised, not by any Affront they had offered me personally, but by the Horror their blaspheming Tongues fill'd me with; however, I was doubtful in my Thoughts, whether the Resentment I retain'd was not all upon my own private Account, for they had given me a great deal of ill Language too, I mean Personally; but after some Pause, and having a Weight of Grief upon my Mind, I retir'd my self, as soon as I came home, for I slept not that Night, and giving God most humble Thanks for my Preservation in the eminent Danger I had been in, I set my Mind seriously, and with the utmost Earnestness, to pray for those desperate Wretches, that God would pardon them, open their Eyes, and effectually humble them.

By this I not only did my Duty, namely, to pray for those who dispitefully used me, but I fully try'd my own Heart, to my full Satisfaction; that it was not fill'd with any Spirit of Resentment as they had offended me in particular; and I humbly recommend the Method to all those that would know, or be certain, how to distinguish between their real Zeal for the Honour of God, and the Effects of their private Passions and Resentment.

But I must go back here to the particular Incidents which occur to my Thoughts of the Time of the Visitation, and particularly, to the Time of their shutting up Houses, in the first Part of the Sickness; for before the Sickness was come to its Height, People had more Room to make their Observations, than they had afterward: But when it was in the Extremity, there was no such Thing as Communication with one another, as before.

During the shutting up of Houses, as I have said, some Violence was offered to the Watchmen; as to Soldiers, there were none to be found; the few Guards which the King then had, which were nothing like the Number entertain'd since, were disperss'd, either at *Oxford* with the Court, or in Quarters in the remoter Parts of the Country; small detachments excepted, who did Duty at the Tower, and at *White-Hall*, and these but very few; neither am I positive, that there was any other Guard at the Tower, than the *Warders*, as they call'd them, who stand at the Gate with Gowns and Caps, the same as the Yeomen of the Guard; except the ordinary Gunners, who were 24, and the Officers appointed to look after the Magazine, who were call'd Armourers: as to Traind-Bands, there was no Possibility of raising any, neither if the Lieutenancy, either of *London* or *Middlesex* had ordered the Drums to beat for the Militia, would any of the Companies, I believe, have drawn together, whatever Risque they had run.

This made the Watchmen be the less regarded, and perhaps, occasioned the greater Violence to be used against them; I mention it on this Score, to observe that the setting Watchmen thus to keep the People in, was (1st) of all, not effectual, but that the People broke out, whether by Force or by Stratagem, even almost as often as they pleas'd: And (2d) that those that did thus break out, were generally People infected, who in their Desperation, running about from one Place to another, valued not who they injur'd, and which perhaps, as I have said, might give Birth to Report, that it was natural to the infected People to desire to infect others, which Report was really false.

And I know it so well, and in so many several Cases, that I could give several Relations of good, pious, and religious People, who, when they have had the Distemper, have been so far from being forward to infect others, that they have forbid their own Family to come near them, in Hopes of their being preserved; and have even died without seeing their nearest Relations, lest they should be instrumental to give them the Distemper, and infect or endanger them: If then there were Cases wherein the infected People were careless of the Injury they did to others, this was certainly one of them, if not the chief, namely, when People, who had the Distemper, had broken out from Houses which were so shut up, and having been driven to Extremities for Provision, or for Entertainment, had endeavoured to conceal their Condition, and have been thereby Instrumental involuntarily to infect others who have been ignorant and unwary.

This is one of the Reasons why I believed then, and do believe still, that the shutting up Houses thus by Force, and restraining, or rather imprisoning People in their own Houses, as is said above, was of little or no Service in the Whole; nay, I am of Opinion, it was rather hurtful, having forc'd those desperate People to wander abroad with the Plague upon them, who would otherwise have died quietly in their Beds.

I remember one Citizen, who having thus broken out of his House in *Aldersgate-Street*, or thereabout, went along the Road to *Islington*, he attempted to have gone in at the *Angel-Inn*, and after that, at the *White-Horse*, two Inns known still by the same Signs, but was refused; after which he came to the *Pyed Bull*, an Inn also still continuing the same Sign; he asked them for Lodging for one Night only, pretending to be going into *Lincolnshire*, and assuring them of his being very sound, and free from the Infection, which also, at that Time, had not reached much that Way.

They told him they had no Lodging that they could spare, but one Bed, up in the Garret, and that they could spare that Bed but for one Night, some Drovers being expected the next Day with Cattle; so, if he would accept of that Lodging, he might have it, which he did; so a Servant was sent up with a Candle with him, to shew him the Room; he was very well dress'd, and look'd like a Person not used to lie in a Garret, and when he came to the Room he fech'd a deep Sigh, and said to the Servant, I have seldom lain in such a Lodging as this; however the Servant assuring him again, that they had no better. Well, says he, I must make shift; this is a dreadful Time, but it is but for one Night; so he sat down upon the Bedside, and bad the maid, *I think it was*, fetch him up a Pint of warm Ale; accordingly the Servant went for the Ale; but some Hurry in the House, which perhaps employed her otherways, put it out of her Head; and she went up no more to him.

The next Morning seeing no Appearance of the Gentleman, some Body in the House asked the Servant that had shewed him up Stairs, what was become of him? She started; Alas says she, I never thought more of him: He bad me carry him some warm Ale, but I forgot; upon which, not the Maid, but some other Person, was sent up to see after him, who coming into the Room found him stark dead, and almost cold, stretch'd out cross the Bed; his Cloths were pulled off, his Jaw fallen, his Eyes open in a most frightful Posture, the Rug of the Bed being grasped hard in one of his Hands; so that it was plain he died soon after the Maid left him, and 'tis probable, had she gone up with the Ale, she had found him dead in a few Minutes after he sat down upon the Bed. The Alarm was great in the House, as any one may suppose, they having been free from the Distemper, till that Disaster, which bringing the Infection to the House, spread it immediately to other Houses round about it. I do not remember how many died in the House it self, but I think the Maid Servant, who went up first with him, fell presently ill by the Fright, and several others; for whereas there died but two in *Islington* of the Plague the Week before, there died 17 the Week after, whereof 14 were of the Plague; this was in the Week from the 11th of *July* to the 18th.

There was one Shift that some Families had, and that not a few, when their Houses happened to be infected, *and that was this*; The Families, who in the first breaking out of the Distemper, fled away into the Country, and had Retreats among their Friends, generally found some or other of their Neighbours or Relations to commit the Charge of those Houses to, for the Safety of the Goods, and the like. Some Houses were indeed, entirely lock'd up, the Doors padlockt, the Windows and Doors having Deal-Boards nail'd over them, and only the Inspection of them committed to the ordinary Watchmen and Parish Officers; but these were but few.

It was thought that there were not less than 10000 Houses forsaken of the Inhabitants in the City and Suburbs, including what was in the Out Parishes, and in Surrey, or the Side of the

Water they call'd *Southwark*. This was besides the Numbers of Lodgers, and of particular Persons who were fled out of other Families; so that in all it was computed that about 200000 People were fled[1] and gone in all: But of this I shall speak again: But I mention it here on this Account, namely, that it was a Rule with those who had thus two Houses in their Keeping, or Care, that if any Body was taken sick in a Family, before the Master of the Family let the Examiners, or any other Officer, know of it, he immediately would send all the rest of his Family whether Children or Servants, as it fell out to be, to such other House which he had so in Charge, and then giving Notice of the sick Person to the Examiner, have a Nurse, or Nurses appointed; and have another Person to be shut up in the House with them (which many for Money would do) so to take Charge of the House, in case the Person should die.

This was in many Cases the saving a whole Family, who, if they had been shut up with the sick Person, would inevitably have perished: But on the other Hand, this was another of the Inconveniencies of shutting up Houses; for the Apprehensions and Terror of being shut up, made many run away with the rest of the Family, who, tho' it was not publickly known, and they were not quite sick, had yet the Distemper upon them; and who by having an uninterrupted Liberty to go about, but being obliged still to conceal their Circumstances, or perhaps not knowing it themselves, gave the Distemper to others, and spread the Infection in a dreadful Manner, as I shall explain farther hereafter.

And here I may be able to make an Observation or two of my own, which may be of use hereafter to those, into whose Hands this may come, if they should ever see the like dreadful Visitation. (1.) The Infection generally came into the Houses of the Citizens, by the Means of their Servants, who, they were obliged to send up and down the Streets for Necessaries, that is to say, for Food, or Physick, to Bake-houses, Brew-houses, Shops, &c. and who going necessarily thro' the Streets into Shops, Markets, and the like, it was impossible, but that they should one way or other, meet with distempered people, who conveyed the fatal Breath[1] into them, and they brought it Home to the Families, to which they belonged. (2.) It was a great Mistake, that such a great City as this had but one Pest-House; for had there been, instead of one Pest-House *viz.* beyond *Bunhil-Fields*, where, at most, they could receive, perhaps, 200 or 300 People; I say, had there instead of that one been several Pest-houses, every one able to contain a thousand People without lying two in a Bed, or two Beds in a Room; and had every Master of a Family, as soon as any Servant especially, had been taken sick in his House, been obliged to send them to the next Pest-House, if they were willing, as many were, and had the Examiners done the like among the poor People, when any had been stricken with the Infection; I say, had this been done where the People were willing, (not otherwise) and the Houses not been shut, I am perswaded, and was all the While of that Opinion, that not so many, by several Thousands, had died; for it was observed, and I could give several Instances within the Compass of my own Knowledge, where a Servant had been taken sick, and the Family had either Time to send them out, or retire from the House, and leave the sick Person, *as I have said above*, they had all been preserved; whereas, when upon one, or more, sickning in a Family, the House has been shut up, the whole Family have perished, and the Bearers been oblig'd to go in to fetch out the Dead Bodies, none being able to bring them to the Door; and at last none left to do it.

(3.) This put it out of Question to me, that the Calamity was spread by Infection, that is to say, by some certain Steams, or Fumes, which the Physicians call *Effluvia*,[2] by the Breath, or by the Sweat, or by the Stench of the Sores of the sick Persons, or some other way, perhaps, beyond even the Reach of the Physicians themselves, which *Effluvia* affected the Sound, who come within certain Distances of the Sick, immediately penetrating the Vital Parts of the said sound Persons, putting their Blood into an immediate ferment, and agitating their Spirits to that Degree which it was found they were agitated; and so those newly infected Persons communicated it in the same Manner to others; and this I shall give some Instances of, that cannot but convince those who seriously consider it; and I cannot but with some Wonder, find some People, now the Contagion is over, talk of its being an immediate Stroke from Heaven,[1] without the Agency of Means, having Commission to strike this and that particular Person, and none other; which I look upon with Contempt, as the Effect of manifest Ignorance and Enthusiasm; likewise the Opinion of others, who talk of infection being carried on by the Air only, by carrying with it vast Numbers of Insects,[2] and invisible Creatures, who enter into the Body with the Breath, or even at the Pores with the Air, and there generate, or emit most accute Poisons, or poisonous Ovæ, or Eggs, which mingle themselves with the Blood, and so infect the Body; a Discourse full of learned Simplicity, and manifested to be so by universal Experience; but I shall say more to this Case in its Order.

I must here take farther Notice that Nothing was more fatal to the Inhabitants of this City, than the Supine Negligence of the People themselves,[3] who during the long Notice, or Warning they had of the Visitation, yet made no Provision for it, by laying in Store of Provisions, or of other Necessaries; by which they might have liv'd retir'd, and within their own Houses, as I have observed, others did, and who were in a great Measure preserv'd by that Caution; nor were they, after they were a little hardened to it so shye of conversing with one another, when actually infected, as they were at first, no tho' they knew it.

I acknowledge I was one of those thoughtless Ones, that had made so little Provision, that my Servants were obliged to go out of Doors to buy every Trifle by Penny and Half-penny, just as before it begun, even till my Experience shewing me the Folly, I began to be wiser so late, that I had scarce Time to store my self sufficient for our common Subsistence for a Month.

I had in Family only an antient Woman, that managed the

House, a Maid-Servant, two Apprentices, and my self; and the Plague beginning to encrease about us, I had many sad Thoughts about what Course I should take, and how I should act; the many dismal Objects, which happened everywhere as I went about the Streets, had fill'd my Mind with a great deal of Horror, for fear of the Distemper it self, which was indeed, very horrible in it self, and in some more than in others, the swellings which were generally in the Neck, or Groin, when they grew hard, and would not break, grew so painful, that it was equal to the most exquisite Torture; and some not able to bear the Torment, threw themselves out at Windows, or shot themselves, or otherwise made themselves away, and I saw several dismal Objects of that Kind: Others unable to contain themselves, vented their Pain by incessant Roarings, and such loud and lamentable Cries were to be heard as we walk'd along the Streets, that would Pierce the very Heart to think of, especially when it was to be considered, that the same dreadful Scourge might be expected every Moment to seize upon our selves.

I cannot say, but that now I began to faint in my Resolutions, my Heart fail'd me very much, and sorely I repented of my Rashness: When I had been out, and met with such terrible Things as these I have talked of; I say, I repented my Rashness in venturing to abide in Town: I wish'd often, that I had not taken upon me to stay, but had gone away with my Brother and his Family.

Terrified by those frightful Objects, I would retire Home sometimes, and resolve to go out no more, and perhaps, I would keep those Resolutions for three or four Days, which Time I spent in the most serious Thankfulness for my Preservation, and the Preservation of my Family, and the constant Confession of my Sins, giving my self up to God every Day, and applying to him with Fasting, Humiliation, and Meditation: Such intervals as I had, I employed in reading Books, and in writing down my Memorandums of what occurred to me every Day, and out of which, afterwards, I [took] most of this Work as it relates to my Observations without

Doors: What I wrote of my private Meditations I reserve for private Use, and desire it may not be made publick on any Account whatever.

I also wrote other Meditations upon Divine Subjects,[1] such as occurred to me at that Time, and were profitable to my self, but not fit for any other View, and therefore I say no more of that.

I had a very good Friend, a Physician,[2] whose Name was *Heath*, who I frequently visited during this dismal Time, and to whose Advice I was very much oblig'd for many Things which he directed me to take, by way of preventing the Infection when I went out, as he found I frequently did, and to hold in my Mouth when I was in the Streets; he also came very often to see me, and as he was a good Christian, as well as a good Physician, his agreeable Conversation was a very great Support to me in the worst of this terrible Time.

It was now the Beginning of *August*, and the Plague grew very violent and terrible in the Place where I liv'd,[3] and Dr. *Heath* coming to visit me, and finding that I ventured so often out in the Streets, earnestly perswaded me to lock my self up and my Family, and not to suffer any of us to go out of Doors; to keep all our Windows fast, Shutters and Curtains close, and never to open them; but first to make a very strong Smoke in the Room, where the Window, or Door was to be opened, with Rozen and Pitch, Brimstone,[4] or Gunpowder, and the like; and we did this for some Time: But as I had not laid in a Store of Provision for such a retreat, it was impossible that we could keep within Doors entirely; however, I attempted, tho' it was so very late, to do something towards it; and first, as I had Convenience both for Brewing and Baking, I went and bought two Sacks of Meal, and for several Weeks, having an Oven, we baked all our own Bread; also I bought Malt, and brew'd as much Beer as all the Casks I had would hold, and which seem'd enough to serve my House for five or six Weeks; also I laid in a Quantity of Salt-butter and *Cheshire* Cheese; but I had no Flesh-meat, and the Plague raged so violently among the Butchers, and Slaughter-Houses, on the other Side of our Street, where they are known to dwell in great Numbers, that it was not advisable, so much as to go over the Street among them.

And here I must observe again, that this Necessity of going out of our Houses to buy Provisions, was in a great Measure the Ruin of the whole City, for the People catch'd the Distemper, on those Occasions, one of another, and even the Provisions themselves were often tainted, at least I have great Reason to believe so; and therefore I cannot say with Satisfaction what I know is repeated with great Assurance, that the Market People, and such as brought Provisions, to Town, were never infected: I am certain, the Butchers of *White-Chapel*[1] where the greatest Part of the Flesh-meat was killed, were dreadfully visited, and that at last to such a Degree, that few of their Shops were kept open, and those that remain'd of them, kill'd their Meat at *Mile-End*, and that Way, and brought it to Market upon Horses.

However, the poor People cou'd not lay up Provisions, and there was a necessity, that they must go to Market to buy, and others to send Servants or their Children; and as this was a Necessity which renew'd it self daily; it brought abundance of unsound People to the Markets, and a great many that went thither Sound, brought Death Home with them.

It is true, People us'd all possible Precaution, when any one bought a Joint of Meat in the Market, they would not take it of the Butchers Hand, but take it off of the Hooks themselves. On the other Hand, the Butcher would not touch the Money, but have it put into a Pot full of Vinegar[2] which he kept for that purpose. The Buyer carry'd always small Money to make up any odd Sum, that they might take no Change. They carry'd Bottles for Scents, and Perfumes in their Hands, and all the Means that could be us'd, were us'd: But then the Poor cou'd not do even these things, and they went at all Hazards.

Innumerable dismal Stories we heard every Day on this very Account: Sometimes a Man or Woman dropt down Dead in the very Markets; for many People that had the Plague upon them, knew nothing of it;[1] till the inward Gangreen had affected their Vitals and they dy'd in a few Moments; this caus'd, that many died frequently in that Manner in the Streets suddainly, without any warning: Others perhaps had Time to go to the next Bulk or Stall; or to any Door, Porch, and just sit down and die, as I have said before.

These Objects were so frequent in the Streets, that when the Plague came to be very raging, on one Side, there was scarce any passing by the Streets, but that several dead Bodies would be lying here and there upon the Ground; on the other hand it is observable, that tho' at first, the People would stop as they went along, and call to the Neighbours to come out on such an Occasion; yet, afterward, no Notice was taken of them; but that, if at any Time we found a Corps lying, go cross the Way, and not come near it; or if in a narrow Lane or Passage, go back again, and seek some other Way to go on the Business we were upon; and in those Cases, the Corps was always left, till the Officers had notice, to come and take them away; or till Night, when the Bearers attending the Dead-Cart would take them up, and carry them away: Nor did those undaunted Creatures, who performed these Offices, fail to search their Pockets, and sometimes strip off their Cloths, if they were well drest, as sometimes they were, and carry off what they could get.

But to return to the Markets; the Butchers took that Care, that if any Person dy'd in the Market, they had the Officers always at Hand, to take them up upon Hand-barrows, and carry them to the next Church-Yard; and this was so frequent that such were not entred in the weekly Bill, found Dead in the Streets or Fields, as is the Case now; but they went into the general Articles of the great Distemper.

But now the Fury of the Distemper encreased to such a Degree, that even the Markets were but very thinly furnished with Provisions, or frequented with Buyers, compair'd to what they were before; and the Lord-Mayor caused the Country-People who brought Provisions, to be stop'd in the Streets leading into the Town, and to sit down there with their

Goods, where they sold what they brought, and went immediately away; and this Encourag'd the Country People greatly to do so, for they sold their Provisions at the very Entrances into the Town, and even in the Fields; as particularly in the Fields beyond *White-Chappel*, in *Spittle-fields*. Note, *Those Streets now called* Spittle-Fields, *were then indeed open Fields*: Also in St. *George's-fields* in *Southwark*, in *Bun-Hill* Fields, and in a great Field, call'd *Wood's-Close* near *Islington*; thither the Lord-Mayor, Aldermen, and Magistrates, sent their Officers and Servants to buy for their Families, themselves keeping within Doors as much as possible; and the like did many other People; and after this Method was taken, the Country People came with great chearfulness, and brought Provisions of all Sorts, and very seldom got any harm; which I suppose, added also to that Report of their being Miraculously preserv'd.

As for my little Family, having thus as I have said, laid in a Store of Bread, Butter, Cheese, and Beer, I took my Friend and Physician's Advice, and lock'd my self up, and my Family, and resolv'd to suffer the hardship of Living a few Months without Flesh-Meat, rather than to purchase it at the hazard of our Lives.

But tho' I confin'd my Family, I could not prevail upon my unsatisfy'd Curiosity to stay within entirely my self; and tho' I generally came frighted and terrified Home, yet I cou'd not restrain; only that indeed, I did not do it so frequently as at first.

I had some little Obligations indeed upon me, to go to my Brothers House, which was in *Coleman's-street* Parish, and which he had left to my Care, and I went at first every Day, but afterwards only once, or twice a Week.

In these Walks I had many dismal Scenes before my Eyes, as particularly of Persons falling dead in the Streets, terrible Shrieks and Skreekings of Women, who in their Agonies would throw open their Chamber Windows, and cry out in a dismal Surprising Manner; it is impossible to describe the Variety of Postures, in which the Passions of the Poor People would Express themselves.

Passing thro' *Token-House-Yard* in *Lothbury*, of a sudden a Casement violently opened just over my Head, and a Woman gave three frightful Skreetches, and then cry'd, *Oh! Death, Death, Death!* in a most inimitable Tone, and which struck me with Horror and a Chilness, in my very Blood. There was no Body to be seen in the whole Street, neither did any other Window open; for People had no Curiosity now in any Case; nor could any Body help one another; so I went on to pass into *Bell-Alley*.

Just in *Bell-Alley*, on the right Hand of the Passage, there was a more terrible Cry than that, tho' it was not so directed out at the Window, but the whole Family was in a terrible Fright, and I could hear Women and Children run skreaming about the Rooms like distracted, when a Garret Window opened, and some body from a Window on the other Side the Alley, call'd and ask'd, *What is the Matter?* upon which, from the first Window it was answered, *O Lord, my Old Master has hang'd himself!* The other ask'd again, *Is he quite dead?* and the first answer'd, *Ay, ay, quite dead; quite dead and cold!* This Person was a Merchant, and a Deputy Alderman, and very rich. I care not to mention the Name, tho' I knew his Name too, but that would be an Hardship to the Family, which is now flourishing again.

But, this is but one; it is scarce credible what dreadful Cases happened in particular Families every Day; People in the Rage of the Distemper, or in the Torment of their Swellings, which was indeed intollerable, running out of their own Government, raving and distracted,[1] and oftentimes laying violent Hands upon themselves, throwing themselves out at their Windows, shooting themselves, &c. Mothers murthering their own Children, in their Lunacy, some dying of meer Grief, as a Passion, some of meer Fright and Surprize, without any Infection at all; others frighted into Idiotism, and foolish Distractions, some into despair and Lunacy; others into mellancholy Madness.

The Pain of the Swelling was in particular very violent, and to some intollerable; the Physicians and Surgeons may be

said to have tortured many poor Creatures,[1] even to Death.
The Swellings in some grew hard, and they apply'd violent
drawing Plasters, or Pultices, to break them; and if these did
not do, they cut and scarified them in a terrible Manner: In
some, those Swellings were made hard, partly by the Force
of the Distemper, and partly by their being too violently
drawn, and were so hard, that no Instrument could cut them,
and then they burnt them with Causticks, so that many died
raving mad with the Torment; and some in the very Operation. In these Distresses, some for want of Help to hold them
down in their Beds, or to look to them, laid Hands upon
themselves, as above. Some broke out into the Streets,
perhaps naked, and would run directly down to the River, if
they were not stopt by the Watchmen, or other Officers, and
plunge themselves into the Water, wherever they found it.

It often pierc'd my very Soul to hear the Groans and Crys
of those who were thus tormented, but of the Two, this was
counted the most promising Particular in the whole Infection;
for, if these Swellings could be brought to a Head, and to
break and run,[2] or as the Surgeons call it, to digest, the Patient
generally recover'd; whereas those, who like the Gentlewoman's Daughter, were struck with Death at the Beginning,
and had the Tokens come out upon them, often went about
indifferent easy, till a little before they died, and some till the
Moment they dropt down, as in Apoplexies and Epilepsies, is
often the Case; such would be taken suddenly very sick, and
would run to a Bench or Bulk, or any convenient Place that
offer'd it self, or to their own Houses, if possible, *as I mentioned
before*, and there sit down, grow faint and die. This kind of
dying was much the same, as it was with those who die of
common Mortifications, who die swooning, and as it were, go
away in a Dream; such as died thus, had very little Notice of
their being infected at all, till the Gangreen was spread thro'
their whole Body; nor could Physicians themselves, know
certainly how it was with them, till they opened their Breasts,
or other Parts of their Body, and saw the Tokens.

We had at this Time a great many frightful Stories told us

of Nurses[1] and Watchmen, who looked after the dying People, *that is to say*, hir'd Nurses, who attended infected People, using them barbarously, starving them, smothering them, or by other wicked Means, hastening their End, *that is to say*, murthering of them: And Watchmen being set to guard Houses that were shut up, when there has been but one person left, and perhaps, that one lying sick, that they have broke in and murthered that Body, and immediately thrown them out into the Dead-Cart! and so they have gone scarce cold to the Grave.

I cannot say, but that some such Murthers were committed, and I think two were sent to Prison for it, but died before they could be try'd; and I have heard that three others, at several Times, were excused for Murthers of that kind; but I must say I believe nothing of its being so common a Crime, as some have since been pleas'd to say, nor did it seem to be so rational, where the People were brought so low as not to be able to help themselves, for such seldom recovered, and there was no Temptation to commit a Murder, at least, none equal to the Fact where they were sure Persons would die in so short a Time; and could not live.

That there were a great many Robberies and wicked Practises committed even in this dreadful Time I do not deny; the Power of Avarice was so strong in some, that they would run any Hazard to steal and to plunder, and particularly in Houses where all the Families, or Inhabitants have been dead, and carried out, they would break in at all Hazards, and without Regard to the Danger of Infection, take even the Cloths off, of the dead Bodies, and the Bed-cloaths from others where they lay dead.

This, *I suppose*, must be the Case of a Family in *Houndsditch*, where a Man and his Daughter, *the rest of the Family being, as I suppose, carried away before by the Dead-Cart*, were found stark naked, one in one Chamber, and one in another, lying Dead on the Floor; and the Cloths of the Beds, from whence, 'tis supposed they were roll'd off by Thieves, stoln, and carried quite away.

It is indeed to be observ'd, that the Women were in all this Calamity, the most rash, fearless, and desperate Creatures; and as there were vast Numbers that went about as Nurses, to tend those that were sick, they committed a great many petty Thieveries in the Houses where they were employed; and some of them were publickly whipt for it, when perhaps, they ought rather to have been hanged for Examples; for Numbers of Houses were robbed on these Occasions, till at length, the Parish Officers were sent to recommend Nurses to the Sick, and always took an Account who it was they sent, so as that they might call them to account, if the House had been abused where they were placed.

But these Robberies extended chiefly to Wearing-Cloths, Linen, and what Rings, or Money they could come at, when the Person dyed who was under their Care, but not to a general Plunder of the Houses; and I could give an Account of one of these Nurses, who several Years after, being on her Death-bed, confest with the utmost Horror, the Robberries she had committed at the Time of her being a Nurse, and by which she had enriched her self to a great Degree: But as for murthers, I do not find that there was ever any Proof of the Facts, in the manner, as it has been reported, *except as above*.

They did tell me indeed of a Nurse in one place, that laid a wet Cloth upon the Face of a dying Patient, who she tended, and so put an End to his Life, who was just expiring before: And another that smother'd a young Woman she was looking to, when she was in a fainting fit, and would have come to her self: Some that kill'd them by giving them one Thing, some another, and some starved them by giving them nothing at all: But these Stories had two Marks of Suspicion that always attended them, which caused me always to slight them, and to look on them as meer Stories, that People continually frighted one another with. (1.) That wherever it was that we heard it, they always placed the Scene at the farther End of the Town, opposite, or most remote from where you were to hear it: If you heard it in *White-Chapel*, it had happened at St. *Giles*'s, or at *Westminster*, or *Holborn*, or that End of the

Town; if you heard of it at that End of the Town, then it was done in *White-Chapel*, or the *Minories*, or about *Cripplegate* Parish: If you heard of it in the City, why, then it had happened in *Southwark*; and if you heard of it in *Southwark*, then it was done in the City, and the like.

In the next Place, of what Part soever you heard the Story, the Particulars were always the same, especially that of laying a wet double Clout on a dying Man's Face, and that of smothering a young Gentlewoman; so that it was apparent, at least to my Judgment, that there was more of Tale than of Truth in those Things.

However, I cannot say, but it had some Effect upon the People, and particularly that, *as I said before*, they grew more cautious who they took into their Houses, and who they trusted their Lives with; and had them always recommended, if they could; and where they could not find such, for they were not very plenty, they applied to the Parish Officers.

But here again, the Misery of that Time lay upon the Poor, who being infected, had neither Food or Physick; neither Physician or Appothecary to assist them, or Nurse to attend them: Many of those died calling for help, and even for Sustenance out at their Windows, in a most miserable and deplorable manner; but it must be added, that when ever the Cases of such Persons or Families, were represented to my Lord-Mayor, they always were reliev'd.

It is true, in some Houses where the People were not very poor; yet, where they had sent perhaps their Wives and Children away; and if they had any Servants, they had been dismist; *I say it is true, that* to save the Expences, many such as these shut themselves in, and not having Help, dy'd alone.

A Neighbour and Acquaintance of mine, having some Money owing to him from a Shopkeeper in *White-Cross-street*, or thereabouts, sent his Apprentice, a youth about 18 Years of Age, to endeavour to get the Money: He came to the Door, and finding it shut, knockt pretty hard, and as he thought, heard some Body answer within, but was not sure, So he waited, and after some stay knockt again, and then a third Time, when he heard some Body coming down Stairs.

At length the Man of the House came to the Door; he had on his Breeches or Drawers, and a yellow Flannel Wastcoat; no Stockings, a pair of Slipt-Shoes, a white Cap on his head; and as the young Man said, Death in his Face.

When he open'd the Door, says he, *what do you disturb me thus for?* the Boy, tho' a little surpriz'd, reply'd, *I come from such a one, and my Master sent me for the Money, which he says you know of: Very well Child,* returns the living Ghost, *call as you go by at* Cripplegate *Church, and bid them ring the Bell,* and with those Words, shut the Door again, and went up again and Dy'd, The same Day; nay, perhaps the same Hour. This, the young Man told me himself, and I have Reason to believe it. This was while the Plague was not come to a Height: I think it was in *June;* Towards the latter End of the Month, it must be before the Dead Carts came about, and while they used the Ceremony of Ringing the Bell for the Dead, which was over for certain, in that Parish at least, before the Month of *July;* for by the 25*th* of *July,* there died 550 and upward in a Week, and then they cou'd no more bury in Form, Rich or Poor.

I have mention'd above, that notwithstanding this dreadful Calamity; yet the Numbers of Thieves were abroad upon all Occasions, where they had found any Prey; and that these were generally Women. It was one Morning about 11 a Clock, I had walk'd out to my Brothers House in *Coleman's-street* Parish, as I often did, to see that all was Safe.

My Brother's House had a little Court before it, and a Brick-Wall with a Gate in it; and within that, several Warehouses, where his Goods of several Sorts lay: It happen'd, that in one of these Ware-houses, were several Packs of Womens high-Crown'd Hats, which came out of the Country; and were, as I suppose, for Exportation; whither I know not.

I was surpriz'd that when I came near my Brother's Door, which was in a Place they call'd *Swan-Alley,* I met three or four Women with High-crown'd Hats on their Heads; and as I remembred afterwards, one, if not more, had some Hats likewise in their Hands: but as I did not see them come out at my Brother's Door, and not knowing that my Brother had any such Goods in his Ware-house, I did not offer to say any Thing to them, but went cross the Way to shun meeting them, as was usual to do at that Time, for fear of the Plague. But when I came nearer to the Gate, I met another Woman with more Hats come out of the Gate. *What Business Mistress*, said I, *have you had there?* There are more People there, said she, I have had no more Business there than they. I was hasty to get to the Gate then, and said no more to her; by which means she got away. But just as I came to the Gate, I saw two more coming cross the Yard to come out with Hats also on their Heads, and under their Arms; at which I threw the Gate too behind me, which having a Spring Lock fastened it self; and turning to the Women, forsooth said I, what are ye *doing here?* and seiz'd upon the Hats, and took them from them. One of them, who I confess, did not look like a Thief, indeed says she, we are wrong; but we were told, they were Goods that had no Owner; be pleas'd to take them again, and look yonder, there are more such Customers as we: She cry'd and look'd pitifully; so I took the Hats from her, and opened the Gate, and bad them be gone, for I pity'd the Women indeed; But when I look'd towards the Ware-house, as she directed, there were six or seven more, all Women, fitting themselves with Hats, as unconcerned and quiet, as if they had been at a Hatters Shop, buying for their Money.

I was surpriz'd, not at the Sight of so many Thieves only, but at the Circumstances I was in; being now to thrust my self in among so many People, who for some Weeks, had been so shye of my self, that if I met any Body in the Street, I would cross the Way from them.

They were equally surpriz'd, tho' on another Account: They all told me, they were Neighbours, that they had heard any one might take them, that they were no Bodies Goods, and the like. I talk't big to them at first; went back to the Gate, and took out the Key; so that they were all my

Prisoners; threaten'd to Lock them all into the Ware-house, and go and fetch my Lord Mayor's Officers for them.

They beg'd heartily, protested they found the Gate open, and the Ware-house Door open; and that it had no doubt been broken open by some, who expected to find Goods of greater Value; which indeed, was reasonable to believe, because the Lock was broke, and a Padlock that hung to the Door on the out-side also loose; and not abundance of the Hats carry'd away.

At length I consider'd, that this was not a Time to be Cruel and Rigorous; and besides that, it would necessarily oblige me to go much about, to have several People come to me, and I go to several, whose Circumstances of Health, I knew nothing of; and that even at this Time the Plague was so high, as that there dy'd 4000 a Week; so that in showing my Resentment, or even in seeking Justice for my Brother's Goods, I might lose my own Life; so I contented my self, with taking the Names and Places where some of them lived, who were really Inhabitants in the Neighbourhood; and threatning that my Brother should call them to an Account for it, when he return'd to his Habitation.

Then I talk'd a little upon another Foot with them; and ask'd them how they could do such Things as these, in a Time of such general Calamity; and as it were, in the Face of Gods most dreadful Judgments, when the Plague was at their very Doors; and it may be in their very Houses; and they did not know, but that the Dead-Cart might stop at their Doors in a few Hours, to carry them to their Graves.

I cou'd not perceive that my Discourse made much Impression upon them all that while; till it happened, that there came two Men of the Neighbourhood, hearing of the Disturbance, and knowing my Brother, for they had been both dependants upon his Family, and they came to my Assistance: These being as I said Neighbours, presently knew three of the Women, and told me who they were, and where they liv'd; and it seems, they had given me a true Account of themselves before.

This brings these two Men to a farther Remembrance: The Name of one was *John Hayward*,[1] who was at that Time under-Sexton, of the Parish of St. *Stephen Coleman-street*; by under-Sexton, was understood at that Time Grave-digger and Bearer of the Dead. This Man carry'd or assisted to carry all the Dead to their Graves, which were bury'd in that large Parish, and who were carried in Form; and after that Form of Burying was stopt, went with the Dead Cart and the Bell, to fetch the dead Bodies from the Houses where they lay, and fetch'd many of them out of the Chambers and Houses; for the Parish was, and is still remarkable, particularly above all the Parishes in *London*, for a great Number of Alleys, and Thorough-fares[2] very long, into which no Carts cou'd come, and where they were oblig'd to go and fetch the Bodies a very long Way; which Alleys now remain to Witness it; such as *Whites-Alley*, *Cross-Key-Court*, *Swan-Alley*, *Bell-Alley*, *White-Horse-Alley*, and many more: Here they went with a kind of Hand-Barrow, and lay'd the Dead Bodies on it, and carry'd them out to the Carts; which work he performed, and never had the Distemper at all, but liv'd above 20 Year after it, and was Sexton of the Parish to the Time of his Death. His Wife at the same time was a Nurse to infected People, and tended many that died in the Parish, being for her honesty recommended by the Parish Officers, yet she never was infected neither.

He never used any Preservative against the Infection, other than holding *Garlick* and *Rue*[3] in his Mouth, and smoking Tobacco;[4] this I also had from his own Mouth; and his Wife's Remedy was washing her Head in Vinegar, and sprinkling her Head-Cloths so with Vinegar, as to keep them always Moist; and if the smell of any of those she waitd on was more than ordinary Offensive, she snuft Vinegar up her Nose, and sprinkled Vinegar upon her Head-Cloths, and held a Hand-kerchief wetted with Vinegar to her Mouth.

It must be confest, that tho' the Plague was chiefly among the Poor;[5] yet, were the Poor the most Venturous and Fearless of it, and went about their Employment, with a Sort of brutal

Courage; I must call it so, for it was founded neither on Religion or Prudence; scarce did they use any Caution, but run into any Business, which they could get Employment in, tho' it was the most hazardous; such was that of tending the Sick, watching Houses shut up, carrying infected Persons to the Pest-House; and which was still worse, carrying the Dead away to their Graves.

It was under this *John Hayward's* Care, and within his Bounds, that the Story of the Piper,[1] with which People have made themselves so merry, happen'd, and he assur'd me that it was true. It is said, that it was a blind Piper; but as *John* told me, the Fellow was not blind, but an ignorant weak poor Man, and usually walked his Rounds about 10 a-Clock at Night, and went piping along from Door to Door, and the People usually took him in at Public Houses where they knew him, and would give him Drink and Victuals, and sometimes Farthings; and he in Return, would Pipe and Sing, and talk simply, which diverted the People, and thus he liv'd: It was but a very bad Time for this Diversion, while Things were as I have told; yet the poor Fellow went about as usual, but was almost starv'd; and when any Body ask'd how he did, he would answer, the Dead Cart had not taken him yet, but that they had promised to call for him next Week.

It happen'd one Night, that this poor Fellow, whether some body had given him too much Drink or no, *John Hayward* said, he had not Drink in his House; but that they had given him a little more Victuals than ordinary at a Public House in *Coleman-street*; and the poor Fellow having not usually had a Bellyfull, or perhaps not a good while, was laid all along upon the Top of a Bulk or Stall, and fast a sleep at a Door, in the Street near *London-Wall*, towards *Cripplegate*, and that upon the same Bulk or Stall, the People of some House, in the Alley of which the House was a Corner, hearing a Bell, which they always rung before the Cart came, had laid a Body really dead of the Plague just by him, thinking too, that this poor Fellow had been a dead Body as the other was, and laid there by some of the Neighbours.

Accordingly when *John Hayward* with his Bell and the Cart came along, finding two dead Bodies lie upon the Stall they took them up with the Instrument they used, and threw them into the Cart; and all this while the Piper slept soundly.

From hence they passed along, and took in other dead Bodies, till, as honest *John Hayward* told me, they almost burried him alive, in the Cart, yet all this While he slept soundly; at length the Cart came to the Place where the Bodies were to be thrown into the Ground, which, as I do remember, was at *Mount-mill*; and as the Cart usually stopt some Time before they were ready to shoot out the melancholly Load they had in it, as soon as the Cart stop'd, the Fellow awaked, and struggled a little to get his Head out from among the dead Bodies, when raising himself up in the Cart, he called out, *Hey! where am I?* This frighted the Fellow that attended about the Work, but after some Pause *John Hayward* recovering himself said, *Lord bless us. There's some Body in the Cart not quite dead!* So another call'd to him and said, *Who are you?* the Fellow answered, *I am the poor Piper. Where am I? Where are you!* says *Hayward; why, you are in the Dead-Cart, and we are a-going to bury you. But I an't dead tho', am I?* says the Piper; which made them laugh a little, tho' as *John* said, they were heartily frighted at first; so they help'd the poor Fellow down, and he went about his Business.

I know the Story goes, he set up his Pipes in the Cart, and frighted the Bearers, and others, so that they ran away; but *John Hayward* did not tell the Story so, nor say any Thing of his Piping at all; but that he was a poor Piper, and that he was carried away as above I am fully satisfied of the Truth of.

It is to be noted here, that the Dead Carts in the City were not confin'd to particular Parishes, but one Cart went thro' several Parishes, according as the Numbers of Dead presented; nor were they ty'd to carry the Dead to their respective Parishes, but many of the Dead, taken up in the City, were carried to the Burying Ground in the Out-parts, for want of Room.

I have already mentioned the Surprize, that this Judgment

was at first among the People. I must be allowed to give some of my Observations on the more serious and religious Part. Surely never City, at least, of this Bulk and Magnitude, was taken in a Condition so perfectly unprepar'd for such a dreadful Visitation, whether I am to speak of the Civil Preparations, or Religious; they were indeed, as if they had had no Warning, no Expectation, no Apprehensions, and consequently the least Provision imaginable, was made for it in a publick Way; for Example.

The Lord Mayor and Sheriffs had made no Provision as Magistrates, for the Regulations which were to be observed; they had gone into no Measures for Relief of the Poor.

The Citizens had no publick Magazines, or Store-Houses for Corn, or Meal, for the Subsistence of the Poor; which, if they had provided themselves, as in such Cases is done abroad, many miserable Families, who were now reduc'd to the utmost Distress, would have been reliev'd, and that in a better Manner, than now could be done.

The Stock of the City's Money, I can say but little to, the Chamber of *London* was said to be exceeding rich;[1] and it may be concluded, that they were so, by the vast Sums of Money issued from thence, in the re-building the publick Edifices after the Fire of *London*, and in Building new Works, such as, for the first Part, the *Guild-Hall*, *Blackwell-Hall*, Part of *Leaden-Hall*, Half the *Exchange*, the *Session-House*, the *Compter*; the Prisons of *Ludgate*, *Newgate*, &c. several of the Wharfs, and Stairs, and Landing-places on the River; all which were either burnt down or damaged by the great Fire of *London*, the next Year after the Plague; and of the second Sort, the Monument, *Fleet-ditch* with its Bridges, and the Hospital of *Bethlem*, or *Bedlam*, &c. But possibly the Managers of the City's Credit, at that Time, made more Conscience of breaking in upon the Orphan's Money[2] to shew Charity to the distress'd Citizens than the Managers in the following Years did, to beautify the City, and re-edify the Buildings, tho' in the first Case, the Losers would have thought their Fortunes better bestow'd, and the Publick

Faith of the City have been less subjected to Scandal and Reproach.

It must be acknowledg'd that the absent Citizens, who, tho' they were fled for Safety into the Country, were yet greatly interested in the Welfare of those who they left behind,[1] forgot not to contribute liberally to the Relief of the Poor, and large Sums were also collected among Trading-Towns in the remotest Parts of *England*; and as I have heard also, the Nobility and the Gentry, in all Parts of *England*, took the deplorable Condition of the City into their Consideration, and sent up large Sums of Money in Charity, to the Lord Mayor and Magistrates, for the Relief of the Poor; the King also, as I was told, ordered a thousand Pounds a Week to be distributed in four Parts; one Quarter to the City and Liberties of *Westminster*; one Quarter, or Part, among the Inhabitants of the *Southwark* Side of the Water; one Quarter to the Liberty and Parts within of the City, exclusive of the City within the Walls; and, one fourth Part to the Suburbs in the County of *Middlesex*, and the East and North Parts of the City; But this latter I only speak of as a Report.

Certain it is, the greatest Part of the Poor, or Families, who formerly liv'd by their Labour, or by Retail-Trade, liv'd now on Charity; and had there not been prodigious Sums of Money given by charitable, well-minded Christians, for the Support of such, the City could never have subsisted. There were, no Question, Accounts kept of their Charity, and of the just Distribution of it by the Magistrates: But as such Multitudes of those very Officers died, thro' whose Hands it was distributed; and also that, as I have been told, most of the Accounts of those Things were lost in the great Fire which happened in the very next Year, and which burnt even the Chamberlain's Office, and many of their Papers; so I could never come at the particular Account, which I used great Endeavours to have seen.

It may, however, be a Direction in Case of the Approach of a like Visitation, which God keep the City from; I say, it may be of use to observe that by the Care of the Lord Mayor and Aldermen, at that Time, in distributing Weekly, great Sums of Money, for Relief of the Poor, a Multitude of People, who would otherwise have perished, were relieved, and their Lives preservd. And here let me enter into a brief State of the Case of the Poor at that Time, and what was apprehended from them, from whence may be judg'd hereafter, what may be expected, if the like Distress should come upon the City.

At the Beginning of the Plague, when there was now no more Hope, but that the whole City would be visited, when, as I have said, all that had Friends or Estates in the Country, retired with their Families, and when, indeed, one would have thought the very City it self was running out of the Gates, and that there would be no Body left behind, you may be sure, from that Hour, all Trade, except such as related to immediate Subsistence, was, *as it were*, at a full Stop.

This is so lively a Case, and contains in it so much of the real Condition of the People; that I think, I cannot be too particular in it; and therefore I descend to the several Arrangements or Classes of People, who fell into immediate Distress upon this Occasion: For Example,

1. *All Master Work-men in Manufactures; especially such as belong'd to Ornament, and the less necessary Parts of the People's dress Cloths and Furniture for Houses; such as Riband Weavers, and other Weavers; Gold and Silverlace-makers, and Gold and Silverwyer-drawers, Sempstresses, Milleners, Shoe-makers, Hat-makers and Glove-makers: Also Upholsterers, Joyners, Cabinet-makers, Looking-glass-makers; and innumerable Trades which depend upon such as these; I say the Master Workmen in such, stopt their Work, dismist their Journeymen, and Workmen, and all their Dependants.*

2. *As Merchandizing was at a full stop, for very few Ships ventur'd to come up the River, and none at all went out; so all the extraordinary Officers of the Customes, likewise the Watermen, Carmen, Porters, and all the Poor, whose Labour depended upon the Merchants, were at once dismist, and put out of Business.*

3. *All the Tradesmen usually employ'd in building or repareing of Houses, were at a full Stop, for the People were far from wanting to build Houses, when so many thousand Houses were at once stript of their Inhabitants; so that this one Article turn'd all the ordinary Work-men of that Kind out of Business; such as Brick-layers, Masons, Carpenters, Joyners, Plasterers, Painters, Glaziers, Smiths, Plumbers; and all the Labourers depending on such.*

4. *As Navigation was at a Stop; our Ships neither coming in, or going out as before; so the Seamen were all out of Employment, and many of them in the last and lowest Degree of Distress, and with the Seamen, were all the several Tradesmen, and Workmen belonging to and depending upon the building, and fitting out of Ships; such as Ship Carpenters, Caulkers, Rope-makers, Dry-Coopers, Sail-makers, Anchor-Smiths, and other Smiths; Block-makers, Carvers, Gun Smiths, Ship-Chandlers, Ship-Carvers and the like; The Masters of those perhaps might live upon their Substance; but the Traders were Universally at a Stop, and consequently all their Work-men discharged: Add to these, that the River was in a manner without Boats, and all or most part of the Watermen, Lightermen, Boat-builders, and Lighter-builders in like manner idle, and laid by.*

5. *All Families retrench'd their living as much as possible, as well those that fled, as those that stay'd; so that an innumerable Multitude of Footmen, Serving Men, Shop-keepers, Journey-men, Merchants-Book-keepers, and such Sort of People, and especially poor Maid Servants were turn'd off, and left Friendless and Helpless without Employment, and without Habitation; and this was really a dismal Article.*

I might be more particular as to this Part: But it may suffice to mention in general; all Trades being stopt, Employment ceased; the Labour, and by that, the Bread of the Poor were cut off; and at first indeed, the Cries of the poor were most lamentable to hear; tho' by the Distribution of Charity, their Misery that way was greatly abated: Many indeed fled into the Countries; but thousands of them having stay'd in *London*, till nothing but Desperation sent them away; Death overtook them on the Road, and they serv'd for no better than the Messengers of Death, indeed, others carrying the Infection along with them; spreading it very unhappily into the remotest Parts of the Kingdom.

Many of these were the miserable Objects of Despair which I have mention'd before, and were remov'd by the Destruction which followed; these might be said to perish, not by the Infection it self, but by the Consequence of it; indeed, namely, by Hunger and Distress, and the Want of all Things; being without Lodging, without Money, without Friends, without Means to get their Bread, or without any one to give it them, for many of them were without what we call legal Settlements,[1] and so could not claim of the Parishes, and all the Support they had, was by Application to the Magistrates for Relief, which Relief was, (to give the Magistrates their Due) carefully and chearfully administred, as they found it necessary; and those that stay'd behind never felt the Want and Distress of that Kind, which they felt, who went away in the manner above-noted.

Let any one who is acquainted with what Multitudes of People get their daily Bread in this City by their Labour, whether Artificers or meer Workmen; I say, let any Man consider, what must be the miserable Condition of this Town, if on a sudden, they should be all turned out of Employment, that Labour should cease, and Wages for Work be no more.

This was the Case with us at that Time, and had not the Sums of Money, contributed in Charity by well disposed People, of every Kind, as well abroad as at home, been prodigiously great, it had not been in the Power of the Lord Mayor and Sheriffs, to have kept the Publick Peace; nor were they without Apprehensions as it was, that Desperation should push the People upon Tumults, and cause them to rifle the Houses of rich Men, and plunder the Markets of Provisions; in which Case the Country People, who brought Provisions very freely and boldly to Town, would ha' been terrified from coming any more, and the Town would ha' sunk under an unavoidable Famine.

But the Prudence of my Lord Mayor, and the Court of Aldermen within the City, and of the Justices of Peace in the Out-parts was such, and they were supported with Money from all Parts so well, that the poor People were kept quiet, and their Wants every where reliev'd, as far as was possible to be done.

Two Things, besides this, contributed to prevent the Mob doing any Mischief: One was, that really the Rich themselves had not laid up Stores of Provisions in their Houses, as indeed, they ought to have done, and which if they had been wise enough to have done, and lock'd themselves entirely up, as some few did, they had perhaps escaped the Disease better: But as it appear'd they had not, so the Mob had no Notion of finding Stores of Provisions there, if they had broken in, as it is plain they were sometimes very near doing, and which, if they had, they had finish'd the Ruin of the whole City, for there were no regular Troops to ha' withstood them, nor could the Traind-Bands have been brought together to defend the City, no Men being to be found to bear Arms.

But the Vigilance of the Lord Mayor, and such Magistrates as could be had, for some, even of the Aldermen were Dead, and some absent, prevented this; and they did it by the most kind and gentle Methods they could think of, as particularly by relieving the most desperate with Money, and putting others into Business, and particularly that Employment of watching Houses that were infected and shut up; and as the Number of these were very great, for it was said, there was at one Time, ten thousand Houses shut up, and every House had two Watchmen to guard it, *viz* one by Night, and the other by Day; this gave Opportunity to employ a very great Number of poor Men at a Time.

The Women, and Servants, that were turned off from their Places, were likewise employed as Nurses to tend the Sick in all Places; and this took off a very great Number of them.

And, which tho' a melancholy Article in it self, yet was a

Deliverance in its Kind, namely, the Plague which raged in a dreadful Manner from the Middle of *August* to the Middle of *October*, carried off in that Time thirty or forty Thousand of these very People,[1] which had they been left, would certainly have been an unsufferable Burden, by their Poverty, *that is to say*, the whole City could not have supported the Expence of them, or have provided Food for them; and they would in Time have been even driven to the Necessity of plundering either the City it self, or the Country adjacent, to have subsisted themselves, which would first or last, have put the whole Nation, as well as the City, into the utmost Terror and Confusion.

It was observable then, that this Calamity of the People made them very humble; for now, for about nine Weeks together, there died near a thousand a-Day, one Day with another, even by the Account of the weekly Bills, which yet I have Reason to be assur'd never gave a full Account, by many thousands; the Confusion being such, and the Carts working in the Dark, when they carried the Dead, that in some Places no Account at all was kept, but they work'd on; the Clerks and Sextons not attending for Weeks together, and not knowing what Number they carried. This Account is verified by the following Bills of Mortality.

				Of all Diseases.	*Of the Plague.*
	Aug. 8 to *Aug.*	15	— 5319	— 3880
		to 22	— 5568	— 4237
		to 29	— 7496	— 6102
From	*Aug.* 29 to *Sept.*	5	— 8252	— 6988
		to 12	— 7690	— 6544
		to 19	— 8297	— 7165
		to 26	— 6460	— 5533
	Sept. 26 to *Oct.*	3	— 5720	— 4929
		to 10	— 5068	— 4227
			59870	49705

So that the Gross of the People were carried off in these two Months; for as the whole Number which was brought in, to die of the Plague, was but 68590 here, is fifty thousand of them, within a Trifle, in two Months; I say 50000, because, as there wants 295 in the Number above, so there wants two Days of two Months, in the Account of Time.

Now when, I say, that the Parish Officers did not give in a full Account, or were not to be depended upon for their Account, let any one but consider how Men could be exact in such a Time of dreadful Distress, and when many of them were taken sick themselves, and perhaps died in the very Time when their Accounts were to be given in, I mean the Parish-Clerks; besides inferior Officers; for tho' these poor Men ventured at all Hazards, yet they were far from being exempt from the common Calamity, especially, if it be true, that the Parish of *Stepney* had within the Year, one hundred and sixteen Sextons, Grave-diggers, and their Assistants, that is to say, Bearers, Bell-men, and Drivers of Carts, for carrying off the dead Bodies.

Indeed the Work was not of a Nature to allow them Leisure, to take an exact Tale of the dead Bodies, which were all huddled together in the Dark into a Pit; which Pit, or Trench, no Man could come nigh, but at the utmost Peril. I observ'd often, that in the Parishes of *Aldgate*, and *Cripplegate*, *White-Chappel* and *Stepney*, there was five, six, seven, and eight hundred in a Week, in the Bills, whereas if we may believe the Opinion of those that liv'd in the City, all the Time, as well as I, there died sometimes 2000 a-Week in those Parishes; and I saw it under the Hand of one, that made as strict an examination into that Part as he could, that there really died an hundred thousand People of the Plague, in it that one Year, whereas the Bills, the Articles of the Plague, was but 68590.

If I may be allowed to give my Opinion, by what I saw with my Eyes, and heard from other People that were Eye Witnesses, I do verily believe the same, *viz.* that there died, at least, 100000 of the Plague only, besides other Distempers, and besides those which died in the Fields, and High-ways, and secret Places, out of the Compass of the Communication,

as it was called; and who were not put down in the Bills, tho'
they really belonged to the Body of the Inhabitants. It was
known to us all, that abundance of poor despairing Creatures,
who had the Distemper upon them, and were grown stupid,
or melancholly by their Misery, as many were, wandred away
into the Fields, and Woods, and into secret uncouth Places,
almost any where to creep into a Bush, or Hedge, and DIE.

The Inhabitants of the Villages adjacent would in Pity,
carry them Food, and set it at a Distance, that they might
fetch it, if they were able, and sometimes they were not able;
and the next Time they went, they should find the poor
Wretches lie dead, and the Food untouch'd. The Number of
these miserable Objects were many, and I know so many that
perish'd thus, and so exactly where, that I believe I could go
to the very Place and dig their Bones up still; for the Country
People would go and dig a Hole at a Distance from them, and
then with long Poles, and Hooks at the End of them, drag the
Bodies into these Pits, and then throw the Earth in Form as
far as they could cast it to cover them; taking notice how the
Wind blew, and so coming on that Side which the Sea-men
call *to-Wind-ward*, that the Scent of the Bodies might blow
from them; and thus great Numbers went out of the World,
who were never known or any Account of them taken, as well
within the Bills of Mortality as without.

This indeed I had, in the main, only from the Relation of
others; for I seldom walk'd into the Fields, except towards
Bednal-green and *Hackney*; or as hereafter: But when I did
walk I always saw a great many poor Wanderers at a Distance,
but I could know little of their Cases; for whether it were in
the Street, or in the Fields, if we had seen any Body coming,
it was a general Method to walk away; yet I believe the
Account is exactly true.

As this puts me upon mentioning my walking the Streets
and Fields, I cannot omit taking notice what a desolate Place
the City was at that Time: The great Street I liv'd in, which
is known to be one of the broadest of all the Streets of *London*,
I mean of the Suburbs as well as the Liberties; all the Side

where the Butchers lived, especially without the Bars was more like a green Field than a paved Street, and the People generally went in the middle with the Horses and Carts: It is true, that the farthest End towards *White-Chappel* Church, was not all pav'd, but even the Part that was pav'd was full of Grass also; but this need not seem strange since the great Streets within the City, such as *Leaden-hall-Street*, *Bishop-gate-Street*, *Cornhill*, and even the *Exchange* it self, had Grass growing in them,[1] in several Places; neither Cart or Coach were seen in the Streets from Morning to Evening, except some Country Carts to bring Roots and Beans, or Pease, Hay and Straw, to the Market, and those but very few, compared to what was usual: As for Coaches they were scarce used, but to carry sick People to the Pest-House, and to other Hospitals; and some few to carry Physicians to such Places as they thought fit to venture to visit; for really Coaches were dangerous things,[2] and People did not Care to venture into them, because they did not know who might have been carried in them last; and sick infected People were, *as I have said*, ordinarily carried in them to the Pest-Houses, and sometimes People expired in them as they went along.

It is true, when the Infection came to such a Height as I have now mentioned, there were very few Physicians, which car'd to stir abroad to sick Houses, and very many of the most eminent of the Faculty were dead as well as the Surgeons also, for now it was indeed a dismal time, and for about a Month together, not taking any Notice of the Bills of Mortality, I believe there did not die less than 1500 or 1700 a-Day, one Day with another.

One of the worst Days we had in the whole Time, as I thought, was in the Beginning of *September*, when indeed good People began to think, that God was resolved to make a full End of the People in this miserable City. This was at that Time when the Plague was fully come into the Eastern Parishes: The Parish of *Aldgate*, if I may give my Opinion buried above a thousand a Week for two Weeks, tho' the Bills did not say so many; but it surrounded me at so dismal a rate, that there was not a House in twenty uninfected; in the *Minories*, in *Houndsditch*, and in those Parts of *Aldgate* Parish about the *Butcher-Row*,[1] and the Alleys over against me, I say in those places Death reigned in every Corner. *White Chapel* Parish was in the same Condition, and tho' much less than the Parish I liv'd in; yet bury'd near 600 a Week by the Bills; and in my Opinion, near twice as many; whole Families, and indeed, whole Streets of Families were swept away together; insomuch, that it was frequent for Neighbours to call to the Bellman, to go to such and such Houses, and fetch out the People, for that they were all Dead.

And indeed, the Work of removing the dead Bodies by Carts, was now grown so very odious and dangerous, that it was complain'd of, that the Bearers did not take Care to clear such Houses, where all the Inhabitants were dead; but that sometimes the Bodies lay several Days unburied, till the neighbouring Families were offended with the Stench, and consequently infect'd; and this neglect of the Officers was such, that the Church Wardens and Constables were summon'd to look after it; and even the Justices of the *Hamlets*, were oblig'd to venture their Lives among them, to quicken and encourage them; for innumerable of the Bearers dy'd of the Distemper, infected by the Bodies they were oblig'd to come so near; and had it not been, that the Number of poor People who wanted Employment, and wanted Bread, (as I have said before,) was so great, that Necessity drove them to undertake any Thing, and venture any thing, they would never have found People to be employ'd; and then the Bodies of the dead would have lain above Ground, and have perished and rotted in a dreadful Manner.

But the Magistrates cannot be enough commended in this, that they kept such good Order for the burying of the Dead, that as fast as any of those they employ'd to carry off, and bury the dead, fell sick or dy'd, as was many Times the Case, they immediately supply'd the places with others; which by reason of the great Number of Poor that was left out of Business, *as above*, was not hard to do: This occasion'd, that notwithstanding the infinite Number of People which dy'd, and were sick almost all together, yet, they were always clear'd away, and carry'd off every Night; so that it was never to be said of *London*, that the living were not able to bury the Dead.

As the Desolation was greater, during those terrible Times, so the Amazement of the People encreas'd; and a thousand unaccountable Things they would do in the violence of their Fright, as others did the same in the Agonies of their Distemper, and this part was very affecting; some went roaring, and crying, and wringing their Hands along the Street; some would go praying, and lifting up their Hands to Heaven, calling upon God for Mercy. I cannot say indeed, whether this was not in their Distraction; *but be it so*, it was still an indication of a more serious Mind, when they had the use of their Senses, and was much better, *even as it was*, than the frightful yellings and cryings that every Day, and especially in the Evenings, were heard in some Streets. I suppose the World has heard of the famous *Soloman Eagle* an Enthusiast:[1] He tho' not infected at all, but in his Head, went about denouncing of Judgment upon the City in a frightful manner; sometimes quite naked, and with a Pan of burning Charcoal on his Head: What he said or pretended, indeed I could not learn.

I will not say, whether that Clergyman was distracted or not: Or whether he did it in pure Zeal for the poor People who went every Evening thro' the Streets of *White-Chapel*; and with his Hands lifted up, repeated that Part of the *Liturgy* of the Church continually; *Spare us good Lord, spare thy People whom thou hast redeemed with thy most precious Blood*, I say, I cannot speak positively of these Things; because these were only the dismal Objects which represented themselves to me as I look'd thro' my Chamber Windows (for I seldom opened the Casements) while I confin'd my self within Doors, during that most violent rageing of the Pestilence; when indeed, as I have said, many began to think, and even to say, that there would none escape; and indeed, I began to think so too; and therefore kept within Doors, for about a Fortnight, and never stirr'd out: But I cou'd not hold it: Besides, there were some

People, who notwithstanding the Danger, did not omit
publickly to attend the Worship of God,[1] even in the most
dangerous Times; and tho' it is true, that a great many
Clergymen did shut up their Churches, and fled as other
People did, for the safety of their Lives; yet, all did not do so,
some ventur'd to officiate, and to keep up the Assemblies of
the People by constant Prayers; and sometimes Sermons, or
Brief Exhortations to Repentance and Reformation, and this
as long as any would come to hear them; and Dissenters did
the like also, and even in the very Churches,[2] where the Parish
Ministers were either Dead or fled, nor was there any Room
for making Difference, at such a Time as this was.

It was indeed a lamentable Thing to hear the miserable
Lamentations of poor dying Creatures, calling out for Ministers to Comfort them, and pray with them, to Counsel them,
and to direct them, calling out to God for Pardon and Mercy,
and confessing aloud their past Sins. It would make the
stoutest Heart bleed to hear how many Warnings were then
given by dying Penitents, to others not to put off and delay
their Repentance to the Day of Distress, that such a Time of
Calamity as this, was no Time for Repentance; was no Time
to call upon God. I wish I could repeat the very Sound of those
Groans, and of those Exclamations that I heard from some
poor dying Creatures, when in the Hight of their Agonies and
Distress; and that I could make him that read this hear, as I
imagine I now hear them, for the Sound seems still to Ring
in my Ears.

If I could but tell this Part, in such moving Accents as
should alarm the very Soul of the Reader, I should rejoice
that I recorded those Things, however short and imperfect.

It pleased God that I was still spar'd, and very hearty and
sound in Health, but very impatient of being pent up within
Doors without Air, as I had been for 14 Days or thereabouts;
and I could not restrain my self, but I would go to carry a
Letter for my Brother to the Post-House; then it was indeed,
that I observ'd a profound Silence in the Streets; when I
came to the Post-House, as I went to put in my Letter, I saw

a Man stand in one Corner of the Yard, and talking to another at a Window; and a third had open'd a Door belonging to the Office; In the middle of the Yard lay a small Leather Purse, with two Keys hanging at it, and Money in it, but no Body would meddle with it: I ask'd how long it had lain there; the Man at the Window said, it had lain almost an Hour; but that they had not meddled with it, because they did not know, but the Person who dropt it, might come back to look for it. I had no such need of Money, nor was the Sum so big, that I had any Inclination to meddle with it, or to get the Money at the hazard it might be attended with; so I seem'd to go away, when the Man who had open'd the Door, said he would take it up; but so, that if the right Owner came for it, he should be sure to have it: So he went in, and fetched a pail of Water, and set it down hard by the Purse; then went again, and fetch'd some Gun-powder, and cast a good deal of Powder upon the Purse, and then made a Train from that which he had thrown loose upon the Purse; the train reached about two Yards; after this he goes in a third Time, and fetches out a pair of Tongs red hot, and which he had prepar'd, I suppose on purpose; and first setting Fire to the Train of Powder, that sing'd the Purse and also smoak'd the Air sufficiently: But he was not content with that; but he then takes up the Purse with the Tongs, holding it so long till the Tongs burnt thro' the Purse, and then he shook the Money out into the Pail of Water, so he carried it in. The Money, as I remember, was about thirteen Shillings, and some smooth Groats, and Brass Farthings.

There might perhaps, have been several poor People, *as I have observ'd above*, that would have been hardy enough to have ventured for the sake of the Money; but you may easily see by what I have observ'd, that the few People, who were spar'd, were very careful of themselves, at that Time when the Distress was so exceeding great.

Much about the same Time I walk'd out into the Fields towards *Bow*; for I had a great mind to see how things were managed in the River, and among the Ships; and as I had some Concern in Shipping, I had a Notion that it had been one of the best Ways of securing ones self from the Infection to have retir'd into a Ship, and musing how to satisfy my Curiosity, in that Point, I turned away over the Fields, from *Bow* to *Bromley*, and down to *Blackwall*, to the Stairs, which are there for landing, or taking Water.

Here I saw a poor Man walking on the Bank, or Sea-wall, as they call it, by himself. I walked a while also about, seeing the Houses all shut up; at last I fell into some Talk, at a Distance, with this poor Man; first I asked him, how People did thereabouts? *Alas, Sir!* says he, *almost all desolate; all dead or sick: Here are very few Families in this Part, or in that Village*, pointing at *Poplar, where half of them are not dead already, and the rest sick.* Then he pointed to one House, *There they are all dead*, said he, *and the House stands open; no Body dares go into it. A poor Thief*, says he, *ventured in to steal something, but he paid dear for his Theft; for he was carried to the Church Yard too, last Night.* Then he pointed to several other Houses. *There*, says he, *they are all dead; the Man and his Wife, and five Children. There*, says he, *they are shut up, you see a Watchman at the Door*; and so of other Houses. *Why*, says I, *What do you here all alone? Why*, says he, *I am a poor desolate Man; it has pleased God I am not yet visited, tho' my Family is, and one of my Children dead. How do you mean then*, said I, *that you are not visited. Why*, says he, *that's my House*, pointing to a very little low boarded House, *and there my poor Wife and two Children live*, said he, *if they may be said to live; for my Wife and one of the Children are visited, but I do not come at them.* And with that Word I saw the Tears run very plentifully down his Face; and so they did down mine too, I assure you.

But said I, *Why do you not come at them? How can you abandon your own Flesh, and Blood? Oh, Sir!* says he, *the Lord forbid; I do not abandon them; I work for them as much as I am able; and blessed be the Lord, I keep them from Want*; and with that I observ'd, he lifted up his Eyes to Heaven, with a Countenance that presently told me, I had happened on a

Man that was no Hypocrite, but a serious, religious good Man, and his Ejaculation was an Expression of Thankfulness, that in such a Condition as he was in, he should be able to say his Family did not want. *Well, says I, honest Man, that is a great Mercy as things go now with the Poor: But how do you live then, and how are you kept from the dreadful Calamity that is now upon us all? Why Sir,* says he, *I am a Waterman, and there's my Boat,* says he, *and the Boat serves me for a House; I work in it in the Day, and I sleep in it in the Night; and what I get, I lay down upon that Stone,* says he, shewing me a broad Stone on the other Side of the Street, a good way from his House, and then, says he, *I halloo, and call to them till I make them hear; and they come and fetch it.*

Well Friend, says I, *but how can you get any Money as a Waterman? does any Body go by Water these Times? Yes Sir,* says he, *in the Way I am employ'd there does. Do you see there,* says he, *five Ships lie at Anchor,* pointing down the River, a good way below the Town, *and do you see,* says he, *eight or ten Ships lie at the Chain, there, and at Anchor yonder,* pointing above the Town. *All those Ships have Families on board, of their Merchants and Owners, and such like, who have lock'd themselves up, and live on board, close shut in, for fear of the Infection; and I tend on them to fetch Things for them, carry Letters, and do what is absolutely necessary, that they may not be obliged to come on Shore; and every Night I fasten my Boat on board one of the Ship's Boats, and there I sleep by my self, and blessed be God, I am preserv'd hitherto.*

Well, said I, *Friend, but will they let you come on board, after you have been on Shore here, when this is such a terrible Place, and so infected as it is?*

Why, as to that, said he, *I very seldom go up the Ship Side, but deliver what I bring to their Boat, or lie by the Side, and they hoist it on board; if I did, I think they are in no Danger from me, for I never go into any House on Shore, or touch any Body, no, not of my own Family; But I fetch Provisions for them.*

Nay, says I, *but that may be worse, for you must have those Provisions of some Body or other; and since all this Part of the*

Town is so infected, it is dangerous so much as to speak with any Body; for this Village, said I, *is as it were, the Beginning of* London, *tho' it be at some Distance from it.*

That is true, added he, *but you do not understand me Right, I do not buy Provisions for them here; I row up to* Greenwich *and buy fresh Meat there, and sometimes I row down the River to* Woolwich *and buy there; then I go to single Farm Houses on the Kentish Side, where I am known, and buy Fowls and Eggs, and Butter, and bring to the Ships, as they direct me, sometimes one, sometimes the other; I seldom come on Shore here; and I came now only to call to my Wife, and hear how my little Family do, and give them a little Money, which I receiv'd last Night.*

Poor Man! said I, *and how much hast thou gotten for them?*

I have gotten four Shillings, said he, *which is a great Sum, as things go now with poor Men; but they have given me a Bag of Bread too, and a Salt Fish and some Flesh; so all helps out.*

Well, said I, *and have you given it them yet?*

No, said he, *but I have called, and my Wife has answered, that she cannot come out yet, but in Half an Hour she hopes to come, and I am waiting for her: Poor Woman!* says he, *she is brought sadly down; she has a Swelling, and it is broke, and I hope she will recover; but I fear the Child will die; but* it is the Lord! —— Here he stopt, and wept very much.

Well, honest Friend, said I, *thou hast a sure Comforter, if thou hast brought thy self to be resign'd to the will of God, he is dealing with us all in Judgment.*

Oh, Sir, says he, *it is infinite Mercy, if any of us are spar'd; and who am I to repine!*

Sayest thou so, said I, *and how much less is my Faith than thine?* And here my Heart smote me, suggesting how much better this Poor Man's Foundation was, on which he staid in the Danger, than mine; that he had no where to fly; that he had a Family to bind him to Attendance, which I had not; and mine was meer Presumption, his a true Dependance, and a Courage resting on God: and yet, that he used all possible Caution for his Safety.

I turn'd a little way from the Man, while these Thoughts

engaged me, for indeed, I could no more refrain from Tears than he.

At length, after some farther Talk, the poor Woman opened the Door, and call'd, *Robert, Robert*; he answered and bid her stay a few Moments, and he would come; so he ran down the common Stairs to his Boat, and fetch'd up a Sack in which was the Provisions he had brought from the Ships; and when he returned, he hallooed again; then he went to the great Stone which he shewed me, and emptied the Sack, and laid all out, every Thing by themselves, and then retired; and his Wife came with a little Boy to fetch them away; and he call'd, and said, such a Captain had sent such a Thing, and such a Captain such a Thing, and at the End adds, *God has sent it all, give Thanks to him*. When the Poor Woman had taken up all, she was so weak, she could not carry it at once in, *tho' the Weight was not much neither*; so she left the Biscuit which was in a little Bag, and left a little Boy to watch it till she came again.

Well, but says I to him, *did you leave her the four Shillings too, which you said was your Week's Pay?*

YES, YES, says he, *you shall hear her own it*. So he calls again, *Rachel, Rachel*, which it seems was her Name, *did you take up the Money? YES*, said she. *How much was it*, said he? *Four Shillings and a Groat*, said she. *Well, well*, says he, *the Lord keep you all*; and so he turned to go away.

As I could not refrain contributing Tears to this Man's Story, so neither could I refrain my Charity for his Assistance; so I call'd him, *Hark thee Friend*, said I, *come hither; for I believe thou art in Health, that I may venture thee*; so I pull'd out my Hand, which was in my Pocket before, *here*, says I, *go and call thy* Rachel *once more, and give her a little more Comfort from me. God will never forsake a Family that trust in him as thou dost*; so I gave him four other Shillings, and bad him go lay them on the Stone and call his Wife.

I have not Words to express the poor Man's thankfulness, neither could he express it himself; but by Tears running down his Face; he call'd his Wife, and told her God had mov'd the Heart of a Stranger upon hearing their Condition, to give them all that Money; and a great deal more such as that, he said to her. The Woman too, made Signs of the like Thankfulness, as well to Heaven, as to me, and joyfully pick'd it up; and I parted with no Money all that Year, that I thought better bestow'd.

I then ask'd the poor Man if the Distemper had not reach'd to *Greenwich*: He said it had not, till about a Fortnight before; but that then he feared it had; but that it was only at that End of the Town, which lay South towards *Deptford*-Bridge; that he went only to a Butchers-Shop, and a Grocers, where he generally bought such Things as they sent him for; but was very careful.

I ask'd him then, how it came to pass, that those People who had so shut themselves up in the Ships, had not laid in sufficient Stores of all things necessary? He said some of them had, but on the other Hand, some did not come on board till they were frighted into it, and till it was too dangerous for them to go to the proper People, to lay in Quantities of Things, and that he waited on two Ships which he shewed me, that had lay'd in little or nothing but Biscuit Bread, and Ship Beer; and that he had bought every Thing else almost for them. I ask'd him, if there was any more Ships that had separated themselves, as those had done. He told me yes, all the way up from the Point, right against *Greenwich*, to within the Shore of *Lime-house* and *Redriff*, all the Ships that could have Room, rid two and two in the middle of the Stream; and that some of them had several Families on Board. I ask'd him, if the Distemper had not reached them? He said he believ'd it had not, except two or three Ships, whose People had not been so watchful, to keep the Seamen from going on Shore as others had been; and he said it was a very fine Sight to see how the Ships lay up the Pool.

When he said he was going over to *Greenwich*, as soon as the Tide began to come in, I ask'd if he would let me go with him, and bring me back, for that I had a great mind to see how the Ships were ranged as he had told me? He told me if

I would assure him on the Word of a Christian, and of an honest Man, that I had not the Distemper, he would: I assur'd him, that I had not, that it had pleased God to preserve me, That I liv'd in *White-Chapel*, but was too Impatient of being so long within Doors, and that I had ventured out so far for the Refreshment of a little Air; but that none in my House had so much as been touch't with it.

Well, Sir, says he, as your Charity has been mov'd to pity me and my poor Family; sure you cannot have so little pity left, as to put your self into my Boat if you were not Sound in Health, which would be nothing less than killing me, and ruining my whole Family. The poor Man troubled me so much, when he spoke of his Family with such a sensible Concern, and in such an affectionate Manner, that I cou'd not satisfy my self at first to go at all. I told him, I would lay aside my Curiosity, rather than make him uneasy; tho' I was sure, and very thankful for it, that I had no more Distemper upon me, than the freshest Man in the World: *Well*, he would not have me put it off neither, but to let me see how confident he was, that I was just to him, he now importuned me to go; so when the Tide came up to his Boat, I went in, and he carry'd me to *Greenwich*: While he bought the Things which he had in his Charge to buy, I walk'd up to the Top of the Hill, under which the Town stands, and on the East-Side of the Town, to get a Prospect of the River: But it was a surprising Sight to see the Number of Ships which lay in Rows, two and two, and some Places, two or three such Lines in the Breadth of the River, and this not only up quite to the Town, between the Houses which we call *Ratclif* and *Redriff*, which they name the *Pool*, but even down the whole River, as far as the Head of *Long-Reach*, which is as far as the Hills give us Leave to see it.

I cannot guess at the Number of Ships, but I think there must be several Hundreds of Sail; and I could not but applaud the Contrivance, for ten thousand People,[1] and more, who attended Ship Affairs, were certainly sheltered here from the Violence of the Contagion, and liv'd very safe and very easy.

I returned to my own Dwelling very well satisfied with my Days Journey, and particularly with the poor Man; also I rejoyced to see that such little Sanctuaries were provided for so many Families, in a Time of such Desolation. I observ'd also, that as the Violence of the Plague had encreased, so the Ships which had Families on Board, remov'd and went farther off, till, as I was told, some went quite away to Sea, and put into such Harbours, and safe Roads on the *North* Coast, as they could best come at.

But it was also true, that all the People, who thus left the Land, and liv'd on Board the Ships, were not entirely safe from the Infection, for many died, and were thrown over board into the River, some in Coffins, and some, as I heard, without Coffins, whose Bodies were seen sometimes to drive up and down, with the Tide in the River.

But I believe, I may venture to say, that in those Ships which were thus infected, it either happened where the People had recourse to them too late, and did not fly to the Ship till they had stayed too long on Shore, and had the Distemper upon them, tho' perhaps, they might not perceive it, and so the Distemper did not come to them, on Board the Ships, but they really carried it with them; OR it was in these Ships, where the poor Waterman said they had not had Time to furnish themselves with Provisions, but were obliged to send often on Shore to buy what they had Occasion for, or suffered Boats to come to them from the Shore; and so the Distemper was brought insensibly among them.

And here I cannot but take notice that the strange Temper of the People of *London* at that Time contributed extremely to their own Destruction. The Plague began, as I have observed, at the other End of the Town, namely, in *Long-Acre*, *Drury-Lane*, &c. and came on towards the City very gradually and slowly. It was felt at first in *December*, then again in *February*, then again in *April*, and always but a very little at a Time; then it stopt till *May*, and even the last Week in *May*, there was but 17, and all at that End of the Town; and all this while, even so long, as till there died above 3000 a-Week; yet had the People in *Redriff*, and in *Wapping*, and *Ratcliff* on both Sides the River, and almost all *Southwark-Side*, a mighty Fancy, that they should not be visited, or at least, that it would not be so violent among them. Some People fancied, the smell of the Pitch and Tar, and such other things, as Oil and Rosin, and Brimstone, which is so much used by all Trades relating to Shipping, would preserve them. Others argued it, because it was in its extreamest Violence in *Westminster*, and the Parishes of St. *Giles*'s and St. *Andrew*'s, &c. and began to abate again, before it came among them, which was true indeed, in Part: *For Example.*

From the 8th to the 15th of *August.*			Total this Week.
St. *Giles*'s in the Fields } 242	Stepney	197	
	St. Mag. Bermondsey	24 }	4030
Cripplegate 886	Rotherhith	3	

From the 15th to the 22d of *August.*			Total this Week.
St. *Giles*'s in the Fields } 175	Stepney	273	
	St. Mag. Bermondsey	36 }	5319
Cripplegate 847	Rotherhith	2	

N.B. That it was observ'd the Numbers mention'd in *Stepney* Parish, at that time, were generally all on that Side where *Stepney* Parish joined to *Shoreditch*, which we now call *Spittle-fields*, where the Parish of *Stepney*, comes up to the very Wall of *Shoreditch* Church-Yard, and the Plague at this Time was abated at St. *Giles*'s *in the Fields*, and raged most violently in *Cripplegate*, *Bishopsgate* and *Shoreditch* Parishes, but there was not 10 People a-Week that died of it in all that Part of *Stepney* Parish, which takes in *Lime-House*, *Ratcliff-high-way*, and which are now the Parishes of *Shadwell* and *Wapping*, even to St. *Katherines* by the Tower, till after the whole Month of *August* was expired; but they paid for it afterwards, as I shall observe by and by.

This, I say, made the People of *Redriff* and *Wapping*, *Ratcliff* and *Lime-House* so secure, and flatter themselves so much with the Plague's going off, without reaching them, that they took no Care, either to fly into the Country, or shut themselves up; nay, so far were they from stirring, that they rather receiv'd their Friends and Relations from the City into their Houses; and several from other Places really took Sanctuary in that Part of the Town, as a Place of Safety, and as a Place which they thought God would pass over and not visit as the rest was visited.

And this was the Reason, that when it came upon them they were more surprized, more unprovided and more at a Loss what to do than they were in other Places, for when it came among them really, and with Violence, as it did indeed, in *September* and *October*, there was then no stirring out into the Country, no Body would suffer a Stranger to come near them, no nor near the Towns where they dwelt; and as I have been told, several that wandred into the Country on *Surry* Side were found starv'd to Death in the Woods and Commons, that Country being more open and more woody, than any other Part so near *London*; especially about *Norwood*, and the Parishes of *Camberwell*, *Dullege*, and *Lusum*, where it seems no Body durst relieve the poor distress'd People for fear of the Infection.

This Notion having, as I said, prevailed with the People in that Part of the Town, was in Part the Occasion, *as I said before*, that they had Recourse to Ships for their Retreat; and where they did this early, and with Prudence, furnishing themselves so with Provisions, that they had no need to go on Shore for Supplies, or suffer Boats to come on Board to bring them; I say where they did so they had certainly the safest Retreat of any People whatsoever: But the Distress was such, that People ran on Board in their Fright without Bread to eat, and some into Ships, that had no Men on Board to remove them farther off, or to take the Boat and go down the River to buy Provisions where it might be done safely; and these often suffered, and were infected on board as much as on Shore.

As the richer Sort got into Ships, so the lower Rank got into Hoys, Smacks, Lighters, and Fishing-boats; and many, especially Watermen, lay in their Boats; but those made sad Work of it, especially the latter, for going about for Provision, and perhaps to get their Subsistence, the Infection got in among them and made a fearful Havock; many of the Water-men died alone in their Wherries, as they rid at their Roads, as well above-Bridge as below, and were not found sometimes till they were not in Condition for any Body to touch or come near them.

Indeed the Distress of the People at this Sea-faring End of the Town was very deplorable, and deserved the greatest Commiseration: But alas! this was a Time when every one's private Safety lay so near them, that they had no Room to pity the Distresses of others; for every one had Death, as it were, at his Door, and many even in their Families, and knew not what to do, or whither to fly.

This, I say, took away all Compassion; self Preservation indeed appear'd here to be the first Law. For the Children ran away from their Parents, as they languished in the utmost Distress: And in some Places, tho' not so frequent as the other, Parents did the like to their Children; nay, some dreadful Examples there were, and particularly two in one Week of distressed Mothers, raveing and distracted, killing their own Children; one whereof was not far off from where I dwelt; the poor lunatick Creature not living herself long enough to be sensible of the Sin of what she had done, much less to be punish'd for it.

It is not indeed to be wondred at, for the Danger of imme-diate Death to ourselves, took away all Bowels of Love, all Concern for one another: I speak in general, for there were many Instances of immovable Affection, Pity, and Duty in many, and some that came to my Knowledg; that is to say, by here-say.

For I shall not take upon me to vouch the Truth of the Particulars.

To introduce one, let me first mention, that one of the most deplorable Cases, in all the present Calamity, was, that of Women with Child; who when they came to the Hour of their

Sorrows, and their Pains came upon them, cou'd neither have help of one Kind or another; neither Midwife or Neighbouring Women to come near them; most of the Midwives were dead; especially, of such as serv'd the poor; and many, if not all the Midwives of Note were fled into the Country: So that it was next to impossible for a poor Woman that cou'd not pay an immoderate Price to get any Midwife to come to her, and if they did, those they cou'd get were generally unskilful and ignorant Creatures; and the Consequence of this was, that a most unusual and incredible Number of Women were reduc'd to the utmost distress. Some were deliver'd and spoil'd by the rashness and ignorance of those who pretended to lay them. Children without Number, were, I might say murthered by the same, but a more justifiable ignorance, pretending they would save the Mother, whatever became of the Child; and many Times, both Mother and Child were lost in the same Manner; and especially, where the Mother had the Distemper, there no Body would come near them, and both sometimes perish'd: Sometimes the Mother has died of the Plague; and the Infant, it may be half born, or born but not parted from the Mother. Some died in the very Pains of their Travail, and not deliver'd at all; and so many were the Cases of this Kind, that it is hard to Judge of them.

Something of it will appear in the unusual Numbers which are put into the Weekly Bills (tho' I am far from allowing them to be able to give any Thing of a full Account) under the Articles of

> *Child-Bed.*
> *Abortive* and *Stilborn.*
> *Chrisoms* and *Infants.*

Take the Weeks in which the Plague was most violent, and compare them with the Weeks before the Distemper began, even in the same Year: *For Example:*

		Child bed.	Abort.	Stil-born.
From {	Jan. 3 to Jan. 10	— 7	— 1	— 13
	to 17	— 8	— 6	— 11
	to 24	— 9	— 5	— 15
	to 31	— 3	— 2	— 9
	Jan. 31 to Feb. 7	— 3	— 3	— 8
	to 14	— 6	— 2	— 11
	to 21	— 5	— 2	— 13
	to 28	— 2	— 2	— 10
	Feb. 7 to March 7	— 5	— 1	— 10
		48	— 24	—100
From {	Aug. 1 to Aug. 8	— 25	— 5	— 11
	to 15	— 23	— 6	— 8
	to 22	— 28	— 4	— 4
	to 29	— 40	— 6	— 10
	Aug. 1 to Sept. 5	— 38	— 2	— 11
	to 12	— 39	— 23	— 00
	to 19	— 42	— 5	— 17
	to 26	— 42	— 6	— 10
	Aug. 1 to Octob. 3	— 14	— 4	— 9
		291	— 61	— 80

To the Disparity of these Numbers, is to be considered and allow'd for, that according to our usual Opinion, who were then upon the Spot, there were not one third of the People in the Town, during the Months of *August* and *September*, as were in the Months of *January* and *February*: In a Word, the usual Number that used to die of these three Articles; and as I hear, did die of them the Year before, was thus:

1664 {	Child-bed. - - - - - - -	189	1665 {	Child-bed. - - - - -	625
	Abortive and Stil-born.	458		Abort. & Stil-born.	617
		647			1242

This inequallity, I say, is exceedingly augmented, when the Numbers of People are considered: I pretend not to make any exact Calculation of the Numbers of People, which

were at this Time in the City; but I shall make a probable
Conjecture at that part by and by: What I have said now, is
to explain the misery of those poor Creatures above; so that
it might well be said as in the Scripture. *Wo! be to those who
are with Child; and to those which give suck in that Day.*[1] For
indeed, it was a Wo to them in particular.

I was not conversant in many particular Families where
these things happen'd; but the Out-cries of the miserable,
were heard afar off. As to those who were with Child, we have
seen some Calculation made, 291 Women dead in Child bed
in nine Weeks; out of one third Part of the Number, of whom
there usually dy'd in that Time, but 48 of the same Disaster.
Let the Reader calculate the Proportion.

There is no Room to doubt but the Misery of those that
gave Suck was in Proportion as great. Our Bills of Mortality
cou'd give but little Light in this; yet, some it did, there were
several more than usual starv'd at Nurse, But this was nothing:
The Misery was, where they were (1*st*) starved for want of a
Nurse, the Mother dying, and all the Family and the Infants
found dead by them, meerly for want; and if I may speak my
Opinion, I do believe, that many hundreds of Poor helpless
Infants perish'd in this manner. (2*dly*) Not starved (but
poison'd) by the Nurse, Nay even where the Mother has been
Nurse, and having receiv'd the Infection, has poison'd, that
is, infected the Infant with her Milk, even before they knew
they were infected themselves; nay, and the Infant has dy'd
in such a Case before the Mother. I cannot but remember to
leave this Admonition upon Record, if ever such another
dreadful Visitation should happen in this City; that all
Women that are with Child or that give Suck should be gone,
if they have any possible Means out of the Place; because
their Misery if infected, will so much exceed all other Peoples.

I could tell here dismal Stories of living Infants being
found sucking the Breasts of their Mothers, or Nurses, after
they have been dead of the Plague. Of a Mother, in the Parish
where I liv'd, who having a Child that was not well, sent for
an Apothecary to View the Child, and when he came, as the

Relation goes, was giving the Child suck at her Breast, and to all Appearance, was her self very well: But when the Apothecary came close to her, he saw the Tokens upon that Breast, with which she was suckling the Child. He was surpriz'd enough to be sure; but not willing to fright the poor Woman too much, he desired she would give the Child into his Hand; so he takes the Child, and going to a Cradle in the Room lays it in, and opening its Cloths, found the Tokens upon the Child too, and both dy'd before he cou'd get Home, to send a preventative Medicine to the Father of the Child, to whom he had told their Condition; whether the Child infected the Nurse-Mother, or the Mother the Child was not certain, but the last the most likely.

Likewise of a Child brought Home to the Parents from a Nurse that had dy'd of the Plague; yet, the tender Mother would not refuse to take in her Child, and lay'd it in her Bosom, by which she was infected, and dy'd with the Child in her Arms dead also.

It would make the hardest Heart move at the Instances that were frequently found of tender Mothers, tending and watching with their dear Children, and even dying before them, and sometimes taking the Distemper from them, and dying when the Child, for whom the affectionate Heart had been sacrificed, has got over it and escap'd.

The like of a Tradesman in *East-Smith-field*, whose Wife was big with Child of her first Child, and fell in Labour, having the Plague upon her: He cou'd neither get Midwife to assist her, or Nurse to tend her; and two Servants which he kept fled both from her. He ran from House to House like one distracted, but cou'd get no help; the utmost he could get was, that a Watchman who attended at an infected House shut up, promis'd to send a Nurse in the Morning: The poor Man with his Heart broke, went back, assisted his Wife what he cou'd, acted the part of the Midwife; brought the Child dead into the World; and his Wife in about an Hour dy'd in his Arms, where he held her dead Body fast till the Morning, when the Watchman came and brought the Nurse as he had promised; and coming up the Stairs, for he had left the Door open, or only latched: They found the Man sitting with his dead Wife in his Arms; and so overwhelmed with Grief, that he dy'd in a few Hours after, without any Sign of the Infection upon him, but meerly sunk under the Weight of his Grief.

I have heard also of some, who on the Death of their Relations, have grown stupid with the insupportable Sorrow, and of one in particular, who was so absolutely overcome with the Pressure upon his Spirits, that by Degrees, his Head sunk into his Body, so between his Shoulders, that the Crown of his Head was very little seen above the Bones of his Shoulders; and by Degrees, loseing both Voice and Sense, his Face looking forward, lay against his Collar-Bone, and cou'd not be kept up any otherwise, unless held up by the Hands of other People; and the poor Man never came to himself again, but languished near a Year in that Condition and died: Nor was he ever once seen to lift up his Eyes, or to look upon any particular Object.

I cannot undertake to give any other than a Summary of such Passages as these, because it was not possible to come at the Particulars, where sometimes the whole Families, where such Things happen'd, were carry'd off by the Distemper: But there were innumerable Cases of this Kind, which presented to the Eye, and the Ear; even in passing along the Streets, as I have hinted above, nor is it easy to give any Story of this, or that Family, which there was not divers parallel Stories to [be] met with of the same Kind.

But as I am now talking of the Time, when the Plague rag'd at the Easter-most Part of the Town; how for a long Time the People of those Parts had flattered themselves that they should escape; and how they were surprized, when it came upon them as it did; for indeed, it came upon them like an armed Man, when it did come. I say, this brings me back to the three poor Men, who wandered from *Wapping*, not knowing whither to go, or what to do, and who I mention'd before; one a Biscuit-Baker, one a Sail-Maker, and the other a Joiner; all of *Wapping*, or thereabouts.

The Sleepiness and Security of that Part as I have observ'd, was such that they not only did not shift for themselves as others did; but they boasted of being safe, and of Safety being with them; and many People fled out of the City, and out of the infected Suburbs, to *Wapping*, *Ratcliff*, *Lime-house*, *Poplar*, and such Places, as to Places of Security; and it is not at all unlikely, that their doing this, help'd to bring the Plague that way faster, than it might otherwise have come. For tho' I am much for Peoples flying away and emptying such a Town as this, upon the first Appearance of a like Visitation, and that all People that have any possible Retreat, should make use of it in Time, and begone; yet, I must say, when all that will fly are gone, those that are left and must stand it, should stand stock still where they are, and not shift from one End of the Town, or one Part of the Town to the other; for that is the Bane and Mischief of the whole, and they carry the Plague from House to House in their very Clothes.

Wherefore, were we ordered to kill all the Dogs and Cats:[1] But because as they were domestick Animals, and are apt to run from House to House, and from Street to Street; so they are capable of carrying the Effluvia or Infectious Steams of Bodies infected, even in their Furrs and Hair; and therefore, it was that in the beginning of the Infection, an Order was published by the Lord Mayor, and by the Magistrates, according to the Advice of the Physicians; that all the Dogs and Cats should be imediately killed, and an Officer was appointed for the Execution.

It is incredible, if their Account is to be depended upon, what a prodigious Number of those Creatures were destroy'd: I think they talk'd of forty thousand Dogs, and five times as many Cats, few Houses being without a Cat, and some having several, and sometimes five or six in a House. All possible Endeavours were us'd also to destroy the Mice and Rats, especially the latter; by laying Rats-Bane, and other Poisons for them, and a prodigious multitude of them were also destroy'd.

I often reflected upon the unprovided Condition, that the

whole Body of the People were in at the first coming of this Calamity upon them, and how it was for Want of timely entring into Measures, and Managements, as well publick as private, that all the Confusions that followed were brought upon us; and that such a prodigious Number of People sunk in that Disaster, which if proper Steps had been taken, might, Providence concurring, have been avoided, and which, if Posterity think fit, they may take a Caution, and Warning from: But I shall come to this Part again.

I come back to my three Men: Their Story has a Moral in every Part of it, and their whole Conduct, and that of some who they join'd with, is a Pattern for all poor Men to follow, or Women either, if ever such a Time comes again; and if there was no other End in recording it, I think this a very just one, whether my Account be exactly according to Fact or no.

Two of them are said to be Brothers, the one an old Soldier, but now a Biscuit Baker; the other a lame Sailor, but now a Sail-Maker; the Third a Joiner. Says *John* the Biscuit Baker, one Day to *Thomas* his Brother, the Sail-maker, *Brother* Tom, *what will become of us? The Plague grows hot in the City, and encreases this way: What shall we do?*

Truly, says *Thomas,* *I am at a great Loss what to do, for I find, if it comes down into* Wapping, *I shall be turn'd out of my Lodging:* And thus they began to talk of it beforehand.

John, *Turn'd out of your Lodging,* Tom! *if you are, I don't know who will take you in; for People are so afraid of one another now, there's no getting a Lodging any where.*

Tho. *Why? The People where I lodge are good civil People, and have Kindness enough for me too; but they say I go abroad every Day to my Work, and it will be dangerous; and they talk of locking themselves up, and letting no Body come near them.*

John, *Why, they are in the right to be sure, if they resolve to venture staying in Town.*

Tho. *Nay, I might e'en resolve to stay within Doors too, for, except a Suit of Sails that my Master has in Hand, and which I am just a finishing, I am like to get no more Work a great while;*

there's no Trade stirs now; Workmen and Servants are turned off every where, so that I might be glad to be lock'd up too: But I do not see they will be willing to consent to that, any more than to the other.

John, *Why, what will you do then Brother? and what shall I do? for I am almost as bad as you; the People where I lodge are all gone into the Country but a Maid, and she is to go next Week, and to shut the House quite up, so that I shall be turn'd a drift to the wide World before you, and I am resolved to go away too, if I knew but where to go.*

Tho. *We were both distracted we did not go away at first, then we might ha' travelled any where; there's no stirring now; we shall be starv'd if we pretend to go out of Town; they won't let us have Victuals, ño, not for our Money, nor let us come into the Towns, much less into their Houses.*

John, *And that which is almost as bad, I have but little Money to help my self with neither.*

Tho. *As to that we might make shift; I have a little, tho' not much; but I tell you there's no stirring on the Road. I know a Couple of poor honest Men in our Street have attempted to travel, and at Barnet, or Whetston, or there about, the People offered to fire at them if they pretended to go forward; so they are come back again quite discourag'd.*

John, *I would have ventured their Fire, if I had been there; If I had been denied Food for my Money they should ha' seen me take it before their Faces; and if I had tendred Money for it, they could not have taken any Course with me by Law.*

Tho. *You talk your old Soldier's Language, as if you were in the Low-Countries now, but this is a serious thing. The People have good Reason to keep any Body off, that they are not satisfied are sound, at such a Time as this; and we must not plunder them.*

John, *No Brother, you mistake the Case, and mistake me too, I would plunder no Body; but for any Town upon the Road to deny me Leave to pass thro' the Town in the open High-Way, and deny me Provisions for my Money, is to say the Town has a Right to starve me to Death, which cannot be true.*

Tho. But they do not deny you Liberty to go back again from whence you came, and therefore they do not starve you.

John, *But the next Town behind me will by the same Rule deny me leave to go back, and so they do starve me between them; besides there is no Law to prohibit my travelling wherever I will on the Road.*

Tho. But there will be so much Difficulty in disputing with them at every Town on the Road, that it is not for poor Men to do it, or to undertake it at such a Time as this is especially.

John, *Why Brother? Our Condition at this Rate is worse than any Bodies else; for we can neither go away nor stay here; I am of the same Mind with the Lepers of* Samaria,[1] If we stay here we are sure to die; *I mean especially, as you and I are stated, without a Dwelling-House of our own, and without Lodging in any Bodies else; there is no lying in the Street at such a Time as this; we had as good go into the Dead Cart at once: Therefore I say,* if we stay here we are sure to die, *and if we go away* we can but die: *I am resolv'd to be gone.*

Tho. You will go away: Whither will you go? and what can you do? I would as willingly go away as you, if I knew whither: But we have no Acquaintance, no Friends. Here we were born, and here we must die.

John, *Look you* Tom, *the whole Kingdom is my Native Country as well as this Town. You may as well say, I must not go out of my House if it is on Fire, as that I must not go out of the Town I was born in, when it is infected with the Plague. I was born in* England, *and have a Right to live in it if I can.*

Tho. But you know every vagrant Person may by the Laws of England, *be taken up, and pass'd back to their last legal Settlement.*[2]

John, *But how shall they make me vagrant; I desire only to travel on, upon my lawful Occasions.*

Tho. What lawful Occasions can we pretend to travel, or rather wander upon, they will not be put off with Words.

John, *Is not flying to save our Lives, a Lawful Occasion! and do they not all know that the Fact is true: We cannot be said to dissemble.*

Tho. *But suppose they let us pass, Whither shall we go?*

John, *Any where to save our Lives: It is Time enough to consider that when we are got out of this Town. If I am once out of this dreadful Place I care not where I go.*

Tho. *We shall be driven to great Extremities. I know not what to think of it.*

John, *Well* Tom, *consider of it a little.*

This was about the Beginning of *July*,[1] and tho' the Plague was come forward in the West and North Parts of the Town, yet all *Wapping*, as I have observed before, and *Redriff*, and *Ratcliff*, and *Lime-House*, and *Poplar*, in short, *Deptford* and *Greenwich*, all both Sides of the River from the *Hermitage*, and from over against it, quite down to *Blackwall*, was intirely free, there had not one Person died of the Plague in all *Stepney* Parish, and not one on the South Side of *White-Chappel* Road, no, not in any Parish; and yet the Weekly Bill was that very Week risen up to 1006.

It was a Fortnight after this, before the two Brothers met again, and then the Case was a little altered, and the Plague was exceedingly advanced, and the Number greatly encreased, the Bill was up at 2785, and prodigiously encreasing, tho' still both Sides of the River, as below, kept pretty well: But some began to die in *Redriff*, and about five or six in *Ratclif-High-Way*, when the Sail Maker came to his Brother *John*, express, and in some Fright, for he was absolutely warn'd out of his Lodging, and had only a Week to provide himself. His Brother *John* was in as bad a Case, for he was quite out, and had only beg'd Leave of his Master the Biscuit Baker to lodge in an Out-House belonging to his Work-house, where he only lay upon Straw, with some Biscuit Sacks, or Bread Sacks, as they call'd them, laid upon it, and some of the same Sacks to cover him.

Here they resolved, seeing all Employment being at an End, and no Work, or Wages to be had, they would make the best of their Way to get out of the Reach of the dreadful Infection; and being as good Husbands as they could, would endeavour to live upon what they had as long as it would last, and then work for more, if they could get Work any where, of any Kind, let it be what it would.

While they were considering to put this Resolution in Practice, in the best Manner they could, the third Man, who was acquainted very well with the Sail Maker, came to know of the Design, and got Leave to be one of the Number, and thus they prepared to set out.

It happened that they had not an equal share of Money, but as the Sail-maker, who had the best Stock, was besides his being Lame, the most unfit to expect to get any thing by Working in the Country, so he was content that what Money they had should all go into one publick Stock, on Condition, that whatever any one of them could gain more than another, it should, without any grudging, be all added to the same publick Stock.

They resolv'd to load themselves with as little Baggage as possible, because they resolv'd at first to travel on Foot; and to go a great way, that they might, if possible, be effectually Safe; and a great many Consultations they had with themselves, before they could agree about what Way they should travel, which they were so far from adjusting, that even to the Morning they set out, they were not resolv'd on it.

At last the Seaman put in a Hint that determin'd it; First, says he, the Weather is very hot, and therefore I am for travelling North, that we may not have the Sun upon our Faces and beating on our Breasts, which will heat and suffocate us; and I have been told, says he, that it is not good to over-heat our Blood at a Time when, for ought we know, the Infection may be in the very Air. In the next Place, says he, I am for going the Way that may be contrary to the Wind as it may blow when we set out, that we may not have the Wind blow the Air of the City on our Backs as we go. These two Cautions were approv'd of; if it could be brought so to hit, that the Wind might not be in the South when they set out to go North.

John the Baker, who had been a Soldier, then put in his

Opinion; First, says he, we none of us expect to get any Lodging on the Road, and it will be a little too hard to lie just in the open Air; tho' it be warm Weather, yet it may be wet, and damp, and we have a double Reason to take care of our Healths at such a time as this; and therefore, says he, you, Brother *Tom*, that are a Sail-maker, might easily make us a little Tent, and I will undertake to set it up every Night, and take it down, and a Fig for all the Inns in *England*; if we have a good Tent over our Heads, we shall do well enough.

The Joyner oppos'd this, and told them, let them leave that to him, he would undertake to build them a House every Night with his Hatchet and Mallet, tho' he had no other Tools, which should be fully to their satisfaction, and as good as a Tent.

The Soldier and the Joyner disputed that Point some time, but at last the Soldier carry'd it for a Tent; the only Objection against it was, that it must be carry'd with them, and that would encrease their Baggage too much, the Weather being hot; but the Sail-maker had a piece of good Hap [befall him] which made that easie, for, his Master who he work'd for having a Rope-Walk as well as his Sail-making Trade, had a little poor Horse that he made no use of then, and being willing to assist the three honest Men, he gave them the Horse for the carrying their Baggage; also for a small Matter of three Days Work that his Man did for him before he went, he let him have an old Top-gallant Sail that was worn out, but was sufficient and more than enough to make a very good Tent: The Soldier shew'd how to shape it, and they soon by his Direction made their Tent, and fitted it with Poles or Staves for the purpose, and thus they were furnish'd for their Journey; *viz.* three Men, one Tent, one Horse, one Gun, for the Soldier would not go without Arms, for now he said he was no more a Biscuit-Baker, but a Trooper.

The Joyner had a small Bag of Tools, such as might be useful if he should get any Work abroad, as well for their Subsistence as his own: What Money they had, they brought all into one publick Stock, and thus they began their Journey.

It seems that in the Morning when they set out, the Wind blew as the Saylor said by his Pocket Compass, at N. W. by W. So they directed, or rather resolv'd to direct their Course N. W.

But then a Difficulty came in their Way, that as they set out from the hither end of *Wapping* near the *Hermitage*, and that the Plague was now very Violent, especially on the North side of the City, as in *Shoreditch* and *Cripplegate* Parish, they did not think it safe for them to go near those Parts; so they went away East through *Radcliff* High-way, as far as *Radcliff-Cross*, and leaving *Stepney* Church still on their Left-hand, being afraid to come up from *Radcliff-Cross* to *Mile-end*, because they must come just by the Church-yard, and because the Wind that seemed to blow more from the West, blow'd directly from the side of the City where the Plague was hottest. So I say, leaving *Stepney*, they fetched a long Compass, and going to *Poplar* and *Bromley*, came into the great Road just at *Bow*.

Here the Watch plac'd upon *Bow* Bridge would have question'd them; but they crossing the Road into a narrow Way that turns out at the hither End of the Town of *Bow* to *Old-Ford*, avoided any Enquiry there, and travelled to *Old-Ford*. The Constables every where were upon their Guard, not so much it seems to stop People passing by, as to stop them from taking up their Abode in their Towns, and withal because of a Report that was newly rais'd at that time, and that indeed was not very improbable, *viz*. That the poor People in *London* being distress'd and starv'd for want of Work, and by that means for want of Bread, were up in Arms, and had raised a Tumult, and that they would come out to all the Towns round to plunder for Bread. This, I say, was only a Rumour, and it was very well it was no more; but it was not so far off from being a Reality, as it had been thought, for in a few Weeks more the poor People became so Desperate by the Calamity they suffer'd, that they were with great difficulty kept from running out into the Fields and Towns, and tearing all in pieces where-ever they came; and, as I have observed before, nothing hinder'd them but that the Plague rag'd so violently, and fell in upon them so furiously, that they rather went to the Grave by Thousands than into the Fields in Mobs by Thousands: For in the Parts about the Parishes of St. *Sepulchres, Clerkenwell, Cripplegate, Bishopsgate* and *Shoreditch*, which were the Places where the Mob began to threaten, the Distemper came on so furiously, that there died in those few Parishes, even then, before the Plague was come to its height, no less than 5361 People in the first three Weeks in *August*,[1] when at the same time, the Parts about *Wapping, Radcliffe*, and *Rotherhith*, were, as before describ'd, hardly touch'd, or but very lightly; so that in a Word, tho', as I said before, the good Management of the Lord Mayor and Justices did much to prevent the Rage and Desperation of the People from breaking out in Rabbles and Tumults, and in short, from the Poor plundering the Rich; I say, tho' they did much, the Dead Carts did more, for as I have said, that in five Parishes only there died above 5000 in 20 Days, so there might be probably three times that Number Sick all that time; for some recovered, and great Numbers fell sick every Day and died afterwards. Besides, I must still be allowed to say, that if the Bills of Mortality said five Thousand, I always believ'd it was near twice as many in reality; there being no room to believe that the Account they gave was right, or that indeed, they were, among such Confusions as I saw them in, in any Condition to keep an exact Account.

But to return to my Travellers; Here they were only examined, and as they seemed rather coming from the Country than from the City, they found the People the easier with them; that they talk'd to them, let them come into a publick House where the Constable and his Warders were, and gave them Drink and some Victuals, which greatly refreshed and encourag'd them; and here it came into their Heads to say, when they should be enquir'd of afterwards, not that they came from *London*, but that they came out of *Essex*.

To forward this little Fraud, they obtain'd so much Favour of the Constable at *Old-Ford*, as to give them a Certificate of their passing from *Essex* thro' that Village, and that they had not been at *London*; which tho' false in the common acceptation of *London* in the County, yet was literally true; *Wapping* or *Radcliff* being no part either of the City or Liberty.

This Certificate directed to the next Constable that was at *Hummerton*, one of the Hamlets of the Parish of *Hackney*, was so serviceable to them, that it procured them not a free Passage there only, but a full Certificate of Health from a Justice of the Peace; who, upon the Constable's Application, granted it without much Difficulty; and thus they pass'd through the long divided Town of *Hackney*, (for it lay then in several separated Hamlets) and travelled on till they came into the great North Road on the top of *Stamford-Hill*.

By this time they began to be weary, and so in the back Road from *Hackney* a little before it opened into the said great Road, they resolv'd to set up their Tent and encamp for the first Night; which they did accordingly, with this addition, that finding a Barn, or a Building like a Barn, and first searching as well as they could to be sure there was no Body in it, they set up their Tent, with the Head of it against the Barn; this they did also because the Wind blew that Night very high, and they were but young at such a way of Lodging, as well as the managing their Tent.

Here they went to Sleep, but the Joyner, a grave and sober Man, and not pleased with their lying at this loose rate the first Night, could not sleep, and resolv'd, after trying to Sleep to no purpose, that he would get out, and taking the Gun in his Hand stand Centinel and Guard his Companions: So with the Gun in his Hand he walk'd to and again before the Barn, for that stood in the Field near the Road, but within the Hedge. He had not been long upon the Scout, but he heard a Noise of People coming on as if it had been a great Number, and they came on, as he thought, directly towards the Barn. He did not presently awake his Companions, but in a few Minutes more their Noise growing louder and louder, the Biscuit-Baker call'd to him and ask'd him what was the Matter, and quickly started out too:

The other being the Lame Sail-maker and most weary, lay still in the Tent.

As they expected, so the People who they had heard, came on directly to the Barn, when one of our Travellers challenged, like Soldiers upon the Guard, with *Who comes there?* The People did not Answer immediately, but one of them speaking to another that was behind him, *Alas! Alas! we are all disappointed*, says he, *here are some People before us, the Barn is taken up.*

They all stopp'd upon that as under some Surprize, and it seems there was about Thirteen of them in all, and some Women among them: They consulted together what they should do, and by their Discourse our Travellers soon found they were poor distress'd People too like themselves, seeking Shelter and Safety; and besides, our Travellers had no need to be afraid of their coming up to disturb them; for as soon as they heard the Words, *Who comes there*, these could hear the Women say, *as if frighted, Do not go near them, how do you know but they may have the Plague?* And when one of the Men said, *Let us but speak to them*; the Women said, *No, don't by any means, we have escap'd thus far* by the Goodness of God, *do not let us run into Danger now, we beseech you.*

Our Travellers found by this that they were a good sober sort of People and flying for their Lives as they were; and, as they were encourag'd by it, so *John* said to the Joyner his Comrade, *Let us Encourage them too as much as we can*: So he called to them, *Hark ye good People* says the Joyner, we find by your Talk, that you are fleeing from the same dreadful Enemy as we are, do not be afraid of us, we are only three poor Men of us, if you are free from the Distemper you shall not be hurt by us; we are not in the Barn, but in a little Tent here in the outside, and we will remove for you, we can set up our Tent again immediately any where else; and upon this a Parly began between the Joyner, whose Name was *Richard*, and one of their Men, who said his Name was *Ford*.

Ford. And do you assure us that you are all Sound Men.

Rich. Nay, we are concern'd to tell you of it, that you may not be uneasy, or think your selves in Danger; but you see we do not desire you should put your selves into any Danger; and therefore I tell you, that as we have not made use of the Barn, so we will remove from it, that you may be Safe and we also.

Ford. That is very kind and charitable; But, if we have Reason to be satisfied that you are Sound and free from the Visitation, why should we make you remove now you are settled in your Lodging, and it may be are laid down to Rest? we will go into the Barn if you please, to rest our selves a while, and we need not disturb you.

Rich. Well, but you are more than we are, I hope you will assure us that you are all of you Sound too, for the Danger is as great from you to us, as from us to you.

Ford. Blessed be God that some do escape tho' it is but few; what may be our Portion still we know not, but hitherto we are preserved.

Rich. What part of the Town do you come from? Was the Plague come to the Places where you liv'd?

Ford. Ay ay, in a most frightful and terrible manner, or else we had not fled away as we do; but we believe there will be very few left alive behind us.

Rich. What Part do you come from?

Ford. We are most of us of *Cripplegate* Parish, only two or three of *Clerkenwell* Parish, but on the hither side.

Rich. How then was it that you came away no sooner?

Ford. We have been away some time, and kept together as well as we could at the hither End of *Islington*, where we got leave to lie in an old uninhabited House, and had some Bedding and Conveniencies of our own that we brought with us, but the Plague is come up into *Islington* too, and a House next Door to our poor Dwelling was Infected and shut up, and we are come away in a Fright.

Rich. And what Way are you going?

Ford. As our Lott shall cast us, we know not whither, but God will Guide those that look up to him.

They parlied no further at that time, but came all up to the Barn, and with some Difficulty got into it: There was nothing but Hay in the Barn, but it was almost full of that, and they accommodated themselves as well as they cou'd, and went to Rest; but our Travellers observ'd, that before they went to Sleep, an antient Man, who it seems was Father of one of the Women, went to Prayer with all the Company, recommending themselves to the Blessing and Direction of Providence, before they went to Sleep.

It was soon Day at that time of the Year; and as *Richard* the Joyner had kept Guard the first part of the Night, so *John* the Soldier Reliev'd him, and he had the Post in the Morning, and they began to be acquainted with one another. It seems, when they left *Islington*, they intended to have gone North away to *Highgate*, but were stop'd at *Holloway*, and there they would not let them pass; so they cross'd over the Fields and Hills to the Eastward, and came out at the *Boarded-River*,[1] and so avoiding the Towns, they left *Hornsey* on the left Hand, and *Newington* on the right Hand, and came into the great Road about *Stamford-Hill* on that side, as the three Travellers had done on the other side: And now they had Thoughts of going over the River in the Marshes, and make forwards to *Epping* Forest, where they hoped they should get leave to Rest. It seems they were not Poor, at least not so Poor as to be in Want; at least they had enough to subsist them moderately for two or three Months, when, as they said, they were in Hopes the cold Weather would check the Infection, or at least the Violence of it would have spent itself, and would abate, if it were only for want of People left alive to be Infected.

This was much the Fate of our three Travellers; only that they seemed to be the better furnish'd for Travelling, and had it in their View to go further off; for as to the first, they did not propose to go farther than one Day's Journey, that so they might have Intelligence every two or three Days how Things were at *London*.

But here our Travellers found themselves under an unexpected Inconvenience namely, that of their Horse, for by means of the Horse to carry their Baggage, they were obliged to keep in the Road, whereas the People of this other Band

went over the Fields or Roads, Path or no Path, Way, or no
Way, as they pleased; neither had they any Occasion to pass
thro' any Town, or come near any Town, other than to buy
such Things as they wanted for their necessary Subsistence,
and in that indeed they were put to much Difficulty: Of which
in its Place.

But our three Travellers were oblig'd to keep the Road, or
else they must commit Spoil and do the Country a great deal
of Damage in breaking down Fences and Gates, to go over
enclosed Fields, which they were loth to do if they could
help it.

Our three Travellers however had a great Mind to join
themselves to this Company, and take their Lot with them;
and after some Discourse, they laid aside their first Design
which look'd Northward, and resolv'd to follow the other into
Essex; so in the Morning they took up their Tent and loaded
their Horse, and away they travelled all together.

They had some Difficulty in passing the Ferry at the River
side, the Ferry-Man being afraid of them; but after some
Parly at a Distance, the Ferry-Man was content to bring his
Boat to a Place distant from the usual Ferry, and leave it there
for them to take it; so putting themselves over, he directed
them to leave the Boat, and he having another Boat, said he
would fetch it again, which it seems however he did not do
for above Eight Days.

Here giving the Ferry-Man Money before-hand, they had
a supply of Victuals and Drink, which he brought and left in
the Boat for them, but not without, as I said, having receiv'd
the Money before-hand. But now our Travellers were at a
great Loss and Difficulty how to get the Horse over, the Boat
being small and not fit for it, and at last cou'd not do it without
unloading the Baggage, and making him swim over.

From the River they travelled towards the Forest, but when
they came to *Walthamstow* the People of that Town denied
to admit them, as was the Case every where: The Constables
and their Watchmen kept them off at a Distance, and Parly'd
with them; they gave the same Account of themselves as

before, but these gave no Credit to what they said, giving it for a Reason that two or three Companies had already come that Way and made the like Pretences, but that they had given several People the Distemper in the Towns where they had pass'd, and had been afterwards so hardly us'd by the Country, tho' with Justice too, as they had deserv'd; that about *Brent-Wood* or that Way, several of them Perish'd in the Fields, whether of the Plague, or of mere Want and Distress, they could not tell.

This was a good Reason indeed why the People of *Waltham-stow* shou'd be very cautious, and why they shou'd resolve not to entertain any Body that they were not well satisfied of. But as *Richard* the Joyner, and one of the other Men who parly'd with them told them, it was no Reason why they should block up the Roads, and refuse to let People pass thro' the Town, and who ask'd nothing of them, but to go through the Street: That if their People were afraid of them, they might go into their Houses and shut their Doors, they would neither show them Civility nor Incivility, but go on about their Business.

The Constables and Attendants, not to be perswaded by Reason, continued Obstinate, and wou'd hearken to nothing; so the two Men that talk'd with them went back to their Fellows, to consult what was to be done: It was very discouraging in the whole, and they knew not what to do for a good while: But at last *John* the Soldier and Biscuit-Baker considering a-while, Come, says he, leave the rest of the Parly to me; he had not appear'd yet, so he sets the Joyner *Richard* to Work to cut some Poles out of the Trees, and shape them as like Guns as he could, and in a little time he had five or six fair Muskets, which at a Distance would not be known; and about the Part where the Lock of a Gun is he caused them to wrap Cloths and Rags, such as they had, as Soldiers do in wet Weather, to preserve the Locks of their Pieces from Rust, the rest was discolour'd with Clay or Mud, such as they could get; and all this while the rest of them sat under the Trees by his Direction, in two or three Bodies, where they made Fires at a good Distance from one another.

While this was doing, he advanc'd himself and two or three with him, and set up their Tent in the Lane within sight of the Barrier which the Town's Men had made, and set a Centinel just by it with the real Gun, the only one they had, and who walked to and fro with the Gun on his Shoulder, so as that the People of the Town might see them; also he ty'd the Horse to a Gate in the Hedge just by, and got some dry Sticks together and kindled a Fire on the other side of the Tent, so that the People of the Town cou'd see the Fire and the Smoak, but cou'd not see what they were doing at it.

After the Country People had look'd upon them very earnestly a great while, and by all that they could see, cou'd not but suppose that they were a great many in Company, they began to be uneasie, not for their going away, but for staying where they were; and above all perceiving they had Horses and Arms, for they had seen one Horse and one Gun at the Tent, and they had seen others of them walk about the Field on the inside of the Hedge, by the side of the Lane with their Muskets, as they took them to be, Shoulder'd: I say, upon such a Sight as this, you may be assured they were Alarm'd and terribly Frighted; and it seems they went to a Justice of the Peace to know what they should do; what the Justice advis'd them to I know not, but towards Evening they call'd from the Barrier, as above, to the Centinel at the Tent.

What do ye want? says *John**

Why, what do ye intend to do? says the Constable.

To do, says John, *What wou'd you have us to do?*

Const. Why don't you be gone? what do you stay there for?

John. Why do you stop us on the King's Highway,[1] and pretend to refuse us Leave to go on our Way?

Const. We are not bound to tell you our Reason, though we did let you know, it was because of the Plague.

* It seems *John* was in the Tent, but hearing them call he steps out, and taking the Gun upon his Shoulder, talk'd to them as if he had been the Centinel plac'd there upon the Guard by some Officer that was his Superior.

John. We told you we were all sound, and free from the Plague, which we were not bound to have satisfied you of, and yet you pretend to stop us on the Highway.

Const. We have a Right to stop it up, and our own Safety obliges us to it; besides this is not the King's Highway, 'tis a Way upon Sufferance; you see here is a Gate, and if we do let People pass here, we make them pay Toll.

John. We have a Right to seek our own Safety as well as you, and you may see we are flying for our Lives, and 'tis very unchristian and unjust to stop us.

Const. You may go back from whence you came; we do not hinder you from that.

John. No, it is a stronger Enemy than you that keeps us from doing that; or else we should not ha' come hither.

Const. Well, you may go any other way then.

John. No, no: I suppose you see we are able to send you going, and all the People of your Parish, and come thro' your Town, when we will; but since you have stopt us here, we are content; you see, we have encamp'd here, and here we will live: we hope you will furnish us with Victuals.

Const. We furnish you! What mean you by that?

John. Why you would not have us Starve, would you? If you stop us here, you must keep us.

Const. You will be ill kept at our Maintenance.

John. If you stint us, we shall make ourselves the better Allowance.

Const. Why you will not pretend to quarter upon us by Force, will you?

John. We have offer'd no Violence to you yet, why do you seem to oblige us to it? I am an old Soldier, and cannot starve, and if you think that we shall be obliged to go back for want of Provisions, you are mistaken.

Const. Since you threaten us, we shall take Care to be strong enough for you: I have Orders to raise the County upon you.

John. It is you that threaten, not we: And since you are

for Mischief, you cannot blame us, if we do not give you time for it; we shall begin our March in a few Minutes.*

Const. What is it you demand of us?

John. At first we desir'd nothing of you, but Leave to go thro' the Town; we should have offer'd no Injury to any of you, neither would you have had any Injury or Loss by us. We are not Thieves, but poor People in distress, and flying from the dreadful Plague in *London*, which devours thousands every Week: We wonder how you could be so unmerciful!

Const. Self-preservation obliges us.

John. What! to shut up your Compassion in a Case of such Distress as this?

Const. Well, if you will pass over the Fields on your Left-hand, and behind that part of the Town, I will endeavour to have Gates open'd for you.

John. Our Horsemen cannot† pass with our Baggage that Way; it does not lead into the Road that we want to go; and why should you force us out of the Road? besides, you have kept us here all Day without any Provisions, but such as we brought with us; I think you ought to send us some Provisions for our Relief.

Const. If you will go another Way, we will send you some Provisions.

John. That is the way to have all the Towns in the County stop up the Ways against us.

Const. If they all furnish you with Food, what will you be the worse, I see you have Tents, you want no Lodging.

John. Well, what quantity of Provisions will you send us?

Const. How many are you?

John. Nay, we do not ask enough for all our Company, we are in three Companies; if you will send us Bread for twenty Men, and about six or seven Women for three Days, and shew us the Way over the Field you speak of, we desire not to put your People into any fear for us, we will go out of

---

* This frighted the Constable and the People that were with him, that they immediately chang'd their Note.

† They had but one Horse among them.

our Way to oblige you, tho' we are as free from Infection as you are.

Const. And will you assure us that your other People shall offer us no new Disturbance.

John. No, no, you may depend on it.

Const. You must oblige your self too that none of your People shall come a step nearer than where the Provisions we send you shall be set down.

John. I answer for it we will not.*

Accordingly they sent to the Place twenty Loaves of Bread, and three or four large pieces of good Beef, and opened some Gates thro' which they pass'd, but none of them had Courage so much as to look out to see them go, and, as it was Evening, if they had looked they cou'd not have seen them so as to know how few they were.

This was *John* the Soldier's Management. But this gave such an Alarm to the County, that had they really been two or three Hundred, the whole County would have been rais'd upon them, and they wou'd ha' been sent to Prison, or perhaps knock'd on the Head.

They were soon made sensible of this, for two Days afterwards they found several Parties of Horsemen and Footmen also about, in pursuit of three Companies of Men arm'd, *as they said*, with Muskets, who were broke out from *London*, and had the Plague upon them; and that were not only spreading the Distemper among the People, but plundering the Country.

As they saw now the Consequence of their Case, they soon saw the Danger they were in, so they resolv'd by the Advice also of the old Soldier, to divide themselves again. *John* and his two Comrades with the Horse, went away as if towards *Waltham*; the other in two Companies, but all a little asunder, and went towards *Epping*.

The first Night they Encamp'd all in the Forest, and not

* Here he call'd to one of his Men, and bade him order Capt. *Richard* and his People to March the Lower Way on the side of the Marshes, and meet them in the Forest; which was all a Sham, for they had no Captain *Richard*, or any such Company.

far off of one another, but not setting up the Tent, lest that should discover them: On the other hand *Richard* went to work with his Axe and his Hatchet, and cutting down Branches of Trees, he built three Tents or Hovels, in which they all Encamp'd with as much Convenience as they could expect.

The Provisions they had had at *Walthamstow* serv'd them very plentifully this Night, and as for the next they left it to Providence; they had far'd so well with the old Soldier's Conduct, that they now willingly made him their Leader; and the first of his Conduct appear'd to be very good: He told them that they were now at a proper Distance enough from *London*; that as they need not be immediately beholden to the County for Relief, so they ought to be as careful the Country did not infect them, as that they did not infect the Country; that what little Money they had they must be as frugal of as they could; that as he would not have them think of offering the Country any Violence, so they must endeavour to make the Sense of their Condition go as far with the Country as it could: They all referr'd themselves to his Direction; so they left their 3 Houses standing, and the next Day went away towards *Epping*; the Captain also, for so they now called him, and his two Fellow Travellers laid aside their Design of going to *Waltham*, and all went together.

When they came near *Epping* they halted, choosing out a proper Place in the open Forest, not very near the High-way, but not far out of it on the North-side, under a little cluster of low Pollard-Trees: Here they pitched their little Camp, which consisted of three large Tents or Hutts made of Poles, which their Carpenter, and such as were his Assistants, cut down and fix'd in the Ground in a Circle, binding all the small Ends together at the Top, and thickning the sides with Boughs of Trees and Bushes, so that they were compleatly close and warm. They had besides this, a little Tent where the Women lay by themselves, and a Hutt to put the Horse in.

It happened that the next day, or next but one was Market-day at *Epping*; when Capt. *John*, and one of the other Men, went to Market, and bought some Provisions, that is to say

Bread, and some Mutton and Beef; and two of the Women went separately, as if they had not belong'd to the rest, and bought more. *John* took the Horse to bring it Home, and the Sack (which the Carpenter carry'd his Tools in) to put it in: The Carpenter went to Work and made them Benches and Stools to sit on, such as the Wood he cou'd get wou'd afford, and a kind of a Table to dine on.

They were taken no Notice of for two or three Days, but after that, abundance of People ran out of the Town to look at them, and all the Country was alarmed about them. The People at first seem'd afraid to come near them, and on the other Hand they desir'd the People to keep off, for there was a Rumour that the Plague was at *Waltham*, and that it had been in *Epping* two or three Days. So *John* called out to them not to come to them, *For*, says he, *we are all whole and sound People here, and we would not have you bring the Plague among us, nor pretend we brought it among you.*

After this the Parish Officers came up to them and parly'd with them at a Distance, and desir'd to know who they were, and by what Authority they pretended to fix their Stand at that Place? *John* answered very frankly, they were poor distressed People from *London*, who foreseeing the Misery they should be reduc'd to, if the Plague spread into the City, had fled out in time for their Lives, and having no Acquaintance or Relations to fly to, had first taken up at *Islington*, but the Plague being come into that Town, were fled further, and as they suppos'd that the People of *Epping* might have refus'd them coming into their Town, they had pitch'd their Tents thus in the open Field, and in the Forest, being willing to bear all the Hardships of such a disconsolate Lodging, rather than have any one think or be afraid that they should receive Injury by them.

At first the *Epping* People talk'd roughly to them, and told them they must remove; that this was no Place for them; and that they pretended to be Sound and Well, but that they might be infected with the Plague for ought they knew, and might infect the whole Country, and they cou'd not suffer them there.

John argu'd very calmly with them a great while, and told them, 'That *London* was the Place by which they, that is, the Townsmen of *Epping* and all the Country round them, subsisted; to whom they sold the produce of their Lands, and out of whom they made the Rent of their Farms; and to be so cruel to the Inhabitants of *London*, or to any of those by whom they gain'd so much was very hard, and they would be loth to have it remembered hereafter, and have it told how barbarous, how unhospitable and how unkind they were to the People of *London*, when they fled from the Face of the most terrible Enemy in the World; that it would be enough to make the Name of an *Epping*-Man hateful thro' all the City, and to have the Rabble Stone them in the very Streets, whenever they came so much as to Market; that they were not yet secure from being Visited themselves, and that as he heard, *Waltham* was already; that they would think it very hard that when any of them fled for Fear before they were touch'd, they should be deny'd the Liberty of lying so much as in the open Fields.'

The *Epping* Men told them again, That they, indeed, said they were sound and free from the Infection, but that they had no assurance of it; and that it was reported, that there had been a great Rabble of People at *Walthamstow*, who made such Pretences of being sound, as they did, but that they threaten'd to plunder the Town, and force their Way whether the Parish Officers would or no; That they were near 200 of them, and had Arms and Tents like Low-Country Soldiers; that they extorted Provisions from the Town by threatning them with living upon them at free Quarter, shewing their Arms, and talking in the Language of Soldiers; and that several of them being gone away towards *Rumford* and *Brent-Wood*, the Country had been infected by them, and the Plague spread into both those large Towns, so that the People durst not go to Market there as usual; that it was very likely they were some of that Party, and if so, they deserv'd to be sent to the County Jail, and be secur'd till they had made Satisfaction for the Damage they had done, and for the Terror and Fright they had put the Country into.

John answered, That what other People had done was nothing to them; that he assured them they were all of one Company; that they had never been more in Number than they saw them at that time; (which by the way was very true) that they came out in two separate Companies, but joyn'd by the Way, their Cases being the same; that they were ready to give what Account of themselves any Body cou'd desire of them, and to give in their Names and Places of Abode, that so they might be call'd to an Account for any Disorder that they might be guilty of; that the Townsmen might see they were content to live hardly, and only desir'd a little Room to breathe in on the Forest where it was wholsome, for where it was not they cou'd not stay, and wou'd decamp if they found it otherwise there.

But, said the Townsmen, we have a great charge of Poor upon our Hands already, and we must take care not to encrease it; we suppose you can give us no Security against your being chargeable to our Parish and to the Inhabitants, any more than you can of being dangerous to us as to the Infection.

'Why look you, *says John*, as to being chargeable to you, we hope we shall not; if you will relieve us with Provisions for our present Necessity, we will be very thankful; as we all liv'd without Charity when we were at Home, so we will oblige ourselves fully to repay you, if God please to bring us back to our own Families and Houses in Safety, and to restore Health to the People of *London*.

'As to our dying here, we assure you, if any of us die, we that survive, will bury them, and put you to no Expence, except it should be that we should all die, and then indeed the last Man not being able to bury himself, would put you to that single Expence, which I am perswaded, says *John*, he would leave enough behind him to pay you for the Expence of.

'On the other Hand, says *John*, if you will shut up all Bowels of Compassion and not relieve us at all, we shall not extort any thing by Violence, or steal from any one; but when what little we have is spent, if we perish for want, God's Will be done.'

John wrought so upon the Townsmen by talking thus rationally and smoothly to them, that they went away; and tho' they did not give any consent to their staying there, yet they did not molest them; and the poor People continued there three or four Days longer without any Disturbance. In this time they had got some remote Acquaintance with a Victualling-House at the out-skirts of the Town, to whom they called at a Distance to bring some little Things that they wanted, and which they caus'd to be set down at a Distance, and always paid for very honestly.

During this Time, the younger People of the Town came frequently pretty near them, and wou'd stand and look at them, and sometimes talk with them at some Space between; and particularly it was observed, that the first Sabbath Day the poor People kept retir'd, worship'd God together, and were heard to sing Psalms.

These Things and a quiet inoffensive Behaviour, began to get them the good Opinion of the Country, and People began to pity them and speak very well of them; the Consequence of which was, that upon the occasion of a very wet rainy Night, a certain Gentleman who liv'd in the Neighbourhood, sent them a little Cart with twelve Trusses or Bundles of Straw, as well for them to lodge upon, as to cover and thatch their Huts, and to keep them dry: The Minister of a Parish not far off, not knowing of the other, sent them also about two Bushels of Wheat, and half a Bushel of white Peas.

They were very thankful to-be-sure for this Relief, and particularly the Straw was a very great Comfort to them; for tho' the ingenious Carpenter had made Frames for them to lie in like Troughs, and fill'd them with Leaves of Trees, and such Things as they could get, and had cut all their Tent-cloth out to make them Coverlids, yet they lay damp, and hard, and unwholesome till this Straw came, which was to them like Feather-beds, and, as *John* said, more welcome than Feather-beds wou'd ha' been at another time.

This Gentleman and the Minister having thus begun and given an Example of Charity to these Wanderers, others quickly followed, and they receiv'd every Day some Benevolence or other from the People, but chiefly from the Gentlemen who dwelt in the Country round about; some sent them Chairs, Stools, Tables, and such Houshold Things as they gave Notice they wanted; some sent them Blankets, Rugs and Coverlids; some Earthen-ware; and some Kitchin-ware for ordering their Food.

Encourag'd by this good Usage, their Carpenter in a few Days, built them a large Shed or House with Rafters, and a Roof in Form, and an upper Floor in which they lodged warm, for the Weather began to be damp and cold in the beginning of *September*; But this House being very well Thatch'd, and the Sides and Roof made very thick, kept out the Cold well enough: He made also an earthen Wall at one End, with a Chimney in it; and another of the Company, with a vast deal of Trouble and Pains, made a Funnel to the Chimney to carry out the Smoak.

Here they liv'd very comfortably, tho' coarsely, till the beginning of *September*, when they had the bad News to hear, whether true or not, that the Plague, which was very hot at *Waltham-Abby* on one side, and at *Rumford* and *Brent-Wood* on the other side; was also come to *Epping*, to *Woodford*, and to most of the Towns upon the Forest, and which, as they said, was brought down among them chiefly by the Higlers[1] and such People as went to and from *London* with Provisions.

If this was true, it was an evident Contradiction to that Report which was afterwards spread all over *England*, but which, *as I have said*, I cannot confirm of my own Knowledge, namely, That the Market People carrying Provisions to the City, never got the Infection or carry'd it back into the Country; both which I have been assured, has been false.

It might be that they were preserv'd even beyond Expectation, though not to a Miracle, that abundance went and come, and were not touch'd, and that was much for the Encouragement of the poor People of *London*, who had been compleatly miserable, if the People that brought Provisions to the Markets had not been many times wonderfully preserv'd, or at least more preserv'd than cou'd be reasonably expected.

But now these new Inmates began to be disturb'd more effectually, for the Towns about them were really infected, and they began to be afraid to trust one another so much as to go abroad for such things as they wanted, and this pinch'd them very hard; for now they had little or nothing but what the charitable Gentlemen of the Country supply'd them with: But for their Encouragement it happen'd, that other Gentlemen in the Country who had not sent 'em any thing before, began to hear of them and supply them, and one sent them a large Pig, that is to say a Porker; another two Sheep; and another sent them a Calf: In short, they had Meat enough, and, sometimes had Cheese and Milk, and all such things; They were chiefly put to it for Bread, for when the Gentlemen sent them Corn they had no where to bake it, or to grind it: This made them eat the first two Bushel of Wheat that was sent them in parched Corn, as the *Israelites* of old did without grinding or making Bread of it.[1]

At last they found means to carry their Corn to a Windmill near *Woodford*, where they had it ground; and afterwards the Biscuit Baker made a Hearth so hollow and dry that he cou'd bake Biscuit Cakes tolerably well; and thus they came into a Condition to live without any assistance or supplies from the Towns; and it was well they did, for the Country was soon after fully Infected, and about 120 were said to have died of the Distemper in the Villages near them, which was a terrible thing to them.

On this they call'd a new Council, and now the Towns had no need to be afraid they should settle near them, but on the contrary several Families of the poorer sort of the Inhabitants quitted their Houses, and built Hutts in the Forest after the same manner as they had done: But it was observ'd, that several of these poor People that had so remov'd, had the Sickness even in their Hutts or Booths; the Reason of which was plain, namely, not because they removed into the Air, but because they did not remove time enough, that is to say, not till by openly conversing with the other People their Neighbours, they had the Distemper upon them, or, (as may be said) among them, and so carry'd it about them whither they went: Or, (2.) Because they were not careful enough after they were safely removed out of the Towns, not to come in again and mingle with the diseased People.

But be it which of these it will, when our Travellers began to perceive that the Plague was not only in the Towns, but even in the Tents and Huts on the Forest near them, they began then not only to be afraid, but to think of decamping and removing; for had they stay'd, they wou'd ha' been in manifest Danger of their Lives.

It is not to be wondered that they were greatly afflicted, as being obliged to quit the Place where they had been so kindly receiv'd, and where they had been treated with so much Humanity and Charity; but Necessity, and the hazard of Life, which they came out so far to preserve, prevail'd with them, and they saw no Remedy. *John* however thought of a Remedy for their present Misfortune, namely, that he would first acquaint that Gentleman who was their principal Benefactor, with the Distress they were in, and to crave his Assistance and Advice.

The good charitable Gentleman encourag'd them to quit the Place, for fear they should be cut off from any Retreat at all, by the Violence of the Distemper; but whither they should go, that he found very hard to direct them to. At last *John* ask'd of him, whether he (being a Justice of the Peace) would give them Certificates of Health to other Justices who they might come before, that so whatever might be their Lot they might not be repulsed now they had been also so long from *London*. This his Worship immediately granted, and gave them proper Letters of Health, and from thence they were at Liberty to travel whither they pleased.

Accordingly they had a full Certificate of Health, intimating, That they had resided in a Village in the County of *Essex* so long, that being examined and scrutiniz'd sufficiently, and having been retir'd from all Conversation for above 40 Days, without any appearance of Sickness, they were therefore certainly concluded to be Sound Men, and might be safely entertain'd any where, having at last remov'd rather for fear of the Plague, which was come into *such a Town*, rather than for having any signal of Infection upon them, or upon any belonging to them.

With this Certificate they remov'd, tho' with great Reluctance; and *John* inclining not to go far from Home, they mov'd towards the Marshes on the side of *Waltham*: But here they found a Man, who it seems kept a Weer or Stop upon the River, made to raise the Water for the Barges which go up and down the River, and he terrified them with dismal Stories of the Sickness having been spread into all the Towns on the River, and near the River, on the side of *Middlesex* and *Hertfordshire*; that is to say, into *Waltham*, *Waltham-Cross*, *Enfield* and *Ware*, and all the Towns on the Road, that they were afraid to go that way; tho' it seems the Man impos'd upon them, for that the thing was not really true.

However it terrified them, and they resolved to move cross the Forest towards *Rumford* and *Brent-Wood*; but they heard that there were numbers of People fled out of *London* that way, who lay up and down in the Forest call'd *Henalt* Forest, reaching near *Rumford*, and who having no Subsistence of Habitation, not only liv'd oddly, and suffered great Extremities in the Woods and Fields for want of Relief, but were said to be made so desperate by those Extremities, as that they offer'd many Violences to the County, robb'd and plunder'd, and kill'd Cattle, and the like; that others building Hutts and Hovels by the Road-side Begg'd, and that with an Importunity next Door to demanding Relief; so that the County was very uneasy, and had been oblig'd to take some of them up.

This, in the first Place intimated to them, that they would be sure to find the Charity and Kindness of the County, which they had found here where they were before, hardned and shut up against them; and that on the other Hand, they would be question'd where-ever they came, and would be in Danger of Violence from others in like Cases as themselves.

Upon all these Considerations, *John*, their Captain, in all their Names, went back to their good Friend and Benefactor, who had reliev'd them before, and laying their Case truly before him, humbly ask'd his Advice; and he as kindly advised them to take up their old Quarters again, or if not, to remove but a little further out of the Road, and directed them to a proper Place for them; and as they really wanted some House rather than Huts to shelter them at that time of the Year, it growing on towards *Michaelmas*, they found an old decay'd House, which had been formerly some Cottage or little Habitation, but was so out of repair as scarce habitable, and by the consent of a Farmer to whose Farm it belong'd, they got leave to make what use of it they could.

The ingenious Joyner and all the rest by his Directions, went to work with it, and in a very few Days made it capable to shelter them all in case of bad Weather, and in which there was an old Chimney, and an old Oven, tho' both lying in Ruins, yet they made them both fit for Use, and raising Additions, Sheds, and Leantoo's on every side, they soon made the House capable to hold them all.

They chiefly wanted Boards to make Window-shutters, Floors, Doors, and several other Things; but as the Gentlemen above favour'd them, and the Country was by that Means made easy with them, and above all, that they were known to be all sound and in good health, every Body help'd them with what they could spare.

Here they encamp'd for good and all, and resolv'd to remove no more; they saw plainly how terribly alarm'd that County was every where, at any Body that came from *London*; and that they should have no admittance any where but with the utmost Difficulty, at least no friendly Reception and Assistance as they had receiv'd here.

Now altho' they receiv'd great Assistance and Encouragement from the Country Gentlemen and from the People round about them, yet they were put to great Straits, for the Weather grew cold and wet in *October* and *November*, and they had not been us'd to so much hardship; so that they got

Colds in their Limbs, and Distempers, but never had the Infection: And thus about *December* they came home to the City again.

I give this Story thus at large, principally to give an Account what became of the great Numbers of People which immediately appear'd in the City as soon as the Sickness abated: For, as I have said, great Numbers of those that were able and had Retreats in the Country, fled to those Retreats; So when it was encreased to such a frightful Extremity as I have related, the midling People who had not Friends, fled to all Parts of the Country where they cou'd get shelter, as well those that had Money to relieve themselves; as those that had not. Those that had Mony always fled farthest, because they were able to subsist themselves; but those who were empty, suffer'd, as I have said, great Hardships, and were often driven by Necessity to relieve their Wants at the Expence of the Country: By that Means the Country was made very uneasie at them, and sometimes took them up, tho' even then they scarce knew what to do with them, and were always very backward to punish them, but often too they forced them from Place to Place, till they were oblig'd to come back again to *London*.

I have, since my knowing this Story of *John* and his Brother, enquir'd and found, that there were a great many of the poor disconsolate People, as above, fled into the Country every way, and some of them got little Sheds, and Barns, and Out-houses to live in, where they cou'd obtain so much Kindness of the Country, and especially where they had any the least satisfactory Account to give of themselves, and particularly that they did not come out of *London* too late. But others, and that in great Numbers, built themselves little Hutts and Retreats in the Fields and Woods, and liv'd like Hermits in Holes and Caves, or any Place they cou'd find; and where, we may be sure, they suffer'd great Extremities, such that many of them were oblig'd to come back again whatever the Danger was; and so those little Huts were often found empty, and the Country People suppos'd the Inhabitants lay Dead in them of the Plague, and would not go near them for fear, no not in a great while; nor is it unlikely but that some of the unhappy Wanderers might die so all alone, even sometimes for want of Help, as particularly in one Tent or Hutt, was found a Man dead, and on the Gate of a Field just by, was cut with his Knife in uneven Letters, the following Words, by which it may be suppos'd the other Man escap'd, or that one dying first, the other bury'd him as well as he could;

O mIsErY!
We BoTH ShaLL DyE,
WoE, WoE.

I have given an Account already of what I found to ha' been the Case down the River among the Sea-faring Men, how the Ships lay in the *Offing*, as 'tis call'd, in Rows or Lines a-stern of one another, quite down from the *Pool* as far as I could see. I have been told, that they lay in the same manner quite down the River as low as *Gravesend*, and some far beyond, even every where, or in every Place where they cou'd ride with Safety as to Wind and Weather; Nor did I ever hear that the Plague reach'd to any of the People on board those Ships, except such as lay up in the *Pool*, or as high as *Deptford* Reach, altho' the People went frequently on Shoar to the Country Towns and Villages, and Farmers Houses, to buy fresh Provisions, Fowls, Pigs, Calves, and the like for their Supply.

Likewise I found that the Watermen on the River above the Bridge, found means to convey themselves away up the River as far as they cou'd go; and that they had, many of them, their whole Families in their Boats, cover'd with Tilts and Bales,[1] as they call them, and furnish'd with Straw within for their Lodging; and that they lay thus all along by the Shoar in the Marshes, some of them setting up little Tents with their Sails, and so lying under them on Shoar in the Day, and going into their Boats at Night; and in this manner, as I have heard, the River-sides were lin'd with Boats and People as long as they had any thing to subsist on, or cou'd get any thing of the

Country; and indeed the Country People, as well Gentlemen as others, on these and all other Occasions, were very forward to relieve them, but they were by no means willing to receive them into their Towns and Houses, and for that we cannot blame them.

There was one unhappy Citizen, within my Knowledge, who had been Visited in a dreadful manner, so that his Wife and all his Children were Dead, and himself and two Servants only left, with an elderly Woman a near Relation, who had nurs'd those that were dead as well as she could: This disconsolate Man goes to a Village near the Town, tho' not within the Bills of Mortality, and finding an empty House there, enquires out the Owner, and took the House: After a few Days he got a Cart and loaded it with Goods, and carries them down to the House; the People of the Village oppos'd his driving the Cart along, but with some Arguings, and some Force, the Men that drove the Cart along, got through the Street up to the Door of the House, there the Constable resisted him again, and would not let them be brought in. The Man caus'd the Goods to be unloaden and lay'd at the Door, and sent the Cart away; upon which they carry'd the Man before a Justice of Peace; that is to say, they commanded him to go, which he did. The Justice order'd him to cause the Cart to fetch away the Goods again, which he refused to do; upon which the Justice order'd the Constable to pursue the Carters and fetch them back, and make them re-load the Goods and carry them away, or to set them in the Stocks till they came for farther Orders; and if they could not find them, nor the Man would not consent to take them away, they should cause them to be drawn with Hooks from the House-Door and burnt in the Street. The poor distress'd Man upon this fetch'd the Goods again, but with grievous Cries and Lamentations at the hardship of his Case. But there was no Remedy; Self-preservation oblig'd the People to those Severities, which they wou'd not otherwise have been concern'd in: Whether this poor Man liv'd or dy'd I cannot tell, but it was reported that he had the Plague upon him at that time; and perhaps the

People might report that to justify their Usage of him; but it was not unlikely, that either he or his Goods, or both, were dangerous, when his whole Family had been dead of the Distemper so little a while before.

I kno' that the Inhabitants of the Towns adjacent to *London*, were much blamed for Cruelty to the poor People that ran from the Contagion in their Distress; and many very severe things were done, as may be seen from what has been said; but I cannot but say also that where there was room for Charity and Assistance to the People, without apparent Danger to themselves, they were willing enough to help and relieve them. But as every Town were indeed Judges in their own Case, so the poor People who ran abroad in their Extremities, were often ill-used and driven back again into the Town; and this caused infinite Exclamations and Out-cries against the Country Towns, and made the Clamour very popular.

And yet more or less, maugre all their Caution, there was not a Town of any Note within ten (or I believe twenty) Miles of the City, but what was more or less Infected, and had some died among them. I have heard the Accounts of several; such as they were reckon'd up as follows.

In *Enfield*	32	*Hertford*	90	*Brent-Wood*	70
In *Hornsey*	58	*Ware*	160	*Rumford*	109
In *Newington*	17	*Hodsdon*	30	*Barking* abt.	200
In *Tottenham*	42	*Waltham* Ab.	23	*Branford*	432
In *Edmonton*	19	*Epping*	26	*Kingston*	122
In *Barnet* and		*Deptford*	623	*Stanes*	82
Hadly	43	*Greenwich*	231	*Chertsey*	18
In St. *Albans*	121	*Eltham* and		*Windsor*	103
In *Watford*	45	*Lusum*	85		
In *Uxbridge*	117	*Croydon*	61	*cum aliis.*	

Another thing might render the Country more strict with respect to the Citizens, and especially with respect to the Poor; and this was what I hinted at before, namely, that there was a seeming propensity, or a wicked Inclination in those that were Infected to infect others.

There have been great Debates among our Physicians, as to the Reason of this; some will have it to be in the Nature of the Disease, and that it impresses every one that is seized upon by it, with a kind of a Rage, and a hatred against their own Kind, as if there was a malignity, not only in the Distemper to communicate it self, but in the very Nature of Man, prompting him with evil Will, or an evil Eye, that *as they say* in the Case of a mad Dog, who tho' the gentlest Creature before of any of his Kind, yet then will fly upon and bite any one that comes next him and those as soon as any, who had been most observ'd by him before.

Others plac'd it to the Account of the Coruption of humane Nature, which cannot bear to see itself more miserable than others of its own Species, and has a kind of involuntary Wish, that all Men were as unhappy, or in as bad a Condition as itself.

Others say, it was only a kind of Desperation, not knowing or regarding what they did, and consequently unconcern'd at the Danger or Safety, not only of any Body near them, but even of themselves also: And indeed when Men are once come to a Condition to abandon themselves, and be unconcern'd for the Safety, or at the Danger of themselves, it cannot be so much wondered that they should be careless of the Safety of other People.

But I choose to give this grave Debate a quite different turn, and answer it or resolve it all by saying, *That I do not grant the Fact.* On the contrary, I say, that the Thing is not really so, but that it was a general Complaint rais'd by the People inhabiting the out-lying Villages against the Citizens, to justify, or at least excuse those Hardships and Severities so much talk'd of, and in which Complaints, both Sides may be said to have injur'd one another; that is to say, the Citizens pressing to be received and harbour'd in time of Distress, and with the Plague upon them, complain of the Cruelty and Injustice of the Country People, in being refused Entrance, and forc'd back again with their Goods and Families; and the Inhabitants finding themselves so imposed upon, and the Citizens breaking in as it were upon them whether they would

or no, complain, that when they were infected, they were not
only regardless of others, but even willing to infect them;
neither of which were really true, that is to say, in the Colours
they were describ'd in.

It is true, there is something to be said for the frequent
Alarms which were given to the Country, of the resolution of
the People in *London* to come out by Force, not only for Relief,
but to Plunder and Rob, that they ran about the Streets with
the Distemper upon them without any control; and that no
Care was taken to shut up Houses, and confine the sick People
from infecting others; whereas, to do the *Londoners* Justice,
they never practised such things, except in such particular
Cases as I have mention'd above, and such-like. On the other
Hand every thing was managed with so much Care, and such
excellent Order was observ'd in the whole City and Suburbs,
by the Care of the Lord Mayor and Aldermen; and by the
Justices of the Peace, Churchwardens, *&c.* in the out-Parts;
that *London* may be a Pattern to all the Cities in the World for
the good Government and the excellent Order that was every
where kept, even in the time of the most violent Infection;
and when the People were in the utmost Consternation and
Distress. But of this I shall speak by itself.

One thing, it is to be observ'd, was owing principally to the
Prudence of the Magistrates, and ought to be mention'd to
their Honour, (*viz.*) The Moderation which they used in the
great and difficult Work of shutting up of Houses: It is true,
as I have mentioned, that the shutting up of Houses was a
great Subject of Discontent, and I may say indeed the only
Subject of Discontent among the People at that time; for the
confining the Sound in the same House with the Sick, was
counted very terrible, and the Complaints of People so confin'd were very grievous; they were heard into the very Streets,
and they were sometimes such that called for Resentment, tho'
oftner for Compassion; they had no way to converse with any
of their Friends but out at their Windows, where they wou'd
make such piteous Lamentations, as often mov'd the Hearts of
those they talk'd with, and of others who passing by heard

their Story; and as those Complaints oftentimes reproach'd the Severity, and sometimes the Insolence of the Watchmen plac'd at their Doors, those Watchmen wou'd answer saucily enough; and perhaps be apt to affront the People who were in the Street talking to the said Families; for which, or for their ill Treatment of the Families, I think seven or eight of them in several Places were kill'd; I know not whether I shou'd say murthered or not, because I cannot enter into the particular Cases. It is true, the Watchmen were on their Duty, and acting in the Post where they were plac'd by a lawful Authority; and killing any publick legal Officer in the Execution of his Office, is always in the Language of the Law call'd Murther. But as they were not authoriz'd by the Magistrate's Instructions, or by the Power they acted under, to be injurious or abusive, either to the People who were under their Observation, or to any that concern'd themselves for them; so when they did so, they might be said to act themselves, not their Office; to act as private Persons, not as Persons employ'd; and consequently if they brought Mischief upon themselves by such an undue Behaviour, that Mischief was upon their own Heads; and indeed they had so much the hearty Curses of the People, whether they deserv'd it or not, that whatever befel them no body pitied them, and every Body was apt to say, they deserv'd it, whatever it was; nor do I remember that any Body was ever punish'd, at least to any considerable Degree, for whatever was done to the Watchmen that guarded their Houses.

What variety of Stratagems were used to escape and get out of Houses thus shut up, by which the Watchmen were deceived or overpower'd, and that the People got away, I have taken notice of already, and shall say no more to that: But I say the Magistrates did moderate and ease Families upon many Occasions in this Case, and particularly in that of taking away, or suffering to be remov'd the sick Persons out of such Houses, when they were willing to be remov'd either to a Pest-House, or other Places, and sometimes giving the well Persons in the Family so shut up, leave to remove upon Information given that they were well, and that they would confine themselves in such Houses where they went, so long as should be requir'd of them. The Concern also of the Magistrates for the supplying such poor Families as were infected; I say, supplying them with Necessaries, as well Physick as Food, was very great, and in which they did not content themselves with giving the necessary Orders to the Officers appointed, but the Aldermen in Person, and on Horseback frequently rid to such Houses, and caus'd the People to be ask'd at their Windows, whether they were duly attended, or not? Also, whether they wanted any thing that was necessary, and if the Officers had constantly carry'd their Messages, and fetch'd them such things as they wanted, or not? And if they answered in the Affirmative, all was well; but if they complain'd, that they were ill supply'd, and that the Officer did not do his Duty, or did not treat them civilly, they (the Officers) were generally remov'd, and others plac'd in their stead.

It is true, such Complaint might be unjust, and if the Officer had such Arguments to use as would convince the Magistrate, that he was right, and that the People had injur'd him, he was continued, and they reproved. But this part could not well bear a particular Inquiry, for the Parties could very ill be brought face to face, and a Complaint could not be well heard and answer'd in the Street, from the Windows, as was the Case then; the Magistrates therefore generally chose to favour the People, and remove the Man, as what seem'd to be the least Wrong, and of the least ill Consequence; seeing, if the Watchman was injur'd yet they could readily make him amends by giving him another Post of the like Nature; but if the Family was injur'd, there was no Satisfaction could be made to them, the Damage perhaps being irreparable, as it concern'd their Lives.

A great variety of these Cases frequently happen'd between the Watchmen and the poor People shut up, besides those I formerly mention'd about escaping; sometimes the Watchmen were absent, sometimes drunk, sometimes asleep when the People wanted them, and such never fail'd to be punish'd severely, as indeed they deserv'd.

But after all that was or could be done in these Cases, the shutting up of Houses, so as to confine those that were well with those that were sick, had very great Inconveniences in it, and some that were very tragical, and which merited to have been consider'd if there had been room for it; but it was authoriz'd by a Law, it had the publick Good in view, as the End chiefly aim'd at, and all the private Injuries that were done by the putting it in Execution, must be put to the account of the publick Benefit.

It is doubtful to this day, whether in the whole it contributed any thing to the stop of the Infection, and indeed, I cannot say it did; for nothing could run with greater Fury and Rage than the Infection did when it was in its chief Violence; tho' the Houses infected were shut up as exactly, and as effectually as it was possible. Certain it is, that if all the infected Persons were effectually shut in, no sound Person could have been infected by them, because they could not have come near them. But the Case was this, and I shall only touch it here, namely, that the Infection was propagated insensibly, and by such Persons as were not visibly infected, who neither knew who they infected, or who they were infected by.

A House in *White-Chapel* was shut up for the sake of one Infected Maid, who had only Spots, not the Tokens come out upon her, and recover'd; yet these People obtain'd no Liberty to stir, neither for Air or Exercise forty Days; want of Breath, Fear, Anger, Vexation, and all the other Griefs attending such an injurious Treatment, cast the Mistress of the Family into a Fever, and Visitors came into the House, and said it was the Plague, tho' the Physicians declar'd it was not; however the Family were oblig'd to begin their Quarantine anew, on the Report of the Visitor or Examiner, tho' their former Quarantine wanted but a few Days of being finish'd. This oppress'd them so with Anger and Grief, and, *as before*, straiten'd them also so much as to Room, and for want of Breathing and free Air, that most of the Family fell sick, one of one Distemper, one of another, chiefly Scorbutick Ailments; *only one a violent Cholick*, 'till after several prolongings of their

Confinement, some or other of those that came in with the Visitors to inspect the Persons that were ill, in hopes of releasing them, brought the Distemper with them, and infected the whole House, and all or most of them died, not of the Plague, as really upon them before, but of the Plague that those People brought them, who should ha' been careful to have protected them from it; and this was a thing which frequently happen'd, and was indeed one of the worst Consequences of shutting Houses up.

I had about this time a little Hardship put upon me, which I was at first greatly afflicted at, and very much disturb'd about; tho' as it prov'd, it did not expose me to any Disaster; and this was being appointed by the Alderman of *Portsoken* Ward, one of the Examiners of the Houses in the Precinct where I liv'd; we had a large Parish, and had no less than eighteen Examiners, as the Order call'd us, the People call'd us Visitors. I endeavour'd with all my might to be excus'd from such an Employment, and used many Arguments with the Alderman's Deputy to be excus'd; particularly I alledged, that I was against shutting up Houses at all, and that it would be very hard to oblige me, to be an Instrument in that which was against my Judgment, and which I did verily believe would not answer the End it was intended for, but all the Abatement I could get was only, that whereas the Officer was appointed by my Lord Mayor to continue two Months, I should be obliged to hold it but three Weeks, on Condition, nevertheless that I could then get some other sufficient House-keeper to serve the rest of the Time for me, which was, in short, but a very small Favour, it being very difficult to get any Man to accept of such an Employment, that was fit to be intrusted with it.

It is true that shutting up of Houses had one Effect, which I am sensible was of Moment, namely, it confin'd the distemper'd People, who would otherwise have been both very troublesome and very dangerous in their running about Streets with the Distemper upon them, which when they were delirious, they would have done in a most frightful manner;

and as indeed they began to do at first very much, 'till they were thus restrain'd; nay, so very open they were, that the Poor would go about and beg at peoples Doors, and say they had the Plague upon them, and beg Rags for their Sores, or both, or any thing that delirious Nature happen'd to think of.

A poor unhappy Gentlewoman, a substantial Citizen's Wife was (if the Story be true) murther'd by one of these Creatures in *Aldersgate-street*, or that Way: He was going along the Street, raving mad to be sure, and singing, the People only said, he was drunk; but he himself said, he had the Plague upon him, which, it seems, was true; and meeting this Gentlewoman, he would kiss her; she was terribly frighted as he was only a rude Fellow, and she run from him, but the Street being very thin of People, there was no body near enough to help her: When she saw he would overtake her, she turn'd, and gave him a Thrust so forcibly, he being but weak, and push'd him down backward: But very unhappily, she being so near, he caught hold of her, and pull'd her down also; and getting up first, master'd her, and kiss'd her; and which was worst of all, when he had done, told her he had the Plague, and why should not she have it as well as he. She was frighted enough before, being also young with Child; but when she heard him say, he had the Plague, she scream'd out and fell down in a Swoon, or in a Fit, which tho' she recover'd a little, yet kill'd her in a very few Days, and I never heard whether she had the Plague or no.

Another infected Person came, and knock'd at the Door of a Citizen's House, where they knew him very well; the Servant let him in, and being told the Master of the House was above, he ran up, and came into the Room to them as the whole Family was at supper: They began to rise up a little surpriz'd, not knowing what the Matter was, but he bid them sit still, he only came to take his leave of them. They ask'd him, Why Mr. —— where are you going? Going, says he, I have got the Sickness, and shall die to morrow Night. 'Tis easie to believe, though not to describe the Consternation they were all in, the

Women and the Man's Daughters which were but little Girls, were frighted almost to Death, and got up, one running out at one Door, and one at another, some down-Stairs and some up-Stairs, and getting together as well as they could, lock'd themselves into their Chambers, and screamed out at the Window for Help, as if they had been frighted out of their Wits: The Master more compos'd than they, tho' both frighted and provok'd, was going to lay Hands on him, and thro' him down Stairs, being in a Passion, but then considering a little the Condition of the Man and the Danger of touching him, Horror seiz'd his Mind, and he stood still like one astonished. The poor distemper'd Man all this while, being as well diseas'd in his Brain as in his Body, stood still like one amaz'd; at length he turns round, *Ay! says he*, with all the seeming calmness imaginable, *Is it so with you all! Are you all disturb'd at me? why then I'll e'en go home and die there*. And so he goes immediately down Stairs: The Servant that had let him in goes down after him with a Candle, but was afraid to go past him and open the Door, so he stood on the Stairs to see what he wou'd do; the Man went and open'd the Door, and went out and flung the Door after him: It was some while before the Family recover'd the Fright, but as no ill Consequence attended, they have had occasion since to speak of it (you may be sure) with great Satisfaction. Tho' the Man was gone it was some time, nay, as I heard, some Days before they recover'd themselves of the Hurry they were in, nor did they go up and down the House with any assurance, till they had burnt a great variety of Fumes and Perfumes in all the Rooms, and made a great many Smoaks of Pitch, of Gunpowder, and of Sulphur, all separately shifted; and washed their Clothes, and the like: As to the poor Man whether he liv'd or dy'd I don't remember.

It is most certain, that if by the Shutting up of Houses the sick had not been confin'd, multitudes who in the height of their Fever were Delirious and Distracted, wou'd ha' been continually running up and down the Streets, and even as it was, a very great number did so, and offer'd all sorts of Violence to those they met, even just as a mad Dog runs on and bites at every one he meets; nor can I doubt but that shou'd one of those infected diseased Creatures have bitten any Man or Woman, while the Frenzy of the Distemper was upon them, they, I mean the Person so wounded, wou'd as certainly ha' been incurably infected, as one that was sick before and had the Tokens upon him.

I heard of one infected Creature, who running out of his Bed in his Shirt, in the anguish and agony of his Swellings, of which he had three upon him, got his Shoes on and went to put on his Coat, but the Nurse resisting and snatching the Coat from him, he threw her down, run over her, run down Stairs and into the Street directly to the *Thames* in his Shirt, the Nurse running after him, and calling to the Watch to stop him; but the Watchmen frighted at the Man, and afraid to touch him, let him go on; upon which he ran down to the Still-yard Stairs, threw away his Shirt, and plung'd into the *Thames*, and, being a good swimmer, swam quite over the River; and the Tide being coming in, as they call it, that is running West-ward, he reached the Land not till he came about the Falcon Stairs, where landing, and finding no People there, it being in the Night, he ran about the Streets there, Naked as he was, for a good while, when it being by that time High-water, he takes the River again, and swam back to the Still-yard, landed, ran up the Streets again to his own House, knocking at the Door, went up the Stairs, and into his Bed again; and that this terrible Experiment cur'd him of the Plague, that is to say, that the violent Motion of his Arms and Legs stretch'd the Parts where the Swellings he had upon him were, that is to say under his Arms and his Groin, and caused them to ripen and break; and that the cold of the Water abated the Fever in his Blood.

I have only to add, that I do not relate this any more than some of the other, as a Fact within my own Knowledge, so as that I can vouch the Truth of them, and especially that of the Man being cur'd by the extravagant Adventure, which I confess I do not think very possible, but it may serve to confirm the many desperate Things which the distress'd People falling into, Deliriums, and what we call Lightheadedness, were frequently run upon at that time, and how infinitely more such there wou'd ha' been, if such People had not been confin'd by the shutting up of Houses; and this I take to be the best, *if not the only good thing* which was perform'd by that severe Method.

On the other Hand, the Complaints and the Murmurings were very bitter against the thing itself.

It would pierce the Hearts of all that came by to hear the piteous Cries of those infected People, who being thus out of their Understandings by the Violence of their Pain, or the heat of their Blood, were either shut in, or perhaps ty'd in their Beds and Chairs, to prevent their doing themselves Hurt, and who wou'd make a dreadful outcry at their being confin'd, and at their being not permitted to die at large, as they call'd it, and as they wou'd ha' done before.

This running of distemper'd People about the Streets was very dismal, and the Magistrates did their utmost to prevent it, but as it was generally in the Night and always sudden, when such attempts were made, the Officers cou'd not be at hand to prevent it, and even when any got out in the Day, the Officers appointed did not care to meddle with them, because, as they were all grievously infected to *be sure* when they were come to that Height, so they were more than ordinarily infectious, and it was one of the most dangerous Things that cou'd be to touch them; on the other Hand, they generally ran on, not knowing what they did, till they dropp'd down stark Dead, or till they had exhausted their Spirits so, as that they wou'd fall and then die in perhaps half an Hour or an Hour, and which was most piteous to hear, they were sure to come to themselves intirely in that half Hour or Hour, and then to make most grievous and piercing Cries and Lamentations in the deep afflicting Sense of the Condition they were in. This was much of it before the Order for shutting up of Houses was strictly put in Execution, for at first the Watchmen were not so vigorous and severe, as they were afterward in the keeping the People in; that is to say, before they were, I mean some of them, severely punish'd for their Neglect, failing in their Duty, and letting People who were under their Care slip away, or conniving at their going abroad whether sick or well. But after they saw the Officers appointed to examine into their Conduct, were resolv'd to have them do their Duty, or be punish'd for the omission, they were more exact, and the People were strictly restrain'd; which was a thing they took so ill, and bore so impatiently, that their Discontents can hardly be describ'd: But there was an absolute Necessity for it, that must be confess'd, unless some other Measures had been timely enter'd upon, and it was too late for that.

Had not this particular of the Sick's been restrain'd as above, been our Case at that time, *London* wou'd ha' been the most dreadful Place that ever was in the World; there wou'd for ought I know have as many People dy'd in the Streets as dy'd in their Houses; for when the Distemper was at its height, it generally made them Raving and Delirious, and when they were so, they wou'd never be perswaded to keep in their Beds but by Force; and many who were not ty'd, threw themselves out of Windows, when they found they cou'd not get leave to go out of their Doors.

It was for want of People conversing one with another, in this time of Calamity, that it was impossible any particular Person cou'd come at the Knowledge of all the extraordinary Cases that occurr'd in different Families; and particularly I believe it was never known to this Day how many People in their Deliriums drowned themselves in the *Thames*, and in the River which runs from the Marshes by *Hackney*, which we generally call'd *Ware* River, or *Hackney* River; as to those which were set down in the Weekly Bill, they were indeed few; nor cou'd it be known of any of those, whether they drowned themselves by Accident or not: But I believe, I might reckon up more, who, within the compass of my Knowledge or Observation, really drowned themselves in that Year, than are put down in the Bill of all put together, for many of the Bodies were never found, who yet were known to be so lost; and the like in other Methods of Self-Destruction. There was also One Man in or about *Whitecross-street*, burnt himself to Death in his Bed; some said it was done by himself, others that it was by the Treachery of the Nurse that attended him; but that he had the Plague upon him was agreed by all.

It was a merciful Disposition of Providence also, and which I have many times thought of at that time, that no Fires, or no considerable ones at least, happen'd in the City, during that Year, which, if it had been otherwise, would have been very dreadful; and either the People must have let them alone unquenched, or have come together in great Crowds and Throngs, unconcern'd at the Danger of the Infection, not concerned at the Houses they went into, at the Goods they handled, or at the Persons or the People they came among: But so it was that excepting that in *Cripplegate* Parish, and two or three little Eruptions of Fires, which were presently extinguish'd, there was no Disaster of that kind happen'd in the whole Year. They told us a Story of a House in a Place call'd *Swan-Alley*, passing from *Goswell-street* near the End of *Oldstreet* into *St. John-street*, that a Family was infected there, in so terrible a Manner that every one of the House died; the last Person lay dead on the Floor, and as it is supposed, had laid her self all along to die just before the Fire; the Fire, it seems had fallen from its Place, being of Wood, and had taken hold of the Boards and the Joists they lay on, and burnt as far as just to the Body, but had not taken hold of the dead Body, tho' she had little more than her Shift on, and had gone out of itself, not hurting the Rest of the House, tho' it was a slight Timber House. How true this might be, I do not determine, but the City being to suffer severely the next Year by Fire, this Year it felt very little of that Calamity.

Indeed considering the Deliriums, which the Agony threw People into, and how I have mention'd in their Madness, when they were alone, they did many desperate Things; it was very strange there were no more Disasters of that kind.

It has been frequently ask'd me, and I cannot say, that I

ever knew how to give a direct Answer to it, How it came to pass that so many infected People appear'd abroad in the Streets, at the same time that the Houses which were infected were so vigilantly searched, and all of them shut up and guarded as they were.

I confess, I know not what Answer to give to this, unless it be this, that in so great and populous a City as this is, it was impossible to discover every House that was infected as soon as it was so, or to shut up all the Houses that were infected: so that People had the Liberty of going about the Streets, even where they pleased, unless they were known to belong to such and such infected Houses.

It is true, that as several Physicians told my Lord Mayor, the Fury of the Contagion was such at some particular Times, and People sicken'd so fast, and died so soon, that it was impossible and indeed to no purpose to go about to enquire who was sick and who was well, or to shut them up with such Exactness, as the thing required; almost every House in a whole Street being infected, and in many Places every Person in some of the Houses; and that which was still worse, by the time that the Houses were known to be infected, most of the Persons infected would be stone dead, and the rest run away for Fear of being shut up; so that it was to very small Purpose, to call them infected Houses and shut them up; the Infection having ravaged, and taken its Leave of the House, before it was really known, that the Family was any way touch'd.

This might be sufficient to convince any reasonable Person, that as it was not in the Power of the Magistrates, or of any human Methods or Policy, to prevent the spreading the Infection; so that this way of shutting up of Houses was perfectly insufficient for that End. Indeed it seemed to have no manner of publick Good in it, equal or proportionable to the grievous Burthen that it was to the particular Families, that were so shut up; and as far as I was employed by the publick in directing that Severity, I frequently found occasion to see, that it was incapable of answering the End. For Example as I was desired as a Visitor or Examiner to enquire into the

Particulars of several Families which were infected, we scarce came to any House where the Plague had visibly appear'd in the Family, but that some of the Family were Fled and gone; the Magistrates would resent this, and charge the Examiners with being remiss in their Examination or Inspection: But by that means Houses were long infected before it was known. Now, as I was in this dangerous Office but half the appointed time, which was two Months, it was long enough to inform myself, that we were no way capable of coming at the Knowledge of the true state of any Family, but by enquiring at the Door, or of the Neighbours; as for going into every House to search, that was a part no Authority wou'd offer to impose on the Inhabitants, or any Citizen wou'd undertake, for it wou'd ha' been exposing us to certain Infection and Death, and to the Ruine of our own Families as well as of ourselves, nor wou'd any Citizen of Probity, and that cou'd be depended upon, have staid in the Town, if they had been made liable to such a Severity.

Seeing then that we cou'd come at the certainty of Things by no Method but that of Enquiry of the Neighbours, or of the Family, and on that we cou'd not justly depend, it was not possible, but that the incertainty of this Matter wou'd remain as above.

It is true, Masters of Families were bound by the Order, to give Notice to the Examiner of the Place wherein he liv'd, within two Hours after he shou'd discover it, of any Person being sick in his House, that is to say, having Signs of the Infection, but they found so many ways to evade this, and excuse their Negligence, that they seldom gave that Notice, till they had taken Measures to have every one Escape out of the House, who had a mind to Escape, whether they were Sick or Sound; and while this was so, it is easie to see, that the shutting up of Houses was no way to be depended upon, as a sufficient Method for putting a stop to the Infection, because, as I have said elsewhere, many of those that so went out of those infected Houses, had the Plague really upon them, tho' they might really think themselves Sound: And some of these were the People that walk'd the Streets till they fell down Dead, not that they were suddenly struck with the Distemper, as with a Bullet that kill'd with the Stroke, but that they really had the Infection in their Blood long before, only, that, as it prey'd secretly on the Vitals, it appear'd not till it seiz'd the Heart with a mortal Power, and the Patient died in a Moment, as with a sudden Fainting, or an Apoplectick Fit.

I know that some, even of our Physicians, thought, for a time, that those People that so died in the Streets, were seiz'd but that Moment they fell, as if they had been touch'd by a Stroke from Heaven, as Men are kill'd by a flash of Lightning; but they found Reason to alter their Opinion afterward; for upon examining the Bodies of such after they were Dead, they always either had Tokens upon them, or other evident Proofs of the Distemper having been longer upon them, than they had otherwise expected.

This often was the Reason that, as I have said, we, that were Examiners, were not able to come at the Knowledge of the Infection being enter'd into a House, till it was too late to shut it up; and sometimes not till the People that were left, were all Dead. In *Petticoat-Lane* two Houses together were infected, and several People sick; but the Distemper was so well conceal'd, the Examiner, who was my Neighbour, got no Knowledge of it, till Notice was sent him that the People were all Dead, and that the Carts should call there to fetch them away. The two Heads of the Families concerted their Measures, and so order'd their Matters, as that when the Examiner was in the Neighbourhood, they appeared generally one at a time, and answered, that is, lied for one another, or got some of the Neighbourhood to say they were all in Health, and perhaps knew no better, till Death making it impossible to keep it any longer as a Secret, the dead-Carts were call'd in the Night, the Houses to both, and so it became publick: But when the Examiner order'd the Constable to shut up the Houses, there was no Body left in them but three People, two in one House, and one in the other just dying, and a Nurse in each House, who acknowledg'd that they had buried five before, that the Houses had been infected nine or ten Days, and that for all the rest of the two Families, which were many, they were gone, some sick, some well, or whether sick or well could not be known.

In like manner, at another House in the same Lane, a Man having his Family infected, but very unwilling to be shut up, when he could conceal it no longer, shut up himself; that is to say, he set the great red Cross upon his Door with the words LORD HAVE MERCY UPON US; and so deluded the Examiner, who suppos'd it had been done by the Constable, by Order of the other Examiner, for there were two Examiners to every District or Precinct; by this means he had free egress and regress into his House again, and out of it, as he pleas'd not-withstanding it was infected; till at length his Stratagem was found out, and then he, with the sound part of his Servants and Family, made off and escaped; so they were not shut up at all.

These things made it very hard, if not impossible, *as I have said*, to prevent the spreading of an Infection by the shutting up of Houses, unless the People would think the shutting up of their Houses no Grievance, and be so willing to have it done, as that they wou'd give Notice duly and faithfully to the Magistrates of their being infected, as soon as it was known by themselves: But as that can not be expected from them, and the Examiners can not be supposed, as above, to go into their Houses to visit and search, all the good of shutting up Houses, will be defeated, and few Houses will be shut up in time, except those of the Poor, who can not conceal it, and of some People who will be discover'd by the Terror and Consterna-tion which the Thing put them into.

I got myself discharg'd of the dangerous Office I was in, as soon as I cou'd get another admitted, who I had obtain'd for a little Money to accept of it; and so, instead of serving the two Months, which was directed, I was not above three Weeks in it; and a great while too, considering it was in the Month of *August*, at which time the Distemper began to rage with great Violence at our end of the Town.[1]

In the execution of this Office, I cou'd not refrain speaking my Opinion among my Neighbours, as to this shutting up the People in their Houses; in which we saw most evidently the Severities that were used *tho' grievous in themselves*, had also this particular Objection against them, namely, that they did not answer the End, *as I have said*, but that the distemper'd People went Day by Day about the Streets; and it was our united Opinion, that a Method to have removed the Sound from the Sick in Case of a particular House being visited, wou'd ha' been much more reasonable on many Accounts, leaving no Body with the sick Persons, but such as shou'd on such Occasion request to stay and declare themselves content to be shut up with them.

Our Scheme for removing those that were Sound from those that were Sick, was only in such Houses as were infected, and confining the sick was no Confinement; those that cou'd not stir, wou'd not complain, while they were in their Senses, and while they had the Power of judging: Indeed, when they came to be Delirious and Light-headed, then they wou'd cry out of the Cruelty of being confin'd; but for the removal of those that were well, we thought it highly reasonable and just, for their own sakes, they shou'd be remov'd from the Sick, and that, for other People's Safety, they shou'd keep retir'd for a while, to see that they were sound, and might not infect others; and we thought twenty or thirty Days enough for this.

Now certainly, if Houses had been provided on purpose for those that were sound to perform this demy Quarantine in, they wou'd have much less Reason to think themselves injur'd in such a restraint, than in being confin'd with infected People, in the Houses where they liv'd.

It is here, however, to be observ'd, that after the Funerals became so many, that People could not Toll the Bell, Mourn, or Weep, or wear Black for one another, as they did before; no, nor so much as make Coffins for those that died; so after a while the fury of the Infection appeared to be so encreased, that in short, they shut up no Houses at all; it seem'd enough that all the Remedies of that Kind had been used till they were found fruitless, and that the Plague spread itself with an irresistible Fury, so that, as the Fire the succeeding Year, spread itself and burnt with such Violence, that the Citizens in Despair, gave over their Endeavours to extinguish it, so in the Plague, it came at last to such Violence that the People sat still looking at one another, and seem'd quite abandon'd to Despair; whole Streets seem'd to be desolated, and not to be shut up only, but to be emptied of their Inhabitants; Doors were left open, Windows stood shattering with the Wind in empty Houses, for want of People to shut them: In a Word, People began to give up themselves to their Fears, and to think that all regulations and Methods were in vain, and that there was nothing to be hoped for, but an universal Desolation; and it was even in the height of this general Despair, that it pleased God to stay his Hand, and to slacken the Fury of the Contagion, in such a manner as was even surprizing like its beginning, and demonstrated it to be his own particular Hand, and that above, if not without the Agency of Means, as I shall take Notice of in its proper Place.

But I must still speak of the Plague as in its height, raging even to Desolation, and the People under the most dreadful Consternation, even, as I have said, to Despair. It is hardly credible to what Excesses the Passions of Men carry'd them in this Extremity of the Distemper; and this Part, I think, was as moving as the rest; What cou'd affect a Man in his full Power of Reflection; and what could make deeper Impressions on the Soul, than to see a Man almost Naked and got out of his House, or perhaps out of his Bed into the Street, come out of *Harrow-Alley*, a populous Conjunction or Collection of Alleys, Courts, and Passages, in the Butcher-row in *White-chappel*? I say, What could be more Affecting, than to see this poor Man come out into the open Street, run Dancing and Singing, and making a thousand antick Gestures, with five or six Women and Children running after him, crying, and calling upon him, for the Lord's sake to come back, and entreating the help of others to bring him back, but all in vain, no Body daring to lay a Hand upon him, or to come near him.

This was a most grievous and afflicting thing to me, who saw it all from my own Windows; for all this while, the poor afflicted Man, was, as I observ'd it, even then in the utmost Agony of Pain, having, as they said, two Swellings upon him, which cou'd not be brought to break, or to suppurate; but by laying strong Causticks on them, the Surgeons had, it seems, hopes to break them, which Causticks were then upon him, burning his Flesh as with a hot Iron: I cannot say what became of this poor Man, but I think he continu'd roving about in that manner till he fell down and Died.

No wonder the Aspect of the City itself was frightful, the usual concourse of People in the Streets, and which used to be supplied from our end of the Town, was abated; the Exchange was not kept shut indeed,[1] but it was no more frequented; the Fires were lost;[2] they had been almost extinguished for some Days by a very smart and hasty Rain: But that was not all, some of the Physicians insisted that they were not only no Benefit, but injurious to the Health of People:[3] This they made a loud Clamour about, and complain'd to the Lord Mayor about it: On the other Hand, others of the same Faculty, and Eminent too, oppos'd them, and gave their Reasons why the Fires were and must be useful to asswage the Violence of the Distemper. I cannot give a full Account of their Arguments on both Sides, only this I remember, that they cavil'd very much with one another; some were for Fires, but that they must be made of Wood and not Coal,[4] and of particular sorts of Wood too, such as Fir in particular, or Cedar, because of the strong effluvia of Turpentine; Others were for Coal and not Wood, because of the Sulphur and Bitumen; and others were for neither one or other. Upon the whole, the Lord Mayor ordered no more Fires, and especially on this Account, namely, that the Plague was so fierce that they saw evidently it defied all Means and rather seemed to encrease than decrease upon any application to check and abate it; and yet this Amazement of the Magistrates, proceeded rather from want of being able to apply any Means successfully, than from any unwillingness either to expose themselves, or undertake the Care and Weight of Business; for, to do them Justice, they neither spared their Pains or their Persons; but nothing answer'd, the Infection rag'd, and the People were now frighted and terrified to the last Degree, so that, as I may say, they gave themselves up, and, as I mention'd above, abandon'd themselves to their Despair.

But let me observe here, that when I say the People abandon'd themselves to Despair, I do not mean to what Men call a religious Despair, or a Despair of their eternal State, but I mean a Despair of their being able to escape the Infection, or to out-live the Plague, which they saw was so raging and so irresistible in its Force, that indeed few People that were touch'd with it in its height about *August*, and *September*, escap'd: And, which is very particular, contrary to its ordinary Operation in *June* and *July*, and the beginning of *August*, when, as I have observ'd many were infected, and continued so many Days, and then went off, after having had the Poison in their Blood a long time; but now on the contrary, most of the People who were taken during the two last Weeks in *August*, and in the three first Weeks in *September*, generally died in two or three Days at farthest, and many the very same Day they were taken; Whether the Dog-days, or as our Astrologers pretended to express themselves, the Influence of the Dog-Star[1] had that malignant Effect; or all those who had the seeds of Infection before in them, brought it up to a maturity at that time altogether I know not; but this was the time when it was reported, that above 3000 People died in one Night; and they that wou'd have us believe they more critically observ'd it, pretend to say, that they all died within the space of two Hours, (*viz.*) Between the Hours of One and three in the Morning.

As to the Suddenness of People's dying at this time more than before, there were innumerable Instances of it, and I could name several in my Neighbourhood; one Family without the Barrs, and not far from me, were all seemingly well on the Monday, being Ten in Family, that Evening one

Maid and one Apprentice were taken ill, and dy'd the next Morning, when the other Apprentice and two Children were touch'd, whereof one dy'd the same Evening, and the other two on Wednesday: In a Word, by Saturday at Noon, the Master, Mistress, four Children and four Servants were all gone, and the House left entirely empty, except an ancient Woman, who came in to take Charge of the Goods for the Master of the Family's Brother, who liv'd not far off, and who had not been sick.

Many Houses were then left desolate, all the People being carry'd away dead, and especially in an Alley farther, on the same Side beyond the Barrs, going in at the Sign of *Moses* and *Aaron*; there were several Houses together, which (they said) had not one Person left alive in them, and some that dy'd last in several of those Houses, were left a little too long before they were fetch'd out to be bury'd; the Reason of which was not as some have written very untruly, that the living were not sufficient to bury the dead; but that the Mortality was so great in the Yard or Alley, that there was no Body left to give Notice to the Buriers or Sextons, that there were any dead Bodies there to be bury'd. It was said, how true I know not, that some of those Bodies were so much corrupted, and so rotten, that it was with Difficulty they were carry'd; and as the Carts could not come any nearer than to the Alley-Gate in the high Street, it was so much the more difficult to bring them along; but I am not certain how many Bodies were then left, I am sure that ordinarily it was not so.

As I have mention'd how the People were brought into a Condition to despair of Life and abandon themselves, so this very Thing had a strange Effect among us for three or four Weeks, that is, it made them bold and venturous, they were no more shy of one another, or restrained within Doors, but went any where and every where, and began to converse; one would say to another, I do not ask you how you are, or say how I am, it is certain we shall all go, so 'tis no Matter who is sick or who is sound, and so they run desperately into any Place or any Company.

As it brought the People into publick Company, so it was surprizing how it brought them to crowd into the Churches, they inquir'd no more into who they sat near to, or far from, what offensive Smells they met with, or what condition the People seemed to be in, but looking upon themselves all as so many dead Corpses, they came to the Churches without the least Caution, and crowded together, as if their Lives were of no Consequence, compar'd to the Work which they came about there: Indeed, the Zeal which they shew'd in Coming, and the Earnestness and Affection they shew'd in their Attention to what they heard, made it manifest what a Value People would all put upon the Worship of God, if they thought every Day they attended at the Church that it would be their Last.

Nor was it without other strange Effects, for it took away all Manner of Prejudice at, or Scruple about the Person who they found in the Pulpit when they came to the Churches. It cannot be doubted, but that many of the Ministers of the Parish-Churches were cut off among others in so common and so dreadful a Calamity; and others had not Courage enough to stand it, but removed into the Country as they found Means for Escape; as then some Parish-Churches were quite vacant and forsaken, the People made no Scruple of desiring such Dissenters as had been a few Years before depriv'd of their Livings, by Virtue of the Act of Parliament call'd *The Act of Uniformity*,[1] to preach in the Churches, nor did the Church Ministers in that Case make any Difficulty of accepting their Assistance, so that many of those who they called silenced Ministers, had their Mouths open'd on this Occasion, and preach'd publickly to the People.

Here we may observe, and I hope it will not be amiss to take notice of it, that a near View of Death would soon reconcile Men of good Principles one to another, and that it is chiefly owing to our easy Scituation in Life, and our putting these Things far from us, that our Breaches are fomented, ill Blood continued, Prejudices, Breach of Charity and of Christian Union so much kept and so far carry'd on among us, as it is:

Another Plague Year would reconcile all these Differences, a close conversing with Death, or with Diseases that threaten Death, would scum off the Gall from our Tempers, remove the Animosities among us, and bring us to see with differing Eyes, than those which we look'd on Things with before; as the People who had been used to join with the Church, were reconcil'd at this Time, with the admitting the Dissenters to preach to them: So the Dissenters, who with an uncommon Prejudice, had broken off from the Communion of the Church of England, were now content to come to their Parish-Churches, and to conform to the Worship which they did not approve of before; but as the Terror of the Infection abated, those Things all returned again to their less desirable Channel, and to the Course they were in before.

I mention this but historically, I have no mind to enter into Arguments to move either, or both Sides to a more charitable Compliance one with another; I do not see that it is probable such a Discourse would be either suitable or successful; the Breaches seem rather to widen, and tend to a widening farther, than to closing, and who am I that I should think myself able to influence either one Side or other? But this I may repeat again, that 'tis evident Death will reconcile us all; on the other Side the Grave we shall be all Brethren again: In Heaven, whither I hope we may come from all Parties and Perswasions, we shall find neither Prejudice or Scruple; there we shall be of one Principle and of one Opinion, why we cannot be content to go Hand in Hand to the Place where we shall join Heart and Hand without the least Hesitation, and with the most compleat Harmony and Affection; I say, why we cannot do so here I can say nothing to, neither shall I say any thing more of it, but that it remains to be lamented.

I could dwell a great while upon the Calamities of this dreadful time, and go on to describe the Objects that appear'd among us every Day, the dreadful Extravagancies which the Distraction of sick People drove them into; how the Streets began now to be fuller of frightful Objects, and Families to be made even a Terror to themselves: But after I have told you, as I have above, that One Man being tyed in his Bed, and finding no other Way to deliver himself, set the Bed on fire with his Candle, which unhappily stood within his reach, and Burnt himself in his Bed. And how another, by the insufferable Torment he bore, daunced and sung naked in the Streets, not knowing one Extasie from another, I say, after I have mention'd these Things, What can be added more? What can be said to represent the Misery of these Times, more lively to the Reader, or to give him a more perfect Idea of a complicated Distress?

I must acknowledge that this time was Terrible, that I was sometimes at the End of all my Resolutions, and that I had not the Courage that I had at the Beginning. As the Extremity brought other People abroad, it drove me Home, and except, having made my Voyage down to *Blackwall* and *Greenwich*, as I have related, which was an Excursion, I kept afterwards very much within Doors, as I had for about a Fortnight before; I have said already, that I repented several times that I had ventur'd to stay in Town, and had not gone away with my Brother, and his Family, but it was too late for that now; and after I had retreated and stay'd within Doors a good while, before my Impatience led me Abroad, then they call'd me, as I have said, to an ugly and dangerous Office, which brought me out again; but as that was expir'd, while the hight of the Distemper lasted, I retir'd again, and continued close ten or twelve Days more. During which many dismal Spectacles represented themselves in my View, out of my own Windows, and in our own Street, as that particularly from *Harrow-Alley*, of the poor outrageous Creature which danced and sung in his Agony, and many others there were: Scarce a Day or Night pass'd over, but some dismal Thing or other happened at the End of that *Harrow-Alley*, which was a Place full of poor People, most of them belonging to the Butchers, or to Employments depending upon the Butchery.

Sometimes Heaps and Throngs of People would burst out of that Alley, most of them Women, making a dreadful Clamour, mixt or Compounded of Skreetches, Cryings and

Calling one another, that we could not conceive what to make of it; almost all the dead Part of the Night the dead Cart stood at the End of that Alley, for if it went in it could not well turn again, and could go in but a little Way. There, I say, it stood to receive dead Bodies, and as the Church-Yard was but a little Way off, if it went away full it would soon be back again: It is impossible to describe the most horrible Cries and Noise the poor People would make at their bringing the dead Bodies of their Children and Friends out to the Cart, and by the Number one would have thought, there had been none left behind, or that there were People enough for a small City liveing in those Places: Several times they cryed Murther, sometimes Fire; but it was easie to perceive it was all Distraction, and the Complaints of Distress'd and distemper'd People.

I believe it was every where thus at that time, for the Plague rag'd for six or seven Weeks beyond all that I have express'd; and came even to such a height, that in the Extremity, they began to break into that excellent Order, of which I have spoken so much, in behalf of the Magistrates, namely, that no dead Bodies were seen in the Streets or Burials in the Day-time for there was a Necessity, in this Extremity, to bear with its being otherwise, for a little while.

One thing I cannot omit here, and indeed I thought it was extraordinary, at least, it seemed a remarkable Hand of Divine Justice, (*viz.*) That all the Predictors, Astrologers, Fortune-tellers, and what they call'd cunning-Men, Conjurers, and the like; calculators of Nativities, and dreamers of Dreams, and such People, were gone and vanish'd, not one of them was to be found: I am, verily, perswaded that a great Number of them fell in the heat of the Calamity, having ventured to stay upon the Prospect of getting great Estates; and indeed their Gain was but too great for a time through the Madness and Folly of the People; but now they were silent, many of them went to their long Home, not able to foretel their own Fate, or to calculate their own Nativities; some have been critical enough to say, that every one of them dy'd; I dare not affirm that; but this I must own, that I never heard of one of them that ever appear'd after the Calamity was over.

But to return to my particular Observations, during this dreadful part of the Visitation: I am now come, as I have said, to the Month of *September*, which was the most dreadful of its kind, I believe, that ever *London* saw; for by all the Accounts which I have seen of the preceding Visitations which have been in *London*, nothing has been like it; the Number in the Weekly Bill amounting to almost 40,000[1] from the 22d of *August*, to the 26th of *September*, being but five Weeks, the particulars of the Bills are as follows, (*viz.*)

From *August* the 22d to the 29th -	7496
To the 7th of *September* - - - - - -	8252
To the 12th - - - - - - - - - - - - -	7690
To the 19th - - - - - - - - - - - - -	8297
To the 26th - - - - - - - - - - - - -	6460
	————
	38195

This was a prodigious Number of itself, but if I should add the Reasons which I have to believe that this Account was deficient, and how deficient it was, you would with me, make no Scruple to believe that there died above ten Thousand a Week for all those Weeks, one Week with another, and a proportion for several Weeks both before and after: The Confusion among the People, especially within the City at that time, was inexpressible; the Terror was so great at last, that the Courage of the People appointed to carry away the Dead, began to fail them; nay, several of them died altho' they had the Distemper before, and were recover'd; and some of them drop'd down when they have been carrying the Bodies even at the Pitside, and just ready to throw them in; and this Confusion was greater in the City, because they had flatter'd themselves with Hopes of escaping: And thought the bitterness of Death was past: One Cart they told us, going up *Shoreditch*, was forsaken of the Drivers, or being left to one Man to drive, he died in the Street, and the Horses going on, overthrew the Cart, and left the Bodies, some thrown out here, some there, in a dismal manner; Another Cart was it seems found in the great Pit in *Finsbury* Fields, the Driver being Dead, or having been gone and abandon'd it, and the Horses running too near it, the Cart fell in and drew the Horses in also: It was suggested that the Driver was thrown in with it, and that the Cart fell upon him, by Reason his Whip was seen to be in the Pit among the Bodies; but that, I suppose, cou'd not be certain.

In our Parish of *Aldgate*, the dead-Carts were several times, as I have heard, found standing at the Church-yard Gate, full of dead Bodies, but neither Bell man or Driver, or any one else with it; neither in these, or many other Cases, did they know what Bodies they had in their Cart, for sometimes they were let down with Ropes out of Balconies and out of Windows; and sometimes the Bearers brought them to the Cart, sometimes other People; nor, *as the Men themselves said*, did they trouble themselves to keep any Account of the Numbers.

The Vigilance of the Magistrate was now put to the utmost Trial, and it must be confess'd, can never be enough acknowledg'd on this Occasion also; whatever Expence or Trouble they were at, two Things were never neglected in the City or Suburbs either.

1. Provisions were always to be had in full Plenty, and the Price not much rais'd neither, hardly worth speaking.

2. No dead Bodies lay unburied or uncovered; and if one walk'd from one end of the City to another, no Funeral or sign of it was to be seen in the Day-time,[1] except a little, as I have said above, in the three first Weeks in *September*.

This last Article perhaps will hardly be believ'd, when some Accounts which others have published since that shall be seen, wherein they say, that the Dead lay unburied, which I am assured was utterly false; at least, if it had been any where so, it must ha' been in Houses where the Living were gone from the Dead, having found means, as I have observed, to Escape, and where no Notice was given to the Officers: All which amounts to nothing at all in the Case in Hand; for this

I am positive in, having myself been employ'd a little in the Direction of that part in the Parish in which I liv'd, and where as great a Desolation was made in proportion to the Number of Inhabitants as was any where. I say, I am sure that there were no dead Bodies remain'd unburied; that is to say, none that the proper Officers knew of; none for want of People to carry them off, and Buriers to put them into the Ground and cover them; and this is sufficient to the Argument; for what might lie in Houses and Holes as in *Moses* and *Aaron* Alley is nothing; for it is most certain, they were buried as soon as they were found. As to the first Article, namely, of Provisions, the scarcity or dearness, tho' I have mention'd it before, and shall speak of it again; yet I must observe here,

(1.) The Price of Bread in particular was not much raised;[1] for in the beginning of the Year (*viz.*) In the first Week in *March*, the Penny Wheaten Loaf was ten Ounces and a half; and in the height of the Contagion, it was to be had at nine Ounces and an half, and never dearer, no not all that Season: And about the beginning of *November* it was sold ten Ounces and a half again; the like of which, I believe, was never heard of in any City, under so dreadful a Visitation before.

(2.) Neither was there (which I wondred much at) any want of Bakers or Ovens kept open to supply the People with Bread; but this was indeed alledg'd by some Families, *viz.* That their Maid-Servants going to the Bake-houses with their Dough to be baked, which was then the Custom, sometimes came Home with the Sickness, that is to say, the Plague upon them.

In all this dreadful Visitation, there were, as I have said before, but two Pest-houses[2] made use of, *viz.* One in the Fields beyond *Old-Street*, and one in *Westminster*; neither was there any Compulsion us'd in carrying People thither: Indeed there was no need of Compulsion in the Case, for there were Thousands of poor distressed People, who having no Help, or Conveniences, or Supplies but of Charity, would have been very glad to have been carryed thither, and been taken Care of, which indeed was the only thing that, I think, was wanting in the whole publick Management of the City; seeing no Body was here allow'd to be brought to the Pest-house, but where Money was given, or Security for Money, either at their introducing, or upon their being cur'd and sent out; for very many were sent out again whole, and very good Physicians were appointed to those Places, so that many People did very well there, of which I shall make Mention again. The principal Sort of People sent thither were, as I have said, Servants, who got the Distemper by going of Errands to fetch Necessaries to the Families where they liv'd; and who in that Case, if they came Home sick, were remov'd to preserve the rest of the House; and they were so well look'd after there in all the time of the Visitation, that there was but 156 buried in all at the *London* Pest-house, and 159 at that of *Westminster*.

By having more Pest-houses, I am far from meaning a forcing all People into such Places. Had the shutting up of Houses been omitted, and the Sick hurried out of their Dwellings to Pest-houses, as some proposed it seems, at that time as well as since, it would certainly have been much worse than it was; the very removing the Sick would have been a spreading of the Infection, and the rather because that removing could not effectually clear the House, where the sick Person was, of the Distemper, and the rest of the Family being then left at Liberty would certainly spread it among others.

The Methods also in private Families, which would have been universally used to have concealed the Distemper, and to have conceal'd the Persons being sick, would have been such that the Distemper would sometimes have seiz'd a whole Family before any Visitors or Examiners could have known of it: On the other hand, the prodigious Numbers which would have been sick at a time, would have exceeded all the Capacity of publick Pest-houses to receive them, or of publick Officers to discover and remove them.

This was well considered in those Days, and I have heard them talk of it often: The Magistrates had enough to do to bring People to submit to having their Houses shut up, and many Ways they deceived the Watchmen, and got out, as I have observed: But that Difficulty made it apparent, that they would have found it impracticable to have gone the other way to Work; for they could never have forced the sick People out of their Beds and out of their Dwellings; it must not have been my Lord Mayor's Officers, but an Army of Officers that must have attempted it; and the People, on the other hand, would have been enrag'd and desperate, and would have kill'd those that should have offered to have meddled with them or with their Children and Relations, whatever had befallen them for it; so that they would have made the People, who, *as it was*, were in the most terrible Distraction imaginable; I say, they would have made them stark mad; whereas the Magistrates found it proper on several Accounts to treat them with Lenity and Compassion, and not with Violence and Terror, such as dragging the Sick out of their Houses, or obliging them to remove themselves would have been.

This leads me again to mention the Time, when the Plague first began, that is to say, when it became certain that it would spread over the whole Town, when, as I have said, the better sort of People first took the Alarm, and began to hurry themselves out of Town: It was true, as I observ'd in its Place, that the Throng was so great, and the Coaches, Horses, Waggons and Carts were so many, driving and dragging the People away, that it look'd as if all the City was running away; and had any Regulations been publish'd that had been terrifying at that time, especially such as would pretend to dispose of the People, otherwise than they would dispose of themselves, it would have put both the City and Suburbs into the utmost Confusion.

But the Magistrates wisely caus'd the People to be encourag'd, made very good By-Laws for the regulating the Citizens, keeping good Order in the Streets, and making every thing as eligible as possible to all Sorts of People.

In the first Place, the Lord Mayor and the Sheriffs, the Court of Aldermen, and a certain Number of the Common

Council-Men, or their Deputies came to a Resolution and published it, *viz.* 'That *they* would not quit the City themselves, but that they would be always at hand for the preserving good Order in every Place, and for the doing Justice on all Occasions; as also for the distributing the publick Charity to the Poor; and in a Word, for the doing the Duty, and discharging the Trust repos'd in them by the Citizens to the utmost of their Power.'

In Pursuance of these Orders, the Lord Mayor, Sheriffs, &c. held Councils every Day more or less, for making such Dispositions as they found needful for preserving the Civil Peace; and tho' they used the People with all possible Gentleness and Clemency, yet all manner of presumptuous Rogues, such as Thieves, House-breakers, Plunderers of the Dead, or of the Sick, were duly punish'd, and several Declarations were continually publish'd by the Lord Mayor and Court of Aldermen against such.

Also all Constables and Church-wardens were enjoin'd to stay in the City upon severe Penalties, or to depute such able and sufficient House-keepers, as the Deputy Aldermen, or Common Council-men of the Precinct should approve, and for whom they should give Security; and also Security in case of Mortality, that they would forthwith constitute other Constables in their stead.

These things re-establish'd the Minds of the People very much, especially in the first of their Fright, when they talk'd of making so universal a Flight, that the City would have been in Danger of being entirely deserted of its Inhabitants, except the Poor; and the Country of being plunder'd and laid waste by the Multitude. Nor were the Magistrates deficient in performing their Part as boldly as they promised it; for my Lord Mayor and the Sheriffs were continually in the Streets, and at places of the greatest Danger; and tho' they did not care for having too great a Resort of People crouding about them, yet, in emergent Cases, they never denyed the People Access to them, and heard with Patience all their Grievances and Complaints; my Lord Mayor had a low Gallery built on purpose in his Hall, where he stood a little remov'd from the Croud when any Complaint came to be heard, that he might appear with as much Safety as possible.

Likewise the proper Officers, call'd *my Lord Mayor's Officers*, constantly attended in their Turns, as they were *in waiting*; and if any of them were sick or infected, as some of them were, others were instantly employed to fill up and officiate in their Places, till it was known whether the other should live or die.

In like manner the Sheriffs and Aldermen did in their several Stations and Wards, where they were placed by Office; and the Sheriff's Officers or Sergeants were appointed to receive Orders from the respective Aldermen in their Turn; so that Justice was executed in all Cases without Interruption. In the next Place, it was one of their particular Cares, to see the Orders for the Freedom of the Markets observ'd; and in this part either the Lord Mayor, or one or both of the Sheriffs, were every Market-day on Horseback to see their Orders executed, and to see that the Country People had all possible Encouragement and Freedom in their coming to the Markets, and going back again; and that no Nusances or frightful Objects should be seen in the Streets to terrify them, or make them unwilling to come. Also the Bakers were taken under particular Order, and the Master of the Bakers Company[1] was, with his Court of Assistance, directed to see the Order of my Lord Mayor for their Regulation put in Execution, and the due Assize of Bread, which was weekly appointed by my Lord Mayor, observ'd, and all the Bakers were oblig'd to keep their Ovens going constantly, on pain of losing the Privileges of a Freeman of the City of *London*.

By this means, Bread was always to be had in Plenty, and as cheap as usual, as I said above; and Provisions were never wanting in the Markets, even to such a Degree, that I often wonder'd at it, and reproach'd my self with being so timorous and cautious in stirring abroad, when the Country People came freely and boldly to Market, as if there had been no manner of Infection in the City, or Danger of catching it.

It was indeed one admirable piece of Conduct in the said Magistrates, that the Streets were kept constantly clear, and free from all manner of frightful Objects, dead Bodies, or any such things as were indecent or unpleasant, unless where any Body fell down suddenly or died in the Streets, *as I have said above*, and these were generally covered with some Cloth or Blanket, or remov'd into the next Church-yard, till Night: All the needful Works, that carried Terror with them, that were both dismal and dangerous, were done in the Night; if any diseas'd Bodies were remov'd, or dead Bodies buried, or infected Cloths burnt, it was done in the Night; and all the Bodies, which were thrown into the great Pits in the several Church-yards, or burying Grounds, *as has been observ'd*, were so remov'd in the Night; and every thing was covered and closed before Day: So that in the Day-time there was not the least Signal of the Calamity to be seen or heard of, except what was to be observ'd from the Emptiness of the Streets, and sometimes from the passionate Outcries and Lamentations of the People, out at their Windows, and from the Numbers of Houses and Shops shut up.

Nor was the Silence and Emptiness of the Streets so much in the City as in the Out-parts, except just at one particular time, when, as I have mention'd, the Plague came East, and spread over all the City: It was indeed a merciful Disposition of God, that as the Plague began at one End of the Town first, *as has been observ'd at large*, so it proceeded progressively to other Parts, and did not come on this way or Eastward, till it had spent its Fury in the West part of the Town; and so as it came on one way, it abated another. *For Example.*

It began at St. *Giles*'s and the *Westminster* End of the Town, and it was in its Height in all that part by about the Middle of *July*, *viz.* in St. *Giles* in the *Fields*, St. *Andrew's Holborn*, St. *Clement-Danes*, St. *Martins* in the *Fields*, and in *Westminster*: The latter End of *July* it decreased in those Parishes, and coming East, it encreased prodigiously in *Cripplegate*, St. *Sepulchers*, St. *Ja. Clarkenwell*, and St. *Brides*, and *Aldersgate*; while it was in all these Parishes, the City and all the Parishes of the *Southwark* Side of the Water, and all *Stepney*, *White-Chapel*, *Aldgate*, *Wapping*, and *Ratcliff* were very little touch'd; so that People went about their Business unconcern'd, carried on their Trades, kept open their Shops, and conversed freely with one another in all the City, the East and North-East Suburbs, and in *Southwark*, almost as if the Plague had not been among us.

Even when the North and North-west Suburbs were fully infected, *viz.* *Cripplegate*, *Clarkenwell*, *Bishopsgate*, and *Shoreditch*, yet still all the rest were tolerably well. For Example,

> From 25th *July* to 1st *August* the Bill stood thus
> of all Diseases;
>
> | | |
> |---|---:|
> | St. *Giles Cripplegate* - - - - - - - - - - - | 554 |
> | St. *Sepulchers* - - - - - - - - - - - - - - - | 250 |
> | *Clarkenwell* - - - - - - - - - - - - - - - - | 103 |
> | *Bishopsgate* - - - - - - - - - - - - - - - | 116 |
> | *Shoreditch* - - - - - - - - - - - - - - - - | 110 |
> | *Stepney* Parish - - - - - - - - - - - - - - | 127 |
> | *Aldgate* - - - - - - - - - - - - - - - - - | 92 |
> | *White-Chappel* - - - - - - - - - - - - - | 104 |
> | All the 97 Parishes within the Walls - - - | 228 |
> | All the Parishes in *Southwark* - - - - - - | 205 |
> | | 1889 |

So that in short there died more that Week in the two Parishes of *Cripplegate* and St. *Sepulchers* by 48 than in all the City, and all the East Suburbs, and all the *Southwark* Parishes put together: This caused the Reputation of the City's Health to continue all over *England*, and especially in the Counties and Markets adjacent, from whence our Supply of Provisions chiefly came, even much longer than that Health it self continued; for when the People came into the Streets from the Country, by *Shoreditch* and *Bishopsgate*, or by *Old-street* and *Smithfield*, they would see the out Streets empty, and the Houses and Shops shut, and the few People that were stirring there walk in the Middle of the Streets; but when

they came within the City, *there things look'd better*, and the
Markets and Shops were open, and the People walking about
the Streets as usual, tho' not quite so many; and this continued till the latter End of *August*, and the Beginning of
September.

But then the Case alter'd quite, the Distemper abated in
the West and North-West Parishes, and the Weight of the
Infection lay on the City and the Eastern Suburbs and the
Southwark Side, and this in a frightful manner.

Then indeed the City began to look dismal, Shops to be
shut, and the Streets desolate; in the High-Street indeed
Necessity made People stir abroad on many Occasions; and
there would be in the middle of the Day a pretty many People,
but in the Mornings and Evenings scarce any to be seen, even
there, no not in *Cornhill* and *Cheapside*.

These Observations of mine were abundantly confirm'd
by the Weekly Bills of Mortality for those Weeks, an Abstract
of which, as they respect the Parishes which I have mention'd,
and as they make the Calculations I speak of very evident,
take as follows.

The Weekly Bill, which makes out this Decrease of the
Burials in the West and North side of the City, stand thus.

From the 12th of *September* to the 19th.

St. *Giles's Cripplegate* - - - - - - - - - - -	456
St. *Giles* in the Fields - - - - - - - - - - -	140
Clarkenwell - - - - - - - - - - - - - - - - -	77
St. *Sepulchers* - - - - - - - - - - - - - - - -	214
St. *Leonard Shoreditch* - - - - - - - - - - -	183
Stepney Parish - - - - - - - - - - - - - -	716
Aldgate - - - - - - - - - - - - - - - - - -	623
White-Chapel - - - - - - - - - - - - - - -	532
In the 97 Parishes within the Walls - - -	1493
In the 8 Parishes on *Southwark* Side - -	1636

	6060

Here is a strange change of Things indeed, and a sad
Change it was, and had it held for two Months more than it

did, very few People would have been left alive: But then such, I say, was the merciful Disposition of God, that when it was thus the West and North part which had been so dreadfully visited at first, grew *as you see*, much better; and as the People disappear'd here, they began to look abroad again there; and the next Week or two altered it still more, that is, more to the Encouragement of the other Part of the Town. *For Example:*

From the 19th of *September* to the 26th;

St. *Giles's Cripplegate* - - - - - - - - - - -	277
St. *Giles* in the Fields - - - - - - - - - - -	119
Clarkenwell - - - - - - - - - - - - - - - -	76
St. *Sepulchers* - - - - - - - - - - - - - - -	193
St. *Leonard Shoreditch* - - - - - - - - - - -	146
Stepney Parish - - - - - - - - - - - - - -	616
Aldgate - - - - - - - - - - - - - - - - - -	496
White-Chapel - - - - - - - - - - - - - - -	346
In the 97 Parishes within the Walls - - -	1268
In the 8 Parishes on *Southwark* Side - -	1390

	4900

From the 26th of *Septemb.* to the 3^d of *October.*

St. *Giles's Cripplegate* - - - - - - - - - - -	196
St. *Giles* in the Fields - - - - - - - - - - -	95
Clarkenwell - - - - - - - - - - - - - - - -	48
St. *Sepulchers* - - - - - - - - - - - - - - -	137
St. *Leonard Shoreditch* - - - - - - - - - - -	128
Stepney Parish - - - - - - - - - - - - - -	674
Aldgate - - - - - - - - - - - - - - - - - -	372
White-Chapel - - - - - - - - - - - - - - -	328
In the 97 Parishes within the Walls - - -	1149
In the 8 Parishes on *Southwark* Side - -	1201

	4328

And now the Misery of the City, and of the said East and South Parts was complete indeed; for as you see the Weight of the Distemper lay upon those Parts, that is to say, the City, the eight Parishes over the River, with the Parishes of *Aldgate*,

White-Chapel, and *Stepney*, and this was the Time that the Bills came up to such a monstrous Height, as that I mention'd before; and that Eight or Nine, and, as I believe, Ten or Twelve Thousand a Week died; for 'tis my settled Opinion, that they never could come at any just Account of the Numbers, for the Reasons which I have given already.

Nay one of the most eminent Physicians, who has since publish'd in Latin[1] an Account of those Times, and of his Observations, says, that in one Week there died twelve Thousand People, and that particularly there died four Thousand in one Night;[2] tho' I do not remember that there ever was any such particular Night, so remarkably fatal, as that such a Number died in it: However all this confirms what I have said above of the Uncertainty of the Bills of Mortality, *&c.*, of which I shall say more hereafter.

And here let me take leave to enter again, tho' it may seem a Repetition of Circumstances, into a Description of the miserable Condition of the City it self, and of those Parts where I liv'd at this particular Time: The City, and those other Parts, not withstanding the great Numbers of People that were gone into the Country, was vastly full of People, and perhaps the fuller, because People had for a long time a strong Belief, that the Plague would not come into the City, nor into *Southwark*, no nor into *Wapping*, or *Ratcliff* at all; nay such was the Assurance of the People on that Head, that many remov'd from the Suburbs on the West and North Sides, into those Eastern and South Sides as for Safety, and as I verily believe, carry'd, the Plague amongst them there, perhaps sooner than they would otherwise have had it.

Here also I ought to leave a farther Remark for the use of Posterity, concerning the Manner of Peoples infecting one another; namely, that it was not the sick People only, from whom the Plague was immediately receiv'd by others that were sound, but THE WELL. *To explain my self*; by *the sick* People I mean those who were known to be sick, had taken their Beds, had been under Cure, or had Swellings and Tumours upon them, and the like; these every Body could beware of, they were either in their Beds, or in such Condition as cou'd not be conceal'd.

By *the Well*, I mean such as had received the Contagion, and had it really upon them, and in their Blood, yet did not shew the Consequences of it in their Countenances, nay even were not sensible of it themselves, *as many were not* for several Days: These breathed Death in every Place, and upon every Body who came near them; nay their very Cloaths retained the Infection, their Hands would infect the Things they touch'd, especially if they were warm and sweaty, and they were generally apt to sweat too.

Now it was impossible to know these People, nor did they sometimes, as I have said, know themselves to be infected: These were the People that so often dropt down and fainted in the Streets; for oftentimes they would go about the Streets to the last, till on a sudden they would sweat, grow faint, sit down at a Door and die: It is true, finding themselves thus, they would struggle hard to get Home to their own Doors, or at other Times would be just able to go in to their Houses and die instantly; other Times they would go about till they had the very Tokens come out upon them, and yet not know it, and would die in an Hour or two after they came Home, but be well as long as they were Abroad: These were the dangerous People, these were the People of whom the well People ought to have been afraid; but then *on the other side* it was impossible to know them.

And this is the Reason why it is impossible in a Visitation to prevent the spreading of the Plague by the utmost human Vigilance, (*viz.*) that it is impossible to know the infected People from the sound; or that the infected People should perfectly know themselves: I knew a Man who conversed freely in *London* all the Season of the Plague in 1665, and kept about him an Antidote or Cordial, on purpose to take when he thought himself in any Danger, and he had such a Rule to know, or have warning of the Danger by, as indeed I never met with before or since, how far it may be depended on I know not: He had a Wound in his Leg, and whenever he came among any People that were not sound, and the Infection began to affect him, he said he could know it by that Signal, (*viz.*) That his Wound in his Leg would smart, and look pale and white; so as soon as ever he felt it smart, it was time for him to withdraw, or to take care of himself, taking his Drink, which he always carried about him for that Purpose. Now it seems he found his Wound would smart many Times when he was in Company with such, who thought themselves to be sound, and who appear'd so to one another; but he would presently rise up, and say publickly, Friends, here is some Body in the Room that has the Plague, and so would immediately break up the Company. This was indeed a faithful Monitor to all People, that the Plague is not to be avoided by those that converse promiscuously in a Town infected, and People have it when they know it not, and that they likewise give it to others when they know not that they have it themselves; and in this Case, shutting up the WELL or removing the SICK will not do it, unless they can go back and shut up all those that the Sick had Convers'd with, even before they knew themselves to be sick, and none knows how far to carry that back, or where to stop; for none knows when, or where, or how they may have received the Infection, or from whom.

This I take to be the Reason, which makes so many People talk of the Air being corrupted and infected,[1] and that they need not be cautious of whom they converse with, for that the Contagion was in the Air. I have seen them in strange Agitations and Surprises on this Account, I have never come near any infected Body! *says the disturbed Person*, I have Convers'd with none, but sound healthy People, and yet I have gotten the Distemper! I am sure I am struck from Heaven, *says another*, and he falls to the serious Part; again the first goes on exclaiming, I have come near no Infection, or any infected Person, *I am sure it is in the Air*; We draw in Death when we breath[e], and therefore 'tis the Hand of God, there is no withstanding it; and this at last made many People, being hardened to the Danger, grow less concern'd at it, and less cautious towards the latter End of the Time, and when it was come to its height, than they were at first; then with a kind of a *Turkish* Predestinarianism,[1] they would say, if it pleas'd God to strike them, it was all one whether they went Abroad or staid at Home, they cou'd not escape it, and therefore they went boldly about even into infected Houses, and infected Company; visited sick People, and in short, lay in the Beds with their Wives or Relations when they were infected; and what was the Consequence? But the same that is the Consequence in *Turkey*, and in those Countries where they do those Things; namely, that they were infected too, and died by Hundreds and Thousands.

I would be far from lessening the Awe of the Judgments of God, and the Reverence to his Providence, which ought always to be on our Minds on such Occasions as these; doubtless the Visitation it self is a Stroke from Heaven upon a City, or Country, or Nation where it falls; a Messenger of his Vengeance, and a loud Call to that Nation, or Country, or City, to Humiliation and Repentance, according to that of the Prophet *Jeremiah* xviii. 7, 8. *At what instant I shall speak concerning a Nation, and concerning a Kingdom to pluck up, and to pull down, and destroy it : If that Nation against whom I have pronounced, turn from their evil, I will repent of the evil that I thought to do unto them.* Now to prompt due Impressions of the Awe of God on the Minds of Men on such Occasions, and not to lessen them it is that I have left those Minutes upon Record.

I say, therefore I reflect upon no Man for putting the Reason of those Things upon the immediate Hand of God, and the Appointment and Direction of his Providence; nay, on the contrary, there were many wonderful Deliverances of Persons from Infection, and Deliverances of Persons when Infected, which intimate singular and remarkable Providence, in the particular Instances to which they refer, and I esteem my own Deliverance to be one next to miraculous, and do record it with Thankfulness.

But when I am speaking of the Plague, as a Distemper

arising from natural Causes,[1] we must consider it as it was really propagated by natural Means, nor is it at all the less a Judgment for its being under the Conduct of human Causes and Effects; for as the divine Power has form'd the whole Scheme of Nature, and maintains Nature in its Course; so the same Power thinks fit to let his own Actings with Men, whether of Mercy or Judgment, go on in the ordinary Course of natural Causes, and he is pleased to act by those natural Causes as the ordinary Means; excepting and reserving to himself nevertheless a Power to act in a supernatural Way when he sees occasion: Now 'tis evident, that in the Case of an Infection, there is no apparent extraordinary occasion for supernatural Operation, but the ordinary Course of Things appears sufficiently arm'd, and made capable of all the Effects that Heaven usually directs by a Contagion. Among these Causes and Effects this of the secret Conveyance of Infection imperceptible, and unavoidable, is more than sufficient to execute the Fierceness of divine Vengeance, without putting it upon Supernaturals and Miracle.

The acute penetrating Nature of the Disease it self was such, and the Infection was receiv'd so imperceptibly, that the most exact Caution could not secure us while in the Place: But I must be allowed to believe, and I have so many Examples fresh in my Memory, to convince me of it, that I think none can resist their Evidence; *I say*, I must be allowed to believe, that no one in this whole Nation ever receiv'd the Sickness or Infection, but who receiv'd it in the ordinary Way of Infection from some Body, or the Cloaths, or touch, or stench of some Body that was infected before.

The Manner of its coming first to *London*, proves this also, (*viz.*) by Goods brought over from *Holland*, and brought thither from the *Levant*; the first breaking of it out in a House in *Long-Acre*, where those Goods were carried, and first opened; its spreading from that House to other Houses, by the visible unwary conversing with those who were sick, and the infecting the Parish Officers who were employed about the Persons dead, *and the like*; these are known Authorities for this great Foundation Point, that it went on, and proceeded from Person to Person, and from House to House, and no otherwise: In the first House that was infected there died four Persons, a Neighbour hearing the Mistress of the first House was sick, went to visit her, and went Home and gave the Distemper to her Family, and died, and all her Houshold. A Minister call'd to pray with the first sick Person in the second House, was said to sicken immediately, and die with several more in his House: Then the Physicians began to consider, for they did not at first dream of a general Contagion. But the Physicians being sent to inspect the Bodies, they assur'd the People that it was neither more or less than *the Plague* with all its terrifying Particulars, and that it threatned an universal Infection, so many People having already convers'd with the Sick or Distemper'd, and having, as might be suppos'd, received Infection from them, that it would be impossible to put a stop to it.

Here the Opinion of the Physicians agreed with my Observation afterwards, namely, that the Danger was spreading insensibly; for the Sick cou'd infect none but those that came within reach of the sick Person; but that one Man, who may have really receiv'd the Infection, and knows it not, but goes Abroad, and about as a sound Person, may give the Plague to a thousand People, and they to greater Numbers in Proportion, and neither the Person giving the Infection, or the Persons receiving it, know any thing of it, and perhaps not feel the Effects of it for several Days after.

For Example, Many Persons in the Time of this Visitation never perceiv'd that they were infected, till they found to their unspeakable Surprize, the Tokens come out upon them, after which they seldom liv'd six Hours; for those Spots they call'd the Tokens were really gangreen Spots, or mortified Flesh in small Knobs as broad as a little silver Peny, and hard as a piece of Callous or Horn; so that when the Disease was come up to that length, there was nothing could follow but certain Death, and yet *as I said* they knew nothing of their being Infected, nor found themselves so much as out of Order, till those mortal Marks were upon them: But every Body must allow, that they were infected in a high Degree before, and must have been so some time; and consequently their Breath, their Sweat, their very Cloaths were contagious for many Days before.

This occasion'd a vast Variety of Cases, which Physicians would have much more opportunity to remember than I; but some came within the Compass of my Observation, or hearing, of which I shall name a few.

A certain Citizen who had liv'd safe, and untouch'd, till the Month of *September*, when the Weight of the Distemper lay more in the City than it had done before, was mighty chearful, and something too bold, as I think it was, in his Talk of how secure he was, how cautious he had been, and how he had never come near any sick Body: Says another Citizen, a Neighbour of his to him, one Day, *Do not be too confident* Mr. —— *it is hard to say who is sick and who is well; for we see Men alive, and well to outward Appearance one Hour, and dead the next.* That is true, says the first Man, for he was not a Man presumptuously secure, but had escap'd a long while, and Men, as I said above, especially in the City, began to be over-easie upon that Score. *That is true*, says he, I do not think my self secure, *but I hope I have not been in Company with any Person that there has been any Danger in.* No! Says his Neighbour, *was not you at the* Bull-head *Tavern in* Gracechurch Street *with Mr.* —— *the Night before last:* YES, says the first, *I was,* but *there was no Body there, that we had any Reason to think dangerous:* Upon which his Neighbour said no more, being unwilling to surprize him; but this made him more inquisitive, and as his Neighbour appear'd backward, he was the more impatient, and in a kind of Warmth, says he aloud, *why he is not dead, is he!* upon which his Neighbour still was silent, but cast up his Eyes, and said something to himself; at which the first Citizen turned pale, and said no more but this, *then I am a dead Man too*, and went Home immediately, and sent for a neighbouring Apothecary to give him something preventive, for he had not yet found himself ill; but the

Apothecary opening his Breast, fetch'd a Sigh, and said no more, but this, *look up to God*; and the Man died in a few Hours.

Now let any Man judge from a Case like this, if it is possible for the Regulations of Magistrates, either by shutting up the Sick, or removing them, to stop an Infection, which spreads it self from Man to Man, even while they are perfectly well, and insensible of its Approach, and may be so for many Days.

It may be proper to ask here, how long it may be supposed, Men might have the Seeds of the Contagion in them, before it discover'd it self in this fatal Manner; and how long they might go about seemingly whole, and yet be contagious to all those that came near them? I believe the most experienc'd Physicians cannot answer this Question directly, any more than I can; and something an ordinary Observer may take notice of, which may pass their Observation. The opinion of Physicians Abroad seems to be, that it may lye Dormant in the Spirits, or in the Blood Vessels, a very considerable Time; why else do they exact a Quarentine of those who come into their Harbours, and Ports, from suspected Places? Forty Days is, one would think, too long for Nature to struggle with such an Enemy as this, and not conquer it, or yield to it: But I could not think by my own Observation that they can be infected so, as to be contagious to others, above fifteen or sixteen Days at farthest; and on that score it was, that when a House was shut up in the City, and any one had died of the Plague, but no Body appear'd to be ill in the Family for sixteen or eighteen Days after, they were not so strict, but that they would connive at their going privately Abroad; nor would People be much afraid of them afterward, but rather think they were fortified the better, having not been vulnerable when the Enemy was in their own House; but we sometimes found it had lyen much longer conceal'd.

Upon the foot of all these Observations, I must say, that tho' Providence seem'd to direct my Conduct to be otherwise; yet it is my opinion, and I must leave it as a Prescription, (*viz.*) *that the best Physick against the Plague is to run away from it.* I know People encourage themselves, by saying, God is able to keep us in the midst of Danger, and able to overtake us when we think our selves out of Danger; and this kept Thousands in the Town, whose Carcasses went into the great Pits by Cart Loads; and who, if they had fled from the Danger, had, I believe, been safe from the Disaster; at least 'tis probable they had been safe.

And were this very Fundamental only duly consider'd by the People, on any future occasion of this, or the like Nature, I am persuaded it would put them upon quite different Measures for managing the People, from those that they took in 1665, or than any that have been taken Abroad that I have heard of; in a Word, they would consider of separating the People into smaller Bodies, and removing them in Time farther from one another, and not let such a Contagion as this, which is indeed chiefly dangerous to collected Bodies of People, find a Million of People in a Body together, as was very near the Case before, and would certainly be the Case, if it should ever appear again.

The Plague like a great Fire, if a few Houses only are contiguous where it happens, can only burn a few Houses; or if it begins in a single, or as we call it a lone House, can only burn that lone House where it begins: But if it begins in a close built Town, or City, and gets a Head, there its Fury encreases, it rages over the whole Place, and consumes all it can reach.

I could propose many Schemes, on the foot of which the Government of this City, if ever they should be under the Apprehensions of such another Enemy, (God forbid they should) might ease themselves of the greatest Part of the dangerous People that belong to them; I mean such as the begging, starving, labouring Poor, and among them chiefly those who in Case of a Siege, are call'd the useless Mouths; who being then prudently, and to their own Advantage dispos'd of, and the wealthy Inhabitants disposing of themselves, and of their Servants, and Children, the City and its adjacent Parts would be so effectually evacuated, that there would not be above a tenth Part of its People left together, for the Disease to take hold upon: But suppose them to be a fifth Part, and that two Hundred and fifty Thousand People were left, and if it did seize upon them, they would by their living so much at large, be much better prepar'd to defend themselves against the Infection, and be less liable to the Effects of it, than if the same Number of People lived close together in one smaller City, such as *Dublin*, or *Amsterdam*, or the like.

It is true, Hundreds, yea Thousands of Families fled away at this last Plague, but then of them, many fled too late, and not only died in their Flight, but carried the Distemper with them into the Countries where they went, and infected those whom they went among for Safety; which confounded the Thing, and made that be a Propagation of the Distemper, which was the best means to prevent it; and this too is an Evidence of it, and brings me back to what I only hinted at before, but must speak more fully to here; namely, that Men went about apparently well, many Days after they had the taint of the Disease in their Vitals, and after their Spirits were so seiz'd, as that they could never escape it; and that all the while they did so, they were dangerous to others. *I say*, this proves, *that so it was*; for such People infected the very Towns they went thro', as well as the Families they went among, and it was by that means, that almost all the great Towns in *England* had the Distemper among them, more or less; and always they would tell you such a *Londoner* or such a *Londoner* brought it down.

It must not be omitted, that when I speak of those People who were really thus dangerous, I suppose them to be utterly ignorant of their own Condition, for if they really knew their Circumstances to be such as indeed they were, they must have been a kind of *willful Murtherers*, if they would have gone Abroad among healthy People, and it would have verified indeed the Suggestion *which I mention'd above, and which I thought seem'd untrue*, (*viz.*) That the infected People were utterly careless as to giving the Infection to others, and rather forward to do it than not;

and I believe it was partly from this very Thing that they raised that Suggestion, which I hope was not really true in Fact.

I confess no particular Case is sufficient to prove a general, but I cou'd name several People within the Knowledge of some of their Neighbours and Families yet living, who shew'd the contrary to an extream. One Man, a Master of a Family in my Neighbourhood, having had the Distemper, he thought he had it given him by a poor Workman whom he employ'd, and whom he went to his House to see, or went for some Work that he wanted to have finished, and he had some Apprehensions even while he was at the poor Workman's Door, but did not discover it fully, but the next Day it discovered it self, and he was taken very ill; upon which he immediately caused himself to be carried into an out Building which he had in his Yard, and where there was a Chamber over a Work-house, the Man being a Brazier; here he lay, and here he died, and would be tended by none of his Neighbours, but by a Nurse from Abroad, and would not suffer his Wife, or Children, or Servants, to come up into the Room lest they should be infected, but sent them his Blessing and Prayers for them by the Nurse, who spoke it to them at a Distance, and all this for fear of giving them the Distemper, and without which, he knew as they were kept up, they could not have it.

And here I must observe also, that the Plague, as I suppose all Distempers do, operated in a different Manner on differing Constitutions; some were immediately overwhelm'd with it, and it came to violent Fevers, Vomitings, unsufferable Headachs, Pains in the Back, and so up to Ravings and Ragings with those Pains: Others with Swellings and Tumours in the Neck or Groyn, or Arm-pits, which till they could be broke, put them into insufferable Agonies and Torment; while others, as I have observ'd, were silently infected, the Fever preying upon their Spirits insensibly, and they seeing little of it, till they fell into swooning, and faintings, and Death without pain.

I am not Physician enough to enter into the particular

Reasons and Manner of these differing Effects of one and the same Distemper, and of its differing Operation in several Bodies; nor is it my Business here to record the Observations, which I really made, because the Doctors themselves, have done that part much more effectually than I can do, and because my opinion may in some things differ from theirs: I am only relating what I know, or have heard, or believe of the particular Cases, and what fell within the Compass of my View, and the different Nature of the Infection, as it appeared in the particular Cases which I have related; but this may be added too, that tho' the former Sort of those Cases, namely those openly visited, were the worst for themselves as to Pain, I mean those that had such Fevers, Vomitings, Head-achs, Pains and Swellings, because they died in such a dreadful Manner, yet the latter had the worst State of the Disease; for in the former they frequently recover'd, especially if the Swellings broke,[1] but the latter was inevitable Death; no cure, no help cou'd be possible, nothing could follow but Death; and it was worse also to others, because as, above, it secretly, and unperceiv'd by others, or by themselves, communicated Death to those they convers'd with, the penetrating Poison insinuating it self into their Blood in a Manner, which it is impossible to describe, or indeed conceive.

This infecting and being infected, without so much as its being known to either Person, is evident from two Sorts of Cases, which frequently happened at that Time; and there is hardly any Body living who was in *London* during the Infection, but must have known several of the Cases of both Sorts.

1. Fathers and Mothers have gone about as if they had been well, and have believ'd themselves to be so, till they have insensibly infected, and been the Destruction of their whole Families: Which they would have been far from doing, if they had the least Apprehensions of their being unsound and dangerous themselves. A Family, whose Story I have heard, was thus infected by the Father, and the Distemper began tȯ appear upon some of them, even before he found it upon himself; but searching more narrowly, it appear'd he

had been infected some Time, and as soon as he found that
his Family had been poison'd by himself, he went distracted,
and would have laid violent Hands upon himself, but was
kept from that by those who look'd to him, and in a few Days
died.

2. The other Particular is, that many People having been
well to the best of their own Judgment, or by the best Observation which they could make of themselves for several Days,
and only finding a Decay of Appetite, or a light Sickness upon
their Stomachs; nay, some whose Appetite had been strong,
and even craving, and only a light Pain in their Heads; have
sent for Physicians to know what ail'd them, and have been
found to their great Surprize, at the brink of Death, the
Tokens upon them, or the Plague grown up to an incurable
Height.

It was very sad to reflect, how such a Person *as this last
mentioned above*, had been a walking Destroyer, perhaps for
a Week or Fortnight before that; how he had ruin'd those, that
he would have hazarded his Life to save, and had been breathing Death upon them, even perhaps in his tender Kissing and
Embracings of his own Children: Yet thus certainly it was,
and often has been, and I cou'd give many particular Cases
where it has been so; if then the Blow is thus insensibly
striking, if the Arrow flies thus unseen, and cannot be discovered; to what purpose are all the Schemes for shutting
up or removing the sick People? those Schemes cannot take
place, but upon those that appear to be sick, or to be infected;
whereas there are among them, at the same time, Thousands
of People, who seem to be well, but are all that while carrying
Death with them into all Companies which they come into.

This frequently puzzled our Physicians, and especially the
Apothecaries and Surgeons, who knew not how to discover
the Sick from the Sound; they all allow'd *that it was really so*,
that many People had the Plague in their very Blood, and
preying upon their Spirits, and were in themselves but
walking putrified Carcasses, whose Breath was infectious,[1]
and their Sweat Poison; and yet were as well to look on as

other People, and even knew it not themselves: I say, they all allowed that it was really true in Fact, but they knew not how to propose a Discovery.

My Friend Doctor *Heath* was of Opinion, that it might be known by the smell of their Breath; but then, *as he said*, who durst Smell to that Breath for his Information? Since to know it, he must draw the Stench of the Plague up into his own Brain, in order to distinguish the Smell! I have heard, it was the opinion of others, that it might be distinguish'd by the Party's breathing upon a piece of Glass, where the Breath condensing, there might living Creatures be seen by a Microscope of strange monstrous and frightful Shapes, such as Dragons, Snakes, Serpents, and Devils, horrible to behold: But this I very much question the Truth of, and we had no Microscopes at that Time,[1] as I remember, to make the Experiment with.

It was the opinion also of another learned Man, that the Breath of such a Person would poison, and instantly kill a Bird; not only a small Bird, but even a Cock or Hen, and that if it did not immediately kill the latter, it would cause them to be roupy *as they call it*; particularly that if they had laid any Eggs at that Time, they would be all rotten: But those are Opinions which I never found supported by any Experiments, or heard of others that had seen it; so I leave them as I find them, only with this Remark; namely, that I think the Probabilities are very strong for them.

Some have proposed that such Persons should breathe hard upon warm Water, and that they would leave an unusual Scum upon it, or upon several other things, especially such as are of a glutinous Substance and are apt to receive a Scum and support it.

But from the whole I found, that the Nature of this Contagion was such, that it was impossible to discover it at all, or to prevent its spreading from one to another by any human Skill.

Here was indeed one Difficulty, which I could never thoroughly get over to this time, and which there is but one way of answering that I know of, and it is this, *viz*. The first Person that died of the Plague was in *Decemb*. 20th, or thereabouts 1664, and in, or about *Long-acre*, whence the first Person had the Infection, was generally said to be, from a Parcel of Silks imported from *Holland*, and first opened in that House.

But after this we heard no more of any Person dying of the Plague, or of the Distemper being in that Place, till the 9th of *February*; which was about 7 Weeks after, and then one more was buried out of the same House: Then it was hush'd, and we were perfectly easy as to the publick, for a great while; for there were no more entred in the Weekly Bill to be dead of the Plague, till the 22^d of *April*, when there was 2 more buried not out of the same House, but out of the same Street; and as near as I can remember, it was out of the next House to the first: this was nine Weeks asunder, and after this we had No more till a Fortnight, and then it broke out in several Streets and spread every way. Now the Question seems to lye thus, *where lay the Seeds of the Infection all this while? How came it to stop so long, and not stop any longer?* Either the Distemper did not come immediately by Contagion from Body to Body, or if it did, then a Body may be capable to continue infected, without the Disease discovering itself, many Days, nay Weeks together, even not a Quarantine of Days only, but Soixantine, not only 40 Days but 60 Days or longer.

It's true, there was, as I observed at first, and is well known to many yet living, a very cold Winter, and a long Frost,[1] which continued three Months, and this, the Doctors say, might check the Infection; but then the learned must allow me to say, that if according to their Notion, the Disease was, as I may say, only frozen up, it would like a frozen River, have returned to its usual Force and Current when it thaw'd, whereas the principal Recess of this Infection, which was from *February* to *April*, was after the Frost was broken, and the Weather mild and warm.

But there is another way of solving all this Difficulty, which I think my own Remembrance of the thing will supply; and that is, the Fact is not granted, namely, that there died none in those long Intervals, *viz.* from the 20th of *December* to the 9th of *February*, and from thence to the 22^d of *April*. The Weekly Bills are the only Evidence on the other side, and those Bills were not of Credit enough, at least with me, to support an *Hypothesis*, or determine a Question of such Importance as this: For it was our receiv'd Opinion at that time, and I believe upon very good Grounds, that the Fraud lay in the Parish Officers, Searchers, and Persons appointed to give Account of the Dead, and what Diseases they died of: And as People were very loth at first to have the Neighbours believe their Houses were infected, so they gave Money to procure, or otherwise procur'd the dead Persons to be return'd as dying of other Distempers; and this I know was practis'd afterwards in many Places, I believe I might say in all Places, where the Distemper came, as will be seen by the vast Encrease of the Numbers plac'd in the Weekly Bills under other Articles of Diseases, during the time of the Infection: *For Example*, in the Month of *July* and *August*, when the Plague was coming on to its highest Pitch; it was very ordinary to have from a thousand to twelve hundred, nay to almost fifteen Hundred a Week of other Distempers; not that the Numbers of those Distempers were really encreased to such a Degree: But the great Number of Families and Houses where really the Infection was, obtain'd the Favour to have their dead be return'd of other Distempers to prevent the shutting up their Houses. *For Example*,

Dead of other Diseases besides the *Plague*.

From the 18th to the 25th *July* - - - - -	942
to the 1st *August* - - - -	1004
to the 8th - - - - - - - -	1213
to the 15th - - - - - - -	1439
to the 22d - - - - - - -	1331
to the 29th - - - - - - -	1394
to the 5th *September* - -	1264
to the 12th - - - - - - -	1056
to the 19th - - - - - - -	1132
to the 26th - - - - - - -	927

Now it was not doubted, but the greatest part of these, or a great part of them, were dead of the Plague, but the Officers were prevail'd with to return them as above, and the Numbers of some particular Articles of Distempers discover'd is, as follows;

From the 1st to the 8th of *Aug.*	to the 15th.	to the 22.	to the 29.
Fever	314	353	348	383
Spotted Fever	174	190	166	165
Surfeit	85	87	74	99
Teeth	90	113	111	133
	663	743	699	780

From *August* 29th to the 5th *Sept.*	to the 12.	to the 19.	to the 26.
Fever	364	332	309	268
Spotted Fever	157	97	101	65
Surfeit	68	45	49	36
Teeth	138	128	121	112
	728	602	580	481

There were several other Articles which bare a Proportion to these, and which it is easy to perceive, were increased on the same Account, as *Aged, Consumptions, Vomitings, Imposthumes, Gripes*, and the like, many of which were not doubted to be infected People; but as it was of the utmost Consequence to Families not to be known to be infected, if it was possible to avoid it, so they took all the measures they could to have it not believ'd; and if any died in their Houses to get them return'd to the Examiners, and by the Searchers, as having died of other Distempers.

This, I say, will account for the long Interval, which, *as I have said*, was between the dying of the first Persons that were returned in the Bill to be dead of the Plague, and the time when the Distemper spread openly, and could not be conceal'd.

Besides, the Weekly Bills themselves at that time evidently discover this Truth; for while there was no Mention of the

Plague, and no Increase after it had been mentioned, yet it was apparent that there was an Encrease of those Distempers which bordered nearest upon it, for Example there were Eight, Twelve, Seventeen of the Spotted Fever in a Week, when there were none, or but very few of the Plague; whereas before *One*, *Three*, or *Four*, were the ordinary Weekly Numbers of that Distemper; likewise, as I observed before, the Burials increased Weekly in that particular Parish, and the Parishes adjacent, more than in any other Parish, altho' there were none set down of the Plague; all which tells us, that the Infection was handed on, and the Succession of the Distemper really preserv'd, tho' it seem'd to us at that time to be ceased, and to come again in a manner surprising.

It might be also, that the Infection might remain in other parts of the same Parcel of Goods which at first it came in, and which might not be perhaps opened, or at least not fully, or in the Cloths of the first infected Person; for I cannot think, that any Body could be seiz'd with the Contagion in a fatal and mortal Degree for nine Weeks together, and support his State of Health so well, as even not to discover it to themselves; yet if it were so, the Argument is the stronger in Favour of what I am saying; namely, that the Infection is retain'd in Bodies apparently well, and convey'd from them to those they converse with, while it is known to neither the one nor the other.

Great were the Confusions at that time upon this very Account; and when People began to be convinc'd that the Infection was receiv'd in this surprising manner from Persons apparently well, they began to be exceeding shie and jealous of every one that came near them. Once in a publick Day, whether a Sabbath Day or not I do not remember, in *Aldgate* Church in a Pew full of People, on a sudden, one fancy'd she smelt an ill Smell, immediately she fancies the Plague was in the Pew, whispers her Notion or Suspicion to the next, then rises and goes out of the Pew, it immediately took with the next, and so to them all; and every one of them, and of the two or three adjoining Pews, got up and went out of the

Church, no Body knowing what it was offended them or from whom.

This immediately filled every Bodies Mouths with one Preparation or other, such as the old Women directed, and some perhaps as Physicians directed, in order to prevent Infection by the Breath of others; insomuch that if we came to go into a Church, when it was any thing full of People, there would be such a Mixture of Smells at the Entrance, that it was much more strong, tho' perhaps not so wholesome, than if you were going into an Apothecary's or Druggist's Shop; in a Word, the whole Church was like a smelling Bottle, in one Corner it was all Perfumes, in another Aromaticks, Balsamicks, and Variety of Drugs, and Herbs; in another Salts and Spirits, as every one was furnish'd for their own Preservation; yet I observ'd, that after People were possess'd, *as I have said*, with the Belief or rather Assurance, of the Infection being thus carryed on by Persons apparently in Health, the Churches and Meeting-Houses were much thinner of People than at other times before that they us'd to be; for this is to be said of the People of *London*, that during the whole time of the Pestilence, the Churches or Meetings were never wholly shut up, nor did the People decline coming out to the public Worship of God, except only in some Parishes when the Violence of the Distemper was more particularly in that Parish at that time; and even then no longer, than it continued to be so.

Indeed nothing was more strange, than to see with what Courage the People went to the public Service of God, even at that time when they were afraid to stir out of their own Houses upon any other Occasion; this I mean before the time of Desperation, which I have mention'd already; this was a Proof of the exceeding Populousness of the City at the time of the Infection, notwithstanding the great Numbers that were gone into the Country at the first Alarm, and that fled out into the Forests and Woods when they were farther terrifyed with the extraordinary Increase of it. For when we came to see the Crouds and Throngs of People, which appear'd on the Sabbath Days at the Churches, and especially in those parts of the Town where the Plague was abated, or where it was not yet come to its Height, it was amazing. But of this I shall speak again presently; I return in the mean time to the Article of infecting one another at first; before People came to right Notions of the Infection, and of infecting one another, People were only shye of those that were really sick, a Man with a Cap upon his Head, or with Cloths round his Neck, *which was the Case of those that had Swellings there*; such was indeed frightful: But when we saw a Gentleman dress'd, with his Band on and his Gloves in his Hand, his Hat upon his Head, and his Hair comb'd, of such we had not the least Apprehensions; and People conversed a great while freely, *especially with their Neighbours and such as they knew*. But when the Physicians assured us, that the Danger was as well from the Sound, that is *the seemingly sound*, as the Sick; and that those People, who thought themselves entirely free, were oftentimes the most fatal; and that it came to be generally understood, that People were sensible of it, and of the reason of it: Then I say they began to be jealous of every Body, and a vast Number of People lock'd themselves up, so as not to come abroad into any Company at all, nor suffer any, that had been abroad in promiscuous Company, to come into their Houses, or near them; at least not so near them, as to be within the Reach of their Breath, or of any Smell from them; and when they were oblig'd to converse at a Distance with Strangers, they would always have Preservatives in their Mouths, and about their Cloths to repell and keep off the Infection.

It must be acknowledg'd, that when People began to use these Cautions, they were less exposed to Danger, and the Infection did not break into such Houses so furiously as it did into others before, and thousands of Families were preserved, *speaking with due Reserve to the Direction of Divine Providence*, by that Means.

But it was impossible to beat any thing into the Heads of the Poor, they went on with the usual Impetuosity of their

Tempers full of Outcries and Lamentations when taken, but madly careless of themselves, Fool-hardy and obstinate, while they were well: Where they could get Employment they push'd into any kind of Business, the most dangerous and the most liable to Infection; and if they were spoken to, their Answer would be, *I must trust to God for that; if I am taken, then I am provided for, and there is an End of me*, and the like: OR THUS, *Why, What must I do? I can't starve, I had as good have the Plague as perish for want. I have no Work, what could I do? I must do this or beg*: Suppose it was burying the dead, or attending the Sick, or watching infected Houses, which were all terrible Hazards, but their Tale was generally the same. It is true Necessity was a very justifiable warrantable Plea, and nothing could be better; but their way of Talk was much the same, where the Necessities were not the same: This adventurous Conduct of the Poor was that which brought the Plague among them in a most furious manner, and this join'd to the Distress of their Circumstances, when taken, was the reason why they died so by Heaps; for I cannot say, I could observe one jot of better Husbandry among them, I mean the labouring Poor, while they were well and getting Money, than there was before, but as lavish, as extravagant, and as thoughtless for to-morrow as ever; so that when they came to be taken sick, they were immediately in the utmost Distress as well for want, as for Sickness, as well for lack of Food, as lack of Health.

This Misery of the Poor I had many Occasions to be an Eye-witness of, and sometimes also of the charitable Assistance that some pious People daily gave to such, sending them Relief and Supplies both of Food, Physick and other Help, as they found they wanted; and indeed it is a Debt of Justice due to the Temper of the People of that Day to take Notice here, that not only great Sums, *very great* Sums of Money were charitably sent to the Lord Mayor and Aldermen for the Assistance and Support of the poor distemper'd People; but abundance of private People daily distributed large Sums of Money for their Relief, and sent People about to enquire into the Condition of particular distressed and visited Families, and relieved them; nay some pious Ladies were so transported with Zeal in so good a Work, and so confident in the Protection of Providence in Discharge of the great Duty of Charity, that they went about in person distributing Alms to the Poor, and even visiting poor Families, tho' sick and infected in their very Houses, appointing Nurses to attend those that wanted attending, and ordering Apothecaries and Surgeons, the first to supply them with Drugs or Plaisters, and such things as they wanted; and the last to lance and dress the Swellings and Tumours, where such were wanting; giving their Blessing to the Poor in substantial Relief to them, as well as hearty Prayers for them.

I will not undertake to say, as some do, that none of these charitable People were suffered to fall under the Calamity itself; but this I may say, that I never knew any one of them that miscarried, which I mention for the Encouragement of others in case of the like Distress; and doubtless, *if they that give to the Poor, lend to the Lord, and he will repay them*;[1] those that hazard their Lives to give to the Poor, and to comfort and assist the Poor in such a Misery as this, may hope to be protected in the Work.

Nor was this Charity so extraordinary eminent only in a few; but, (*for I cannot lightly quit this Point*) the Charity of the rich as well in the City and Suburbs as from the Country, was so great, that in a Word, a prodigious Number of People, who must otherwise inevitably have perished for want as well as Sickness, were supported and subsisted by it; and tho' I could never, nor I believe any one else come to a full Knowledge of what was so contributed, yet I do believe, that as I heard one say, that was a critical Observer of that Part, there was not only many Thousand Pounds contributed, but many hundred thousand Pounds, to the Relief of the Poor of this distressed afflicted City; nay one Man affirm'd to me that he could reckon up above one hundred thousand Pounds a Week, which was distributed by the Church Wardens at the several Parish Vestries, by the Lord Mayor and the Aldermen in the several Wards and Precincts, and by the particular Direction of the Court and of the Justices respectively in the parts where they resided; over and above the private Charity distributed by pious Hands in the manner I speak of, and this continued for many Weeks together.

I confess this is a very great Sum; but if it be true, that there was distributed in the Parish of *Cripplegate* only 17800 Pounds[1] in one Week to the Relief of the Poor, as I heard reported, and which I really believe was true, the other may not be improbable.

It was doubtless to be reckon'd among the many signal good Providences which attended this great City, *and of which there were many other worth recording*; I say, this was a very remarkable one, that it pleased God thus to move the Hearts of the People in all parts of the Kingdom, so chearfully to contribute to the Relief and Support of the poor at *London*; the good Consequences of which were felt many ways, and particularly in preserving the Lives and recovering the Health of so many thousands, and keeping so many Thousands of Families from perishing and starving.

And now I am talking of the merciful Disposition of Providence in this time of Calamity, I cannot but mention again, tho' I have spoken several times of it already on other Account, I mean that of the Progression of the Distemper; how it began at one end of the Town, and proceeded gradually and slowly from one Part to another, and like a dark Cloud that passes over our Heads, which as it thickens and overcasts the Air at one End, clears up at the other end: So while the Plague went on raging from West to East, as it went forwards East, it abated in the West, by which means those parts of the Town, which were not seiz'd, or who were left, and where it had spent its Fury, were (as it were) spar'd to help and assist the other; whereas had the Distemper spread it self over the whole City and Suburbs at once, raging in all Places alike, as it has done since in some Places abroad, the whole Body of the People must have been overwhelmed, and there would have died twenty thousand a Day, as they say there did at

Naples,[1] nor would the People have been able to have help'd or assisted one another.

For it must be observ'd that where the Plague was in its full Force, there indeed the People were very miserable, and the Consternation was inexpressible. But a little before it reach'd even to that place, or presently after it was gone, they were quite another Sort of People, and I cannot but acknowledge, that there was too much of that common Temper of Mankind to be found among us all at that time; namely to forget the Deliverance, when the Danger is past: But I shall come to speak of that part again.

It must not be forgot here to take some Notice of the State of Trade, during the time of this common Calamity, and this with respect to Foreign Trade, as also to our Home-trade.

As to Foreign Trade, there needs little to be said; the trading Nations of Europe were all afraid of us, no Port of *France*, or *Holland*, or *Spain*, or *Italy* would admit our Ships or correspond with us; indeed we stood on ill Terms with the *Dutch*, and were in a furious War with them, but tho' in a bad Condition to fight abroad, who had such dreadful Enemies to struggle with at Home.

Our Merchants accordingly were at a full Stop, their Ships could go no where, that is to say to no place abroad; their Manufactures and Merchandise, that is to say, of our Growth, would not be touch'd abroad; they were as much afraid of our Goods, as they were of our People; and indeed they had reason, for our woolen Manufactures are as retentive of Infection as human Bodies,[2] and if pack'd up by Persons infected would receive the Infection, and be as dangerous to touch, as a Man would be that was infected; and therefore when any *English* Vessel arriv'd in Foreign Countries, if they did take the Goods on Shore, they always caused the Bales to be opened and air'd in Places appointed for that Purpose: But from *London* they would not suffer them to come into Port, much less to unlade their Goods upon any Terms whatever; and this Strictness was especially us'd with them in *Spain* and *Italy*. In *Turkey* and the Islands of the *Arches*[3] indeed as they are call'd, as well those belonging to the *Turks* as to the *Venetians*, they were not so very rigid; in the first there was no Obstruction at all; and four Ships, which were then in the River loading for *Italy*, that is for *Leghorn* and *Naples*, being denyed Product, *as they call it*, went on to *Turkey*, and were freely admitted to unlade their Cargo without any Difficulty, only that when they arriv'd there, some of their Cargo was not fit for Sale in that Country, and other Parts of it being consign'd to Merchants at *Leghorn*, the Captains of the Ships had no Right nor any Orders to dispose of the Goods; so that great Inconveniences followed to the Merchants. But this was nothing but what the Necessity of Affairs requir'd, and the Merchants at *Leghorn* and at *Naples* having Notice given them, sent again from thence to take Care of the Effects, which were particularly consign'd to those Ports, and to bring back in other Ships such as were improper for the Markets at *Smyrna* and *Scanderoon*.[1]

The Inconveniences in *Spain* and *Portugal* were still greater; for they would, by no means, suffer our Ships, especially those from *London*, to come into any of their Ports, much less to unlade; there was a Report, that one of our Ships having by Stealth delivered her Cargo, among which was some Bales of *English* Cloth, Cotton, Kersyes, and such like Goods, the *Spaniards* caused all the Goods to be burnt, and punished the Men with Death who were concern'd in carrying them on Shore. This I believe was in Part true, tho' I do not affirm it: But it is not at all unlikely, seeing the Danger was really very great, the Infection being so violent in *London*.

I heard likewise that the Plague was carryed into those Countries by some of our Ships, and particularly to the Port of *Faro* in the Kingdom of *Algarve*, belonging to the King of *Portugal*; and that several Persons died of it there, but it was not confirm'd.

On the other Hand, tho' the *Spaniards* and *Portuguese* were so shie of us, it is most certain, that the Plague, *as has been said*, keeping at first much at that end of the Town next *Westminster*, the merchandising part of the Town, such as the City and the Water-side, was perfectly sound, till at least the Beginning of *July*; and the Ships in the River till the Beginning of *August*; for to the 1st of *July*, there had died but seven within the whole City,[1] and but 60 within the Liberties; but one in all the Parishes of *Stepney*, *Aldgate*, and *White-Chappel*; and but two in all the eight Parishes of *Southwark*. But it was the same thing abroad, for the bad News was gone over the whole World, that the City of *London* was infected with the Plague; and there was no inquiring there, how the Infection proceeded, or at which part of the Town it was begun, or was reach'd to.

Besides, after it began to spread, it increased so fast, and the Bills grew so high, all on a sudden, that it was to no purpose to lessen the Report of it, or endeavour to make the People abroad think it better than it was, the Account which the Weekly Bills gave in was sufficient; and that there died two thousand to three or four thousand a Week, was sufficient to alarm the whole trading part of the World, and the following time being so dreadful also in the very City it self, put the whole World, *I say*, upon their Guard against it.

You may be sure also, that the Report of these things lost nothing in the Carriage, the Plague was it self very terrible, and the Distress of the People very great, as you may observe by what I have said: But the Rumor was infinitely greater, and it must not be wonder'd, that our Friends abroad, as my Brother's Correspondents in particular were told there, namely in *Portugal* and *Italy* where he chiefly traded, that in *London* there died twenty thousand in a Week; that the dead Bodies lay unburied by Heaps; that the living were not sufficient to bury the dead, or the Sound to look after the Sick; that all the Kingdom was infected likewise, so that it was an universal Malady, such as was never heard of in those parts of the World; and they could hardly believe us, when we gave them an Account how things really were, and how there was not above one Tenth part of the People dead; that there was 500000 left that lived all the time in the Town; that now the People began to walk the Streets again, and those, who were

fled, to return, there was no Miss of the usual Throng of
people in the Streets, except as every Family might miss their
Relations and Neighbours, and the like; I say they could not
believe these things; and if Enquiry were now to be made in
Naples, or in other Cities on the Coast of *Italy*, they would
tell you that there was a dreadful Infection in *London* so many
Years ago; in which, *as above*, there died Twenty Thousand
in a Week, &c. Just as we have had it reported in *London*, that
there was a Plague in the City of *Naples*, in the Year 1656, in
which there died 20000 People in a Day, of which I have had
very good Satisfaction, that it was utterly false.

But these extravagant Reports were very prejudicial to our
Trade as well as unjust and injurious in themselves; for it was
a long Time after the Plague was quite over, before our Trade
could recover it self in those parts of the World; and the
Flemings and *Dutch*, but especially the last, made very great
Advantages of it, having all the Market to themselves, and
even buying our Manufactures in the several Parts of *England*
where the Plague was not, and carrying them to *Holland*, and
Flanders, and from thence transporting them to *Spain*, and
to *Italy*, as if they had been of their own making.

But they were detected sometimes and punish'd, that is to
say, their Goods confiscated, and Ships also; for if it was true,
that our Manufactures, as well as our People, were infected,[1]
and that it was dangerous to touch or to open, and receive the
Smell of them; then those People ran the hazard by that
clandestine Trade,[2] not only of carrying the Contagion into
their own Country, but also of infecting the Nations to whom
they traded with those Goods; which, considering how many
Lives might be lost in Consequence of such an Action, must
be a Trade that no Men of Conscience could suffer themselves
to be concern'd in.

I do not take upon me to say, that any harm was done, I
mean of that Kind, by those People: But I doubt I need not
make any such Proviso in the Case of our own Country; for
either by our People of *London*, or by the Commerce, which
made their conversing with all Sorts of People in every

County, and of every considerable Town, necessary, I say, by this means the Plague was first or last spread all over the Kingdom, as well in *London* as in all the Cities and great Towns, especially in the trading Manufacturing Towns, and Sea-Ports; so that first or last, all the considerable Places in *England* were visited more or less, and the Kingdom of *Ireland* in some Places, but not so universally; how it far'd with the People in *Scotland*, I had no opportunity to enquire.

It is to be observ'd, that while the Plague continued so violent in *London*, the *out Ports*, as they are call'd, enjoy'd a very great Trade, especially to the adjacent Countries, and to our own Plantations; for Example, the Towns of *Colchester*, *Yarmouth*, and *Hull*, on that side of *England*, exported to *Holland* and *Hamburgh* the Manufactures of the adjacent Counties for several Months after the Trade with *London* was as it were entirely shut up; likewise the Cities of *Bristol* and *Exeter* with the Port of *Plymouth*, had the like Advantage to *Spain*, to the *Canaries*, to *Guinea*, and to the *West Indies*; and particularly to *Ireland*; but as the Plague spread it self every way after it had been in *London*, to such a Degree as it was in *August* and *September*; so all, or most of those Cities and Towns were infected first or last, and then Trade was as it were under a general Embargo, or at a full stop,¹ as I shall observe farther, when I speak of our home Trade.

One thing however must be observed, that as to Ships coming in from Abroad, as many you may be sure did, some, who were out in all Parts of the World a considerable while before, and some who when they went out knew nothing of an Infection, or at least of one so terrible; these came up the River boldly, and delivered their Cargoes as they were oblig'd to do, except just in the two Months of *August* and *September*, when the Weight of the Infection lying, as I may say, all below Bridge, no Body durst appear in Business for a while: But as this continued but for a few Weeks, the Homeward bound Ships, especially such whose Cargoes were not liable to spoil, came to an Anchor for a Time, short of THE POOL*, or fresh Water part of the River, even as low as the River *Medway*, where several of them ran in, and others lay at the *Nore*, and in the *Hope* below *Gravesend*: So that by the latter end of *October*, there was a very great Fleet of Homeward bound Ships to come up, such as the like had not been known for many Years.

Two particular Trades were carried on by Water Carriage all the while of the Infection, and that with little or no Interruption, very much to the Advantage and Comfort of the poor distressed People of the City, and those were the coasting Trade for Corn, and the *Newcastle* Trade for Coals.[1]

The first of these was particularly carried on by small Vessels, from the Port of *Hull*, and other Places in the *Humber*, by which great Quantities of Corn were brought in from *Yorkshire* and *Lincolnshire*: The other part of this Corn-Trade was from *Lynn* in *Norfolk*, from *Wells*, and *Burnham*, and from *Yarmouth*, all in the same County; and the third Branch was from the River *Medway*, and from *Milton*, *Feversham*, *Margate*, and *Sandwich*, and all the other little Places and Ports round the Coast of *Kent* and *Essex*.

There was also a very good Trade from the Coast of *Suffolk* with Corn, Butter and Cheese; these Vessels kept a constant Course of Trade, and without Interruption came up to that Market known still by the Name of *Bear-Key*, where they supply'd the City plentifully with Corn, when Land Carriage began to fail, and when the People began to be sick of coming from many Places in the Country.

This also was much of it owing to the Prudence and Conduct of the Lord Mayor, who took such care to keep the Masters and Seamen from Danger, when they came up, causing their Corn to be bought off at any time they wanted a Market, (which however was very seldom) and causing the Corn-Factors immediately to unlade and deliver the Vessels loaden with Corn, that they had very little occasion to come

* That Part of the River where the Ships lye up when they come Home, is call'd the *Pool*, and takes in all the River on both Sides of the Water, from the *Tower* to *Cuckold*'s Point, and *Lime-house*.

out of their Ships or Vessels, the Money being always carried on Board to them, and put into a Pail of Vinegar before it was carried.

The second Trade was, that of Coals from *Newcastle* upon *Tyne*; without which the City would have been greatly distressed; for not in the Streets only, but in private Houses and Families, great Quantities of Coals were then burnt, even all the Summer long, and when the Weather was hottest, which was done by the Advice of the Physicians; some indeed oppos'd it, and insisted that to keep the Houses and Rooms hot, was a means to propagate the Distemper, which was a Fermentation and Heat already in the Blood, that it was known to spread, and increase in hot Weather, and abate in cold, and therefore they alledg'd that all contagious Distempers are the worse for Heat, because the Contagion was nourished, and gain'd Strength in hot Weather, and was as it were propagated in Heat.

Others said, they granted, that Heat in the Climate might propagate Infection, as sultry hot Weather fills the Air with Vermine, and nourishes innumerable Numbers, and Kinds of venomous Creatures, which breed in our Food, in the Plants, and even in our Bodies, by the very stench of which, Infection may be propagated; also, that heat in the Air, or heat of Weather, *as we ordinarly call it*, makes Bodies relax and faint, exhausts the Spirits, opens the Pores,[1] and makes us more apt to receive Infection, or any evil Influence, be it from noxious pestilential Vapors, or any other Thing in the Air: But that the heat of Fire, and especially of Coal Fires kept in our Houses, or near us, had a quite different Operation, the Heat being not of the same Kind, but quick and fierce, tending not to nourish but to consume, and dissipate all those noxious Fumes, which the other kind of Heat rather exhaled and stagnated than separated and burnt up; besides it was alledg'd, that the sulphurous and nitrous Particles, that are often found to be in the Coal, with that bituminous Substance which burns, are all assisting to clear and purge the Air, and render it wholsom and safe to breath[e] in, after the noctious Particles as above are dispers'd and burnt up.

The latter Opinion prevail'd at that Time, and as I must confess I think with good Reason, and the Experience of the Citizens confirm'd it, many Houses which had constant Fires kept in the Rooms, having never been infected at all; and I must join my Experience to it, for I found the keeping good Fires kept our Rooms sweet and wholsom, and I do verily believe made our whole Family so, more than would otherwise have been.

But I return to the Coals as a Trade, it was with no little difficulty that this Trade was kept open, and particularly because as we were in an open War with the *Dutch*,[1] at that Time; the *Dutch* Capers at first took a great many of our Collier Ships, which made the rest cautious, and made them to stay to come in Fleets together: But after some time, the Capers were either afraid to take them, or their Masters, the States, were afraid they should, and forbad them, lest the Plague should be among them, which made them fare the better.

For the Security of those *Northern* Traders, the Coal Ships were order'd by my Lord Mayor, not to come up into the *Pool* above a certain Number at a Time, and order'd Lighters, and other Vessels, such as the Wood-mongers, that is the *Wharf* Keepers, or Coal-Sellers furnished, to go down, and take out the Coals as low as *Deptford* and *Greenwich*, and some farther down.

Others deliver'd great Quantities of Coals in particular Places, where the Ships cou'd come to the Shoar, as at *Greenwich*, *Blackwal*, and other Places, in vast Heaps, as if to be kept for Sale; but were then fetch'd away, after the Ships which brought them were gone; so that the Seamen had no Communication with the River-Men, nor so much as came near one another.

Yet all this Caution, could not effectually prevent the Distemper getting among the Colliery, that is to say, among the Ships, by which a great many Seamen died of it; and that which was still worse, was, that they carried it down to *Ipswich*, and *Yarmouth*, to *Newcastle* upon *Tyne*, and other Places on the Coast; where, especially at *Newcastle* and at *Sunderland*, it carried off a great Number of People.

The making so many Fires as above, did indeed consume an unusual Quantity of Coals; and that upon one or two stops of the Ships coming up, whether by contrary Weather, or by the Interruption of Enemies, I do not remember, but the Price of Coals was exceeding dear,[1] even as high as 4 l. a Chalder, but it soon abated when the Ships came in, and as afterwards they had a freer Passage, the Price was very reasonable all the rest of that Year.

The publick Fires[2] which were made on these Occasions, as I have calculated it, must necessarily have cost the City about 200 Chalder of Coals a Week, if they had continued, which was indeed a very great Quantity; but as it was, thought necessary, nothing was spar'd; however as some of the Physicians cry'd them down, they were not kept a-light above four or five Days; the Fires were order'd thus.

One at the *Custom-house*, one at *Billingsgate*, one at *Queenhith*, and one at the *Three Cranes*, one in *Black Friars*, and one at the Gate of *Bridewel*, one at the Corner of *Leadenhal* Street, and *Grace-church*, one at the *North*, and one at the *South* Gate of the *Royal Exchange*, one at *Guild Hall*, and one at *Blackwell-hall* Gate, one at the Lord *Mayor*'s Door, in St. *Helens*, one at the West Entrance into St. *Paul*'s, and one at the Entrance into *Bow* Church: I do not remember whether there was any at the City Gates, but one at the *Bridge* foot there was, just by St. *Magnus* Church.

I know, some have quarrell'd since that at the Experiment, and said, that there died the more People, because of those Fires; but I am persuaded those that say so, offer no Evidence to prove it, neither can I believe it on any Account whatever.

It remains to give some Account of the State of Trade at home in *England* during this dreadful Time, and particularly as it relates to the Manufactures, and the Trade in the City: At the first breaking out of the Infection, there was, as it is easie to suppose, a very great fright among the People, and consequently a general stop of Trade; except in Provisions and Necessaries of Life, and even in those Things, as there was a vast Number of People fled, and a very great Number always sick, besides the Number which died, so there could not be above two Thirds, if above one Half of the Consumption of Provisions in the City as used to be.

It pleas'd God, to send a very plentiful Year of Corn and Fruit, but not of Hay or Grass;[1] by which means, Bread was cheap, by Reason of the Plenty of Corn: Flesh was cheap, by Reason of the Scarcity of Grass; but Butter and Cheese were dear for the same Reason, and Hay in the Market just beyond *White-Chapel* Bars, was sold at 4 l. *per* Load. But that affected not the Poor; there was a most excessive Plenty of all Sorts of Fruit,[2] such as Apples, Pears, Plumbs, Cherries, Grapes; and they were the cheaper, because of the want of People; but this made the Poor eat them to excess, and this brought them into Fluxes, griping of the Guts, Surfeits, and the like, which often precipitated them into the Plague.

But to come to Matters of Trade; first, Foreign Exportation being stopt, or at least very much interrupted, and rendred difficult; a general Stop of all those Manufactories followed of Course, which were usually bought for Exportation; and tho' sometimes Merchants Abroad were importunate for Goods, yet little was sent, the Passages being so generally stop'd, that the *English* Ships would not be admitted, as is said already, into their Port.

This put a stop to the Manufactures, that were for Exportation in most Parts of *England*, except in some out Ports; and even that was soon stop'd, for they all had the Plague in their Turn: But tho' this was felt all over *England*, yet what was still worse, all Intercourse of Trade for Home Consumption of Manufactures, especially those which usually circulated thro' the *Londoners* Hands, was stop'd at once, the Trade of the City being stop'd.

All Kinds of Handicrafts in the City, *&c.* Tradesmen and Mechanicks,[3] were, as I have said before, out of Employ, and this occasion'd the putting off, and dismissing an innumerable Number of Journey-men, and Work-men of all Sorts, seeing nothing was done relating to such Trades, but what might be said to be absolutely necessary.

This caused the Multitude of single People in *London* to be unprovided for; as also of Families, whose living depended upon the Labour of the Heads of those Families; I say, this reduced them to extream Misery; and I must confess it is for the Honour of the City of *London*, and will be for many Ages, as long as this is to be spoken of, that they were able to supply with charitable Provision, the Wants of so many Thousands of those as afterwards fell sick, and were distressed; so that it may be safely aver'd that no Body perished for Want, at least that the Magistrates had any notice given them of.

This Stagnation of our Manufacturing Trade in the Country, would have put the People there to much greater Difficulties, but that the Master-Workmen, Clothiers and others, to the uttermost of their Stocks and Strength, kept on making their Goods to keep the Poor at Work, believing that as soon as the Sickness should abate, they would have a quick Demand in Proportion to the Decay of their Trade at that Time: But as none but those Masters that were rich could do thus, and that many were poor and not able, the Manufacturing Trade in *England* suffer'd greatly, and the Poor were pinch'd all over *England* by the Calamity of the City of *London* only.[1]

It is true, that the next Year made them full amends by another terrible Calamity upon the City; so that the City by one Calamity impoverished and weaken'd the Country, and by another Calamity even terrible too of its Kind, enrich'd the Country[2] and made them again amends: For an infinite Quantity of Houshold Stuff, wearing Apparel, and other Things, besides whole Ware-houses fill'd with Merchandize and Manufacturies, such as come from all Parts of *England*, were consum'd in the Fire of *London*, the next Year after this terrible Visitation: It is incredible what a Trade this made all over the whole Kingdom, to make good the Want, and to supply that Loss: So that, in short, all the manufacturing Hands in the Nation were set on Work, and were little enough, for several Years, to supply the Market and answer the Demands; all Foreign Markets, also were empty of our Goods, by the stop which had been occasioned by the Plague, and before an open Trade was allow'd again; and the prodigious Demand-at Home falling in join'd to make a quick Vent for all Sorts of Goods; so that there never was known such a Trade all over *England* for the Time, as was in the first seven Years after the Plague, and after the Fire of *London*.

It remains now, that I should say something of the merciful Part of this terrible Judgment: The last Week in *September*, the Plague being come to its Crisis, its Fury began to asswage. I remember my Friend Doctor *Heath* coming to see me the Week before, told me, he was sure that the Violence of it would asswage in a few Days; but when I saw the weekly Bill of that Week, which was the highest of the whole Year, being 8297 of all Diseases, I upbraided him with it, and ask'd him, what he had made his Judgment from? His Answer, however, was not so much to seek, as I thought it would have been; look you, *says he*, by the Number which are at this Time sick and infected, there should have been twenty Thousand dead the last Week, instead of eight Thousand, if the inveterate mortal Contagion had been, as it was two Weeks ago; for then it ordinarily kill'd in two or three Days, now not under Eight or Ten; and then not above One in Five recovered; whereas I have observ'd, that now not above Two in Five miscarry; and observe it from me, the next Bill will decrease, and you will see many more People recover than used to do; for tho' a vast Multitude are now every where infected, and as many every Day fall sick; yet there will not so many die as there did, for the Malignity of the Distemper is abated; adding, that he began now to hope, nay more than hope, that the Infection had pass'd its Crisis, and was going off; and accordingly so it was, for the next Week being, as I said, the last in *September*, the Bill decreased almost two Thousand.

It is true, the Plague was still at a frightful Height, and the next Bill was no less than 6460, and the next to that 5720; but still my Friend's Observation was just, and it did appear the People did recover faster, and more in Number, than they used to do; and indeed if it had not been so, what had been the Condition of the City of *London*? for according to my Friend there were not fewer than sixty Thousand People at that Time infected, whereof, as above, 20477 died, and near 40000 recovered; whereas had it been as it was before, Fifty thousand of that Number would very probably have died, if not more, and 50000 more would have sickned; for in a Word, the whole Mass of People began to sicken, and it look'd as if none would escape.

But this Remark of my Friend's appear'd more evident in a few Weeks more; for the Decrease went on, and another Week in *October* it decreas'd 1849. So that the Number dead of the Plague was but 2665, and the next Week it decreased 1413 more, and yet it was seen plainly, that there was abundance of People sick, nay abundance more than ordinary, and abundance fell sick every Day, but (as above) the Malignity of the Disease abated.

Such is the precipitant Disposition of our People, whether it is so or not all over the World, that's none of my particular Business to enquire; but I saw it apparently here, that as upon the first Fright of the Infection, they shun'd one another, and fled from one another's Houses, and from the City with an unaccountable, and, as I thought, unnecessary Fright; so now upon this Notion spreading, (*viz.*) that the Distemper was not so catching as formerly, and that if it was catch'd, it was not so mortal, and seeing abundance of People who really fell sick, recover again daily; they took to such a precipitant Courage, and grew so entirely regardless of themselves, and of the Infection, that they made no more of the Plague than of an ordinary Fever, nor indeed so much; they not only went boldly into Company, with those who had Tumours and Carbuncles upon them, that were running, and consequently contagious, but eat and drank with them, nay into their Houses to visit them, and even, as I was told, into their very Chambers where they lay sick.

This I cou'd not see rational; my Friend Doctor *Heath* allow'd, and it was plain to Experience, that the Distemper was as catching as ever, and as many fell sick, but only he alledg'd, that so many of those that fell sick did not die; but I think that while many did die, and that, at best, the Distemper it self was very terrible, the Sores and Swellings very torment-ing, and the Danger of Death not left out of the Circumstance of Sickness, tho' not so frequent as before; all those things, together with the exceeding Tediousness of the Cure, the Loathsomness of the Disease, and many other Articles, were enough to deter any Man living from a dangerous Mixture with the sick People, and make them as anxious almost to avoid the Infection as before.

Nay there was another Thing which made the meer catch-ing of the Distemper frightful, and that was the terrible burning of the Causticks, which the Surgeons laid on the Swellings to bring them to break, and to run; without which the Danger of Death was very great, even to the last; also the unsufferable Torment of the Swellings, which tho' it might not make People raving and distracted, as they were before, and as I have given several Instances of already, yet they put the Patient to inexpressible Torture; and those that fell into it, tho' they did escape with Life, yet they made bitter Com-plaints of those, that had told them there was no Danger, and sadly repented their Rashness and Folly in venturing to run into the reach of it.

Nor did this unwary Conduct of the People end here, for a great many that thus cast off their Cautions suffered more deeply still; and tho' many escap'd, yet many died; and at least it had this publick Mischief attending it, that it made the Decrease of Burials slower than it would otherwise have been; for as this Notion run like Lightning thro' the City, and People's Heads were possess'd with it, even as soon as the first great Decrease in the Bills appear'd, we found, that the two next Bills did not decrease in Proportion; the Reason I take to be the Peoples running so rashly into Danger, giving up all their former Cautions, and Care, and all the Shyness which they used to practise; depending that the Sickness would not reach them, or that if it did, they should not die.

The Physicians oppos'd this thoughtless Humour of the People with all their Might, and gave out printed Directions, spreading them all over the City and Suburbs, advising the People to continue reserv'd, and to use still the utmost Caution in their ordinary Conduct, notwithstanding the Decrease of the Distemper, terrifying them with the Danger of bringing a Relapse upon the whole City, and telling them how such a Relapse might be more fatal and dangerous than the whole Visitation that had been already; with many Arguments and Reasons to explain and prove that part to them, and which are too long to repeat here.

But it was all to no Purpose, the audacious Creatures were so possess'd with the first Joy, and so surpriz'd with the Satisfaction of seeing a vast Decrease in the weekly Bills, that they were impenetrable by any new Terrors, and would not be persuaded, but that the Bitterness of Death was pass'd; and it was to no more purpose to talk to them, than to an East-wind; but they open'd Shops, went about Streets, did Business, and conversed with any Body that came in their Way to converse with, whether with Business, or without, neither inquiring of their Health, or so much as being Apprehensive of any Danger from them, tho' they knew them not to be sound.

This imprudent rash Conduct cost a great many their Lives, who had with great Care and Caution shut themselves up, and kept retir'd as it were from all Mankind, and had by that means, under God's Providence, been preserv'd thro' all the heat of that Infection.

This rash and foolish Conduct, *I say*, of the People went so far, that the Ministers took notice to them of it at last, and laid before them both the Folly and Danger of it; and this check'd it a little, so that they grew more cautious, but it had another Effect, which they cou'd not check; for as the first

Rumour had spread not over the City only, but into the Country, it had the like Effect, and the People were so tir'd with being so long from *London*, and so eager to come back, that they flock'd to Town[1] without Fear or Forecast, and began to shew themselves in the Streets, as if all the Danger was over: It was indeed surprising to see it, for tho' there died still from a Thousand to eighteen Hundred a Week, yet the People flock'd to Town, as if all had been well.

The Consequence of this was, that the Bills encreas'd again Four Hundred the very first Week in *November*; and if I might believe the Physicians, there was above three Thousand fell sick that Week, most of them new Comers too.

One JOHN COCK, a Barber in St. *Martins le Grand*, was an eminent Example of this; I mean of the hasty Return of the People, when the Plague was abated: This *John Cock* had left the Town with his whole Family, and lock'd up his House, and was gone in the Country, as many others did, and finding the Plague so decreas'd in *November*, that there died but 905 *per* Week of all Diseases, he ventur'd home again; he had in his Family Ten Persons, that is to say, himself and Wife, five Children, two Apprentices, and a Maid Servant; he had not been return'd to his House above a Week, and began to open his Shop, and carry on his Trade, but the Distemper broke out in his Family, and within about five Days they all died, except one, that is to say, himself, his Wife, all his five Children, and his two Apprentices, and only the Maid remain'd alive.

But the Mercy of God was greater to the rest than [we] had Reason to expect; for the Malignity, as I have said, of the Distemper was spent, the Contagion was exhausted, and also the Winter Weather came on apace, and the Air was clear and cold, with some sharp Frosts; and this encreasing still, most of those that had fallen sick recover'd, and the Health of the City began to return: There were indeed some Returns of the Distemper, even in the Month of *December*, and the Bills encreased near a Hundred, but it went off again and so in a short while, Things began to return to their own Channel.

And wonderful it was to see how populous the City was again all on a sudden; so that a Stranger could not miss the Numbers that were lost, neither was there any miss of the Inhabitants as to their Dwellings: Few or no empty Houses were to be seen, or if there were some, there was no want of Tenants for them.

I wish I cou'd say, that as the City had a new Face, so the Manners of the People had a new Appearance: I doubt not but there were many that retain'd a sincere Sense of their Deliverance, and that were heartily thankful to that sovereign Hand, that had protected them in so dangerous a Time; it would be very uncharitable to judge otherwise in a City so populous, and where the People were so devout, as they were here in the Time of the Visitation it self; but except what of this was to be found in particular Families, and Faces, it must be acknowledg'd that the general Practice of the People was just as it was before, and very little Difference was to be seen.

Some indeed said Things were worse, that the Morals of the People declin'd from this very time; that the People harden'd by the Danger they had been in, like Sea-men after a Storm is over, were more wicked and more stupid, more bold and hardened in their Vices and Immoralities than they were before; but I will not carry it so far neither: It would take up a History of no small Length, to give a Particular of all the Gradations, by which the Course of Things in this City came to be restor'd again, and to run in their own Channel as they did before.

Some Parts of *England* were now infected as violently as *London* had been; the Cities of *Norwich*, *Peterborough*, *Lincoln*, *Colchester*,[1] and other Places were now visited; and the Magistrates of *London* began to set Rules for our Conduct, as to corresponding with those Cities: It is true, we could not pretend to forbid their People coming to *London*, because it was impossible to know them assunder, so after many Consultations, the Lord Mayor, and Court of Aldermen were oblig'd to drop it: All they cou'd do, was to warn and caution the People, not to entertain in their Houses, or converse with any People who they knew came from such infected Places.

But they might as well have talk'd to the Air, for the People of *London* thought themselves so Plague-free now, that they were past all Admonitions; they seem'd to depend upon it, that the Air was restor'd, and that the Air was like a Man that had had the Small Pox, not capable of being infected again; this reviv'd that Notion, that the Infection was all in the Air, that there was no such thing as Contagion from the sick People to the Sound; and so strongly did this Whimsy prevail among People, that they run all together promiscuously, sick and well; not the *Mahometans*, who, prepossess'd with the Principle of Predestination value nothing of Contagion, let it be in what it will, could be more obstinate than the People of *London*; they that were perfectly sound, and came out of the wholesome Air, as we call it, into the City, made nothing of going into the same Houses and Chambers nay even into the same Beds, with those that had the Distemper upon them, and were not recovered.

Some indeed paid for their audacious Boldness with the Price of their Lives; an infinite Number fell sick, and the Physicians had more Work than ever, only with this Difference, that more of their Patients recovered; that is to say, they generally recovered, but certainly there were more People infected, and fell sick now, when there did not die above a Thousand, or Twelve Hundred in a Week, than there was when there died Five or Six Thousand a Week; so entirely negligent were the People at that Time, in the great and dangerous Case of Health and Infection; and so ill were they able to take or accept of the Advice of those who cautioned them for their Good.

The People being thus return'd, as it were in general, it was very strange to find, that in their inquiring after their Friends, some whole Families were so entirely swept away, that there was no Remembrance of them left; neither was any Body to be found to possess or shew any Title to that little they had left; for in such Cases, what was to be found was generally embezzled, and purloyn'd, some gone one way, some another.

It was said such abandon'd Effects came to the King as the universal Heir, upon which we were told, and I suppose it was in part true, that the King granted all such as Deodands[1] to the Lord Mayor and Court of Aldermen of *London*, to be applied to the use of the Poor, of whom there were very many: For it is to be observ'd, that tho' the Occasions of Relief, and the Objects of Distress were very many more in the Time of the Violence of the Plague, than now after all was over; yet the Distress of the Poor was more now, a great deal than it was then, because all the Sluces of general Charity were now shut; People suppos'd the main Occasion to be over, and so stop'd their Hands; whereas particular Objects were still very moving, and the Distress of those that were Poor, was very great indeed.

Tho' the Health of the City was now very much restor'd, yet Foreign Trade did not begin to stir, neither would Foreigners admit our Ships into their Ports for a great while; as for the *Dutch*, the Misunderstandings between our Court and them had broken out into a War the Year before; so that our Trade that way was wholly interrupted; but *Spain* and *Portugal*, *Italy* and *Barbary*, as also *Hamburgh*, and all the Ports in the *Baltick*, these were all shy of us a great while, and would not restore Trade with us for many Months.

The Distemper sweeping away such Multitudes, as I have observ'd, many, if not all the out Parishes were oblig'd to make new burying Grounds, besides that I have mention'd in *Bunhil-Fields*, some of which were continued, and remain in Use to this Day; but others were left off, and which, I confess, I mention with some Reflection, being converted into other Uses, or built upon afterwards, the dead Bodies were disturb'd, abus'd, dug up again, some even before the Flesh of them was perished from the Bones, and remov'd like Dung or Rubbish to other Places; some of those which came within the Reach of my Observation, are as follow.

1. A piece of Ground beyond *Goswel* Street, near

Mount-Mill, being some of the Remains of the old Lines or Fortifications of the City, where Abundance were buried promiscuously from the Parishes of *Aldersgate, Clerkenwell*, and even out of the City. This Ground, as I take it, was since made a Physick Garden,[1] and after that has been built upon.

2. A piece of Ground just over the *Black Ditch*, as it was then call'd, at the end of *Holloway Lane*, in *Shoreditch* Parish; it has been since made a Yard for keeping Hogs, and for other ordinary Uses, but is quite out of Use as a burying Ground.

3. The upper End of *Hand-Alley* in *Bishopsgate* Street, which was then a green Field, and was taken in particularly for *Bishopsgate* Parish, tho' many of the Carts out of the City brought their dead thither also, particularly out of the Parish of St. *All-hallows* on the *Wall*; this Place I cannot mention without much Regret, it was, as I remember, about two or three Years after the Plague was ceas'd that Sir *Robert Clayton*[2] came to be possest of the Ground; it was reported, how true I know not, that it fell to the King for want of Heirs, all those who had any Right to it being carried off by the Pestilence, and that Sir *Robert Clayton* obtain'd a Grant of it from King *Charles* II. But however he came by it, certain it is, the Ground was let out to build on, or built upon by his Order: The first House built upon it was a large fair House still standing, which faces the Street, or Way, now call'd *Hand-Alley*, which, tho' call'd an *Alley*, is as wide as a Street: The Houses in the same Row with that House Northward, are built on the very same Ground where the poor People were buried, and the Bodies on opening the Ground for the Foundations, were dug up, some of them remaining so plain to be seen, that the Womens Sculls were distinguish'd by their long Hair, and of others, the Flesh was not quite perished; so that the People began to exclaim loudly against it, and some suggested that it might endanger a Return of the Contagion: After which the Bones and Bodies, as fast as they came at them, were carried to another part of the same Ground, and thrown all together into a deep Pit, dug on purpose, which now is to be known, in that it is not built on, but is a Passage to another House, at

the upper end of *Rose Alley*, just against the Door of a Meeting-house, which has been built there many Years since; and the Ground is palisadoed off from the rest of the Passage, in a little square, there lye the Bones and Remains of near Two thousand Bodies, carried by the Dead-Carts to their Grave in that one Year.

4. Besides this, there was a piece of Ground in *Moorfields*, by the going into the Street which is now call'd *Old Bethlem*, which was enlarg'd much, tho' not wholly taken in on the same occasion.

N.B. The Author of this Journal, lyes buried in that very Ground, being at his own Desire, his Sister having been buried there a few Years before.

5. *Stepney* Parish, extending it self from the East part of *London* to the *North*, even to the very Edge of *Shoreditch* Church-yard, had a piece of Ground taken in to bury their Dead, close to the said Church-yard; and which for that very Reason was left open, and is since, I suppose, taken into the same Church-yard; and they had also two other burying Places in *Spittlefields*, one where since a Chapel or Taber-nacle has been built for ease to this great Parish, and another in *Petticoat-lane*.

There were no less than Five other Grounds made use of for the Parish of *Stepney* at that time; one where now stands the Parish Church of St. *Paul*'s *Shadwel*, and the other, where now stands the Parish Church of St. *John* at *Wapping*, both which had not the Names of Parishes at that time, but were belonging to *Stepney* Parish.[1]

I cou'd name many more, but these coming within my particular Knowledge, the Circumstance I thought made it of Use to record them; from the whole, it may be observ'd, that they were oblig'd in this Time of Distress, to take in new burying Grounds in most of the out Parishes, for lay-ing the prodigious Numbers of People which died in so short a Space of Time; but why Care was not taken to keep those Places separate from ordinary Uses, that so the Bodies might rest undisturb'd, that I cannot answer for, and must confess, I think it was wrong; who were to blame, I know not.

I should have mention'd, that the Quakers had at that time also a burying Ground,[1] set a-part to their Use, and which they still make use of, and they had also a particular *dead Cart* to fetch their Dead from their Houses; and the famous *Solomon Eagle*, who, as I mentioned before, had predicted the Plague as a Judgment, and run naked thro' the Streets, telling the People, that it was come upon them, to punish them for their Sins, had his own Wife died the very next Day of the Plague, and was carried one of the first in the Quakers *dead Cart*, to their new burying Ground.

I might have throng'd this Account with many more remarkable Things, which occur'd in the Time of the Infection, and particularly what pass'd between the Lord Mayor and the Court, which was then at *Oxford*, and what Directions were from time to time receiv'd from the Government for their Conduct on this critical Occasion. But really the Court concern'd themselves so little, and that little they did was of so small Import, that I do not see it of much Moment to mention any Part of it here, except that of appointing a Monthly Fast in the City, and the sending the Royal Charity to the Relief of the Poor, both which I have mention'd before.

Great was the Reproach thrown on those Physicians[2] who left their Patients during the Sickness, and now they came to Town again, no Body car'd to employ them; they were call'd Deserters, and frequently Bills were set up upon their Doors, and written, *Here is a Doctor to be let!* So that several of those Physicians were fain for a while to sit still and look about them, or at least remove their Dwellings, and set up in new Places, and among new Acquaintance; the like was the Case with the Clergy, who the People were indeed very abusive to, writing Verses and scandalous Reflections upon them, setting upon the Church Door, *here is a Pulpit to be let*, or sometimes *to be sold*, which was worse.

It was not the least of our Misfortunes, that with our Infection, when it ceased, there did not cease the Spirit of

Strife and Contention, Slander and Reproach, which was really the great Troubler of the Nation's Peace before: It was said to be the Remains of the old Animosities, which had so lately involv'd us all in Blood and Disorder. But as the late Act of Indemnity[1] had laid asleep the Quarrel it self, so the Government had recommended Family and Personal Peace upon all Occasions, to the whole Nation.

But it cou'd not be obtain'd, and particularly after the ceasing of the Plague in *London*, when any one that had seen the Condition which the People had been in, and how they caress'd one another at that time, promis'd to have more Charity for the future, and to raise no more Reproaches: I say, any one that had seen them then, would have thought they would have come together with another Spirit at last. But, I say, it cou'd not be obtain'd; the Quarrel remain'd, the Church and the Presbyterians were incompatible; as soon as the Plague was remov'd, the dissenting outed Ministers who had supplied the Pulpits, which were deserted by the Incumbents, retir'd, they cou'd expect no other; but that they should immediately fall upon them, and harrass them, with their penal Laws,[2] accept their preaching while they were sick, and persecute them as soon as they were recover'd again, this even we that were of the Church thought was very hard, and cou'd by no means approve of it.

But it was the Government, and we cou'd say nothing to hinder it; we cou'd only say, it was not our doing, and we could not answer for it.

On the other Hand, the Dissenters reproaching those Ministers of the Church with going away, and deserting their Charge, abandoning the People in their Danger, and when they had most need of Comfort and the like, this we cou'd by no means approve; for all Men have not the same Faith, and the same Courage, and the Scripture commands us to judge the most favourably, and according to Charity.

A Plague is a formidable Enemy, and is arm'd with Terrors that every Man is not sufficiently fortified to resist, or prepar'd to stand the Shock against: It is very certain, that a great many of the Clergy, who were in Circumstances to do it, withdrew, and fled for the Safety of their Lives; but 'tis true also, that a great many of them staid, and many of them fell in the Calamity, and in the Discharge of their Duty.

It is true, some of the Dissenting turn'd out Ministers staid, and their Courage is to be commended, and highly valued, but these were not abundant; it cannot be said that they all staid, and that none retir'd into the Country, any more than it can be said of the Church Clergy, that they all went away; neither did all those that went away, go without substituting Curates, and others in their Places, to do the Offices needful, and to visit the Sick, as far as it was practicable; so that upon the whole, an Allowance of Charity might have been made on both Sides, and we should have consider'd, that such a time as this of 1665, is not to be parallel'd in History, and that it is not the stoutest Courage that will always support Men in such Cases; I had not said this, but had rather chosen to record the Courage and religious Zeal of those of both Sides, who did hazard themselves for the Service of the poor People in their Distress, without remembring that any fail'd in their Duty on either side. But the want of Temper among us, has made the contrary to this necessary; some that staid, not only boasting too much of themselves, but reviling those that fled, branding them with Cowardice, deserting their Flocks, and acting the Part of the Hireling, and the like: I recommend it to the Charity of all good People to look back, and reflect duly upon the Terrors of the Time; and whoever does so will see, that it is not an ordinary Strength that cou'd support it; it was not like appearing in the Head of an Army, or charging a Body of Horse in the Field; but it was charging Death it self on his pale Horse;[1] to stay was indeed to die, and it could be esteemed nothing less, especially as things appear'd at the latter End of *August*, and the Beginning of *September*, and as there was reason to expect them at that time; for no Man expected, and I dare say, believed, that the Distemper would take so sudden a Turn as it did, and fall immediately 2000 in a Week, when there was such a prodigious

Number of People sick at that Time, as it was known there was; and then it was that many shifted away, that had stay'd most of the time before.

Besides, if God gave Strength to some more than to others, was it to boast of their Ability to abide the Stroak, and upbraid those that had not the same Gift and Support, or ought not they rather to have been humble and thankful, if they were render'd more useful than their Brethren?

I think it ought to be recorded to the Honour of such Men, as well Clergy as Physicians, Surgeons, Apothecaries, Magistrates and Officers of every kind, as also all useful People, who ventur'd their Lives in Discharge of their Duty, as most certainly all such as stay'd did to the last Degree, and several of all these Kinds did not only venture but lose their Lives on that sad Occasion.

I was once making a List of all such, I mean of all those Professions and Employments, who thus died, as I call it, in the way of their Duty, but it was impossible for a private Man to come at a Certainty in the Particulars; I only remember, that there died sixteen Clergy-men, two Aldermen, five Physicians, thirteen Surgeons, within the City and Liberties before the beginning of *September*: But this being, as I said before, the great Crisis and Extremity of the Infection, it can be no compleat List: As to inferior People, I think there died six and forty Constables and Headboroughs[1] in the two Parishes of *Stepney* and *White-Chapel*; but I could not carry my List on, for when the violent Rage of the Distemper in *September* came upon us, it drove us out of all Measures: Men did then no more die by Tale and by Number,[2] they might put out a Weekly Bill, and call them seven or eight Thousand, or what they pleas'd; 'tis certain they died by Heaps, and were buried by Heaps, that is to say without Account; and if I might believe some People, who were more abroad and more conversant with those things than I, tho' I was public enough for one that had no more Business to do than I had, I say, if I may believe them, there was not many less buried those first three Weeks in *September* than 20000

per Week; however the others aver the Truth of it, yet I rather
chuse to keep to the public Account; seven and eight thousand
per Week[1] is enough to make good all that I have said of the
Terror of those Times; and it is much to the Satisfaction of
me that write, as well as those that read, to be able to say, that
every thing is set down with Moderation, and rather within
Compass than beyond it.

Upon all these Accounts I say I could wish, when we were
recover'd, our Conduct had been more distinguish'd for
Charity and Kindness in Remembrance of the past Calamity,
and not so much a valuing our selves upon our Boldness in
staying, as if all Men were Cowards that fly from the Hand
of God, or that those who stay, do not sometimes owe their
Courage to their Ignorance, and despising the Hand of their
Maker, which is a criminal kind of Desperation, and not a
true Courage.

I cannot but leave it upon Record, that the Civil Officers,
such as Constables, Headboroughs, Lord Mayor's, and
Sheriff's-men, as also Parish-Officers, whose Business it was
to take Charge of the Poor, did their Duties in general with
as much Courage as any, and perhaps with more, because their
Work was attended with more Hazards, and lay more among
the Poor, who were more subject to be infected and in the most
pitiful Plight when they were taken with the Infection: But
then it must be added too, that a great Number of them died,
indeed it was scarce possible it should be otherwise.

I have not said one Word here about the Physick or Preparations that we ordinarily made use of on this terrible
Occasion, I mean we that went frequently abroad up and
down Street, as I did; much of this was talk'd of in the Books
and Bills of our Quack Doctors, of whom I have said enough
already. It may however be added, that the College of Physicians were daily publishing several Preparations, which they
had consider'd of in the Process of their Practice, and which
being to be had in Print, I avoid repeating them for that
reason.

One thing I could not help observing, what befell one of

the Quacks, who publish'd that he had a most excellent Preservative against the Plague, which whoever kept about them, should never be infected, or liable to Infection; this Man, who we may reasonably suppose, did not go abroad without some of this *excellent Preservative* in his Pocket, yet was taken by the Distemper, and carry'd off in two or three Days.

I am not of the Number of the Physic-Haters, or Physic-Despisers; on the contrary, I have often mentioned the regard I had to the Dictates of my particular Friend Dr. *Heath*; but yet I must acknowledge, I made use of little or nothing, except as I have observ'd, to keep a Preparation of strong Scent[1] to have ready, in case I met with any thing of offensive Smells, or went too near any burying place, or dead Body.

Neither did I do, what I know some did, keep the Spirits always high and hot with Cordials, and Wine,[2] and such things, and which, as I observ'd, one learned Physician used himself so much to, as that he could not leave them off when the Infection was quite gone, and so became a Sot for all his Life after.

I remember, my Friend the Doctor us'd to say, that there was a certain Set of Drugs and Preparations, which were all certainly good and useful in the case of an Infection; out of which, or with which, Physicians might make an infinite Variety of Medicines, as the Ringers of Bells make several Hundred different Rounds of Musick by the changing and Order of Sound but in six Bells; and that all these Preparations shall be really very good; therefore, said he, I do not wonder that so vast a Throng of Medicines is offer'd in the present Calamity; and almost every Physician prescribes or prepares a different thing, as his Judgment or Experience guides him: but, says my Friend, let all the Prescriptions of all the Physicians in *London* be examined; and it will be found, that they are all compounded of the same things, with such Variations only, as the particular Fancy of the Doctor leads him to; so that, says he, every Man judging a little of his own Constitution and manner of his living, and Circumstances of his being infected, may direct his own Medicines out of the ordinary Drugs and Preparations: Only that, says he, some recommended one thing as most sovereign, and some another; some, says he, think that *Pill. Ruff.*[1] which is call'd itself the Anti-pestilential Pill, is the best Preparation that can be made; others think that *Venice* Treacle[2] is sufficient of it self to resist the Contagion, and I, says he, think as both these think, *viz.* that the last is good to take beforehand to prevent it, and the last, if touch'd, to expel it. According to this Opinion, I several times took *Venice Treacle* and a sound Sweat upon it, and thought my self as well fortified against the Infection as any one could be fortifyed by the Power of Physic.

As for Quackery and Mountebank, of which the Town was so full, I listened to none of them, and have observ'd often since with some Wonder, that for two Years after the Plague, I scarcely saw or heard of one of them about Town. Some fancied they were all swept away in the Infection to a Man, and were for calling it a particular Mark of God's Vengeance upon them, for leading the poor People into the Pit of Destruction, merely for the Lucre of a little Money they got by them; but I cannot go that Length neither; that Abundance of them died is certain, many of them came within the Reach of my own Knowledge; ·but that all of them were swept off I much question; I believe rather, they fled into the Country, and tryed their Practices upon the People there, who were in Apprehension of the Infection, before it came among them.

This however is certain, not a Man of them appear'd for a great while in or about *London*; there were indeed several Doctors, who published Bills, recommending their several physical Preparations for cleansing the Body, as they call it, after the Plague, and needful, as they said, for such People to take, who had been visited and had been cur'd; whereas I must own, I believe that it was the Opinion of the most eminent Physicians at that time, that the Plague was itself a sufficient Purge; and that those who escaped the Infection needed no Physic to cleanse their Bodies of any other things; the running Sores, the Tumors, *&c.* which were broke and

kept open by the Directions of the Physicians, having sufficiently cleansed them; and that all other Distempers and
Causes of Distempers were effectually carried off that Way;
and as the Physicians gave this as their Opinions, wherever
they came, the Quacks got little Business.

There were indeed several little Hurries, which happen'd
after the Decrease of the Plague, and which whether they
were contriv'd to fright and disorder the People, as some
imagin'd, I cannot say, but sometimes we were told the
Plague would return by such a Time; and the famous *Solomon
Eagle* the naked Quaker,[1] I have mention'd, prophesy'd evil
Tidings every Day; and several others telling us that *London*
had not been sufficiently scourg'd, and the sorer and severer
Strokes were yet behind; had they stop'd there, or had they
descended to Particulars, and told us that the City should the
next Year be destroyed by Fire; then indeed, when we had
seen it come to pass, we should not have been to blame to have
paid more than a common Respect to their Prophetick Spirits,
at least we should have wonder'd at them, and have been more
serious in our Enquiries after the meaning of it, and whence
they had the Fore-knowledge: But as they generally told us
of a Relapse into the Plague, we have had no Concern since
that about them; yet by these frequent Clamours, we were all
kept with some kind of Apprehensions constantly upon us,
and if any died suddenly, or if the spotted Fevers at any time
increased, we were presently alarm'd; much more if the
Number of the Plague encreased, for to the End of the Year,
there were always between 2 and 300 of the Plague; on any
of these Occasions, I say, we were alarm'd anew.

Those who remember the City of *London* before the Fire,
must remember that there was then no such Place as that we
now call *Newgate*-Market. But that in the Middle of the
Street, which is now call'd *Blow-bladder Street*, and which
had its Name from the Butchers, who us'd to kill and dress their
Sheep there; (and who it seems had a Custom to blow up their
Meat with Pipes to make it look thicker and fatter than it was,
and were punish'd there for it by the Lord Mayor) I say, from

the End of the Street towards *Newgate*, there stood two long Rows of Shambles for the selling Meat.

It was in those Shambles, that two Persons falling down dead, as they were buying Meat, gave Rise to a Rumor that the Meat was all infected, which tho' it might affright the People, and spoil'd the Market for two or three Days; yet it appear'd plainly afterwards, that there was nothing of Truth in the Suggestion: But no Body can account for the Possession of Fear when it takes hold of the Mind.

However it pleas'd God by the continuing of the Winter Weather to restore the Health of the City, that by *February* following, we reckon'd the Distemper quite ceas'd,[1] and then we were not so easily frighted again.

There was still a Question among the Learned, and at first it perplex'd the People a little, and that was, in what manner to purge the Houses and Goods, where the Plague had been; and how to render them habitable again, which had been left empty during the time of the Plague; Abundance of Perfumes and Preparations were prescrib'd by Physicians, some of one kind and some of another, in which the People, who listened to them, put themselves to a great, and indeed in my Opinion, to an unnecessary Expence; and the poorer People, who only set open their Windows Night and Day, burnt Brimstone, Pitch, and Gun-powder[2] and such things in their Rooms, did as well as the best; nay, the eager People, who as I said above, came Home in haste and at all Hazards, found little or no Inconvenience in their Houses nor in the Goods, and did little or nothing to them.

However, in general, prudent cautious People did enter into some Measures for airing and sweetning their Houses,[3] and burnt Perfumes, Incense, Benjamin, Rozin, and Sulphur in the Rooms close shut up, and then let the Air carry it all out with a Blast of Gun-powder; others caused large Fires to be made all Day and all Night, for several Days and Nights; by the same Token, that two or three were pleas'd to set their Houses on Fire, and so effectually sweetned them by burning them down to the Ground; as particularly one at *Ratcliff*, one in *Holbourn*, and one at *Westminster*; besides two or three that were set on Fire, but the Fire was happily got out again, before it went far enough to burn down the Houses; and one Citizen's Servant, I think it was in *Thames* Street, carryed so much Gun-powder into his Master's House for clearing it of the Infection, and managed it so foolishly, that he blew up part of the Roof of the House. But the Time was not fully come, that the City was to be purg'd by Fire, nor was it far off; for within Nine Months more I saw it all lying in Ashes; when, as some of our Quacking Philosophers pretend, the Seeds of the Plague were entirely destroy'd[1] and not before; a Notion too ridiculous to speak of here, since, had the Seeds of the Plague remain'd in the Houses, not to be destroyed but by Fire, how has it been, that they have not since broken out? Seeing all those Buildings in the Suburbs and Liberties, and in the great Parishes of *Stepney*, *White-Chapel*, *Aldgate*, *Bishopsgate*, *Shoreditch*, *Cripplegate* and St. *Giles's*, where the Fire never came, and where the Plague rag'd with the greatest Violence, remain still in the same Condition they were in before.

But to leave these things just as I found them, it was certain, that those People, who were more than ordinarily cautious of their Health, did take particular Directions for what they called Seasoning of their Houses, and Abundance of costly Things were consum'd on that Account, which, I cannot but say, not only seasoned those Houses, as they desir'd, but fill'd the Air with very grateful and wholesome Smells, which others had the Share of the Benefit of, as well as those who were at the Expences of them.

And yet after all, tho' the Poor came to Town very precipitantly, as I have said, yet I must say, the rich made no such Haste; the Men of Business indeed came up, but many of them did not bring their Families to Town till the Spring came on, and that they saw Reason to depend upon it, that the Plague would not return.

The Court indeed came up soon after Christmas, but the Nobility and Gentry, except such as depended upon, and had Employment under the Administration, did not come so soon.

I should have taken Notice here, that notwithstanding the Violence of the Plague in *London* and in other Places, yet it was very observable, that it was never on Board the Fleet;[1] and yet for some time there was a strange Press in the River, and even in the Streets for Sea-Men to man the Fleet. But it was in the Beginning of the Year, when the Plague was scarce begun, and not at all come down to that part of the City, where they usually press for Seamen; and tho' a War with the *Dutch* was not at all grateful to the People at that time, and the Seamen went with a kind of Reluctancy into the Service, and many complain'd of being drag'd into it by Force, yet it prov'd in the Event a happy Violence to several of them, who had probably perish'd in the general Calamity, and who after the Summer Service was over, tho' they had Cause to lament the Desolation of their Families, who, when they came back, were many of them in their Graves; yet they had room to be thankful, that they were carried out of the Reach of it, tho' so much against their Wills; we indeed had a hot War with the *Dutch* that Year, and one very great Engagement at Sea,[2] in which the *Dutch* were worsted; but we lost a great many Men and some Ships. But, as I observ'd, the Plague was not in the Fleet, and when they came to lay up the Ships in the River, the violent part of it began to abate.

I would be glad, if I could close the Account of this melancholy Year with some particular Examples historically; I mean of the Thankfulness to God our Preserver for our being delivered from this dreadful Calamity; certainly the Circumstances of the Deliverance, as well as the terrible Enemy we were delivered from, call'd upon the whole Nation for it; the Circumstances of the Deliverance were indeed very remarkable, as I have in part mention'd already, and particularly the dreadful Condition, which we were all in, when we were, to the Surprize of the whole Town, made joyful with the Hope of a Stop of the Infection.

Nothing but the immediate Finger of God, nothing but

omnipotent Power could have done it; the Contagion despised all Medicine, Death rag'd in every Corner; and had it gone on as it did then, a few Weeks more would have clear'd the Town of all, and every thing that had a Soul: Men every where began to despair, every Heart fail'd them for Fear, People were made desperate thro' the Anguish of their Souls, and the Terrors of Death sat in the very Faces and Countenances of the People.

In that very Moment, when we might very well say, Vain was the Help of Man;[1] I say in that very Moment it pleased God, with a most agreeable Surprize, to cause the Fury of it to abate, even of it self, and the Malignity declining, as I have said, tho' infinite Numbers were sick, yet fewer died; and the very first Week's Bill decreased 1843, a vast Number indeed!

It is impossible to express the Change that appear'd in the very Countenances of the People, that *Thursday* Morning, when the Weekly Bill came out; it might have been perceived in their Countenances, that a secret Surprize and Smile of Joy sat on every Bodies Face; they shook one another by the Hands in the Streets, who would hardly go on the same Side of the way with one another before; where the Streets were not too broad, they would open their Windows and call from one House to another, and ask'd how they did, and if they had heard the good News, that the Plague was abated; Some would return when they said good News, and ask, *what good News?* and when they answered, that the Plague was abated, and the Bills decreased almost 2000, they would cry out, *God be praised*; and would weep aloud for Joy, telling them they had heard nothing of it; and such was the Joy of the People that it was as it were Life to them from the Grave. I could almost set down as many extravagant things done in the Excess of their Joy, as of their Grief; but that would be to lessen the Value of it.

I must confess my self to have been very much dejected just before this happen'd; for the prodigious Number that were taken sick the Week or two before, besides those that died, was such, and the Lamentations were so great every where, that a Man must have seemed to have acted even against his Reason, if he had so much as expected to escape; and as there was hardly a House, but mine, in all my Neighbourhood, but what was infected; so had it gone on, it would not have been long, that there would have been any more Neighbours to be infected; indeed it is hardly credible, what dreadful Havock the last three Weeks had made, for if I might believe the Person, whose Calculations I always found very well grounded, there were not less than 30000 People dead, and near 100 thousand fallen sick in the three Weeks I speak of; for the Number that sickened was surprising, indeed it was astonishing, and those whose Courage upheld them all the time before, sunk under it now.

In the Middle of their Distress, when the Condition of the City of *London* was so truly calamitous, just then it pleased God, as it were, by his immediate Hand to disarm this Enemy; the Poyson was taken out of the Sting, it was wonderful, even the Physicians themselves were surprized at it; wherever they visited, they found their Patients better, either they had sweated kindly, or the Tumours were broke, or the Carbuncles went down, and the Inflammations round them chang'd Colour, or the Fever was gone, or the violent Headach was asswag'd, or some good Symptom was in the Case; so that in a few Days, every Body was recovering, whole Families that were infected and down, that had Ministers praying with them, and expected Death every Hour, were revived and healed, and none died at all out of them.

Nor was this by any new Medicine found out, or new Method of Cure discovered, or by any Experience in the Operation, which the Physicians or Surgeons had attain'd to; but it was evidently from the secret invisible Hand of him, that had at first sent this Disease as a Judgment upon us; and let the Atheistic part of Mankind call my Saying this what they please, it is no Enthusiasm; it was acknowledg'd at that time by all Mankind; the Disease was enervated, and its Malignity spent, and let it proceed from whencesoever it will, let the

Philosophers search for Reasons in Nature to account for it by, and labour as much as they will to lessen the Debt they owe to their Maker; those Physicians, who had the least Share of Religion in them, were oblig'd to acknowledge that it was all supernatural,[1] that it was extraordinary, and that no Account could be given of it.

If I should say, that this is a visible Summons to us all to Thankfulness, especially we that were under the Terror of its Increase, perhaps it may be thought by some, after the Sense of the thing was over, an officious canting of religious things, preaching a Sermon instead of writing a History, making my self a Teacher instead of giving my Observations of things; and this restrains me very much from going on here, as I might otherwise do: But if ten Lepers were healed,[2] and but one return'd to give Thanks, I desire to be as that one, and to be thankful for my self.

Nor will I deny, but there were Abundance of People who to all Appearance were very thankful at that time; for their Mouths were stop'd, even the Mouths of those whose Hearts were not extraordinary long affected with it: But the Impression was so strong at that time, that it could not be resisted, no not by the worst of the People.

It was a common thing to meet People in the Street, that were Strangers, and that we knew nothing at all of, expressing their Surprize. Going one Day thro' *Aldgate*, and a pretty many People being passing and repassing, there comes a Man out of the End of the *Minories*, and looking a little up the Street and down, he throws his Hands abroad, *Lord, what an Alteration is here!* Why, last Week I came along here, and hardly any Body was to be seen; another Man, I heard him, adds to his Words, 'tis all wonderful, 'tis all a Dream: Blessed be God, says a third Man, and let us give Thanks to him, for 'tis all his own doing: Human Help and human Skill was at an End. These were all Strangers to one another: But such Salutations as these were frequent in the Street every Day; and in Spight of a loose Behaviour, the very common People went along the Streets, giving God Thanks for their Deliverance.

It was now, as I said before, the People had cast off all Apprehensions, and that too fast; indeed we were no more afraid now to pass by a Man with a white Cap upon his Head, or with a Cloth wrapt round his Neck, or with his Leg limping, occasion'd by the Sores in his Groyn, all which were frightful to the last Degree, but the Week before; but now the Street was full of them, and these poor recovering Creatures, give them their Due, appear'd very sensible of their unexpected Deliverance; and I should wrong them very much, if I should not acknowledge, that I believe many of them were really thankful; but I must own, that for the Generality of the People it might too justly be said of them, as was said of the Children of *Israel*, after their being delivered from the Host of *Pharaoh*, when they passed the *Red-Sea*, and look'd back, and saw the *Egyptians* overwhelmed in the Water, *viz.* That *they sang his Praise, but they soon forgot his Works.*[1]

I can go no farther here, I should be counted censorious, and perhaps unjust, if I should enter into the unpleasant Work of reflecting, whatever Cause there was for it, upon the Unthankfulness and Return of all manner of Wickedness among us, which I was so much an Eye-Witness of my self; I shall conclude the Account of this calamitous Year therefore with a coarse but sincere Stanza of my own, which I plac'd at the End of my ordinary Memorandums, the same Year they were written:

A dreadful Plague in London *was,*

In the Year Sixty Five,

Which swept an Hundred Thousand Souls

Away; yet I alive!

H. F.

FINIS.

EXPLANATORY NOTES

ACKNOWLEDGEMENTS

THE following people assisted Professor Landa in preparing the text and notes: George Rousseau, John Sekora, Mr John Bromley of the London Guildhall Library, Mr Herbert Ward of the Tower Hamlets Central Library, Dr Edwin Clarke of the Wellcome Foundation, Dr R. S. Roberts of Queen Mary College, University of London, Dr John Walker of Worcester College, Oxford, and Mrs Louis Landa.

ABBREVIATED TITLES USED IN THE NOTES

A Collection of Very Valuable and Scarce Pieces relating to the Last Plague in the Year 1665. Cited as *A Collection of Very Valuable and Scarce Pieces.* This *Collection* contains *Necessary Directions for the Prevention and Cure of the Plague, with Divers Remedies of small Charge, by the College of Physicians,* 1721. Cited as *Necessary Directions . . . by the College of Physicians.*

Boghurst, William. *Loimographia, Or an Experimentall Relation of the Plague, of what hath happened Remarkable in the Last Plague in the City of London . . . with a Collection of Choice and Tried Medicines for Preservation and Cure, etc. 1666.* Printed for the Epidemiological Society of London, ed. by Joseph Frank Payne, 1894. Cited as *Loimographia.*

Hodges, Nathaniel. *Loimologia, Or an Historical Account of the Plague in London in 1665 . . . to which is added An Essay on the Different Causes of Pestilential Diseases, and how they become Contagious,* by J. Quincy, M.D., 1720, 3rd edn., 1721. Cited as *Loimologia.*

Kemp, William. *A Brief Treatise of the Nature, Causes, Signs, Preservation from and Cure of the Pestilence,* 1665. Cited as *A Brief Treatise . . . of the Pestilence.*

Kephale, Richard. *Medela Pestilentiae: Wherein is contained Several Theological Queries concerning the Plague, with Approved Antidotes, Signs, and Symptoms: also an Exact Method for curing that Epidemical Distemper*, 1665. Cited as *Medela Pestilentiae*.

Lee, William. *Daniel Defoe: His Life and Recently Discovered Writings, extending from 1716 to 1729*. 3 vols., 1869. Cited as Lee.

Mead, Richard. *A Short Discourse Concerning Pestilential Contagion, and the Methods to be used to Prevent it*, 1720. 6th edn., 1720. Cited as *Short Discourse*.

EXPLANATORY NOTES

Page 1. (1) *again in Holland*: On 4 May 1664 Pepys made the first of several entries in his *Diary* concerning the reappearance of the plague in Holland. As a busy port trading with the plague-infected countries of Asia, Amsterdam was watched with apprehension by the English. In 1663 Amsterdam had 9,752 deaths from plague; in 1664, 24,148. See John Graunt's *Natural and Political Observations . . . upon the Bills of Mortality*, 5th edn., 1676, reprinted in *The Economic Writings of Sir William Petty*, ed. C. H. Hull (1899), ii. 402.

(2) *Candia*: Crete.

(3) *matter'd not . . . whence it come*: Defoe reflects the prevalent view that plagues originated in Asia and Africa. This traditional view was stated by Dr. Richard Mead in his widely read *A Short Discourse Concerning Pestilential Contagion*, 1720, a tract authorized by the English Government soon after the outbreak of plague in Marseilles. Plagues, Mead asserted, 'seem to be of the Growth of the *Eastern* and *Southern* parts of the World, and to be transmitted from them into the colder Climates by Way of Commerce. Nor do I think, that in this *Island* particularly there is any one instance of a *Pestilential* Disease . . . of great Consequence; which we did not receive from other *Infected Places*' (*Short Discourse*, 6th edn., 1720, pp. 4–5). The controversy over the geographical origins of plague was widespread. Dr. Mead was opposed by the anonymous author of *Medicina Flagellata* (1721), pp. 191 ff., as well as by others; but more often writers on the plague of 1665 agreed that it had reached England from Holland by means of imported goods from such places as Grand Cairo, Alexandria, Constantinople, Smyrna, and Aleppo. There was, in fact, an outbreak in Turkey in 1661, from which the plague spread to Greece, and thence moved to Amsterdam in 1663.

(4) *no . . . printed News Papers*: Though the newspaper as a distinct type had not yet developed, there were anticipations. In 1665 the *Oxford*

Gazette (later the *London Gazette*) made its appearance and carried news of the plague, as did *The Intelligencer* and *The Newes* of Sir Roger L'Estrange.

Page 2. (1) *Tokens*: in modern medical parlance external signs, cutaneous lesions, which result from the subcutaneous haemorrhages common in bubonic plague: '. . . otherwise called *Gods Tokens*, [they] are commonly of the bigness of a flea-bitten spot, sometimes much bigger; their colour is according to the predominancy of the humour in the body; red or reddish, if choler; pale blue or dark blue, if flegm; leaden or blackish, if melancholy abound; but they have ever a circle about them: The red ones a purplish circle, and the others a reddish circle: they appear most commonly on the breast and back, and sometimes on the neck, arms and thighs; on the breast and back because the vital spirits strive to breathe out the venom the nearest way. In some bodies there will be many; in some, but one or two, or very few, according to the quantity of the venom, and the strength to drive them out.' See Richard Kephale, *Medela Pestilentiae* (1665), pp. 84–5, no. 1421 in the Farewell–Defoe sale catalogue.

(2) *the Hall*: the Hall of the Company of Parish Clerks located in Broad Lane, Vintry Ward. It was burned in the Great Fire of 1666. The Parish Clerks were licensed as a guild in 1233 and called the Fraternity of St. Nicholas.

(3) *weekly Bill of Mortality*: The weekly Bills of Mortality supplied Defoe with the statistical groundwork of the *Journal*. Dating from the sixteenth century, they appeared irregularly and in various forms until about 1636, when they took the form known to Defoe. Compiled and published by the Company of Parish Clerks, they reported parish by parish the causes and number of deaths in London. As Defoe knew the Bills, they gave the weekly mortality rates for the 97 parishes within the Walls, 16 without the Walls, 12 in Middlesex and Surrey, and 5 in the City and Liberties of Westminster, 130 parishes in all. The accuracy of the Bills has been much disputed, both in Defoe's time and later, and Defoe is frequently critical of them in the *Journal*. In *Applebee's Journal*, 18 Nov. 1721, he has a scathing indictment of what he refers to as 'those ridiculous Legends, call'd Bills of Mortality'. He promises at leisure to 'show the scandalous Deficiency of these Mortality Men in the Time of the late Infection in 1665' (Lee, ii. 453–5). In addition to the weekly Bills, two annual compilations from 1665 were available: *London's Dreadful Visitation: Or, A Collection of all the Bills of Mortality of this present Year . . . according to the Report made to the King's most excellent Majesty, by the Company of Parish Clerks* and John Bell, *London's Remembrancer*. Defoe had access also to John Graunt's *Reflections on the Weekly Bills of Mortality . . . from the Year 1592 to the Great Plague in 1665*, reprinted in *A Collection of Very Valuable and Scarce Pieces relating to the Last Plague in the Year 1665* (1721).

Page 4. *Spotted-Feaver*: 'a politic word' for the plague, so Defoe called it
in *The Review*, no. 151, 29 Jan. 1706, echoing Thomas Dekker's earlier
remark in *London Looke Backe* (1630): 'a fine Gentleman like name . . . as
if it had beene a Beautifull faire skind sickenesse' (Dekker, *Plague Pamphlets*,
ed. F. P. Wilson, 1925, p. 179). The phrase, apparently coined in Spain
in the seventeenth century, was loosely applied in England to typhus or any
fever involving petechial eruptions. Defoe's contemporaries thought it
'cousin-germane' to and a herald of the bubonic plague. The confused
medical views of fever in the period are reflected in Sir Richard Blackmore's
'Account of Malignant Fevers', included in his *A Discourse upon the
Plague* (1721). Dr. Nathaniel Hodges wrote: 'Very many were puzzled
to distinguish aright between these Marks [the tokens of bubonic plague]
and the *Petechiae Pestilentiales*, or Pestilential Appearances in Spotted
Fevers' (*An Account of the First Rise . . . of the Plague*, reprinted in *A Collection of Very Valuable and Scarce Pieces*, 1721, pp. 27–8). Willis, Sydenham, and Richard Morton, contemporary authorities, ranged fevers in a
scale of ascending severity: putrid, malignant, pestilential. Sydenham
wrote of malignant fever: 'Its true affinities are with plague . . . and from
the true plague it is distinguished only by its difference in degree' (*Works*,
ed. R. G. Latham, for the Sydenham Society, 1848, i. 98). John Hancocke,
prebendary of Canterbury and chaplain to the Duke of Bedford, was a
popular proponent of the view that the plague is a fever, curable by cold
water. His book, *Febrifugum Magnum: or, Common Water the best Cure for
Fevers, and probably for the Plague* (1722), went quickly into six editions.
William Boghurst, an apothecary who 'practised' during the Plague,
denied that the plague is a putrid fever: 'though wee may fancy it is putrefaction in the highest degree of exaltation . . . [feaver] is not the essence and
constitution of it, but a consequent and effect' (*Loimographia*, [1666]
p. 10).

Page 5. (1) *Apprehensions . . . Summer being at Hand*: From Hippocrates
descended the idea of a special relationship between climate or seasons and
disease. In the seventeenth and eighteenth centuries the prevailing view
was that plague originated in hot climates and flourished in the heat of
summer: 'All that *Experience* helps us in this Case, is, that in the *Heat of
Summer* this Disease commonly rages more than in the *Cold of Winter*'
(R. Brookes, *History of the Most Remarkable Distempers*, 1721, p. 36).
Dr. George Thomson: 'So efficacious do we find cold Seasons . . . in power-
fully restraining this feral Disease, the Pest, that in this part of the World
there hath seldom any great Mortality reigned amongst us in a very sharp
Winter' (*Loimotomia: Or the Pest Anatomized*, 1666, p. 22). Sir Richard
Blackmore asserted that the feared plague then raging in the south of
France consisted of 'a more exalted and active Poyson' such as might with-
stand the cold of winter. He thought that the rigorous season could check
or abate the malignity of a plague but with the return of hot weather a

pestilence could recover its vigour (*A Discourse upon the Plague*, 1721, pp. 38-9).

(2) *Liberties*: The City (that part of London within the old walls) was almost surrounded by Liberties whose relationship to the City authorities varied: the Minories, the Liberty and precinct of the Tower, St. Katherine's by the Tower, Duke's Place, the Old Artillery Ground, Norton Folgate, Glasshouse Street, St. Martin's-le-Grand, the Temple, Blackfriars, and Whitefriars—all were Liberties. John Graunt estimated the population of the eleven Liberties to be 179,000 in 1661 (*Natural and Political Observations . . . upon the Bills of Mortality*, 5th edn., 1676, reprinted in *The Economic Writings of Sir William Petty*, ed. C. H. Hull, 1899, ii. 401).

Page 6. (1) *Weather . . . hot*: Pepys noted the hot weather on 7 June: 'the hottest day that ever I felt in my life, and it is confessed so by all other people the hottest they ever knew in England in the beginning of June.' On this day Pepys saw for the first time two or three houses in Drury Lane 'marked with a red cross upon the doors, and "Lord have mercy upon us" writ there'. H. F.'s remark that 'the Infection spread in a dreadful Manner' is supported by the Bills of Mortality, which show that deaths from the plague increased from 17 the last week of May to 43 the first week of June, a notably warm week.

(2) *Articles of the Feaver, Spotted-Feaver, and Teeth . . . swell*: not wholly true as indicated by the Bills of Mortality. The mortality figures for the last week of May for the three maladies in the order named are 30, 23, and 19; for the first week in June, 43, 16, 25. But the increase in fever was significant because the plague was considered a 'pestilential fever'. *Teeth*: Dr. John Arbuthnot, Fellow of the College of Physicians and of the Royal Society, and the friend and collaborator of Pope and Swift, wrote: 'Above a tenth part of Infants die in Teething, by the Symptoms proceeding from the Irritation of the Tender Parts of the Jaws, occasioning Inflamations, Fevers, Convulsions, Looseness, with Green Stools . . . and in some, Gangrene . . .' (*Practical Rules of Diet in the Various Constitutions and Diseases of Human Bodies*, 1732, p. 408). Joseph Hurlock, an eighteenth-century surgeon, canvassed the subject of death from 'teeth' in his *Practical Treatise upon Dentition* (1742).

Page 7. (1) *I liv'd without Aldgate*: H. F.'s residence was in that portion of the parish of St. Botolph, Aldgate, outside the Walls, midway between the parish church of Aldgate, St. Botolph (where Defoe was married), and the extremity of London marked by Whitechapel Bars (i.e. 'gate'). The street was Whitechapel, described by Edward Hatton as 'a very extraordinary spacious str. between *White chapel bars* (to which the Freedom reaches) W. and the Road to Mile end E.L.' (*A New View of London*, 1708, i. 90). Hatton says that the part of the parish within the Freedom of the City contained 1,300 houses, the part without, 1,000.

(2) *throng'd out of Town*: Pepys, *Diary*, 21 June 1665: '. . . all the towne

almost going out of towne, the coaches and waggons being all full of people going into the country.'

(3) *Certificates of Health*: Issued by the Lord Mayor and at times by parish officers, these certifications that the bearer was free of the plague were not always honoured by the authorities of some towns and cities, where any traveller from plague-ridden London was suspect. Defoe presents the problem in *Due Preparations for the Plague* (p. 156): 'And though they [the brother and sister] had gotten certificates of health from the Lord Mayor, the city began now to be so infected, that nobody would receive them, no inn would lodge them on the way.'

Page 8. (1) *Turn-pikes*: spiked barriers.

(2) *A Saddler*: a craftsman who made saddles, or, as in H. F.'s case, a tradesman who, in addition to selling saddles, was a dealer in other supplies needed by travellers, as pillows, straps, stirrups, horsecloths, and leather bottles.

Page 9. (1) *Master save thy self*: Matt. xxvii. 40; Mark xv. 30.

(2) *Relations in Northamptonshire*: Defoe's paternal grandparents lived in the villages of Peakirk and Etton, Northamptonshire.

Page 11. Turks and Mahometans . . . predestinating Notions: Whether a Christian may fly from the plague; this was a hotly debated question in 1665, as it had been earlier, dating back at least to Luther and Calvin. By the time of the Plague of 1665 the refusal to fly had become a 'Turkish heresy', or, as Sir Richard Blackmore termed it in 1721, a 'Doctrine of fatal Necessity' (*A Discourse upon the Plague*, 1721, p. 85). In his *A Brief Treatise . . . of the Pestilence* (1665), p. 15, W. Kemp describes Turkish predestinarianism (Defoe's phrase) thus: 'The *Turks* are perswaded, that every ones fate is written in his fore-head, and hath a fatal destiny appointed by God, which is impossible for any to avoid; so that they believe, those that shall die by the Plague, cannot be slain in War, nor drown'd in Water, and those that shall die in Battel, cannot be kill'd by the Plague; by which credulity, they slight and neglect all care of avoiding the infection, conversing with one another, and buying the goods out of infected houses, and wearing the apparel of them that lately died. I shall not trouble my self to confute this Opinion, since at *Grand Cayre* and *Constantinople* there have been thousands that have suffered death, and multitudes that have been executed by the Plague for this Heresie.' Kemp's *Brief Treatise* is listed in the sale catalogue of Defoe's library, no. 212.

Page 12. happen'd to stop . . . 91st Psalm: Sortes Biblicae, divination by means of the Bible, an old practice among Christians and at times condemned by councils of the Church. Defoe used the device in *Robinson Crusoe*, where Crusoe found comfort—and eventual penitence—by randomly opening the Bible at Ps. 50.

Page 15. (1) *none but Magistrates and Servants*: R. Kephale, whose *Medela Pestilentiae* (1665) is listed in the sale catalogue of Defoe's library, no. 1421, answered 'theological queries concerning the Plague'. He includes among those who may not flee without an affront to God both magistrates and servants, magistrates because they are needed 'for keeping good orders', and servants because they 'are under command' (p. 27).

(2) *Court removed . . . June*: The Court, Pepys records in his *Diary* on 29 June, was 'full of waggons and ready to go out of towne'. It went first to Hampton Court and thence to Salisbury (Pepys, 27 July), finally setting out for Oxford the last week of September. The King was back at Whitehall on 1 Feb. (Pepys, 31 Jan. and 2 Feb. 1666, and Anthony Wood, *Life and Times*, ed. Andrew Clark, 1892, ii. 46).

Page 16. (1) *hardly any thing of Reformation*: Observing the King and his courtiers at Oxford during the Plague, Anthony Wood noted in his diary: 'The greater part of the courtiers were high, proud, insolent . . . To give a further character of the court, they thought they were neat and gay in their apparell, yet they were nasty and beastly. . . . Rude, rough, whoremongers; vaine, empty, carelesse' (*Life and Times*, ii. 68).

(2) *crying Vices . . . Judgment*: Cf. Bishop Burnet: 'All the King's enemies, and the enemies of monarchy, said, here [i.e. the plague] was a manifest character of God's displeasure upon the nation; as indeed the ill life the King led, and the viciousness of the whole court, gave but a melancholy prospect . . .' (*History of his own Times*, 1818, i. 242). In *The Review*, no. 4, 12 Aug. 1712, Defoe wrote: '*Some have said*, it [the plague in 1665] was to punish the *Nation*, for the horrid Debaucheries of the King's Party, and yet the *Roundheads* died as fast as the *Cavaliers*.'

(3) *London . . . the whole Mass*: Defoe stood in perpetual astonishment before the spectacle of 'this great and monstrous Thing, called London', as he wrote in his *Tour thro' the Whole Island of Great Britain* (1724-6). In his survey of London he estimates that 'the Extent or Circumference of the continued Buildings of the Cities of *London* and *Westminster*, and the Borough of *Southwark*, all of which, in the common Acceptation, is called *London*, amounts to Thirty Six Miles, Two Furlongs, Thirty Nine Rods' (*Tour*, ed. G. D. H. Cole, 1927, i. 323 ff.).

(4) *City . . . not yet much infected*: Following the week of 2 May when one death from plague was reported, the Bills of Mortality reported no deaths from plague in the City until the week of 6 June (4 reported). Then the subsequent weekly deaths were 10, 4, 23, 28, 56, ascending to 128 in the week of 18 July. The greatest number for a single week in the 97 parishes of the City was 1,189, the week of 12 Sept.

Page 17. *Inns of Court . . . shut*: In the second week of June notices of postponed readings appeared at the Inner Temple, the Middle Temple, and Lincoln's Inn, and shortly thereafter at Gray's Inn.

Page 18. (1) *City and Suburbs . . . prodigiously full*: reliable figures on the population of London at the time of the Great Plague are not available. John Graunt, whose figure from his *Natural and Political Observations . . . upon the Bills of Mortality* is much quoted, estimated about 460,000 in and about London at the beginning of Charles II's reign (see *Economic Writings of Sir William Petty*, 1899, ii. 331, 400–1). See also Norman G. Brett-James, *The Growth of Stuart London* (1935), ch. xx, 'Estimates of London's Population in the Seventeenth Century'; a brief, informative discussion.

(2) *Encrease . . . in London*: Two years or so after writing the *Journal* Defoe refers to Sir William Petty, 'famous for his Political Arithmetick, [who] supposed the City . . . to contain a Million of People' (*Tour thro' the Whole Island of Great Britain*, ed. G. D. H. Cole, 1927, i. 324). In his *Five Essays in Political Arithmetic* (1687), Petty 'proves' that London (the parishes within the Bills of Mortality) contains 'about 696 thousand People' (*Economic Writings of Sir William Petty*, edited C. H. Hull, ii. 533). In 1724 Defoe estimated 1,500,000.

(3) *Jerusalem . . . besieg'd*: by the Roman emperor, Titus, in A.D. 70.

Page 19. (1) *Hundred Thousand Ribband Weavers*: a greatly exaggerated figure. In *The Review*, 20 Mar. 1705, Defoe seems to accept half that figure: 'As to *Spittle-fields*, in about 1679 and 80 . . . 'twas alledg'd then . . . were about 50000 Narrow Weavers, as they call'd them, or in Common *English* Ribbon-Weavers.'

(2) *lived . . . about Spittle-fields*: Spitalfields, the name of a hamlet in the parish of Stepney. The name was often applied to the whole silk-weaving district.

(3) *Akeldama*: 'the field of blood', the name given by the Jews of Jerusalem to the field Judas purchased with the money received from the betrayal of Christ, so called because of his violent death there (Acts i. 19; Matt. xxvii. 8 differs).

(4) *a blazing Star or Comet*: In mid-December 1664, and in early April 1665, the appearance of comets over London was related to the Plague in popular literature and in scientific discussions. Pepys mentions the first comet on 15 Dec. 1664, and the second on 6 April 1665.

Page 20. (1) *the Comet . . . of a faint, dull, languid Colour*: Defoe here follows astrological theory. John Gadbury, the astrologer, reports that astrologers divide comets into seven species: 'Such as are of a *Leaden, Envious, Pale, Ashy Colour*, are termed *Saturnine*. And such was this *Comet* or *Blazing Star* that lately appeared to us' (*De Cometis*, 1665, p. 9).

(2) *foretold a heavy Judgment . . . as . . . Plague*: 'Saturnine Comets . . . always denote, there shall happen in the world many pernicious evils, as *Famine, Plague . . . and absolute Destruction* of all things that grow upon the earth, useful for *man* and beast . . .' (Gadbury, *De Cometis*, 1665, p. 23). See also John Merrifield, who describes himself as a student of 'Heavenly and Sublime Sciences', *Catastasis Mundi* (1684), p. 29: 'Comets of the

nature of Saturn . . . denote many Evils, as . . . Chronick Diseases, and
Melancholy Distempers . . . Leprosie, Palsies, Consumption, and all
Diseases which are of long continuance.' Cf. the sceptical medical opinion
voiced by Dr. Nathaniel Hodges: 'Whoever duly considers it, can never
imagine that this Pestilence [of 1665] had its Origin from any Conjunction
of *Saturn* and *Jupiter*, *in Sagitarius* on the Tenth of October, or from a
Conjunction of *Saturn* and *Mars* in the same sign on the twelfth of *November*, which was the common opinion' (*Loimologia*, 1665, p. 4). It should
be noted that not all comets were sinister. Gadbury lists among the seven
kinds, 'jovial comets': these 'presage a very great *plenty* of all things, a very
fertile year, a pleasant *salubrious Air*' (p. 24). In *Applebee's Journal*, 7 Dec.
1723, Defoe asked why a comet must inevitably foretell calamities. He
attacked 'whining astrologers' and 'Stargazers' as men who have 'no Commission . . . to predict the Plagues, or War, or Famine' from appearances in
the heavens.

   (3) *Warnings of Gods Judgments*: A traditional and widely prevalent view
of comets as signs from heaven of impending scourges. William Turner,
*A Complete History of the most remarkable Providences . . . which have
happened in this Present Age* (1697), reflects the usual view: 'For *Comets*, I
declare, that I do not believe the Governour of the World puts out such
Flambeaus, sets such Beacons on fire in the upper Regions for no purpose:
Nature doth not, saith the Philosopher; and shall the Christian say, the
God of Nature doth anything in vain? Two and fifty years ago . . . there
was a Blazing Star seen, upon which followed the *Irish* Massacre, and the
late Civil Wars. In *December* and *March* 1664, there were two *Comets* seen,
which were followed by that sad and dreadful Plague . . . and that lamentable fire' (p. 61).

   (4) *Fore-tellers . . . Pestilence, War, Fire*: Anthony Wood records the
'blazing star' of December 1664 and adds an account of 'prodigious births'
at Sarum, 'the devill let loose to possess people', 'great innundations and
frosts—war with the Dutch—war between the emperour and the Turk—
general commotions throughout Christendom and the rest of the world—
sudden deaths'. This entry is followed by reference to the plague in 1665,
a monster born at Oxford ('one eye in the forehead, noe nose, and its two
eares in the nape of the neck'), a thorn which bore five different fruits
(cherries, dates, apricots), earthquakes (*Life and Times*, ii. 53-4). In
Applebee's Journal, 7 Dec. 1723, Defoe countered the inevitable gloomy
prognostications of astrologers by listing a number of benign comets, i.e.,
those which appeared at great and happy moments in human history
(Lee, iii. 212-13).

Page 21. (1) *Lilly's . . . Gadbury's . . . Poor Robin's*: three of the well-known
almanacs of the period. William Lilly (1602-81) published his first almanac,
Merlinus Anglicus Junior, in 1644 and continued to publish one annually
until his death. He was also the author of a long series of pamphlets of

prophecy, some of which involved him in difficulties. Though he remained in London during the plague of 1625, he fled in 1665. In the later years of his life he practised both medicine and astrology, having been granted a medical licence through the influence of his friend, Elias Ashmole. John Gadbury (1627–1704) served as apprentice to a tailor, after which he attended Oxford. Born of a Roman Catholic mother, he was eventually a Presbyterian, an Independent, and a member of the 'family of love'. He wrote widely on astrological subjects from 1652, his annual Ephemerides first appearing in 1655. Like other astrologers of the day, he was involved in controversy, religious and political as well as astrological. Two of his better known works are *De Cometis* (1665) and *London's Deliverance from the Plague* (1665). Poor Robin is thought to be the pseudonym of William Winstanley (1628?–1698), a barber turned writer and compiler. The earliest extant issue of his almanac is from 1663, most of it in a humorous and satiric vein directed at other almanacs somewhat in the manner of the Partridge papers of Swift and others. The title is revealing: *An Almanack after a New Fashion, Wherein the Reader may see (if he be not blinde) many remarkable Things worthy of Observation . . . written by Poor Robin, Knight of the Burnt-Island, a Well-Willer to Mathematicks.*

(2) *pretended religious Books: Come out of her, etc.* is from the Bible, Rev. xviii. 4. I have not found a book with this title. *Britain's Remembrancer* is by George Wither, but it was published in 1628. Its sub-title is 'Containing a Narration of the Plague lately Past', and possibly Defoe thought it applied to the plague of 1665. *Fair Warning* may be another instance of confusion: in 1665 Wither published his *Memorandum to London occasioned by the Pestilence, with a Warning Piece to London.* Wither's works on Plague were well known in the seventeenth century.

(3) *Jonah to Ninevah*: Jonah iii. 4.

(4) *run about Naked*: Pepys reports a similar incident in the *Diary*, 29 July 1667. The literature of Quakerism contains many instances of the practice of 'testifying by signs'. London, as the new Babylon, was often the subject of prophetic doom. Defoe had in mind the notorious case of Solomon Eagles (or Eccles) who 'as a sign' ran naked through Bartholomew Fair at Smithfield with a pan of fire or brimstone on his head, crying 'repentance' and 'remember Sodom', but this incident occurred in 1662 (William Braithwaite, *The Second Period of Quakerism*, 1961, p. 25). See also pp. 103 and 241, where Defoe mentions Solomon Eagles by name. Eagles, a musician, was a convert to Quakerism.

(5) *Josephus mentions*: Flavius Josephus, *Works* (1773 edn.), IV. vii. 12.

Page 22. (1) *Apparitions in the Air*: the flaming sword (see Gen. iii. 29) was a favourite in homiletic literature. Defoe refers to 'a comet before the Destruction of *Jerusalem*, which hung for a year . . . directly over the City in the shape of a Flaming Sword' (*Applebee's Journal*, 2 Nov. 1723). Gadbury, the astrologer, reports 'a *great black Coffin* seen in the *Air* at

Hamburgh, and other parts in *Germany* and *Flanders*' before and at the time of the second comet. He also says that one of the newsbooks reported '*terrible Apparitions, and noises in the Air . . .*' (*De Cometis*, 1665, p. 48). The respected Dr. George Thomson, whose post-mortem examination of a plague victim was well known, asserted that apparitions were prophetic: 'apparitions of *Dracones volantes* . . . Coffins carried through the Air . . . raining of blood . . . all of which having something *extra naturam*, are portentous and prodigious' (*Loimotamia: or the Pest Anatomized*, 1666, pp. 55-6). In the sale catalogue of Defoe's library is listed 'Glanvil of Witches and Apparitions, 1682' (no. 970). In his *Essay on the History and Reality of Apparitions* (1727), p. 390, Defoe wrote: 'It is without doubt, that Fancy and Imagination form a World of Apparitions in the Minds of Men and Women . . . when in short the Matter is no more than a Vapour in the Brain, a sick delirious fume of some in the Hypochondria. . . .'

(2) *So Hypocondriac Fancy's represent, etc.*: These lines, slightly modified, are quoted from Defoe's poem, *A New Discovery of an Old Intreague* (1691). Defoe used them twice in *The Review*, 29 Mar. 1705 and 24 May 1712, and again in his *Essay on the History and Reality of Apparitions* (1727), p. 391, where he wrote: 'These sham Apparitions which people put upon themselves are indeed very many; and our Hypochondriack People see more *Devils* at noon-day than *Galilaeus* did Starrs. . . . But this in no ways impeaches the main Proposition . . . that there are really and truly Apparitions of various kinds.'

Page 23. Despisers . . . wander and perish: Acts xiii. 41.

Page 24. Conjunctions of Planets . . . malignant: the malign conjunction of planets as a cause of plague; this view was inherited by Defoe's contemporaries from ancient and medieval times. At the time of the Black Death the Paris Faculty of Medicine gave it respectability; and in Defoe's day astrologers and others gave it credence. Saturn in conjunction with Mars, or perhaps Jupiter, was particularly malignant. Medical thought which ascribed the plague to the corruption of the air held planets responsible in part. Richard Kephale reflects this view of 'unwholesome' air in a quotation. 'When *Mars* in opposition is to Jove/The Air will be infected from above' (*Medela Pestilentiae*, 1665, p. 51). Gadbury, characteristically, writes of the plague of 1625: 'It was the consequence of a great *Conjunction* of *Saturn, Jupiter*, and *Mars*, in the Celestial Sign *Leo*, a sign of the fiery triplicity, and representing the heart in the *Microcosme, Ergo*, the most dangerous' (*London's Deliverance Predicted*, 1665, p. 7).

Page 25. (1) *Conjunctions foretold Drought, Famine, and Pestilence*: John Merrifield, the astrologer, wrote: 'Histories, ancient Writers, and Common Experience in former Ages testifie to us, that these Signs in the Heavens, or appearances of Comets, are the assured forerunners of sterility of the Earth; Famine, Pestilence, War, Alteration of Empires . . .

Winds, Earth-quakes, Inundations, extreme Heat and Drought, with
grievous Diseases, and such like evils; also the Birth of some great Emperors,
Kings, Governors, or Learned Men' (*Catastasis Mundi*, London, 1684,
p. 28).

(2) *Ministers . . . sunk . . . the Hearts*: cf. a typical sermon, such as Defoe
may have heard at the time he was writing the *Journal*: '. . . Multitudes
falling dead in the streets and High-ways . . . Crowds of noisome Carcasses
lie unburied, and rotting above Ground . . . populous Towns and Cities
quite depopulated . . . on every side the Cries and Groans of the Dying
and the Living . . . This famous Mart of Nations spews out her inhabitants,
and the like Desolation over-runs our Country.' This image of the plague
was presented in a sermon preached before the House of Commons by
Erasmus Saunders, 8 Dec. 1721, *A Discourse of the Dangers of Abusing the
Divine Blessings*, p. 30. A similar description was delivered at St. Mary's,
Oxford, 16 Dec. 1720, by Thomas Newlin, a fellow of Magdalene College:
'*The Chambers of the Grave* were not large enough to receive the number
of its Guests, and the *Land of Darkness* could not contain the daily increas-
ing Multitude. *Those that died grievous Deaths had none to lament them,
none to bury them. They are as Dung upon the face of the Earth, and their
Carcasses are meat for the Fowls of Heaven, and for the Beasts of the Earth.*
The City is made *an open Sepulchre*' (*God's Gracious Design in inflicting
National Judgments*, Oxford and London, 1721, p. 14).

(3) *ye will not come*: John v. 40.

(4) *spoke nothing but dismal Things*: In 1723 Defoe attacked the news
writers and others who merely from 'the Pleasure of Writing Dismal
Stories, Exciting Surprize and Horror', exaggerated the horrors of the
plague in southern France, 1720, thus terrifying people and injuring trade
(*Applebee's Journal*, 23 Nov. 1723, in Lee, iii. 207-9).

Page 26. (1) *terrifying the People*: Defoe's indictment of those who create
fear in a time of plague reflects current medical opinion in the period. The
plague tracts of the seventeenth and eighteenth centuries by physicians
and laymen stated again and again that fear, despair, and dejection of
spirits disposed the body to receive the contagion. This view was set forth
by Van Helmont and Athanasius Kircher on the Continent, and was held
firmly in England by doctors such as Mead, Rose, Pye, Thomson, and
Blackmore. The laymen held to it as firmly. In 1665 W. Kemp gives a complicated prescription for an electuary which 'is very excellent both against
Fear, and a good preservative against the Plague' (*A Brief Treatise . . . of
the Pestilence*, 1665, p. 73). In 1721 Sir Richard Blackmore writes: 'There
is another Preservative against Contagion, which is a lively and cheerful
Disposition of Mind; for when the Spirits are put into a pleasing Motion
. . . a Person is better prepar'd for his Defence. . . . timorous, diffident, and
weak-hearted Persons are . . . half dead before the Adversary approaches'
(*Discourse upon the Plague*, 1721, p. 76). George Pye, M.D.: '. . . whoever

is frighted and terrified will become more liable to the Pestilential Impressions' (*A Discourse of the Plague*, 1721, sect. iv, p. 17).

(2) *unhappy Breaches . . . in . . . Religion*: a reference to The Clarendon Code (The Corporation Act, 1661; The Conventicle Act, 1664; The Five-Mile Act, 1665) and The Test Act, 1673, all of which imposed penalties and made worship difficult for anyone not of the Anglican communion. See the note to p. 235 (2).

(3) *Dissenters . . . into the Churches*: Thomas Vincent, *God's Terrible Voice in the City* (1667), refers to the many Anglican clergymen who fled and 'left the greatest part of their flock without food or physick, in the time of their greatest need' (1722 edn., p. 37). Vincent, an ejected minister, preached in Defoe's parish church in Aldgate during the plague. Of the many tracts written about the plague of 1665, his was one of the most frequently reprinted. In an Introduction to this tract, the Reverend John Evans wrote that 'the main Body of the Clergy . . . left their pulpits vacant' and noncomformist clergymen 'preached thro' several parts of the city . . . to vast congregations' (sig. A2). Vincent's eulogy of the dissenting clergy for their courage in ministering to the spiritual needs of the people in the crisis (pp. 55 ff.) is conceivably one of Defoe's sources. Bishop Gilbert Burnet reports that many of the parish churches were shut 'when the inhabitants were in a more than ordinary disposition to profit by good sermons [and] some of the nonconformists upon that went into the empty pulpits, and preached . . . with good success' (*History of his own Time*, 1818 edn., i. 249).

(4) *running about to Fortune-tellers, Cunning-men, and Astrologers*: Dr. Nathaniel Hodges attacked the 'Traitors who frighten the credulous Populace with the Apprehensions of an approaching Plague, by idle and groundless Reports and Predictions; for the Propagation of the late Sickness was too notoriously assisted by this Means, to want any arguments to prove it' (*Loimologia*, 1720, p. 206). Cunning men were pretenders to magical or astrological knowledge.

Page 27. (1) *Fryar Bacon's Brazen-Head*: Roger Bacon's fame in magic and alchemy was legendary in the seventeenth century. The story that he had constructed a brazen head with power of speech often appeared in print, notably in Robert Greene's play, *The Honourable History of Frier Bacon and Frier Bongay* (1594). Ben Jonson refers to it in *Every Man in his Humour* (1598). Sir Thomas Browne discusses it in his *History of Vulgar Errors* (1646), and Samuel Butler mentions Friar Bacon's 'noodle' of brass in *Hudibras* (ii. i. 530–2; ed. J. Wilders, 1967, p. 115).

(2) *Mother Shipton*: a reputed prophetess, possibly a mythical person, whose prophecies were published as early as 1641, one of which presumably foretold the Great Fire of London, 1666. Some of her meteorological predictions were quoted by the astrologer, William Lilly, in his *Collection of Ancient and Modern Prophecies* (1645). In 1667 Richard Head

published what purported to be an account of her Life and Death. Some of her prophecies appeared in chapbooks.

(3) *Merlin's Head*: Merlin Ambrosius, or Myrddin Embrys, a legendary enchanter and bard, first mentioned in the *Historia Britonum* (attributed to Nennius, fl. 796). He came down to later ages mainly from the pages of Geoffrey of Monmouth's *Historia Regum Britanniae* (1137) and the Arthurian romances.

(4) *Band*: a collar or ruff.

Page 28. publick Prayers . . . fasting: In L'Estrange's *Newes*, 13 July 1665, is reported a royal proclamation 'for a *General Fast* to the end that Prayers and Supplications may everywhere be offered up unto Almighty God for the removal of the heavy Judgment of Plague and Pestilence'. The fast was to be kept in the cities of London and Westminster and places adjacent on the first Wednesday of each month until the plague ended. At the same time a form of common prayer and an 'Exhortation fit for the times' were issued, along with an injunction that collections should be made on these fast days for relief of the poor visited by the plague (*Cal. State Papers Dom. Car. II, 1664-1665*, p. 466).

Page 29. (1) *Jack-puddings, Merry-andrews . . . Rope-dancers*: the first two are synonymous terms meaning a clown, buffoon, or jester to a mountebank. Rope-dancing, an ancient 'art', is mentioned by several classical authors, including Terence, who refers to it in the Prologue to his comedy, *Hecyra* (165 B.C.). In the *Supplement* to his *Lexicon Technicum* (1744), Dr. John Harris traces the history of rope-dancing. He quotes Capitolinus as saying that the Emperor Marcus Aurelius had such regard for rope dancers that he ordered quilts to be laid under them to prevent injury. In Defoe's day funambulists (as they were sometimes called, following the Latin form of the word) often exhibited at fairs. They are satirized in *The Spectator*, nos. 28 and 141.

(2) *Second Nineveh*: Jonah iii. 5-10.

Page 30. Plague-Water: The College of Physicians had recommended a plague-water in 1665 which, according to Dr. Hodges, had been used with some success. He printed the formula for it (*Loimologia*, 1720, pp. 173-4). Lady Carteret gave Pepys a bottle of plague-water on 20 July 1665. Some of these 'infallible' remedies were advertised in L'Estrange's *Newes* and *Intelligencer*. A 'Universal Elixer' was advertised in the *Newes*, 22 July 1665 (see Walter G. Bell, *The Great Plague in London, 1665* (rev. edn., 1951), pp. 96 ff., for a number of these remedies). Royal antidotes found favour. The College of Physicians recommended '*The King's Majesty's excellent Receipt for the Plague*' and '*A Drink for the Plague prepared by the Lord Bacon and approved by Queen Elizabeth*'. See *Necessary Directions for the Prevention and Cure of the Plague . . . by the College of Physicians*, reprinted in *A Collection of Very Valuable and Scarce Pieces* (1721), p. 51.

Page 31. poisoned . . . with Mercury: In *Several Choice Histories . . . of the Plague*, 1666 (extracts from Isbrandus Diemerbroeck's *Tractatus de Peste*, in Defoe's library in the edition of 1665), 'The Eleventh Famous History' relates the 'deadly mistake' of 'a certain Chyrurgion' who died within three days after treating himself with mercury (pp. 21-2). Dr. Hodges mentions an amulet used 'by our own Country People': 'a *Walnut* filled with *Mercury*' (*Loimologia*, 1720, p. 220).

Page 32. (1) Dr. Brooks . . . Berwick: Of the four medical men mentioned by H. F., the most interesting so far as Defoe is concerned is Dr. Nathaniel Hodges (1627-88), 'the eminent physician', whose Latin treatise on the plague is referred to in the *Journal*, p. 190. Hodges was educated at Trinity College, Cambridge, and at Christ Church, Oxford. He graduated M.D. in 1659 and was elected a Fellow of the Royal College of Physicians in 1672, a year after his treatise, *Loimologia*, was published. It was translated in 1720 by Dr. John Quincy. He was one of several physicians appointed by the Corporation to minister to the poor during the Plague. Defoe's Dr. Brooks is probably Dr. Humphrey Brooke (1617-93), educated at St. John's College, Cambridge, and elected a Fellow of the Royal College of Physicians in 1674. He was the author of a medical work, *A Conservatory of Health* (1650) and *The Durable Legacy* (1681), some moral and religious directions addressed to his children. Peter Berwick, or Barwick (1619-1705), was physician-in-ordinary to Charles II. Well known for his skill in treating small-pox and fevers, he was elected a Fellow of the Royal College of Physicians in 1655. Like Dr. Hodges, he was appointed by the Corporation to care for the ill in several parishes (London, Guildhall Repertory, 70, 1664-5, ff. 150b, 151a, 152a). Nathaniel Upton, whose medical qualifications are unknown, was master of the City pest-house in 1665.

(2) *Amulets*: widely recommended and widely disapproved in the seventeenth century, they had the authority of Ambrose Paré ('a sachet of some poison over the heart') and Van Helmont, whose use of a toad for the purpose was respectfully mentioned and imitated. A striking instance is found in Dr. George Thomson, whose post-mortem examination of a victim of the plague became a classic. In his *Loitomia* (1666) he relates his personal experience with Van Helmont's amulet on discovering symptoms of the plague in himself: 'I am sufficiently persuaded, That the adjunction of this Bufo [toad] nigh my Stomach, was of wonderful force to master and tame this Venom then domineering in me' (see pp. 86-91). Dr. Richard Brookes, who thought quicksilver hung about the neck in a walnut shell efficacious, also refers to toads: 'Those that use Toads either bore a hole through their Heads, and so hang them about their *Necks*, or make Troches of them, as Helmont' (see his *History of the Most remarkable Pestilential Distempers*, 1721, p. 38). The use of amulets, also called plague cakes, was canvassed early in the century by Dr. Peter Turner (*The Opinion of P. Turner concerning Amulets or Plague Cakes*, 1603). Defoe could have found support

for H. F.'s scepticism in Richard Blackmore's *Discourse upon the Plague* (1721), p. 79, or in Dr. John Quincy's *Lexicon Physico-Medicum*, under 'Amulet': 'anything that is hung about the Neck, or any Part of the Body; supposed to be a Charm against Witchcraft, or Disease. These were often in esteem amongst some Enthusiastick Philosophers, and have been last supported by the Credulity of Mr. *Boyle*; but now have none to appear in their behalf but Empiricks and Mountebanks.' W. Kemp's *A Brief Treatise . . . of the Pestilence* (1665), no. 212 in the sale catalogue of Defoe's library, devotes several pages (61–6) to amulets.

Page 33. (1) *Abracadabra*: a cabalistic word dating from about the second century. It was written in various arrangements and used as a charm to cure agues or ward off calamity. Dr. Johnson, *Dictionary* (1755) and *O.E.D.*

(2) *I H S*: an abbreviation or partial transliteration of the Greek word for Jesus, used as a symbol or monogram of the sacred name (*O.E.D.*). It was read as *Iesus Hominum Salvator*.

(3) *this Mark thus*: this is a printer's device known as a 'flower'. It may have had some cabalistic or mysterious significance; but significantly it is a device used as an ornament in 1721 by James Graves, a bookseller, in a plague tract, *A Discourse on Pestilence and Contagion*. Graves was one of three booksellers who issued Defoe's *Journal* in 1722, and later his *Tour thro' the Whole Island of Great Britain* (1724–7).

(4) *Dead-Carts*: The bearers who collected bodies of the dead in carts or barrows, obviously not the most squeamish of men, were the objects of constant criticism in times of plague for their callousness; Dekker, Wither, and Defoe being three of the better-known writers among the critics. A more serious objection to this method of treating the dead may be seen in *An Hypothetical Notion of the Plague . . .* by Mr. Place (1721), p. 39: 'Were Men to study to help the Plague to do its business, and spread itself, they could not contrive a more effectual Way than *Death-Carts*; to carry Loads of Pestilence through the Streets from End to End of the Town. . . . Were *Plague Seed* cried in the Streets, and every Man that went by obliged to buy, it could not be much worse.' Place was an exponent of the contagionist theory.

Page 35. (1) *appointed Physicians and Surgeons for . . . poor*: The Lord Mayor, Sir John Lawrence, and the Court of Aldermen appointed Dr. Nathaniel Hodges and Dr. Thomas Witherley to serve the poor in the City and its Liberties. To these were added others, some of whom proffered their services without payment. Among these were Edward Learmen, Thomas Grey, Dr. John Glover, Dr. Humphrey Brookes (or Brooke), Dr. Parker, and Dr. Barbon. They were assigned to various wards and parishes (see London, Guildhall Repertory, 70, 1664–5, ff. 144–53).

(2) *Directions for cheap Remedies*: At the request of the Privy Council, not the Lord Mayor (as Defoe states), the College of Physicians published

Necessary Directions, as well for the Cure of the Plague, as for preventing the Infection . . . set down by the College of Physicians by the King's Majesties speciall Command (1665). This was a somewhat revised version of similar *Directions* issued in earlier plagues. Defoe found it reprinted in 1721 in *A Collection of Very Valuable and Scarce Pieces.* A copy is also listed in the sale catalogue of his library, no. 184, p. 51. It contained 'diverse remedies of small charge', but also other medicines 'for the richer sort'. The College of Physicians was founded in the reign of Henry VIII. Its charter gave the College power to license all physicians for practice in the City and in a circuit of seven miles. Originally only those with degrees from Oxford or Cambridge could qualify as· Fellows. Restrictions were eased in the seventeenth century: physicians with degrees from foreign universities became eligible and the number of Fellows was increased from thirty to eighty.

Page 36. several Physicians . . . and . . . Surgeons: the exact number of medical men who remained in London and met death during the plague is difficult to establish. See S. D. Clippingdale, 'A Medical Role of Honour', reprinted from the *British Medical Journal,* 6 Feb. 1909. The doctors mentioned by Defoe (p. 32) lived through the epidemic.

Page 37. (1) *An Act . . . Plague*: 1 Jac. I, c. 31, confirmed an order of 1583 that those stricken by the plague be confined to their houses.

(2) *Pest-House beyond Bunhill-Fields*: H. F. says that only two pest-houses were made use of (p. 181). At least five seemed to exist, two of which were hastily built during the Plague, in the parishes of St. Giles-in-the-Fields and St. Martin-in-the-Fields (see W. G. Bell, *The Great Plague in London, 1665* (rev. edn., 1951), pp. 37–9). A report to the Privy Council early in 1666 remarked on the inadequacy of the existing pest-houses, the ones in Westminster and St. Giles accommodating only sixty each, the one in Soho, only ninety (*Cal. State Papers Dom., Car. II, 1665–1666,* p. xiii).

Page 38. (1) The Orders of the Lord Mayor and Aldermen were reprinted in 1721 in *A Collection of Very Valuable and Scarce Pieces,* used by Defoe. Defoe added the names of the Lord Mayor and the two Sheriffs. Except for slight changes, the Orders issued in 1665 were a repetition of similar orders issued in 1646.

(2) *Examiners*: These officials, sometimes called surveyors in earlier plagues, were appointed by the authorities in 1603, perhaps as early as 1578, to search out and report cases of the plague and to ensure that plague orders were observed. For the reaction of Defoe's saddler on being appointed an examiner, see p. 159.

(3) *The Examiner's Office*: Walter G. Bell found no evidence of examiners appointed in 1665 to search for the plague. A few men designated by that title took over duties of parish officers, such as affording relief and assisting

in burials. He maintains that Defoe's saddler, 'nosing out Plague in 1665
. . . is a figure of fiction, invented by [Defoe] out of the "Orders Conceived
and published"' (*The Great Plague in London, 1665* (rev. edn., 1951),
pp. 105-6).

Page 39. *Searchers: In Applebee's Journal*, 18 Nov. 1721, Defoe attributed
the inaccuracy of the Bills of Mortality to both the parish clerks and the
searchers. The custom of appointing 'ancient women' to be searchers,
whose function in times of plague was to seek out the dead and report the
cause of death to the parish clerks, was strongly criticized by Captain John
Graunt and Defoe, among others. Defoe wrote: '. . . the Searchers are a
sort of old Women, Ignorant, Negligent [and] many Times the Clerks,
who are not above half a Degree better Old Women than the Searchers,
often supply the Searchers Office, and put the Dead down of what Disease
comes next in their Heads. And in short, 'tis not one Time in many that in
some Parishes any Searchers come near a dead Body' (Lee, ii. 455).

Page 40. *Botch, or Purple*: Physicians and writers on the plague attempted
to distinguish the external manifestations of the malady. The various spots,
swellings, tumours were called tokens, botches, carbuncles, buboes, blains.
William Kemp described the botch as 'a swelling about the bignesse of a
Nutmeg, Wallnut, or Hens Egge, and cometh in the Neck, or behind the
Eares, if the Brain be affected; or under the Arm-pits, from the Heart; or
in the Groin, from the Liver; for the cure whereof, pull off the feathers
from the Rump of a Cock, Hen, or Pigeon, and rub the Tayl with Salt, and
hold its Bill, and set the Tayl hard to the swelling, and it will die' (*A Brief
Treatise . . . of the Pestilence*, 1665, p. 92). Tokens of the red variety 'have
often a purple Circle around them' (*Necessary Directions . . . by the College of
Physicians*, p. 39). Spotted fever, with its purple spots, might be mistaken
for the plague, so William Boghurst warned (see *Loimographia*, [1666],
p. 49).

Page 41. (1) *Fire, and . . . Perfumes*: see the note to p. 172 (3). The College
of Physicians recommended fires and fumes: 'Fires made in the Streets, and
often with Stink-Pots, and good Fires kept in and about the Houses of such
as are visited . . . may correct the infectious Air; as also frequent discharging of Guns' (*Necessary Directions . . . by the College of Physicians*,
p. 40). Cf. W. Kemp, *A Brief Treatise . . . of the Pestilence* (1665): 'Some
[physicians] direct to make great Fires in the Streets, as *Hyppocrates* did
in the *Plague* at *Athens*, and burning among them sweet Odors, Spices and
Perfumes, Fragrant Ointments and Compositions, whereby he freed the
City from *Infection*' (p. 43). See also Dr. Philip Rose, a member of the
College of Physicians in 1721: 'you cannot imagine what a deal of Morbifick
Miasmata are destroy'd or carried away by a Fire wisely managed' (*A
Theorico-Practical, Miscellaneous, and Succinct Treatise of the Plague*,
1721, p. 35).

(2) *Shutting . . . House*: Perhaps the most extensively discussed of all preventive measures, the sequestration of the sick and anyone who had contact with them, was common practice in England from 1518. Reflecting the intensity of the controversy over its value, Defoe treats the matter at length in *Due Preparations* as well as in the *Journal*. Even those writers on the plague who defended the practice agreed that it was often evaded. Two typical tracts of 1665 opposing the measure may be cited: (1) Anon., *The Shutting up of Infected Houses as it is practised in England soberly debated*; (2) J. V., *Golgotha . . . with an Humble Witness against the Cruel . . . Practice of Shutting up unto Oppression*. Both argue that the practice is ineffective and inhuman, an argument frequently advanced in the 1720s. Richard Bradley called it 'plain Murder to shut Men up in an infected and destroying Air' (*The Plague of Marseilles Consider'd*, 1721, p. 58). In an extended examination of many aspects of the plague, the *Free-Thinker* contended that more good would accrue by permitting 'the free enjoyment of the open Air' (No. CCCXXXVI, 9 June 1721), a view also defended by Sir John Colbatch, a member of the College of Physicians (see *A Scheme for Proper Methods to be taken should it please God to visit us with the Plague*, 1721, p. 14). The plague tracts of Hodges, Pye, Place, and others contain similar arguments. Even Dr. Mead, whose tract was sanctioned by the Government, wrote that 'the shutting up Houses in this Manner is only keeping so many Seminaries of Contagion' (*Short Discourse*, 6th edn., 1720, p. 35).

Page 42. (1) *Burial . . . before Sun-rising, or after Sun-setting*: In his *Diary*, 12 Aug. 1665, Pepys writes: 'The people die so, that now it seems they are fain to carry the dead to be buried by day-light, the nights not sufficing to do it in.' In the course of that week, according to the Bills of Mortality, London suffered 4,030 deaths, of which 2,817 were of the plague.

(2) *accompany the Corps*: Plague Orders as early as 1569 gave attention to the burial of those who died of the plague. Subsequent Orders limited the number of people who might attend a funeral: for example, in 1603 only six, excluding the minister, the clerk, and the bearers, were permitted.

(3) *Graves . . . six Foot deep*: The authority of Hippocrates and Galen, as well as numberless writers throughout the ages, supported the notion that unburied carcasses corrupt the air and cause diseases. Dr. Richard Mead, writing in 1720, says: 'It has . . . been remarked in all Times, that . . . the Corruption of dead *Carcasses* lying unburied [has] occasioned *infectious Diseases*' (*Short Discourse*, 6th edn., 1720, p. 3). Frequent complaints were made against shallow graves, and especially against 'those Pits or Holes (called the Poor's Holes)' in which the poor were unceremoniously dumped. The complaint in part was against the stench of putrefying bodies, but it was also thought that the 'Pestilential Venom' would receive additional strength from the putrid exhalations (see Anon., *Some Customs consider'd whether Prejudicial to the Health of this City*, London, 1721, pp. 8–9; *The Free-Thinker*, No. CCCXXXIV, 2 June 1720).

Page 43. (1) *marked with a red Cross*: The practice of marking infected houses dates from 1518 in England, earlier on the Continent. The use of a *red* cross for the purpose seems to have developed by 1593 and the inscription, 'Lord Have Mercy upon Us', a little earlier (see F. P. Wilson, *The Plague in Shakespeare's London*, 1963, pp. 61–4).

(2) *a red Rod or Wand*: The earliest English plague orders extant (1543) require that an infected person or anyone in contact with an infected person carry a white wand in his hand. In subsequent Orders the wand continued to be required, sometimes white, sometimes red, the red eventually being ordered for physicians, nurses, and examiners.

Page 46. *Tipling in Taverns*: A Lord Mayor's proclamation, dated 4 July 1665, ordered '*That no Vintner, Innholder, Cook, Ordinary-keeper, Seller of Strong-Waters, Ale-house-keeper, shall henceforward, during the Infection receive or entertain any person or persons . . . to eat or drink in their houses or shops . . .*'

Page 56. (1) *to sweat . . . the ordinary Remedy*: '. . . medicines that cause *Sweat* expel them from the heart to the outside of the body, and rarifie those humours into light and thin vapours, which turn into a watery sweat, as soon as they come out of the skin into the air, and thereby drive out those humours and vapours, which breed the pestilence' (W. Kemp, *A Brief Treatise . . . of the Pestilence*, 1665, p. 54). Cf. Sir Richard Blackmore: '. . . those physicians that prescribe Remedies at the Beginning [of the plague] to promote copious and constant Sweats, act contrary to the Laws of Reason and Observation, and do not assist Nature, but enfeeble it' (*A Discourse upon the Plague*, 1721, pp. 92–3).

(2) *Weekly Bill . . . frighted*: The General Bill of Mortality for 1665 lists 23 deaths under 'Frighted'.

Page 58. *late Wars . . . Low Countries*: the war against Spain in 1655 and against Holland in 1652.

Page 59. (1) *long a-coming*: The Bills of Mortality report the first death from the plague in H. F.'s parish, Aldgate, the week of 27 June to 4 July. At that time 33 of 130 parishes were reported infected, and deaths from the plague totalled 470 during the week.

(2) *such Violence as in . . . Aldgate and White Chapel*: The Bills of Mortality do not fully support H. F.'s statement. Whitechapel and Aldgate were two of the worst sufferers in the severe months of August, September, and October, but Stepney surpassed them in total number of deaths from the plague. The figures for Stepney for the year are 6,583, for Aldgate, 4,051, for Whitechapel, 3,855. Defoe measures the violence of the epidemic in particular parishes by the total number of reported deaths from the plague without regard to the size of the parishes. The parishes varied greatly. A populous parish might have more deaths but still be proportionately less afflicted than a parish less well populated.

(3) *two Weeks . . . 1114 Bodies*: The Bills show 1,159 deaths from the plague in the two weekly reports from 5 to 19 September. It is not credible that all but 45 would have been relegated to the plague pits.

Page 60. (1) *the Pit . . . near the three Nuns Inn*: An excavation in 1859 near the Three Nuns Court revealed what was presumably H. F.'s 'dreadful Gulph' (see *Notes and Queries*, 2nd series, viii, 1859, 288–9).

(2) *Pit in Finsbury*: The great pit in Finsbury Fields, beyond the northern walls, served not only the parish (St. Giles Cripplegate) in which it was located; it took the overflow from other parishes as well. In August and September, when the deaths were at their highest, the Court of Aldermen received complaints from the inhabitants of 'sundry parishes' that their churchyards were 'surcharged with dead Bodies & no place remaining for burials', whereupon the Aldermen ordered that Finsbury Fields be considered (London Guildhall Repertory, 70, f. 153b). In *Due Preparations for the Plague* Defoe describes the pit in Finsbury Fields: 'they dug vast pits, and threw the bodies into them nightly by cartloads, always covering those with earth in the morning . . . and then next night throwing in more bodies and more earth, and so on till the pit was filled, so that it was reported by the parish officers, about 2,200 people were thrown into one of those pits' (ed. Aitken, 1895, xv. 59).

Page 61. *Links . . . Bell-man*: Links were torches used to light people along the streets. The ringing of a bell announced the approach of a dead-cart. A visitor to London in July wrote: 'there dye so many that the bell would hardly ever leave ringing and so they ring not at all' (quoted by W. G. Bell, *The Great Plague in London*, *1665*, rev. edn. 1951, p. 80).

Page 63. *Coffins . . . not to be had*: an exaggeration: Vincent, Pepys, and Evelyn report seeing coffins. In his *Diary* on 7 September, in the worst period of the Plague and just three days before H. F. visits the plague pit, John Evelyn wrote: 'I went all along the city and suburbs from Kent Street to St. James's, a dismal passage, and dangerous to see so many coffins exposed in the streets.' Doubtless coffins were scarce and expensive. W. G. Bell reports that Cripplegate purchased four and that these were used to take the dead to the grave and then returned to be used again (*The Great Plague in London*, *1665*, rev. edn. 1951, p. 148).

Page 66. *enthusiastick*: a pejorative word connoting the irrationality and fanaticism associated with nonconformists.

Page 73. *about 200000 People were fled*: Any estimate must be the merest surmise. Sydenham, referring to the autumn, wrote that at this time 'two thirds of the citizens had retired into the country' (*Works*, 1848, i. 98). In *Due Preparations for the Plague*, Defoe asserts that 'according to the most moderate guess' at least 300,000 had fled (ed. Aitken, 1895, xv. 73). In the same work he wrote that 7,000 houses were empty in the City (p. 24). In the *Journal* this figure became 10,000 in the City and Suburbs.

Page 74. (1) *conveyed the fatal Breath*: Defoe's contagionist view of plague is stated here in brief. Cf. W. Kemp: 'One Cause of the *Sickness*, is the Corruption and Infection of the Air; for when the *Plague* begins to raign in any Place . . . the Sick continually not only breathe out of their Mouths, but send out of their Bodies steams and vapours, which being disperst and scattered in the Air, are soon after drawn in by the breath of others; and thence whole Families are extinguisht, and the *Plague* not only creeps, but runs from one House to another: and hence it is that the *Plague* destroyes more in Cities than in Countries, and more in narrow Streets and Lanes of those Cities, than in open places, because usually there are narrow and little rooms, which are soonest fill'd with infectious vapours . . . for though the Air be never so corrupt, you must draw it in with your breath continually . . .' (*A Brief Treatise . . . of the Pestilence*, 1665, p. 35). See the Introduction, p. xxviii.

(2) *Steams, or Fumes . . . Effluvia*: Sir Richard Blackmore describes the spread of 'Pestilential Putrefaction' thus: 'When the Effluvia or invisible malignant Reeks flow from an infected Body greatly corrupted, the poisonous Particles . . . are endow'd with such Velocity, Activity, and Penetration, that they flie with Ease thro' the Air, maintain their fatal Influence in despight of all Opposition, and convey the Infection from House to House, and from Town to Town, and depopulate great Cities. This high Venom advances with resistless Fury . . . and is so far from being enfeebled while it is ventilated by the Winds . . . that it acquires more Strength by converting into its own Nature the Exhalations and Vapours it meets with in its Way . . .' (*A Discourse upon the Plague*, 1721, pp. 37-8).

Page 75. (1) *immediate Stroke from Heaven*: The wrath of God theory was a venerable one. See Ovid, *Metamorphoses*, vii. 532 ff.; references in Numbers 16, Deuteronomy 28, 2 Samuel 24, 1 Kings 8, and Psalms 89, 91 and 106; Procopius of Caesaria, *History of the Wars*, ii, chapters xxii–xxiii; Boccaccio, introduction to *Decameron*. The theory was still popular in Defoe's day; see Nathaniel Hodges, *Vindiciae Medicinae & Medicorum* (1666), p. 34, and *Loimologia*, pp. 30–1; Sir Richard Blackmore, *A Discourse upon the Plague* (1721), pp. 28–9; William Hendley, *Loimologia Sacra* (1721), pp. 6, 41. The view that divine anger works through natural means is set out in Isbrand de Diemerbroek's *Tractatus de Peste*, translated in 1722 by Thomas Stanton as *A Treatise concerning the Pestilence*. Defoe seems to have possessed a copy.

(2) *infection . . . by . . . Insects, and invisible Creatures*: H. F. here reflects and rejects the theory of infection set forth by Athanasius Kircher and his disciples on the Continent. Kircher's famous work, *Scrutinium Physico-medicum . . . Pestis* (1658), was often referred to in English plague tracts. His theory, based upon concepts of fermentation, generation, and putre-faction, held that organisms of minute size acted as the vehicle of con-tagion. The chief proponent of this theory of 'vermicular' infection in England was Richard Bradley, whose *The Plague at Marseilles Considered*

(1721) was well known when Defoe was working on the *Journal*. Bradley wrote that 'all Pestilential Distempers, whether in Animals or Plants, are occasion'd by poisonous Insects convey'd from Place to Place by the Air, and that by uncleanly Living and poor Diet, Human, and other Bodies are disposed to receive such *Insects* into the Stomach and most noble Parts . . .' (p. 57). The rejection of this view, by Dr. Mead and Dr. Hodges, Defoe probably knew. Hodges refers to the famous Kircher's opinion 'about animated Worms', a view he believed to be 'disconsonant to Reason' (*Loimologia*, 1720, p. 64); and Mead calls it 'a supposition grounded upon no manner of Observation' (*Short Discourse*, 6th edn., 1720, p. 16). Richard Blackmore, who considered the views of Kircher and Bradley in his *Discourse upon the Plague* (1721), maintained that 'Worms are by no means the Cause, but the Effect of Pestilential Putrefaction' (p. 36). See also for a vigorous attack on the theory of 'vermicular infection', Philip Rose, *A Theorico-Practical, Miscellaneous and Succinct Treatise of the Plague* (1721), pp. 43 ff. Rose was a member of the College of Physicians.

(3) *Supine Negligence*: The failure of people to prepare for the plague even though long warned of its approach is extensively treated in Defoe's *Due Preparations*.

Page 77. (1) *Meditations upon Divine Subjects*: Defoe himself composed some meditations upon divine subjects in his youth. See *The Meditations of Daniel Defoe*, ed. George Harris Healey (1946).

(2) *a Physician . . . Heath*: Brayley and others identify him as Dr. Nathaniel Hodges. See p. 32, note 1.

(3) *Plague . . . violent . . . where I liv'd*: The Bills of Mortality reported 81 deaths from the Plague in H.F.'s parish of Aldgate in the first week of August, 173 in the following week.

(4) *Rozen and Pitch, Brimstone*: The fumes of those were among the various recommendations of the College of Physicians. Resin and pitch were 'to be put upon Coals, and consumed with the least Flame that may be', and brimstone, 'though ill to be endured for the present', should be 'burned plentifully'—all for the purpose of correcting the air (*Necessary Directions . . . by the College of Physicians*, 1721, p. 40).

Page 78. (1) *Butchers of White-Chapel*: Defoe came naturally to an interest in butchers: his father was a member of the Butchers' Company and Defoe himself, by virtue of this fact, was admitted freedom of the Company on 12 January 1688. Pepys wrote to Lady Carteret, 4 Sept. 1665: 'The butchers are everywhere visited'. Butcher's Row and the Minories, the location of many butchers, were within a stone's throw of Defoe's parish church, St. Botolph, Aldgate.

(2) *Vinegar*: 'Vinegar is a noble thing in tyme of pestilence' (Thomas Phaer, *A Treatise of the Plague, written about two hundred years ago. Republished with a Preface by a Physician of London*, 1722, p. 6). It was widely recommended as a prophylactic and a fumigant as early as the

fifteenth century. In 1665 the College of Physicians commended it: 'Vapours from Vinegar exhaled in any Room, may [correct the infectious air], especially after it hath been impregnated, by infusing or steeping it in any one or more of these Ingredients; Wormwood, Angelica, Masterwort, Bay-Leaves, Rosemary, Rue, Sage, *Scordium*, or Water-Germander, *Valerium*, or Setwall-Root, Zedoary, Camphire' (*Necessary Directions . . . by the College of Physicians*, 1721, p. 40). But see Richard Boulton, Fellow of Brasenose and author of several medical works: Vinegar 'can only be serviceable, as it cools the Blood and may prevent a Ferment and Agitation by Heat; but if notwithstanding this Distemper should appear, it would but increase the Evil, by rendering the Blood more liable to Stagnation and Coagulation; yet it may be a good service to sprinkle the Rooms with it' (*An Essay on the Plague*, 1721, p. 41). Defoe's tradesman in *Due Preparations* (p. 61) purifies his letters by smoking them with brimstone and gunpowder, then sprinkling them with vinegar. Coins, too, were purified by immersion in vinegar. W. Kemp sings the praises of anti-pestilential vinegar and asserts that he wrote his *Brief Treatise . . . of the Plague* (1665), to demonstrate 'the Vertue of Vinegar' (p. 86).

Page 79. dropt . . . Dead . . . knew nothing of it: William Boghurst took exception to reports of sudden deaths: '. . . none dyed suddenly as stricken with Lightning or an Apoplexy, as Authors write in severall countryes, and Dimerbrooke seems to believe it . . .' (*Loimographia*, [1666], p. 26). Diemerbroeck, in 'The Fifth Famous History', reports the instances of a man 'taken with Feavor' but who had 'no outward Figure of the Plague, so that those of his house did not think he died of the Plague, but within twelve hours after he was put in the Coffin, they saw many black spots . . . in him, certain figures of the Plague'. Diemerbroeck adds: 'Sometimes the poison is so deadly, that they die before Nature can send forth any thing . . . neither Carbuncles nor Blaines, but after they are dead there appeareth black spots' (*Several Choice Histories . . . of the Plague*, 1666, p. 9). This appears to be an instance of septicaemic plague in which the blood-stream is heavily infected.

Page 81. People . . . raving and distracted: cf. Thomas Vincent, *God's Terrible Voice in the City* (1667): '. . . some in their frenzy, rising out of their beds, and leaping about their rooms; others crying and roaring at their windows; some coming forth almost naked, and running into the streets; strange things have others spoken . . . one . . . burnt himself in his bed' (1722 edn., p. 44).

Page 82. (1) *tortured . . . Creatures*: cf. Boghurst: 'Many people by Launcing, Corrosives, actuall Cauteries, Scarifications, and many intollerable applications, put their patients to more paine than the disease did' (*Loimographia*, [1666], p. 29).

(2) *Swellings . . . break and run*: see the note to p. 201.

Page 83. *frightful Stories . . . of Nurses*: From Dekker early in the seventeenth century to Dr. Hodges in 1665 and Dr. Mead in 1720, the brutality and wickedness of the nurse-keepers is a constant theme in plague tracts. Dekker's description of them as 'shee wolves' is echoed by Dr. Hodges: 'These Wretches, out of Greediness to plunder the Dead, would strangle their Patients . . . others would secretly convey the pestilential Taint from Sores of the infected to those who were well; and nothing indeed deterred these abandoned Miscreants from prosecuting their avaritious Purposes by all the Methods their Wickedness could invent . . .' (*Loimologia*, 1720, p. 8).

Page 89. (1) *John Hayward*: mentioned as sexton in 1673 in the Vestry Minutes of St. Stephen Coleman Street (f. 352). His death is recorded in the Register General of the same church on 5 October 1684 (f. 188). Note that H. F.'s brother lived in Coleman Street parish.

(2) *Alleys, and Thorough-fares*: In *London Survey'd* (1677), John Ogilby and William Morgan list Coleman Street as having eight courts and six alleys.

(3) *Garlick and Rue*: in addition to these, other herbs, spices, roots, barks, flowers, and seeds were recommended: aloes, amber, ambergris, angelica, balm, bay leaves, benjamin, campana roots, camphor, cinnamon, citrine sanders, cloves, emula, frankincense, gentian, hyssop, juniper, lavender, mace, marjoram, mint, musk, myrrh, nutmeg, origanum, pennyroyal, rosemary, saffron, sage, sassafras, storax, tansy, thyme, wormwood. All of these may be found scattered through plague tracts as well as in the London Pharmacopoeia. The use of aromatics was supported by the tradition that Hippocrates had conquered the plague of Athens by burning aromatic spices in the streets. An occasional note of scepticism was voiced: J. V., in *Golgotha* (1665), wrote that 'sweet-scented Pomanders were exploded . . . long since, as a costly mischief'. He attacks the excessive claims of the 'Pomandermen'; nevertheless he commends the fumes from 'Rhue, Wormwood, Hartshorn, Amber, Thime or Origany, Rosemary' and a few others. Of all fumes he affirms '*Tobacco* to be the best' (p. 24).

(4) *smoaking Tobacco*: widely recommended as a preventative and fumigant. Kemp's *A Brief Treatise . . . of the Pestilence* (1665) describes it as 'a good Fume against pestilential and infected air'. He commends it for 'All Ages, all Sexes, all Constitutions, Young and Old, Men and Women, the Sanguine, the Cholerick, the Melancholy, the Phlegmatick . . . either by chewing in the leaf, or smoaking in the Pipe' (pp. 46-7). It was believed that no tobacconist had died in the plague of 1665. Richard Bradley wrote: '. . . it is to be remarked, that in the time of the last Plague in *London* . . . that Distemper did not reach those who smoak'd Tobacco every Day' (*The Plague at Marseilles considered*, 1721, pp. 48-9). Among the physicians who maintained that tobacco had kept them immune were Hodges and

Diemerbroeck. Pepys records (*Diary*, 7 June) with apprehension his first sight of an infected house, in Drury Lane: 'It put me into an ill conception of myself and my smell, so that I was forced to buy some roll-tobacco to smell and to chaw, which took away my apprehension.'

(5) *Plague . . . chiefly among the Poor*: '. . . it is incredible to think how the Plague raged amongst the common People, insomuch that it came by some to be called the *Poors Plague*' (Hodges, *Loimologia*, 1720, p. 15). The relationship between poverty (with its undernourishment and lack of sanitation) and disease was recognized: '. . . the contagious Maladies most commonly . . . rage amongst a crouded and penn'd up Herd of Creatures, who by Poverty do wallow in their Dirt and Nastiness; and this being accompany'd with bad Air and Nourishment, if it has not . . . the full Effect to occasion and to breed a contagious Malady of it self, yet . . . such poor miserable People will be much more liable, and their Bodies more dispos'd to receive, harbour, and nourish the malign Atoms of a contagious Malady . . .' (P. Kennedy, M.D., *A Discourse on Pestilence*, 1721, p. 19).

Page 90. *Story of the Piper*: the story of a drunken man interred prematurely was in circulation in one form or another as early as 1603 (in Dekker's *The Wonderfull Yeare*); and versions of it in the seventeenth century are found in the anonymous *The Meeting of Gallants at an Ordinarie*, 1604 (possibly by Dekker or Thomas Middleton), in Sir John Reresby's *Memoirs, 1634–1689*; and in William Austin's *The Anatomy of Pestilence, 1666*). See Wilhelm von Füger, 'Der betrunkene Piper', *Archiv f. n. Sprachen*, ccii. (1965), 28–36.

Page 92. (1) *London . . . exceeding rich*: 'Contrary to all outside appearances, the City was on the verge of bankruptcy. Its liabilities were far in excess of its immediate assets, and its expenditure was constantly in excess of its income' (T. F. Reddaway, *The Rebuilding of London after the Great Fire*, reprinted 1951, p. 171. See chapter vii of this study for the tangled financial affairs of the City and for the cost of rebuilding some of the places mentioned by Defoe). The rebuilding of public edifices to which Defoe refers was spread over eight years.

(2) *breaking in upon the Orphan's Money*: accumulated funds for the care of orphans of London citizens were controlled by the Mayor and the Corporation. These funds, loaned to Charles II, were thought to be endangered, and moves were made in Parliament and elsewhere in the 1670s and later to protect the Orphan's money.

Page 93. *Welfare of those . . . left behind*: Defoe's optimistic account of large sums spent during the Plague in relief of the poor may be unjustified. The picture is confused by the fact that charity was dispensed by various agencies: the livery companies, parishes, the city, private persons. Parliament itself took no action, and the tradition that Charles II 'ordered a thousand Pounds a Week to be distributed' seems to be unsubstantiated. Note that H. F. himself says that he can speak of it only 'as a Report'. Funds coming in from the poor rate and the pest rate, from fast-day collections, from private persons, and from the livery companies (required by a Lord Mayor's Proclamation, 28 July, to devote a third of the money saved from their prohibited dinners and entertainments) cannot be accurately estimated. See W. G. Bell, *The Great Plague in London, 1665* (rev. edn., 1951), pp. 130, 195–9, who discounts Defoe's figures. He does, however, quote from a letter written by Sir Edmund Berry Godfrey who, after indicting some of the courtiers, nobility, and gentry for forgetting 'their charity', says, 'I believe they [i.e., the poor] were never so well relieved in any Plague time whatsoever' (p. 197).

Page 96. legal Settlements: i.e. having a legal residence in a particular parish by virtue of residing in the parish for a certain length of time or paying taxes or serving in an annual office. A legal settlement entitled one to claim against the poor rates. See the note to p. 124 (2).

Page 98. thirty or forty Thousand: If Defoe's estimate of the number of poor who died from the plague in the nine weeks, 8 August to 10 October, is correct, we can understand why the epidemic was called 'the poor's plague'. He has accurately given the figures of total deaths and deaths from the plague as they were reported in the Bills of Mortality, but his estimate that roughly sixty to eighty per cent of the deaths were of the poor can only be a guess, if not his own then from an unidentified source. Such figures were not available.

Page 101. (1) Grass growing: Pepys commented on the desolation in London streets in September: 'But, Lord! what a sad time it is to see no boats upon the River; and grass grows all up and down White Hall court, and nobody but poor wretches in the streets!' (*Diary*, 20 Sept. 1665). Cf. Thomas Vincent: 'Now there is a dismal solitude in *London* streets. . . . Now shops are shut in, people rare, and very few that walk about, insomuch that the grass begins to spring up in some places . . . no rattling coaches, no prancing Horses' (*God's Terrible Voice in the City*, 1722 edn., p. 42). Cf. Defoe, *The Review*, no. 8, 26 Aug. 1712: '. . . Grass grew in the Streets, in the Markets, and on the Exchange; and nothing but death was to be seen in every place.'

(2) *Coaches . . . dangerous things*: H. F.'s remark that coaches were scarce and dangerous is supported by entries in Pepys's *Diary*, 25 July 1665: 'Thence to my office awhile, full of business, and thence by coach to the Duke of Albermarle's, not meeting one coach going nor coming from my house thither and back again, which is very strange.' On 27 November Pepys took a hackney coach: 'the first I have durst to go in many a day, and with great pain now for fear.'

Page 102. *Aldgate . . . about the Butcher-Row*: Petticoat Lane, in this parish, was once known as Hog-Lane. N. Bailey, in *The Antiquities of London* (1726), p. 108, says that the south side of the highway from Aldgate 'is the greatest shambles in Europe'.

Page 103. *Soloman Eagle an Enthusiast*: see the note to p. 21 (4). 'Enthusiast' in the sense of a fanatical dissenter. The fumes of the burning charcoal were intended to purify the pestilential air.

Page 104. (1) *People . . . Danger . . . Worship*: The Bishop of London to Lord Arlington, 19 August 1665: 'Many of those who never attended divine service are now present' (*Cal. State Papers Dom.*, *Car. II*, *1664-1665*, p. 524).

(2) *Dissenters . . . in the very Churches*: the government grew alarmed over the appearance of the ejected clergy in the parish churches. In July, Lord Arlington, Secretary of State, wrote to the Bishop of London: 'The King is informed that many ministers and lecturers having been absent from their posts during this time of contagion, nonconformists have thrust themselves into their pulpits, to preach sedition, and doctrines contrary to the Church; His Majesty wishes to prevent such mischiefs to Church and State' (*Cal. State Papers Dom.*, *Car. II*, *1664-1665*, p. 497). On 19 August the Bishop of London replied that 'the sober clergy remain' and that he 'cannot learn that any nonconformists have invaded the pulpit' (ibid., p. 524).

Page 111. *ten thousand . . . sheltered here*: very unlikely. As W. G. Bell says, Pepys does not mention this massing of ships in the Thames; and I have not found this impressive scene mentioned elsewhere.

Page 118. *Wo . . . Child*: Matt. xxiv. 19. Cf. William Boghurst, *Loimographia*, [1666], p. 25: 'Teeming women fared miserably in the disease . . . scarce one in forty lived, for the disease and sweating forced them to miscarry, and the miscarriage drew in the disease again. . . . Hippocrates saith to this purpose that women with child fare ill in occult and epidemicall diseases.' Richard Kephale, in *Medela Pestilentiae* (1665), maintained that women are more susceptible to the plague than men and that pregnant women are the most susceptible, 'for their bodies are full of excrementious humours, and much heat withal, which is as oyle and flame put together' (pp. 55-6). But virgins fare little better according to Kephale: 'Virgins, that are ripe for marriage, are apt to receive infection; and being stricken, seldom or never escape without great means. . . . Their blood being hot, and their seed retain'd for want of copulation, the one will soon be inflam'd, the other corrupted; from thence infection.' Those least likely to be infected are old folks, 'confident spirits', milch-nurses, those who have the gout, or issues or ulcers or haemorrhoids, or women who 'have their courses abundantly' (pp. 56 ff.).

Page 121. *kill all the Dogs and Cats*: the Plague Orders regularly called for the destruction of domestic animals. In 1543 all dogs, except hounds, spaniels, or mastiffs, were ordered killed or removed from London. The task of killing stray animals was entrusted to a parish official or to one appointed for the purpose. Defoe's figures, forty thousand dogs and five times as many cats, are suspect.

Page 124. (1) *Lepers of Samaria*: 2 Kgs. vii. 3–4; Luke xvii. 12.

(2) *last legal Settlement*: The brief 'legal' quibble in this passage refers to the laws of vagrancy. Elizabethan legislation concerning the poor was amplified by Acts in 1662 and 1667 (14 Car. II, cap. xii; 18–19 Car. II, cap. ix). The remark by Thomas concerns the power of a justice to remove from a parish any newcomer who might become an object of parochial charity. A vagrant's last legal settlement, that is, his established residence, was that parish where he was last domiciled as servant, apprentice, house-holder, or sojourner for a period of forty days. In the early months of 1707 Defoe, writing in the *Review*, was critical of a Bill pending in Parliament designed to modify the Act of Settlement.

Page 125. *Beginning of July*: Defoe's account of the slow spread of the plague follows contemporary accounts. Cf. Boghurst: '. . . it gradually insinuated, and crept down Holborne and the Strand [from the western parishes], and then into the City, and at last to the East end of the Suburbs; soe that it was half a yeare at the West end of the City before the East end and Stepney was infected, which was about the middle of July' (*Loimographia*, [1666], p. 28). H. F.'s statement that no one had died of the plague in Stepney parish is not borne out by the Bills of Mortality. They record three deaths by 4 July.

Page 129. *died . . . 5361 people*: This is the total number of deaths in the five parishes mentioned from all causes during the first three weeks in August. The number dying of the plague alone was 3,570.

Page 133. *the Boarded-River*: The 'river' made by Sir Hugh Middleton, 1608–13, to supply London with water. It was so called because of the wooden arches built to support the troughs carrying the water.

Page 136. *King's Highway*: an ancient and intricate legal concept dating perhaps from the eighth or ninth century, at which time it applied to the four great through roads. It later came to apply to all highways. The concept is related to the concept of the King's Peace and implied the King's protection for his subjects travelling on the King's Highway. 'To the citizen of the twelfth, the fifteenth, or even the eighteenth century, the King's Highway was a more abstract conception. It was not a strip of land, or any corporeal thing, but a legal and customary right—as the lawyers said, "a perpetual *right of passage* in the sovereign, for himself and his subjects, over another's land" . . . What existed, in fact, was not a road, but what we might almost term an easement—a right of way, enjoyed by the public at large from village to village, along a certain customary course, which, if much frequented, became a beaten track.' See Sidney and Beatrice Webb, *English Local Government : The Story of the King's Highway* (1913), pp. 5, 10, n. 2.

Page 145. *Higlers*: i.e. higglers: hucksters.

Page 146. *parched Corn*: Josh. v. 11.

Page 151. *Tilts and Bales*: awnings and bales of merchandise.

Page 169. *Violence . . . Town*: In H. F.'s parish of St. Botolph, Aldgate, 65 died of the plague in the last week of July. The figures for the four weeks in August are 81, 173, 212, 46. Deaths from all causes, which rarely rose above 20 before August, are reported in the Bills as 103, 207, 238, 374. These figures support H. F.'s contention that the Bills did not accurately reflect the number of deaths from the plague.

Page 172. (1) *Exchange . . . not kept shut*: On 18 July Pepys went 'to the 'Change, where a little business and a very thin Exchange'. At the end of July the Exchange was closed for a period of approximately two months.

(2) *Fires . . . lost*: The Lord Mayor's Proclamation of 2 September 1665 ordered fires to be kept burning continuously for three days and nights, beginning 5 September, in all streets, courts, lanes, and alleys of the City and Suburbs. Pepys, going by river to see the Duke of Albemarle, reports 'all the way fires on each side of the Thames' (*Diary*, 6 Sept.). On the 9th he records 'a most cursed rainy afternoon'; this is the rain which extinguished the plague-fires and, as Pepys says, 'almost spoiled my silke breeches'.

(3) *not only no Benefit, but injurious*: Defoe reflects the controversy over the value of fires. In the epidemics of 1563, 1603, and 1625 fires were lit in the streets of London, and the authorities followed suit in 1665. Hodges argued against the practice in 1665, as did Mead and Blackmore in 1721; but the Hippocratic tradition was strong and the legend that Hippocrates had freed Athens of the plague by fires appealed to many. See Philip Rose, *A Therico-Practical, Miscellaneous, and Succinct Treatise of the Plague*, 1721: 'We have an Account of him, that he did free *Greece* from the Plague; for which Service the *Athenians* decreed and paid him the same *Honours* as to *Hercules*. We are informed, that he did set several Forests on fire, to purify the Air; which in my Judgment, was [a] ready way to destroy and carry off the Pestilential Effluviums in a great Measure' (pp. 26-7). Rose was a member of the College of Physicians. To Hodges, fires were 'showy and expensive . . . and of no effect' (*Loimologia*, 1720, p. 19).

(4) *Fires . . . Wood . . . Coal*: Boghurst writes that 'Wood fires are accounted best', and he names twenty-eight kinds of wood suitable. He adds: 'Yet I know noe reason why Sea coale fires also should be discontinued' (*Loimographia*, [1666], pp. 61-2).

Page 173. *Dog-days . . . Dog-Star*: a period of about five weeks commonly said to begin on 3 July with the heliacal rising of Sirius in the Constellation of the Greater Dog, long noted for being a hot and unwholesome period and a time in which malignant influences prevailed.

Page 175. *The Act of Uniformity*: received royal assent 19 May 1662. Its provisions and required oaths led to the ejection of many, perhaps a fifth, of the Anglican beneficed clergy, one of whom was Dr. Samuel Annesley, family pastor of the Foe's, then living in St. Giles, Cripplegate. The family and Defoe (aged 2) followed Annesley out of the Established Church into nonconformity. For a brief general statement of Defoe's attitude toward this Act, the Test Act, and the practice known as occasional conformity, see *The Review*, 22 Nov. 1705.

Page 179. *almost 40,000*: Defoe here uses the number of deaths from all causes as reported in the Bills of Mortality. The number of deaths attributed to the plague for the five weeks was 32,332.

Page 180. *no Funeral . . . in the Day-time*: Pepys reports: 'Thence by water to the Duke of Albemarle's . . . and strange to see in broad daylight two or three burials upon the Bankeside, one at the very heels of another: doubtless all of the plague; and yet at least forty or fifty people going along with every one of them' (*Diary*, 6 Sept. 1665).

Page 181. (1) *Price of Bread . . . not much raised*: The assize of bread by order of the Lord Mayor and the Court of Aldermen was reported weekly in the Bills of Mortality. H. F.'s facts are accurate. To conserve fuel during the Plague and to adjust to the demands of a decreased population, the Bakers' Company ruled in 1665 that 'wives' bread, that is, bread baked from the customer's own dough, would be limited to three days. See Sylvia Thrupp, *A Short History of the Worshipful Company of Bakers of London* (1933), p. 114.

(2) *two Pest-houses*: see p. 37, note 2. The Westminster pest-house was in Tothill Fields.

Page 185. *Bakers Company*: see p. 181, note 1. The government and discipline of the Worshipful Company of Bakers of London were in the hands of the Master and Wardens and the Court of Assistants, the Court consisting of ex-wardens and others chosen from the livery. See Sylvia Thrupp, *A Short History of the Worshipful Company of Bakers of London* (1933), p. 85.

Page 190. (1) *publish'd in Latin*: a reference to Dr. Nathaniel Hodges, a Fellow of the Royal College of Physicians, whose *Loimologia* (1672) was translated by John Quincy and published in 1720. For Hodges, see p. 32, note 1.

(2) *four Thousand in one Night*: the figure is from Dr. Hodges, *Loimologia* (1720), pp. 24-5, where he laments the ill-advised action of the

authorities in ordering fires in the streets for three days. Hodges suggests that the damp weather and the 'suffocative effluvia of the coals' had dire consequences the night of 9 September. H. F.'s scepticism is justified. With 6,988 deaths reported for the entire week it is not likely that 4,000 died in a single night.

Page 192. Air ... corrupted and infected: Here and in the following pages Defoe views the plague from the vantage of a contagionist rather than a miasmatist. The miasmatic conception, to which H. F. takes exception, was well stated by William Boghurst in *Loimographia*, [1666], p. 19: 'The Plague is the perfection of putrefaction, or if you like it better in more words, thus: The Plague or Pestilence is a most subtle, peculiar, insinuating, venomous, deleterious Exhalation of the Foeces of the Earth extracted into the Aire by the heat of the sun, and difflated from place to place by the winds, and most tymes gradually but sometymes immediately agressing apt bodyes.

Page 193. Turkish Predestinarianism: the fatalism displayed by Mohamme-dans because of their belief that Allah had decreed death for each individual at a specific moment, and that this would arrive regardless of all other circumstances. Flight from plague raises questions of Christian and professional morality in Theodore de Beze, *A Shorte, Learned and Pithie Treatise of the Plague* (1580, reprinted 1665); Richard Kephale, *Medela Pestilentiae* (1665); William Hendley, *Loimologia Sacra* (1721); and William Boghurst, *Loimographia* (1666).

Page 194. natural Causes: In his 'Observations on the Bills of Mortality', appended to *London's Remembrancer*, 1665 (a work Defoe may have used), John Bell quotes 'our famous *English* Oratour, Bishop Andrews': 'The *Plague* (saith he) is caused by Gods wrath against Sin. ... So that if there be a Plague, God is angry; and if there be a great Plague, God is very angry, &c. Ask the Physician the cause of it, and he will tell you the cause is in the air; the air is infected, the humours corrupted, the Contagion of the sick, coming to and conversing with the sound, and they be all true causes. But as we acknowledge these to be true, That in all Diseases, and even in this also there is a natural cause, so we say there is somewhat more, some-what Divine and above Nature; as somewhat for the Physician, so some work for the Priest, and more too (it may be) for whosoever doth not acknow-ledge the finger of God in this sickness, over and above all causes Natural, looketh not deeply enough into the cause thereof' (sig. D²). See note 1, p. 75.

Page 201. Swellings broke: Contemporary medicine stressed the necessity of drawing out the pestilential venom concentrated in the swellings symptomatic of bubonic plague. It was contended that this would relieve the pain and perhaps save the patient. Plague tracts, medical and lay, abounded in prescriptions for achieving this by remedies to be taken internally or applied externally. In its official recommendations the Royal College of Physicians declared that 'the Swelling under the Ears, Armpits, or in the Groins . . . must be always drawn forth and ripened, and broke with all speed'. An expert chirurgeon was recommended, but for those not using a physician more than a dozen prescriptions were set down, including some remedies for 'those that are delighted with Chymical Medicines only' (*Necessary Directions . . . by the College of Physicians*, pp. 54 ff.).

Page 202. *Breath . . . infectious*: H. F. reflects the confusion and uncertainty in plague literature over whether the breath of an infected person can transmit the disease. The belief of Dr. Hodges that this might be possible was rejected by Dr. George Pye, in *A Discourse of the Plague* (1721), who asserted that the plague was not contagious in the sense that it can be communicated from one person to another: 'it is not caused, nor propagated in that manner' (p. 3). Cf. Thomas Phaer: 'for the venimous aire it self, is not half so vehement to infect, as is the conversation or breth of them that are already infected . . .' (*A Treatise of the Plague . . .* 1722, p. 12). The bubonic plague in its pneumonic stage is infectious.

Page 203. *no Microscopes*: simple microscopes existed as early as the 1590s.

Page 204. *cold Winter . . . long Frost*: cf. Thomas Sydenham: 'After an extremely cold winter, and after a dry frost that lasted without intermission until spring . . . peripneumonies, pleurisies, quinsies, and all such inflammatory diseases, suddenly caused a great mortality' (*Works*, 1848, i. 97).

Page 211. *lend to the Lord*: Prov. xix. 17.

Page 212. *Cripplegate . . . 17800 Pounds*: an unlikely sum. See note to p. 93.

Page 213. (1) *twenty thousand a Day . . . Naples*: Defoe's source was probably *An Account of the Plague at Naples, in 1656, of which there died in one Day 20,000 Persons*, reprinted in *A Collection of Very Valuable and Scarce Pieces* (1721). In *Due Preparations for the Plague* Defoe repeats this figure with a denial.

(2) *woolen Manufactures . . . retentive*: It was widely believed that certain goods had an affinity with the 'venomous particles' which caused the plague. '. . . even Packs and Bails of Goods carry the poisonous *Miasmata* about with them . . . nothing is more likely to preserve it than animal Substances, as Hair, Wool, Leather, Skins, &c. because the very Manner of its Production, and Nature of its Origin, seems to give it a greater Affinity with such Substances than any other, and to dispose it to rest therein until

by Warmth, Ventilation, or any other Means of Dislodgement, it is put into Motion, and raised again into the ambient Air' (John Quincy, *An Essay on . . . Pestilential Diseases*, 3rd edn., 1720, pp. 52–3). Dr. Mead's list contained, in addition, cotton, hemp, flax, paper or books, silk of all kinds, linen, feathers. He recommended that all such goods should be kept in quarantine and exposed to fresh air for forty days (*Short Discourse*, 6th edn., 1720, pp. 24–5). In *Applebee's Journal*, 29 July 1721, Defoe refers to 'the poor unhappy city of Toulon, who had the Distemper brought among them in a Bale of Silk from Marseilles'. For a denial of this view, see J. Pringle, M.D., *Rational Enquiry into the Nature of the Plague* (1722), pp. 7 ff., and see also the sceptical comments of Joseph Browne, M.D., in *A Practical Treatise of the Plague* (1720), pp. 24–5.

(3) *Islands of the Arches*: the Grecian Archipelago.

Page 214. *Scanderoon*: i.e. Iskanderun, or Alexandretto, a seaport of Asiatic Turkey.

Page 215. *1st of July . . . died . . . seven*: A rare instance in which Defoe's figures differ from the Bills of Mortality. The Bills show 100 deaths from plague to 27 June in the City and Liberties of Westminster and five deaths in the three parishes mentioned.

Page 216. (1) *Manufactures . . . infected*: Since certain goods were thought to retain the 'poisonous effluvia', importations were considered dangerous and the effectiveness of a quarantine was a serious matter. Therefore Defoe supported the rigorous Quarantine Act of 1722. A bill for prohibiting commerce with infected countries received royal assent on 12 February 1722 (8 Geo. I, c. 10). Defoe wrote: 'The Damage of obliging Ships to Quarantine, is . . . very considerable to the Merchants; it spoils their Goods, and many sorts of Goods are perishable, and subject to decay in others. The Profit of the whole Voyage depends upon the Season of coming into Market. . . . [Delay] stagnates Trade . . . encreases the Risk, and every way harasses the Merchant in his Business. Yet all this we cheerfully submit to for the Reason of it; 'tis allow'd to be just, to be necessary. . . . But if one Villain can pass the Barriers set,—if one Man can escape out of these Ships, with a Parcel of any sort of Goods, dangerous to Health, he may lodge the Plague among us . . . and we are all undone' (*Applebee's Journal*, 29 July 1721; Lee, ii. 409–10).

(2) *clandestine Trade*: In his *Short Discourse* Mead warned 'But above all it is necessary, that the Clandestine Importing of Goods be punished with the utmost Rigour' (6th edn., 1720, p. 30). In *Due Preparations for the Plague*, Defoe wrote: 'We have a set of men among us so bent upon their gain, by that we call clandestine trade, that they would even venture to import the plague itself . . . not valuing the horrid injustice that they do to other people' (Aitken edn., p. 11). He approved the bill sponsored by the government 'to prevent the clandestine Running of Goods', (8 Geo. I,

c. 18), which received royal assent 7 March 1722, despite opposition from City Merchants.

Page 217. Trade ... at a full stop: The impact of a quarantine on trade was much discussed in 1721. Dr. George Pye argued, in opposition to Dr. Mead, that 'the Plague may possibly destroy a hundred thousand lives, but the Loss of Trade may starve and destroy ten times a hundred thousand' (*A Discourse of the Plague, wherein Dr. Mead's Notions are Consider'd and Refuted*, 1721, p. 51).

Page 218. coasting Trade for Corn ... Coals: In *A Tour thro' the Whole Island of Great Britain* (1724) Defoe describes the two corn markets in London, Bear Key and Queen Hith, as 'Monsters for Magnitude, and not to be matched in the World'. To Bear Key 'comes all the vast Quantity of Corn that is brought into the City by Sea'. The other market was chiefly for malt. The coal market at Billingsgate was supplied mainly from New-castle and the northern regions. 'The Quantity of Coals, which it is sup-posed are, *Communibus Annis*, burnt and consumed in and about this City, is supposed to be about Five hundred thousand Chalder, every Chalder containing Thirty-six Bushels' (*Tour*, ed. G. D. H. Cole, 1927, i. 347-8).

Page 219. heat ... opens the Pores: cf. W. Kemp, *A Brief Treatise ... of the Pestilence* (1665): 'To guard your self from the corrupted air, you may do well ... to be within doors at noon and the heat of the day, when the pores being more open are apter to receive *Infection*' (p. 47).

Page 220. War with the Dutch: England declared war on the Dutch on 22 February 1665. The 'Capers' were privateers.

Page 221. (1) Price of Coals ... dear: An attempt to control the price of coal during the Plague is evident in an act of the Common Council, 1 June 1665. 'For the benefit and relief of the Poor' the City Companies were required to purchase and store coal between Lady-day and Michaelmas, to be sold 'in dear times, at such prices as the Lord Mayor and Aldermen should direct'. A chalder of coal: a dry measure, varying in amount from 32 to 40 bushels.

(2) *publick Fires*: see p. 172, notes 2 and 3.

Page 222. (1) but not of Hay or Grass: cf. Boghurst, *Loimographia*, [1666]: '... the spring being continuall dry ... which caused a pitifull crop of Hay' (p. 29).

(2) *excessive Plenty ... Fruit*: cf. Hodges, *Loimologia* (1720), p. 20. 'The Year was luxuriant in most Fruits, especially Cherries and Grapes ... at so low a Price, that the common People surfeited with them ...'

(3) *Mechanicks*: manual labourers or men of mean occupations.

Page 223. (1) *Poor ... pinch'd ... London only*: if London manufacturing and trading activity declined, all of England suffered—this was a fixed idea in Defoe's economic thinking. Cf. *The Review*, no. 4, 18 Feb. 1706: '*London* is the great Center of this Circulation . . . hither all the Manu- factures in the Nation from the several and remotest Countries are con- vey'd in gross, as to the vast Center of Trade; and here they pass from the Wholesaler to the Merchant, from the Ware-house to the Shop, and from thence, by a happy Counter-changing again, are transmitted to all the several Parts of the Kingdom again; and upon this Circulation . . . more Families depend, and are maintain'd, than upon the first Working of the whole Manufacture of the Nation.'

(2) *Calamity ... enrich'd the Country*: the economic utility of natural calamities, this is the principle Defoe reflects at this point in his assertion that the Fire of London (1666), by virtue of its destructiveness, created a great demand for goods and services. This is an old principle (related to the make-work principle of modern economic theory) much discussed in both an economic and a religious context in Defoe's day and earlier. Defoe's contemporary, Bernard Mandeville, in his brilliant *The Fable of the Bees* (2nd edn., 1723), has a passage reminiscent of Defoe: 'The Fire of *London* was a great Calamity, but if the Carpenters, Bricklayers, Smiths, and all, not only that are employed in Building but likewise those that made and dealt in the same Manufactures and other Merchandizes that were burnt, and other Trades again that got by them when they were in full Employ, were to Vote against those who lost by the Fire; the rejoicings would equal if not exceed the Complaints. In recruiting what is lost and destroy'd by Fire, Storms, Sea-fights, Sieges, Battles, a considerable part of Trade consists . . .' (*The Fable of the Bees: Or, Private Vices, Public Benefits*, ed. F. B. Kaye, 1924, i. 359).

Page 228. *People ... flock'd to Town*: 'And a delightfull thing it is to see the towne full of people again as now it is; and shops begin to open, though in many places seven or eight together, and more, all shut; but yet the towne is full, compared with what it used to be' (Pepys, *Diary*, 5 Jan. 1665-6). H. F.'s remark that the plague increased by 400 is nearly accurate. The Bills of Mortality report 1,031 deaths from plague in the last week of October and 1,414 in the first week of November. The number of parishes infected increased from 97 to 110.

Page 229. *now infected ... Norwich ... Colchester*: of the provincial towns and cities mentioned by Defoe, Colchester and Norwich were most affected. Colchester particularly suffered from a continuous plague from the summer of 1665 to December of 1666. Creighton calls this 'the greatest of all provincial plagues since the Black Death', with one possible excep- tion (*A History of Epidemics in England*, 2nd edn., 1965, i. 688).

Page 231. *Deodands*: from *deodandum*, a thing to be given to God; in

English law a personal chattel which having occasioned the death of a person was forfeited to the Crown for pious uses (*O.E.D.*).

Page 232. (1) *Physick Garden*: for herbs used in medical prescriptions.

(2) *Sir Robert Clayton*: a wealthy merchant and Whig politician (1629–1707), he served as alderman, Lord Mayor, and member of Parliament. He was much attacked by Tory pamphleteers. Defoe attacks him violently in *Reformation of Manners* (1702), but presents him favourably in *Roxana* (1724), where he acts as a financial adviser to the heroine.

Page 233. *St. Paul's . . . St. John*: The first of these churches was 'made Parochial and distinct from the Parish of Stepney in the Year 1666' and the second in 1694 (Edward Hatton, *A New View of London*, 1708, i. 302; ii. 481).

Page 234. (1) *Quakers . . . burying Ground*: in Bunhill Fields.

(2) *Reproach . . . Physicians*: At the first meeting of the Royal Society after the Plague, 22 January 1666, Pepys heard Dr. Jonathan Goddard defend himself and his fellow physicians who had fled from London: 'their particular patients were most gone out of towne, and they left at liberty' (*Diary*, 22 Jan. 1666). Goddard was Gresham Professor of Physic, an original member of the Royal Society, and inventor of the famous Goddard's drop. Dr. Hodges defended the fleeing physicians on much the same ground: they fled 'not so much for their own Preservation, as the Service of those whom they attend' (*Loimologia*, 1720, p. 23).

Page 235. (1) *Act of Indemnity*: Passed 29 August 1660, it pardoned, with some exceptions, those who had rebelled against the crown to form the Commonwealth.

(2) *penal Laws*: The Clarendon Code, so-called because they were issued under Lord Chancellor Clarendon at the Restoration. The Corporation Act, the Conventicle Act, and the Five-Mile Act aimed at the restriction or abolition of nonconformity.

Page 236. *Death . . . pale Horse*: Rev. vi. 8.

Page 237. (1) *Headboroughs*: officers with the duties of Petty Constables.

(2) *by Tale and by Number*: i.e. by enumeration as distinct from measure or weight.

Page 238. *seven and eight thousand per Week*: the Bills of Mortality report weekly deaths from plague 29 August to 19 September, 6,988, 6,544, 7,165; deaths from all causes, 8,252, 7,690, 8,297.

Page 239. (1) *Preparation of strong Scent*: To ward off offensive smells and to counteract the ill effects of effluvia and infected air the College of Physicians and others recommended perfumes, pomanders, and other concoctions. Among the ingredients were rue, angelica, wormwood, snakeroot, myrrh, camphor, citron, rose leaves, sulphur, oil of amber, and

countless others. These were to be held to the nose or used for anointing
the nostrils. William Boghurst listed among the antidotes of 'little efficacy':
'stuffing the nose with rue, wormwood, or what else' (*Loimographia*,
[1666], p. 55).

(2) *Wine*: an antidote of hoary respectability. Cf. John Lydgate in the
fifteenth century: 'Who will been holle and kepe hym from seckenesse/
And resiste the strok of pestilence/Lat him ... drynk good wyne, & holsom
meetis take' ('A Doctrine for Pestilence', *The Minor Poems of John Lydgate*,
Early English Text Soc., 1934, Pt. II, 702). Diemerbroeck similarly
thought 'a good Draught of *Burnt* Wine, with some *Cinnamon* and *Nutmeg*'
useful (*Several Choice Histories ... of the Plague*, 1665, p. 34). The 'learned
physician' who treated himself with wine and became an addict is presumably Dr. Nathaniel Hodges, who wrote that sack is 'deservedly ...
ranked amongst the principal Antidotes' to the plague. He describes in
detail its virtues and his use of it (*Loimologia*, 1720, p. 225).

Page 240. (1) *Pill. Ruff.*: *Pilulae Rufi*, compounded of aloes and myrrh,
'... to open or keep soluble the Body, the Pills of *Rufus*, commonly called
Pestilential Pills, are ... most proper to be used' (*Necessary Directions ...
by the College of Physicians*, p. 49).

(2) *Venice Treacle*: '*The Treacle* of Andromachus (commonly called
Venice-*Treacle*)' was an electuary compounded of many ingredients
and used in plague after plague. It was commended by the 'Medicus' in
William Bullein's *A Dialogue against the Fever Pestilence* (1564) as 'a
Triacle incomperable ... againste bothe poison and Pestilence' (see
E.E.T.S. edn., Pt. I, 1888, p. 42). In the London *Pharmacopoeia* of 1682
some sixty-five ingredients are listed. It was said to be 'not only the capital
Alexipharmic of our shops, but of all Europe'. Presumably it was devised
by Andromachus, physician to Nero. In *The Complete English Dispensatory*
(1718) an elaborate recipe is given, with the admission that 'there are
abundance of *Recipe*'s extant in Dispensatory-Writers'. It came to be
called Venice-Treacle because of the great quantities made in that city.
John Quincy, the compiler of this pharmacopoeia, rejects the prejudice
of those who maintained that 'this Medicine made in *England* is not so
good as what comes from *Venice*'. He defends viperine juices, an ingredient,
from English vipers as being of quality equal to those of Venice: 'if we
may judge by their poisonous Properties, the Bites of our Vipers, at the
proper time of the Year, which is the hottest, are as efficacious and deadly
as theirs' (*Pharmacopoeia Officinalis et Extemporanea: or, A Complete Dispensatory*, 1718, pp. 441 ff.).

Page 241. *Solomon Eagle*: see p. 21, note 4.

Page 242. (1) *February ... Distemper ... ceas'd*: In fact, death from plague
continued. The Bills of Mortality reported 222 from 30 January to
27 February 1666.

(2) *Gun-powder*: long considered of some efficacy in dissipating the concentration of poisonous effluvia in the air. The virtues of gunpowder were weighed by the anonymous author of *Medicina Flagellata* (1721) who pointed out that 'in the late Plague at Marseilles the constant firing of Guns at Morning and Evening . . . was esteemed to be of great Relief to the inhabitants' (pp. 205-6).

(3) *sweetning their Houses*: see p. 239, note 1. A Lord Mayor's Proclamation on 7 December 1665 ordered that all houses in which plague had been prevalent be thoroughly fumigated and aired before occupancy.

Page 243. Seeds of the Plague . . . destroy'd: Although H. F. scorns the view of some 'Quacking Philosophers', that the Great Fire destroyed the seeds of the plague, a respected scientist, Richard Bradley, F.R.S., held it to be a reasonable hypothesis. In 1721, observing that no plague had occurred in England since 1665, he wrote that this 'might happen from the Destruction of the City by Fire the following Year 1666, and besides the Destroying the Eggs, or Seeds, of those poisonous Animals, might likewise purifie that Air in such a Manner, as to make it unfit for the Nourishment of others of the same Kind, which were Swimming or Driving in the Circumambient Air . . .' (*The Plague of Marseilles Consider'd*, 1721, p. 12).

Page 244. (1) never on Board the Fleet: not true: the Navy Office . . . and Pepys . . . received frequent notices of plague in the fleet (see *Cal. State Papers Dom., Car. II, 1665-1666*, pp. 32, 54, 87, and *passim*). On 11 October John Evelyn, Commissioner for Mariners, reported to the Duke of Albemarle that the plague was spreading at Chatham and requested that the Navy Commissioners be ordered to send two hospital ships 'for this emergent occasion' (ibid., p. 12). As early as 8 April John Allin wrote to Philip Fryth: 'Our fleete is sickly, and ye sicknesse increases at Yarmouth' (*Archaeologia*, xxxvii. 18. 5).

(2) *great Engagement at Sea*: the battle off Lowestoft, 3 June 1665.

Page 245. Vain . . . Man: Ps. lx. 11.

Page 247. (1) Physicians . . . all supernatural: see note to p. 194.

(2) *ten Lepers . . . healed*: Luke xvii. 12-17.

Page 248. sang his Praise: Ps. cvi. 12-13.

A MEDICAL NOTE

Modern epidemiology

Modern knowledge of plague dates from the Hong Kong epidemic of 1894. Shibasaburo Kitasato and Alexandre Yersin discovered the plague bacillus and called it *Pasteurella pestis*. Its correct name is now *Yersinia pestis*.

Plague is not primarily a human disease. *Yersinia pestis* lives in the digestive tract of the fleas *Xenopsylla cheopis* and *Cortophylus* or *Nosopsylla fasciatus*, which live off the black rat, *Rattus rattus*. Other rodents carry infected fleas, but of species which tend not to bite humans. *Yersinia pestis* can also survive in dung, an old nest or even textile bales, for up to twelve months given a moderately high temperature and level of humidity. If plague is contained within flea and rodent populations, it is called enzootic. Periodically the plague bacillus multiplies, blocking the passage of blood to the flea's stomach and threatening starvation; the flea regurgitates blood infected with many bacilli into the bloodstream of its host, causing death. When the secondary hosts, or rodents, die *en masse*, the disease is epizootic: flea and bacillus must then find an alternative host, not always human. *Rattus rattus* is a climbing species which lives close to humans and often inhabits roofing, so people are an obvious alternative.

There are three types of plague, all occurring simultaneously among humans. Bubonic plague accounts for three-quarters of all cases, and is 60–80 per cent fatal. The first symptoms appear between thirty-six hours and ten days (on average, six days) after infection. A black pustule appears where the flea has bitten; there follows enlargement of the lymph glands in the armpits, neck or groin, depending on the location of the bite, and causing headaches, vomiting, and a cutting pain in the vicinity of the swelling, or bubo. In mild cases infection and bubo subside, and if a bubo is treated early, the patient is likely to recover. If not, it turns purple through haemorrhaging under the skin; red lumps (*Petechiae*) appear and the bacillus enters the bloodstream and poisons the nervous system.

Pneumonic, or pulmonary plague, accounts for a fifth of cases but is more frequent in cold weather: a combination of pneumonia and the passage of infected blood into the lungs. Coughing discharges sputum containing *Yersinia pestis*, which may then enter the lungs of other people. The period of incubation is two to three days; the body temperature then falls and the lungs stiffen.

Pneumonic plague, which is 95–100 per cent lethal, is the only kind which can be transmitted by human agency.

Septicaemic plague can be transmitted not only by rat fleas but by the human flea, *Pulex irritans*. The human louse, *Pediculus humanus*, can also carry it. Transmission depends on the access of fleas or lice to sufferers with a high concentration of plague bacilli in their blood. Infected blood can be carried in the flea's mouth and introduced into the bloodstream of the next human the flea bites. This is a rare form of the disease, but it appears to be 100 per cent fatal. A rash develops within hours, and death usually occurs within three days (often in one), before buboes have had time to form.

The plague of 1665 was probably caused not by infected cargoes from the East, but by the seasonal changes in rat and flea ecology outlined above. London had suffered epidemics in 1563, 1593, 1603 and 1625; in the intervening years a steady number of people had died of the disease. Moreover, the first outbreak of the Great Plague was in the west end rather than near the docks in the east. It is true that the number of plague deaths had fallen steadily since 1649, which suggests that a more virulent imported strain of the bacillus attacked a population becoming immune to the resident one; *Yersinia pestis*, however, is striking for the consistency of its virulence. The most likely cause is in a combination of immunity patterns and demographic change. Repeated epidemics over a hundred years build up limited immunity among humans and rodents, but the disease survives to attack virgin populations. Defoe correctly observes that many people moved to London for the first time after the Restoration of the monarchy. This shift in population, with changes in rat and flea ecology, may have caused a major revival of the disease among humans.

The disappearance of the 1665 plague, which is to say the virtual disappearance of the disease from the British Isles, is still harder to explain. We may not need a human explanation; rats may have acquired immunity. Nevertheless, it appears that people of blood group 'A' are more likely to be bitten by fleas than those of other groups; also that 'A' has always been the most common group in the south-east of England, where plague was worst and most durable. The most vulnerable part of the population therefore suffered the most prolonged exposure to the disease: of these, the weaker died while the stronger developed immunities. This may explain why plague established itself far more strongly in London than in any other part of the country. It is also possible that *Yersinia pestis* mutated through regular pulmonary infection into a milder form called *Yersinia pseudo-tuberculosis*, initiating a stable, non-fatal relationship with the human host. This caused a disease with symptoms similar to typhoid which gave partial immunity to plague.

Some popular but wrong explanations of the disappearance of plague should be mentioned. H. F. himself scorns the idea that the Great Fire burned out the infection, if not for the right reasons. Some authorities still accept this idea in one form: that brick and tiles replaced timber and thatch as building materials, so making it hard for rats to nest in human dwellings. The Great Fire, however, destroyed little beyond the walls of the City, whereas the plague was most virulent to the west. Popular too is the notion that the black rat was replaced by the brown rat, which tends to live underground and carries fleas which do not bite humans as readily as *Xenopsylla cheopis*; but the brown rat did not reach Britain in large numbers until the 1730s. It is also doubtful that hygiene improved so much as to eliminate the risk of infection.

Defoe's epidemiology

Defoe's debt to contemporary medical works is traced in Louis Landa's explanatory notes. Some general observations will establish the validity of his epidemiology. The *Journal* is a dramatic account, not a medical tract, so it is occasionally difficult to tell H. F.'s opinions from the rumours of the times. Nevertheless, we can still observe a distinct epidemiological stance. The three types of plague all seem to be present. Most of the victims in the *Journal* suffer from the bubonic kind; H. F.'s observations regarding its treatment are accurate. Defoe also writes about people who, ignorant of their infection, collapsed and died suddenly. This suggests the septicaemic form. Pulmonary plague may be depicted by H. F.'s references to the 'fatal Breath' of victims; here Defoe is closer to modern epidemiology than many of his contemporaries. Descriptions of mental disorder among sufferers reflect plague's tendency to attack the nervous system.

The *Journal* enters an old debate between contagionist and miasmatic theories, and comes down firmly on the side of contagion. Each theory anticipates modern knowledge of the disease in equally important ways. Miasmatists believed that a poisonous cloud of corrupted air settled in times of plague, encouraged by hot weather and insanitary conditions, and sometimes originating (according to the telluric theory) in effusions of gas from the earth's crust. The cloud was said to be inhaled by victims. This theory was popular because it seemed to explain how one could be infected when there were no other people present, and because it sat easily with the more simple-minded theories of plague as a sign of God's anger. Defoe disagreed strongly with its assumption that there existed 'invisible Creatures, who enter into the Body with the Breath' (pp. 74–5). Modern bacteriology has been kinder to miasmatists. Indeed, what the contagionists lacked was precisely the notion of living organisms as instruments of infection; instead they found contagion in inert chemical matter, a view which miasmatists, rightly regarded with suspicion. Defoe's contagionist theory emphasizes the sufferer as the agent of transmission. His position seems categorical: 'no one in this whole Nation ever receiv'd the Sickness or Infection, but who receiv'd it in the ordinary Way of Infection from some Body, or the Cloaths, or touch, or stench of some Body that was infected before' (p. 194). However, this takes the contagionist position so far as to propose a theory of local or personal miasma. H. F.'s insistence that the malodorous excrescences of victims transmitted plague may derive not only from clinical observation, but also from biblical descriptions of leprosy, to which there is one direct reference in the *Journal* (p. 247).

H. F. is correct to argue that plague could be carried in clothes, since fleas can lodge in them. Although he is bemused by prophylactics, he carries his own 'Preparation of strong Scent' in case he comes near an infected person or burying place, and accepts advice to fumigate his house. These measures are known to have some success in deterring fleas and, in the case of fumigation, rats. Escaping to ships moored on the river did not ensure safety, not only because ship-bound people either fled too late or had to trade with infected ones, but also because the black rat can climb up mooring ropes. Quarantine measures for foreign vessels were therefore inadequate, since rats could leave a ship by the same means. It follows that shutting oneself up at home with provisions could not guarantee safety unless the house was secured against rats and fleas. In practice, infected rats might already be nesting in the roof or cellar. The narrator's best schemes for controlling the disease were his most ambitious ones: the building of more pest-houses and the isolation of infected areas would have checked the plague better than anything the miasmatists proposed.

Until the end of the *Journal* H. F. dismisses the theory that plague was the direct instrument of God's wrath: the disease, he says, arose from 'natural Causes' and spread by 'natural Means' (pp. 193–4), exhibiting divine power 'in the Scheme of Nature'. This position is abandoned when the plague departs: 'just then it pleased God, as it were, by his immediate Hand to disarm this Enemy' (p. 246). Defoe often presents medical opinion as the product of dangerous circumstances; in this instance he is also aware of the dangers of being wise after the event: 'perhaps it may be thought by some, after the Sense of the thing was over, an officious canting of religious things . . . and this restrains me very much from going on here, as I might otherwise do' (p. 247). H. F. does not ignore the demands of scepticism in claiming divine intervention.

D. R.

TOPOGRAPHICAL REFERENCES

LONDON AND ENVIRONS

A Journal of the Plague Year contains approximately 175 names of streets, alleys, inns, taverns, buildings, burial grounds, parishes, churches, districts, and liberties in London, of hamlets nearby, and a sprinkling of names of places more remote. Practical necessity, as well as the scope and intention of this edition, will justify, I trust, the selection of a limited number of these for identification, roughly one-third. Most of those not identified are either widely known or merely casually mentioned in the text. In general I have followed three principles in selecting place-names to be identified: (1) places which existed at the time of the Great Plague of London but which no longer exist; (2) places which are of more than casual interest for the narrative; (3) places whose identification may give a reader some geographical orientation. For varied reasons I have also identified . number of other places, some of which will be familiar to the Londoner but less familiar to others. For information I have relied chiefly on the following works: Edward Hatton, *A New View of London*, 1708 (cited as Hatton); Daniel Defoe, *Tour thro' the Whole Island of Great Britain*, 1724-6, ed. G. D. H. Cole (1927; cited as *Tour*); John Stow, *A Survey of the Cities of London and Westminster*, 6th edn. (1754), ed. John Strype (cited as Strype); Henry B. Wheatley and Peter Cunningham, *London Past and Present* (1891); Henry A. Harben, *A Dictionary of London* (1918); Norman G. Brett-James, *The Growth of Stuart London* (1918); Jacob Larwood and John Camden Hotten, *English Inn Signs* (1951). The most useful maps, nearly contemporary, are the Map of London (1677) by John Ogilby and William Morgan; the Plan of London (1682) by Robert Morden and Philip Lea, revised in 1732; and the series of parish and ward plans by Richard Blome (based on Morden and Lea) included in Strype's editions of Stow's *Survey of London* (1720 and 1754-5).

Page 2. Long Acre . . . Drury-Lane: two streets, where the Plague began, in the out parish (i.e. outside the ancient wall of the City of London) of St. Giles-in-the-Fields. The first case of plague reported was in a house at or near the junction of the two streets.

Page 5. Bearbinder-lane . . . Stocks market: the lane was a passage from the market to St. Swithin's Lane. Stocks Market, between Threadneedle Street and the Poultry, dates from the thirteenth century. At first it was a flesh and fish market, later chiefly for fruit, roots, and herbs. Later the Mansion House was built on the site.

Page 7. Crooked-lane: a winding lane in Eastcheap, near London Bridge.

Page 14. Cripplegate: i.e. St. Giles, Cripplegate, the parish in which Defoe is thought to have been born and in which he died.

Page 16. Westminster: in 1665 a city consisting of five parishes and liberties, distinct from London, though contiguous. It was governed by a High Steward and other officers chosen by the Dean and Chapter of the Abbey, in whom all civil jurisdiction resided.

Page 18. Wapping . . . Rotherhith: Wapping and Ratcliff were hamlets in 1665, Rotherhithe (often called Redriff), a manor. All are on the Thames, and the inhabitants were mainly mariners and others associated with shipping. Stepney was at the time a very large parish in the eastern section. It suffered greatly in the Plague.

Page 23. Petty-France: in the parish of Bishopsgate, outside the City wall, a short alley or street once inhabited by Frenchmen. It was east of Moorfields, near to old Bethlehem.

Page 37. Bunhill-Fields . . . Islington: a large open field adjacent to the Artillery Grounds and Upper Moorfields, it became the chief burial ground of nonconformists. Defoe is buried here. Islington in 1665 was rural, a northern suburb, and a favourite Sunday resort as well as a place for duels. Travellers going north out of London went through Islington.

Page 47. Tower-Hamlets: a number of parishes, hamlets, and liberties were at one time within the jurisdiction of the Lieutenant of the Tower. Defoe seems to use the term in a geographical sense, to include parishes in the vicinity of the Tower. Among the Tower hamlets listed by Defoe are his own parish of Aldgate, Trinity Minories, then a small parish of 120 houses named after an abbey of nuns (thirteenth century) of the order of St. Clare, and Saint Catherine, Tower, which included part of Butcher Row, mentioned by Defoe as suffering greatly in the Plague.

Page 48. Houndsditch: a street between Aldgate and Bishopsgate, possibly so named because it ran along the line of the old City moat, into which dogs were thrown before the moat was paved. The parish church of the Defoe family stood at the corner where Houndsditch and Whitechapel Street meet.

Page 55. Throckmoreton Street . . . Drapers Garden: Throckmorton or Throgmorton Street, Hatton writes, contained the houses of 'several Marchants' and 'other great Traders'. It was near the Royal Exchange. The gardens attached to the Hall of the Drapers' Company were extensive, reaching northwards as far as the street named London Wall. The Drapers settled in Throgmorton Street in 1541. The Map of London, 1677, by Ogilby and Morgan, shows the Dutch Church nearby and what may be the houses of the Dutch merchants mentioned by Defoe. The Dutch had moved into this vicinity in the sixteenth century.

Page 60. *three Nuns Inn*: a great coaching inn, opposite the parish church of the Defoe family, St. Botolph, Aldgate.

Page 60. *Finsbury*: see Explanatory Note for p. 60 (2).

Page 61. *Minories*: a street between Aldgate and the Tower, near to the fictional residence of H. F., and then much inhabited by gunners, wheel-wrights, and other artificers connected with the Ordnance.

Page 62. *Pye-Tavern*: in Houndsditch, not far from the Three Nuns Inn and the parish church of the Defoe family, St. Botolph, Aldgate. The Pye had a 'great room' in which plays were occasionally performed in the seventeenth century.

Page 63. *Harrow-Alley . . . Butcher-Row*: Harrow Alley ran southward out of Aldgate High Street. Butcher Row, within sight of the Defoe family parish church, extended along the south side of Aldgate High Street, eastward from the Minories.

Page 71. *Angel Inn . . . White-Horse . . . Pyed Bull*: The Angel, an inn with a long history in the parish of Clerkenwell, was a halting place for travellers approaching London from the north. The White Horse Inn mentioned here (there were many with this name) was probably the one on the north side of Barbican where that street leads out of Aldersgate at its junction with Goswell Street. The Pied Bull, originally a country villa, is often said, on flimsy evidence, to have been once the residence of Sir Walter Raleigh. It was in Church Row, near Islington.

Page 78. *Mile-End*: in 1665 Mile End was a hamlet of Stepney, still in the country and a resort of Londoners for fresh air, cakes, and ale.

Page 80. *Spittle-fields*: Spitalfields, open fields in the east of London, once belonging to the Priory and Hospital of St. Mary Spital, founded in 1197. It began to be built up about 1650, and after 1685 it became the silk-weaving district settled by Huguenot emigrants from France.

Page 80. *St. George's-fields*: in 1665 an extensive open space on the Surrey side of the Thames, lying between Southwark and Lambeth. It was used for large gatherings and by Londoners as a Sunday resort. Its famous Dog and Duck Inn was built in 1642.

Page 80. *Coleman's-street* Parish: Defoe's father appears to have resided in this parish at two different times. Hatton calls Coleman Street, where H. F.'s brother resides, a spacious street of good buildings. In 1665 it was much inhabited by Puritans. It ran between Lothbury and London Wall. In walking from his own residence in Aldgate to his brother's in Swan Alley, Coleman Street, H. F. went from the eastern section of the City to the northern section. Strype says that 'in this street are divers Courts and Alleys, some of which are very good, and others as mean and ordinary'.

Page 81. Token-House-Yard: named for a mint house or office built there for the issue of royal farthing tokens, granted under patent in 1635. It ran north out of Lothbury, in the vicinity of the Bank of England.

Page 81. Bell-Alley: in Coleman Street, a passage to London Wall and Token House Yard in Lothbury (north side of the Bank of England).

Page 91. Mount-mill: in Goswell Street, Aldersgate, the site of one of the Parliamentary forts in 1642-3, a plague pit was dug in 1665.

Page 92. Blackwell-Hall . . . Leaden-Hall . . . Session-House . . . Compter: in 1665 Blackwell Hall was the great cloth market in Basinghall Street. Leadenhall Market dated from the sixteenth century. Defoe describes it at length in the *Tour*, i. 346 ff. Varied products were sold at Leadenhall: meat, poultry, wool, leather goods, etc. The Hall of Justice in the Old Bailey was commonly referred to as the Session House. It was presided over by the Lord Mayor and the Justices of Middlesex County. There were two compters in the City, in Wood Street and in the Poultry, for the detention of debtors and others guilty of misdemeanours.

Page 92. the Monument: the famous column on Fish Street Hill, erected to commemorate the Fire of 1666, was designed by Wren. It was not authorized until three years after the Plague. Defoe wrote: 'It out does all the Obelisks and Pillars of the Ancients, at least that I have seen' (*Tour*, i. 333).

Page 92. Fleet-ditch: the Fleet River, of unsavoury reputation, improved after the Fire of 1666 by being deepened and having four stone bridges built over it. It was navigable as far as Holborn Bridge. The stream, on the western side of London, entered the City in Faringdon Ward Without and flowed south to the Thames. Its unsavoury reputation as a depository of filth continued for almost another century.

Page 92. Bethlem: this old hospital for the insane was not damaged in the Fire of 1666, but its inadequacy was recognized. In 1675 construction of a new and enlarged Bedlam was begun on a site in Moorsfield. Defoe called this one 'the most beautiful Structure for such a Use . . . in the World' (*Tour*, i. 372).

Page 100. Bednal-green: Bethnal Green was a hamlet of Stepney in 1665, well known as the site of the house built by the Blind Beggar of Bednall-green—'so much talked of and sang in ballads', according to Pepys (*Diary*, 26 June 1663).

Page 100. *Hackney*: in 1665 a suburban manor. By Defoe's later years it had grown extensively. He describes it as consisting of twelve hamlets or separate villages 'remarkable for the retreat of Wealthy Citizens' (*Tour*, i. 382).

Page 102. *Hamlets*: i.e. the Tower Hamlets. See topographical note to p. 47.

Page 106. *Bow*: a mile east of Mile End, in 1665 a hamlet of Stepney. This is the Stratford atte Bowe where Chaucer's prioress learned her French. Stowe called it 'a Place anciently celebrated for the Education of young Gentlewomen' (ed. Strype, ii. 768).

Page 106. *Bromley*: then a village in the eastern suburbs. Early it had been part of the great manor of Stepney and was called Bromley-by-Bow. H. F. has turned southward, moving from Bow to Bromley and thence to Thameside.

Page 106. *Blackwall*: in 1665 part of the extensive parish of Stepney, Blackwall, on the Thames at its junction with the Lea river, was noted as a harbour and for shipbuilding.

Page 106. *Poplar*: in 1665 a Thameside hamlet in Stepney engaged in maritime activities.

Page 110. *Lime-house*: like Blackwall, Poplar, and Redriff (Rotherhithe), Limehouse was notable for mariners and shipping. Between Wapping and Poplar, it became a separate parish in 1730.

Page 110. *Pool*: Defoe wrote: 'That Part of the River of *Thames* which is properly the Harbour, and where the Ships usually deliver or unload their Cargoes, is called the *Pool*, and begins at the turning of the River out of *Lime-house* Reach, and extends to Custom-house-Keys' (*Tour*, i. 350).

Page 111. *Long-Reach*: the bend of the Thames near Gravesend, just after Blackwall Reach and just before Gravesend Reach.

Page 119. *East-Smith-field*: earlier an open space east of the Tower, between Little Tower Hill and Ratcliffe Highway. By the time of the Plague in 1665 it was beginning to be well populated.

Page 125. *the Hermitage*: a Thameside area east of the Tower, in Wapping, containing Great Hermitage Street and Little Hermitage Street. Located here were Hermitage landing stairs, a dock, and a bridge.

Page 125. *Ratclif-High-Way*: it ran from East Smithfield, near the Tower, to Shadwell, and was much inhabited by mariners and trades dependent on shipping. Ratcliffe Cross, mentioned on p. 128, was a street leading out of the Highway to Ratcliffe Stairs on the Thames.

Page 128. *Bow Bridge*: built over the Lea in the twelfth century, near Old Ford, it still existed in 1665, though much repaired. For Bow, see topographical note to p. 106.

Page 128. *Old-Ford*: a hamlet near London, 3½ miles north-east of St. Paul's Cathedral, at the end of the Old Ford Road. It marks the site of the old ford over the river Lea. Here the road from Essex entered London before the bridge at Stratford-at-Bow was built.

Page 130. *Stamford-Hill*: in Middlesex, roughly four miles from St. Paul's Cathedral to the north-east, between Stoke Newington and Totten-ham. It was part of the Great North Road often associated with James I, who entered London from Stamford Hill when he came to be crowned.

Page 151. *Gravesend*: described in the *Atlas Maritimus* (1728), a work in which Defoe had a hand, as 'eminent for its being the Place where all the Merchant Ships outward-bound stop to clear . . . that is, to be visited by the Custom-house Officers . . . who may, if they please, search the whole Ship' (p. 20). In the *Tour*, i. 101 ff., Defoe gives a fuller account of the customs inspection at Gravesend.

Page 159. *Portsoken Ward*: the easternmost of the City wards, partly within and partly without the City wall, it coincided in part with the Defoe family parish of St. Botolph, Aldgate.

Page 162. *Still-yard Stairs*: in Upper Thames Street, at the Steelyard and Dowgate Dock. The Steelyard, a hall where Hanseatic merchants once carried on their trading activities. Hatton wrote that it is rightly named, 'vast quantities of Steel having for many years past been landed'. In 1665 a wine house, much frequented by Samuel Pepys, occupied the ground floor and was noted for its Rhenish wines and neat's tongues. The Cannon Street Station is now on the site.

Page 162. *Falcon Stairs*: on the Southwark side of the Thames, near Gravel Lane and Dirty Lane, in the vicinity of St. George's Fields. See topographical note to p. 80. The Falcon Tavern here was visited, so tradi-tion has it, by Shakespeare. Pepys mentions the Stairs and the Tavern several times.

Page 168. *Petticoat-Lane*: now Middlesex Street, once called Hog Lane, this famous market for second-hand wares had not yet developed its present character. It was in the parish of St. Mary, Whitechapel, and thus close to the fictional residence of H. F. If Hatton is right, the west side of Petticoat Lane from Gravel Lane to Whitechapel Bar was in the parish of St. Botolph, Aldgate.

Page 174. *Moses and Aaron*: not identified but apparently an inn in White-chapel. See under *Moses and Aaron Alley* below.

Page 174. *the high Street*: probably Aldgate High Street, which was the beginning of Whitechapel Street.

Page 181. *Moses and Aaron Alley*: it ran off the northern side of White-chapel Street, a passage to Castle Street, Spitalfields.

Page 196. *Bull-head Tavern*: I have not identified a Bull Head Tavern in Gracechurch Street, a street noted for 'many fair Inns for Travellers', according to Strype.

Page 221. *Custom-house*: in 1665 the Custom House was on a quay called Wool Wharf. It was burned in 1666. Rebuilt by Wren, it was burned again in 1714-15.

Page 221. *Queen-hith*: Queenhithe, from the medieval period a quay for the landing of wool, hides, corn, and other products. It was used by ships from the west of England and from overseas. The Queenhithe market, mainly for corn and meal, was in Upper Thames Street.

Page 221. *Three Cranes*: the name was variously applied to a dock, a lane, and a tavern. The unloading of wine at the spot from early times was responsible for 'in the Vintry', a phrase that continued to be used for locating places in the area. One of London's most famous waterside taverns, The Three Cranes in the Vintry, a favourite of Pepys, was located here, in Upper Thames Street.

Page 221. *Black Friars*: the area near Ludgate, once the site of a Dominican monastery seized at the Reformation. Later it was the site of Blackfriar's Theatre, and by 1665 it was mainly occupied by tenements.

Page 221. *Bridewel*: originally a royal palace of Henry VIII, this was granted to the City of London by Edward VI to be used as a workhouse for the poor and idle. It was burned in the Great Fire of 1666 and was rebuilt in 1668.

Page 221. *Lord Mayor's Door*: in 1665 Sir John Lawrence, Lord Mayor of London, lived in Great Saint Helen's Street in Bishopsgate Ward.

Page 221. *Bow Church*: St. Mary Le Bow. This famous old church, dating from the reign of William the Conqueror, located on the south side of Cheapside in Cordwainers Ward, burned in 1666. Wren designed the new one.

Page 221. *Bridge foot*: i.e. London Bridge. The Church of St. Magnus the Martyr, at the north end of the Bridge, was burned in 1666 and was rebuilt by Wren in 1676.

Page 228. *St. Martins le Grand*: a street between Newgate Street and Aldersgate Street. In 1665 the precinct was a liberty of Westminster even though it was in the City of London. Privileges dating from earlier times, such as sanctuary, were abolished in 1815. In medieval times this was the site of a Collegiate Church of Secular Canons.

Page 232. *Black Ditch . . . Holloway Lane*: Contemporary maps do not show *Black Ditch*. Strype's map of the parish of St. Leonard, Shoreditch, shows Holloway Lane running west out of Shoreditch with what appears to be an extension in the direction of Vinegar Yard and Upper Moorfields.

Hatton says that Holloway Lane led to Bunhill Fields. Mrs. Basil Holmes (*The London Burial Grounds*, 1896, p. 125) identifies the burial ground Defoe mentions as the Holywell Mount burial ground, named after the neighbouring Holywell Convent and long in use. This is in the vicinity of Curtain Road and the site of the Curtain, the famous Elizabethan theatre.

Page 232. Hand-Alley: on the east side of Bishopsgate Street Without (now New Street), this was the site of a Presbyterian meeting-house where Defoe's friend, the nonconformist clergyman, Daniel Williams, was minister for twenty-seven years. In his will, Williams provided for the founding of the Daniel Williams Library.

Page 233. Rose Alley: on the eastern side of Bishopsgate Street, near the southern end.

Page 233. Moorfields: low-lying marshy ground to the north outside the Wall of the City, it was 'a most noysome and offensive place' until improved in the reign of James I and Charles II. The new Bethlehem Hospital was built here after the Fire of 1666, and with further improvements (draining and construction of walks) Moorfields became a popular place for many activities. The burial ground referred to by Defoe, on the east side of Moorfields, dated from 1569. It was known as Bethlehem Churchyard.

Page 241. Newgate-Market: before the Fire of 1666 this was chiefly a meal market, apparently of ancient date. A row of sheds accommodated butchers. It served as a meat market until the formation of the Central Market, Smithfield, 1868.

Page 241. Blow-bladder Street: between Cheapside and Newgate Street, so called, according to Stow, because bladders were sold there. Defoe gives a different reason.

THE WORLD'S CLASSICS

A Select List

SERGEI AKSAKOV: A Russian Gentleman
Translated by J. D. Duff
Edited by Edward Crankshaw

HANS ANDERSEN: Fairy Tales
Translated by L. W. Kingsland
Introduction by Naomi Lewis
Illustrated by Vilhelm Pedersen and Lorenz Frølich

JANE AUSTEN: Emma
Edited by James Kinsley and David Lodge

Mansfield Park
Edited by James Kinsley and John Lucas

ROBERT BAGE: Hermsprong
Edited by Peter Faulkner

WILLIAM BECKFORD: Vathek
Edited by Roger Lonsdale

CHARLOTTE BRONTË: Jane Eyre
Edited by Margaret Smith

THOMAS CARLYLE: The French Revolution
Edited by K. J. Fielding and David Sorensen

LEWIS CARROLL: Alice's Adventures in Wonderland
and Through the Looking Glass
Edited by Roger Lancelyn Green
Illustrated by John Tenniel

GEOFFREY CHAUCER: The Canterbury Tales
Translated by David Wright

ANTON CHEKHOV: The Russian Master and Other Stories
Translated by Ronald Hingley

JOSEPH CONRAD: Victory
Edited by John Batchelor
Introduction by Tony Tanner

CHARLES DICKENS: Christmas Books
Edited by Ruth Glancy

Dr. Wortle's School
Edited by John Halperin

Orley Farm
Edited by David Skilton

VILLIERS DE L'ISLE-ADAM: Cruel Tales
Translated by Robert Baldick
Edited by A. W. Raitt

VIRGIL: The Aeneid
Translated by C. Day Lewis
Edited by Jasper Griffin

HORACE WALPOLE: The Castle of Otranto
Edited by W. S. Lewis

IZAAK WALTON and CHARLES COTTON:
The Compleat Angler
Edited by John Buxton
Introduction by John Buchan

OSCAR WILDE: Complete Shorter Fiction
Edited by Isobel Murray

The Picture of Dorian Gray
Edited by Isobel Murray

ÉMILE ZOLA:
The Attack on the Mill and other stories
Translated by Douglas Parmeé

A complete list of Oxford Paperbacks, including The World's Classics, OPUS, Past Masters, Oxford Authors, Oxford Shakespeare, and Oxford Paperback Reference, is available in the UK from the Arts and Reference Publicity Department (RS), Oxford University Press, Walton Street, Oxford OX2 6DP.

In the USA, complete lists are available from the Paperbacks Marketing Manager, Oxford University Press, 200 Madison Avenue, New York, NY 10016.

Oxford Paperbacks are available from all good bookshops. In case of difficulty, customers in the UK can order direct from Oxford University Press Bookshop, Freepost, 116 High Street, Oxford, OX1 4BR, enclosing full payment. Please add 10 per cent of published price for postage and packing.